# Earth
### *and* Sky

## ZAHRA OWENS

*Dreamspinner Press*

Published by
Dreamspinner Press
4760 Preston Road
Suite 244-149
Frisco, TX 75034
http://www.dreamspinnerpress.com/

Earth and Sky

Cover Art by Anne Cain   annecain.art@gmail.com
Cover Design by Mara McKennen

ISBN: 978-1-61581-834-1

Printed in the United States of America
First Edition
June 2011

eBook edition available
eBook ISBN: 978-1-61581-835-8

To Nicky and Emmet,
my yin and yang,
my female and male wordsmiths
who balance everything out for me.

# —1—

"I'M TELLING you, we're missing horses," Hugh told his boss. "Not a lot, but last week I had Tim count again because we were one short, and this week we lost another one."

Hugh and Hunter were riding fences. On a large ranch like Hunter's, this was a job that took most of the day, especially when they needed to dismount from time to time to check something out or to make small repairs. Usually this job was done by two of the workmen, but because of Hugh's concerns, the foreman had invited his boss to ride with him on this crisp spring morning.

Both men were tall and muscled and had practically been born in the saddle. Hugh was the oldest son of a ranch foreman who had worked for Hunter's father and, later, for Hunter. Now that his dad had retired, Hugh was Hunter's foreman. He had a younger brother Tim working with him, and a middle brother Jack, who specialized in horse dentistry. They lived and breathed horses.

Hunter had been born into the ranch as well. His father had been a rancher who had bought up most of the surrounding ranches during a recession—including the one Hugh's father had owned—and who had done rather well for himself until his untimely death. Hunter had only been fourteen at the time, and if it hadn't been for Hugh's father, he wouldn't have kept the ranch afloat. Now Hugh was married to Hunter's older sister, Lisa, so he was practically family. Hunter was an even better businessman than his father, with more horses than ever being born inside the large perimeter of the Blue River Ranch and sold at auction or to other ranches all over the US. He worked hard and enjoyed getting his hands dirty in between all the paperwork and negotiating his job required.

Despite Hunter's concern over the missing horses, a day like today, when he could spend it on horseback, was a treat. Sometimes he wished he could just work the ranch and not have to deal with everything else that came with running a successful business. Today felt like a holiday, something that was rare in Hunter's world. He couldn't remember the last time he'd been away from the ranch for anything other than a rancher's convention or an out-of-town auction. Then again, he really didn't mind. Even on those occasions when he needed to travel, he always felt homesick from the moment he crossed the county line. This was his land, and if he had anything to say about it, he would be buried on it, just like his father. He hoped it would be after a long and full life—not like his dad, who'd been cut down in his prime—but nevertheless, he did not see himself ever moving away from it.

"So are you saying someone is stealing our horses, or are you thinking we have a predator on our hands?" Hunter asked his foreman after a long silence. He had his own idea about the matter, but Hugh didn't spend all his time with his nose in paperwork, so Hunter valued his opinion.

"I'm thinking cougar or mountain lion, possibly with cubs and definitely hungry," Hugh answered calmly. "Only thing we haven't found so far is a carcass. Which would point to a horse thief, but then, if I were him, I'd steal horses that were already trained, not one-year-old colts."

Hunter sighed. They didn't need this. They'd only moved the horses to the higher meadows two weeks ago so they'd get the fresh grass that had been growing all winter. Among them were pregnant mares that would foal later in the year. For now, they were still quick enough to get away from any predator, but if Hugh was right, they wouldn't get the good grass they needed to nourish their offspring in the later stages of pregnancy because they'd have to be moved closer to the house, where predators were less likely to strike. Hunter didn't like this one bit. Then again, he hated losing horses, and not just because it meant less income.

Hunter was still deep in thought when he saw Hugh direct his horse toward a natural incline, where he jumped off.

"I think we've got an inquisitive mountain lion on our hands," Hugh said gruffly. "Let's hope she's just here to feed her babies until her usual prey recuperate from the harsh winter, because if she's been forced out of her habitat for some reason, we're in trouble."

"Are you sure?" Hunter asked from atop his horse.

Hugh was crouching down near a muddy patch on the small hill. "Oh yes, a puma's been standing here, surveying her surroundings. Unless we find the carcass of a horse nearby, we can't be sure she killed as well, but she's definitely been here since the rain, which means within the last two days."

Hunter unconsciously felt for the rifle in his saddlebag. The last thing he wanted was for mama puma to come out of hiding and make a tasty treat out of his foreman. Although mountain lions were notoriously wary of people, this one seemed to be more brazen than most, and it was hard to tell what a desperate puma would do for food.

"Did Tim say which horses we lost?" Hunter asked.

Hugh got up from his crouching position and nodded. "We're not sure about this week's, but last week was a late foal from October."

"Damn!" Hunter cursed. He'd have to make a decision soon. He couldn't afford to lose new foals. They were the ranch's source of income, and every one they lost would show up in the books. He had no choice. They'd have to move the herd away from the outer fields again.

"Do we have enough wranglers to move the herd back down?" Hunter wondered aloud.

Hugh climbed back in the saddle. "In a word, no. We got one drifter walking in after we put out the feelers, and I put him to work in the stables. He's not a bad worker, but I doubt he's much of a wrangler. Haven't seen him ride a horse yet, although according to Tim, he's okay handling them. I suppose if we really needed him, we could give him a try, but that still leaves us two hands short. If you ask me, I'd move the herd in smaller groups, like we did to bring them up here. That way we should be able to handle them. Don't suppose Gable's made a miraculous recovery? We could use his help."

Hunter sighed. "With the state of his leg after that injury he sustained last year, if anything, Gable will need *our* help from now on. Although, I think he found himself a ranch hand." Hunter wanted to ask Hugh how his neighbor, running his ranch single-handedly and in dire straits, had found capable help when they could afford to hire staff but couldn't find any. He didn't, though. Gable had a hard enough time staying afloat, so Hunter didn't begrudge him finding someone to lend a hand.

They trotted along, talking about the goings-on at the ranch while keeping their eyes peeled for anything unusual along the way. It had started to drizzle, and Hunter pulled the collar on his oilskin duster tighter, closing the zipper some more in an attempt to stay dry. He knew it would be futile, but he did it anyway. After a while, both men needed to dismount when they noticed a breach in a stretch of barbed wire. It was easily mended with an extra length and a pair of wire cutters, but Hugh pointed at the flattened high grass beyond the fence. They tied up their horses, and Hunter took out his rifle again before crossing the fence. They took their time, looking at the tracks in the mud and the broken-off bushes here and there, but found no evidence of the missing horses.

The rain started to pick up, so the men packed up to return to the homestead. From where they'd left their horses, they could see the mares with last year's young, grazing. With a hungry predator around, Hunter knew they couldn't leave them there for much longer.

"YOU mean there's a puma eating our horses?" Danny asked eagerly as he scarfed down the mashed potatoes, peas, and roast beef they were having for dinner.

"Do we have to talk about this over dinner?" Lisa, his mother, admonished.

"He's going to find out anyway, Lise," Hunter told his sister. "It's nature's way. The sooner he finds out about it, the better." He turned to the nine-year-old. "You can help move the herd on Saturday, bring them to safety."

"And that's the last I want to hear about it over the dinner table," Lisa cautioned. "We don't eat horse meat, and we don't talk about anything else eating it at this table."

Danny chuckled but stopped as soon as he saw his grandmother, who was clearly of the same opinion as his mother, giving him a stern look.

Even Hunter's face turned serious. Although he loved his mother dearly, she was a woman you didn't trifle with.

"So you're moving the herd back down?" Beth Krause asked her son.

"Yes, ma'am," Hunter answered. "We can't afford to lose more colts to that puma or anything else that feels we've got plenty, and although it's really great grass on those high pastures, we can't keep round-the-clock surveillance to prevent them from becoming a moveable feast for predators. We barely have enough manpower to bring them down again."

"Well, you're not taking Danny if there's a big cat on the loose up there," Lisa added.

"Mom!" Danny protested.

"Come on, sis," Hunter pleaded. "He's big enough to ride more than a pony now, so if anything happens, he can get away. He's been riding Belle down here on the grounds, and you know how beautifully she handles. She's one we got from Gable, so she can be trusted, even carrying a shrimp like Danny." He ruffled Danny's dark, curly hair and winked at him to make his words sound less harsh. "You know we're shorthanded, and he can work the fences. There'll always be someone around to help out, and Hugh and I will take good care of him. Right, Hugh?"

Hunter looked at Hugh across the table. The foreman had been quiet until now, like he always was around his wife and mother-in-law. There wasn't much point in protesting if you couldn't win, so he simply shrugged.

"We'll see," Lisa compromised, silently asking for Hunter's plate to give him seconds.

SATURDAY morning started off early with saddling the horses at dawn. The drizzle that had kept everything pretty much wet for the last few days had ceased, and the sun looked bright as it crept over the horizon.

"Great day to move some horses," Hunter said aloud as he entered the row of stables toward the one that held Davenport, a temperamental gelding that had lost none of his spunk after being neutered. Hunter loved to ride him. It was a battle of wills, and Hugh always shook his head and laughed when he saw what Hunter put up with when it came to that horse.

"He's almost ready," an unfamiliar voice said from behind the brown steed.

Hunter patted Davenport's neck as he rounded him. "And who are… Grant? What are you doing here?"

The tall and strikingly handsome cowboy turned toward Hunter. "Hugh hired me last night. I heard you were a few hands short, and I was in the neighborhood, so I figured I could help out."

"Hugh hired you?"

Hunter didn't wait for an answer. Instead, he paced determinedly in the direction of where he thought Hugh would be: saddling his own horse.

"What the fuck made you hire Grant Jarreau?" Hunter shouted, not bothering to check whether there was anyone else present in the stable.

Hugh, always calm and collected, put his horse's foot down and straightened his back. "We've been looking for help for over a year, and all we found was a halfway decent stable boy. Grant arrived here last night looking for a job, so I hired him."

"And how long is he staying for?" Hunter asked, trying to keep his anger from boiling over.

Hugh shrugged. "Like any other horse wrangler. Until he's found someplace better to work, which around here isn't likely to happen. So I guess until he's ready to move on."

"He'll leave in the dead of night, like after Gable's accident. For all we know, he caused it and left Gable for dead. I don't trust him to cover my back, Hugh."

Hugh calmly looked at Hunter. "All I know is that he's a damn fine wrangler and not too proud to get his hands dirty. He's like us, Hunter. He's welded to his horse, knows their language, and can get them to do just about anything. And on top of that, he doesn't mind mucking out stables or saddling horses for other riders. If he leaves, he leaves. In the meantime, we have had a good worker to carry part of the load. If he doesn't come around on Friday evening for his paycheck, I'll have a drink on him." A shy smile played around Hugh's mouth. "Besides, even Davenport doesn't dare to give him attitude. That was his test. I let him groom your horse last night, and the big shit didn't even flinch. I figured if Grant was good enough for the prince, he would be good enough for you."

Hunter eyed Hugh suspiciously and then conceded. "Fine! But I don't need to like him. He's trouble and he'll prove me right one day. I can't forget what he did to Gable and therefore to us. We had fifty extra horses to take care of because of him."

"Yeah, yeah," Hugh replied with a smile. "You never mind helping Gable out, so it wasn't such a big burden, right?"

Hunter narrowed his eyes at Hugh and then paced out of the stable without saying another word. He slowed his pace as soon as he came near his own horse. Grant was standing with his back toward him, bent over and apparently checking something on Davenport's hoof. Hunter's eyes traveled from the long, narrow back to where a red plaid shirt was tucked into a pair of fitted, slightly worn jeans that showed off a nicely curved ass, and Hunter felt all his blood rush south. He closed his eyes and swerved into the stable to prevent himself from bumping into Grant.

He couldn't do this, couldn't have these feelings. Not right now, and certainly not about Grant. He took a few cleansing breaths and willed himself to calm down. The thoughts would go away. They always did. He'd go out on the town tonight and get laid. He was popular enough and always got plenty of attention, so even if all else failed, he could count on Miranda forgetting he had turned her down so many times before, and she'd sleep with him. Take the edge off. She was good at that.

One more deep breath and Hunter was ready to step outside. He didn't look at Grant this time, although he was aware that Grant had stepped away from the horse. Instead, he took Davenport's reins and mounted him, turning the nervous horse around once. "Grant, you can ride Raven. You should remember him, since I bought him from Gable. I'll meet you, Danny, and Hugh at the first gate." And with that, he sped off.

Now that Hunter was concentrating on keeping his eager gelding in check, he slowly calmed down. This he could do. He could work hard all day, spend time in the open air, move some horses, stay alert to any trouble that was brewing in the herd, and do all this with men who were practically family to him. It would all run smoothly, even with Grant there. Hunter knew Hugh was right. Grant was a good worker and he knew what he was doing. Hunter would set his objections aside and work with him like he worked with all the other wranglers. It didn't matter that he suspected Grant was gay. The other guys didn't know, and Grant had always been discreet, so it wouldn't make a difference.

Hunter shook his head and focused on watching where he was going. Davenport wasn't always to be trusted when he was this eager to run, and Hunter had been thrown off more than once when his horse had decided to jump a fence or a hedge. He pulled the reins and made the gelding stop just before the first gate. He turned the horse around and saw the others trot leisurely over toward him: Hugh and his brother Tim, with little Danny in between them and Grant beside them on the dark horse Hunter had told him to ride. Even from this distance he could see how well Grant sat in the saddle. He almost had a regal seat, aided not only by his clear confidence but also by his tall physique, long, lean back, and broad shoulders. Hunter turned his horse around to force himself to stop looking at the new wrangler. Instead, he opened the gate and entered the lower range.

The mustering went smoothly, with the four experienced riders rounding up the horses and little Danny opening and closing gates. Danny was also putting in some extra effort, running behind the occasional spooked foal and unruly young horse, just so he could prove he was worth his keep. The mare he was riding did a good job protecting her young jockey, which wasn't something that surprised Hunter, since that was the reason he'd bought her off Gable two years earlier. Hunter's father had bought Hunter his first full-grown horse for his seventh birthday, so when Danny, Hunter's godson, turned that age, Hunter had to buy him one too. Although at the time the horse had been a bit big for the seven-year-old, now that Danny was older, Belle proved an excellent choice for the young rider.

After the work was done and Hunter was assured that the herd was safe in the lower fields, the men dismounted and started rubbing down their horses. Although the ranch employed stable boys who were quite capable of grooming the horses and unsaddling them, the general rule was that if they had the time, every wrangler took care of his own mount.

With Hugh and Tim helping out Danny, Hunter was left on the other side of the stable block with Grant. Hunter brushed by Grant as he took Davenport's saddle off.

"So does this mean I can stay?" Grant asked, smiling.

Hunter looked at him briefly, then walked on. When he returned, Grant was still waiting for an answer.

"You're a good wrangler," Hunter answered flatly. "And we're shorthanded, so I'm not about to throw you out, but just realize that I don't trust you. I won't forget what you did to Gable." With that, Hunter turned around and started brushing down Davenport.

Grant moved into his field of vision. "You don't know the full story."

Hunter sighed and avoided looking Grant in the eye. "All I know is that the day he got hurt, you disappeared. If there had been anything missing from Gable's house, the sheriff would have put you on the wanted list, but there wasn't. The rumors were there, though." Hunter didn't elaborate and Grant didn't offer an explanation.

After what seemed like a long time, during which both men silently worked on their horses, Grant spoke again. "I wouldn't trust rumors. Have you ever bothered asking Gable?"

Hunter didn't give an answer, and Grant didn't wait around for one. The tone had been set.

# —2—

SUNDAY morning Hunter woke up, hungover, at the crack of dawn.

The night before, after the roundup, they'd gone into town for a few beers, and Hunter was glad Grant hadn't joined them. He had wanted to relax, and frankly, that was easier with just the usual suspects around. Their regular haunt, a bar called The Barrel Run, had been pretty crowded, and the beer had flowed freely. Jack, Hugh's middle brother, was playing with his band that night, which usually meant that Hunter's always even-tempered foreman would let his proverbial hair down and join his brother on stage for a few songs.

The band had just announced a break when Miranda joined Hunter at his table. Her mass of strawberry blonde hair had hung loosely over her shoulders, and she had been wearing a carefully fitted embroidered blouse over low-cut skinny jeans. "You should come here more often, Hunter," she'd purred, resting her hand possessively on Hunter's thigh.

Hunter didn't mind the attention. Miranda worked in the local elementary school and had been Danny's teacher for the last two years. She was probably the closest thing he'd ever had to a girlfriend, although they didn't really seek out each other's company that often. In fact, they only seemed to bump into one another at the bar, which was pretty much the only time Hunter came into town. Although the clothes she wore at the bar were a lot sexier than the chaste blouses and skirts she wore to school, Miranda never showed too much skin. It was as if she was always holding back, always aware that the people in town trusted her to educate their young children.

There was nothing hesitant about the way she flirted with Hunter, though. Luckily, she never pushed him when he said no, which he had done on more than one occasion. Otherwise Hunter would have wondered if she was after his money, but she never seemed to want more than his attention.

After the band had played their second set and they'd shared a few drinks, Hunter—as usual—had been invited to her house for a nightcap. They always ended up in bed together when he accepted. This was where Miranda showed her true nature. Hunter was happy that she lived in a freestanding house, because she was quite the vixen in bed and was what you would call a screamer. It stoked his ego, but he never stayed for breakfast, preferring to sleep in his own bed.

Hunter woke up, glad to be alone, a few hours later. Although Miranda's ministrations had released quite a bit of tension—and despite his flaming headache—he was rock-hard again. The dreams that had brought him to this state, as usual, had very little to do with the red-haired schoolteacher. Hunter pushed his hand between his legs and enveloped his straining erection, experimentally tugging it a few times. The friction felt good, and he buried his face into his pillow. Closing his eyes brought the images from his dreams back in full force, and he resisted giving in to them. He didn't want to be reminded what had aroused him so, didn't want to see the image of a naked Grant playing in his head. Although he'd only seen Grant fully clothed the day before, he knew what the strong, handsome man looked like. He'd seen him in his full glory a few years earlier, on Gable's ranch, showering at the back of Gable's house. At the time, Grant had caught him looking, but not before he'd given Hunter quite a show. It wasn't until Grant had made it abundantly clear that he knew Hunter was there, hiding in the bushes, that Hunter had run off. They had never spoken about it, and if Hunter had any say in it, they never would, but Hunter was one of the few people who knew that Grant had been more than Gable's hired help. This, too, wasn't something that was openly talked about, so he didn't dare to bring it up, even in jest, but it did mean that his own fantasies were that much harder to keep at bay now that Grant had walked back into his life.

Hunter had never acted on these urges and had vowed he never would. Here in the solitude of his own bachelor bed, he let the images in his mind wash over him. As he squeezed the base of his cock, he pushed his fingers down over the sensitive flesh behind his balls. Thrusting his straining erection into his other hand, effectively fucking it, and biting his pillow to stifle his cry, he came much harder than he had a few hours earlier at the hands of Miranda. After the spasms slowly died down, Hunter rolled onto his back to catch his breath. He was panting hard.

Why? Why did he feel this way? Although they needed Grant's helping hand around the ranch, Hunter was going to have to talk to Hugh about putting as much distance between Grant and him as they could manage. The only question was how he was going to explain it to his brother-in-law.

WHILE the rest of the household was at church, Hunter needed his own kind of distraction, so he determinedly paced to the stable block and started clearing Davenport's box. The horse, sensing his rider's foul mood, protested all the way against everything Hunter did. Eventually Hunter put him in the treadmill, just so Davenport would stop harassing him while he worked.

Hunter set a good pace, knowing that if he worked hard he could get his brain to shut up. He wasn't doing badly, until he heard a familiar voice behind him.

"So what did your horse do to warrant being put in the mill on a Sunday morning?"

Hunter didn't need to look up to know it was Grant. In fact, he didn't want to look up.

"His stable needed a good mucking out," Hunter answered. "He's just a bit of a hyper horse and hates to be tied up outside, so I let him burn off some energy that way."

"So I guess you deserve each other."

Hunter leaned on his pitchfork as he turned around. "Meaning?"

"Well, you clearly needed to burn off some energy as well."

Hunter thought Grant looked too smug for his own good. Part of him wanted to turn back to working, effectively ignoring Grant's taunts, but he was never one to back down from a challenge. "So what if I did?"

"I heard you didn't get much sleep last night."

"And since when is that your business?" Hunter replied gruffly.

Grant raised his hands. "Just wondering if you needed some help." He shrugged. "And trying to make small talk to get to know my new boss a bit better."

This time Hunter did turn his back on Grant. "Hugh's your boss, as far as I'm concerned." He continued to rake up the straw, using long, swift strokes, and hoped Grant would just leave him alone. The last thing he wanted to do was exchange small talk with Grant. He didn't like the man or his morals, so the less he saw of him the better.

Hunter worked himself into such a sweat he needed a shower before he could go to Sunday lunch. His hair still wet and wearing his Sunday shirt and a new pair of jeans, he bumped into his youngest sister on the stairs.

"You weren't at church," she teased. "Rough night?"

Hunter grumbled, although he could never get mad at Bernie. "A bit short, but other than that…."

They walked into the kitchen, and Bernie handed Hunter a cup of coffee before grabbing one for herself. "I see Hugh's taste in men is improving."

Hunter sputtered as the hot coffee went down the wrong way.

"Isn't he the guy that used to work at Gable's?" She pointed her cup out the back window.

Hunter followed her gesture and saw Grant crossing the driveway toward the house.

"Yeah, he's the one that left Gable in the cold after his accident," Hunter answered, fervently hoping Grant was just walking to the house to ask something and wouldn't come inside.

Bernie shrugged. "Cute, though."

"He's too old for you, Bernice," Hunter sighed, using her full name to taunt her. She didn't react, and Hunter looked outside again, unable to keep himself from following Grant with his eyes.

Bernie poked him. "Stop staring at him, then. Besides, he's not that old, and guys my age only want one thing, so you can keep them."

Hunter hoped guys Bernie's age would keep their hands off her, since they were barely legal, but he didn't comment on it. "I'm sure this one is no different. He's got a reputation, Bernie. Don't get involved."

Bernie raised an eyebrow but didn't say anything. Instead she walked out of the kitchen to answer the knock on the front door.

Hunter was tempted to follow her but didn't want Grant to see him. Instead, he opened the fridge and picked at some of the plates of cold cuts they were going to have for lunch.

"You know better than that, Hunter," his mother admonished him. As usual, she'd snuck into the kitchen without Hunter noticing her. "Take them out and put them on the table. It's only polite to eat with everyone, not pick at them like some vagrant off the street."

Hunter felt caught the way only his mother could manage it. He took the Saran-wrapped plates out of the fridge and put them on the counter, trying not to chew too noticeably. When he turned around and faced her, the look his mother gave him made him not only feel eight years old again, but about four feet tall as well, although he was head and shoulders taller than the tiny woman.

"You weren't at church."

Hunter sighed, exasperated. "What it is today? First Bernie and now you. I don't go to church every Sunday. This is nothing new, Mom."

"Well, if that's the mood you're in after a night on the town, I suggest you stay in next week."

And with that, she left him, seething, in the kitchen.

Hunter paced to the window and back. Yes, he was in a foul mood, and he knew that wouldn't do for Sunday lunch, which was generally a happy and relaxed meal around their house. He and Hugh would usually talk shop with Izzie, since she was the sister who most actively worked the ranch with them. If her boyfriend came along, he'd join them too, but he wasn't coming today, since he worked the rodeo circuit. They'd all have lunch and then retreat to the porch while the other girls cleared the table and did the dishes. All in all, a very relaxed affair.

So why was Hunter tense? Was it because he didn't know whether Grant was coming as well? He had to stop fretting over the man so much. Hugh had hired him, and Hunter rarely questioned Hugh's judgment.

"You coming?" Bernie asked as she popped her head into the kitchen. "We're all waiting for you. And the meat, of course," she added happily, pointing at the dishes on the table.

"What did Grant want?"

"Asked for the day off. I called Hugh to give him an answer."

"He only started working here yesterday," Hunter answered, picking up the plates of lunchmeat and pacing after Bernie. "He's got some nerve."

"Hey!" Bernie called out. "I'm only the baby around here. Talk to Hugh!"

Hunter dropped the cold cuts on the table in the dining room, and after seeing Grant standing there talking to Hugh, he paced outside.

Hunter walked straight to the paddock where Davenport was grazing and whistled for the horse, who came closer reluctantly. Hunter walked him back to saddle him and rode out to the other side of the ranch. He'd been riding for a good half hour when he saw Izzie approaching on her trusted golden-brown gelding. Hunter smiled as he realized that no matter where he rode, she could always find him.

He slowed Davenport down so Izzie could ride next to him. She didn't say anything right away, as if she knew that Hunter wasn't in the mood. As they neared a wooded area, she reached into her saddlebag and unearthed a paper-wrapped parcel of sandwiches.

"Figured you'd be hungry after skipping lunch," she said casually. "Don't suppose you had breakfast either. Why don't we sit down here?" She gestured at a shaded area near an upturned trough.

They let the horses graze and sat down next to each other on the slightly rusted water basin.

Izzie was probably Hunter's favorite sister, not just because she more than pulled her weight around the ranch, but also because she knew when to shut up. At least most of the time she did.

"So, what's eating you?" she asked casually as she handed him an overstuffed sandwich.

Hunter shrugged.

"Is it Grant? I heard he was a good worker."

"You remember Grant from when he worked at Gable's, right?"

Izzie nodded as she bit into her bread. "And I also know he hit the road when Gable busted his leg. Is that what's bothering you?"

"I guess," Hunter answered, raising his eyebrows.

"Or is it the fact he was more to Gable than just the hired help?"

Hunter didn't reply immediately. As much as he loved Izzie, he hated the way she always knew what he was thinking. "I don't hate guys like that. You know that, Izzie. I never held Gable's choices against him."

"It's not really a choice, is it?" Izzie responded. As usual, she didn't look at Hunter or urge him to reply. Instead, she continued munching down her lunch.

Although Hunter always felt comfortable around Izzie, he often feared she could read his most carefully hidden thoughts as well as the more obvious ones. This was no different. Did Izzie know the real reason he avoided Grant?

"I just don't trust men who bolt when it gets a bit hot under their feet," Hunter added after a long silence. "I mean, how hard would it have been to stick around and do his job until Gable was healed up? He could have left then."

"You think Grant had something to do with how Gable got injured?" Izzie raised her eyebrows.

"Not necessarily," Hunter answered truthfully. "I just don't trust a man who would do such a thing to a… friend."

"Lover," Izzie corrected.

"L…." Hunter couldn't bring himself to say the word. "Yeah."

"We don't know what happened, Hunter. Maybe they had a row just before the accident. For all we know, they'd split up already when it happened. Gable didn't exactly say much afterward."

Hunter had to admit he was jumping to conclusions. Maybe Izzie was right. Maybe they didn't know the whole story. "Maybe Grant didn't even know what happened that day and he had already left the ranch?"

"Yeah, maybe," Izzie replied, nudging her big brother with her shoulder. "He didn't stay for lunch, you know. He just came to persuade Hugh he needed a day off tomorrow. Some emergency. Hugh let him have it—unpaid, of course." Izzie waited a bit as if to gauge Hunter's reaction before continuing. "At least he asked for it and didn't just 'forget' to show up."

"True," Hunter had to admit. He mentally gave Grant a merit point. "But what if Gable finds out that I employ Grant now?"

Izzie rolled her eyes. "I know Gable's your friend, but this is business. He knows how hard it is to find decent help, and he of all people should know how big a help Grant is. If Grant wants to work here, then who are you to say no?"

"That would be what a friend would do, maybe," Hunter argued.

"Besides, Gable's found new help. Younger guy. Cute too," Izzie quipped. "Of course, I don't stand a chance. Not if he's 'working' for Gable."

"You have the dirtiest mind I've ever seen in a girl," Hunter said, shaking his head.

"Then you clearly haven't had a decent conversation with Miranda," Izzie returned the jest. "Oh, I forgot. You only bone her."

"Izzie!" Hunter shouted, mock strangling his little sister. He didn't deny it, though. He liked this sort of innuendo a lot more than when Izzie underhandedly suggested that maybe he had a soft spot for Gable. She laughed out loud, and Hunter felt some of the tension leave his body.

— 3 —

IT DIDN'T take Grant long to become a valuable asset to the ranch. He worked long hours and kept himself more than occupied, even without Hugh telling him what to do. The other wranglers seemed to get along fine with him, and the stable boys sung his praises as well. Although Hunter still didn't trust him, Hugh was quite happy to be his boss.

Luckily for everyone even remotely close to Hunter, the earlier air-splitting tension between Hunter and Grant also seemed to die down a bit. They avoided each other but were both casual enough about it so it didn't bother anyone.

The one who helped Hunter most in that respect was Izzie, who had taken on the task of showing Grant how things were done around the ranch. The two of them were often seen laughing and enjoying themselves while at the same time doing the work that needed to be done. The news about this lovely understanding Grant and Izzie shared had traveled far beyond the fences lining the Blue River Ranch.

One evening, after a long day—the first hot one of the summer— the wranglers were hosing down their horses with water. Of course, Grant's hose slipped and got Izzie wet, which meant she retaliated, like any girl who grew up on a ranch full of butch cowboys would. She tackled him and dropped him in the water trough.

Most of the wranglers and stable boys stood by in amusement, cheering Izzie on, but one determined young man wasn't laughing.

"Get your fucking hands off my fiancée," he shouted.

"Delco?" Izzie replied. "What the…?"

John Delco was Izzie's boyfriend, not her fiancé, as she pointed out every time he claimed he was. He worked on the rodeo circuit and didn't make a bad living at it, but it meant he was barely ever home, except during the winter break. He wasn't a big guy, like Hunter and Grant or even Hugh, but he had a jealous temper, especially when he saw someone look a certain way at Izzie. They'd had numerous fights about it because Izzie wasn't afraid of him and she claimed she didn't need a guard dog, especially not one who was barely around, but Delco kept defending Izzie against even the smallest of potential threats.

Now Delco was launching himself at Grant, who was still crawling out of the trough, and pulling him out by his shirt.

"Stop it!" Izzie shouted, knowing full well Delco didn't fight fair, especially against bigger and badder guys. She also had to admit she didn't know how Grant would react, and the last thing she wanted was for Grant to get indicted for assault. It wouldn't be the first time Delco had called the local sheriff after losing a fight.

Luckily, Grant didn't fight back. Delco was making a fool of himself, taking on a boxer's stance and raising his fists at Grant, but Grant just shook his head and wrung some of the water out his clothes before walking away.

After a few moments of hesitation, and after realizing none of the ranch hands were running to his aid, Delco followed Grant into the barn.

With his eyes still adjusting to the relative darkness of the barn, Grant turned around to face Delco. "Listen. Izzie and I work together. I have no intention of moving in on your turf. Don't get me wrong. She's a swell girl, but not my type." He turned around to grab a towel out of his locker, but Delco poked him in the back with his finger.

"What are you? A fruit? She's a beautiful woman. Any guy would have a hard time keeping his hands off her, and that's why she needs me to defend her."

Grant chuckled. "Trust me, she can take care of herself."

"But you want her, right?" Delco, with all his bravado, looked like a rooster ready for a fight, the way he was shuffling his feet and shaking his shoulders. "Hey? I bet you want to nail her in a big way. Well, you can't, 'cause she's mine."

Again, Grant shook his head and walked out, leaving Delco to stew in his own fat. Grant determinedly paced in the direction of the crew quarters to get some dry clothes and hoped it would calm his heartbeat down. Delco wasn't worth getting into a fight with, although his instincts had told him to flatten the little runt. It was true that he liked Izzie. She was a nice girl who could work like any of the guys on the ranch, despite her long brown mane and overt femininity. She had a wicked sense of humor, which pleased Grant a lot, and she could take a joke or a taunt like the other guys too, but he didn't lust after her. If he lusted after anyone here, it was her brother, but it was clear that Hunter hated his guts. That was something Grant was just going to have to live with. He wasn't here looking for a partner anyway. He was only here to make a halfway decent living.

In his small room, Grant got rid of his wet shirt and jeans and took out a clean set. He didn't linger, both because he needed to get back to work and because he didn't want to give himself too much time to think. He'd have plenty of time for that later, as he waited for sleep to catch him. Right now he would look for other ways to keep his mind occupied.

On his way out, he bumped into Izzie.

"Listen, Grant, I'm sorry about Delco."

Grant shrugged. "It's okay. He's harmless."

Izzie shook her head. "The thing is, he isn't. He fights mean, and if he can't win he'll find other ways to gain the upper hand."

"Like what?" Grant asked, a little apprehensive about what to expect.

"He'll spread rumors. He managed to get one of the wranglers at the Hope Ranch fired last year," Izzie answered reluctantly. The Hope Ranch was one of the large ranches one county over, and probably Hunter's biggest competition in the area. "The owner's a big rodeo fan, and Delco said that the wrangler put the moves on me in front of him. That's all it took."

Grant sighed. "Phew. Why do you stay with a guy like that, Izzie?"

Izzie shrugged. "Any boyfriend is better than no boyfriend?"

Grant wrapped an arm around Izzie's slender shoulders. "But you deserve better."

Izzie smiled shyly. "I guess if it hadn't been for Hugh getting Lisa pregnant, all of us Krauses would still be bachelors."

"You're practically on your own anyway, with Delco being away ten months out of the year," Grant said as he closed the door behind him and they made their way back toward the stables.

Izzie chuckled. "Yeah, and that's just the way I like it!" She turned to Grant. "Do you see yourself living with someone for the rest of your life?"

Grant pulled a doubtful face. "Haven't met anyone I'd want to live with. Let alone for the rest of my life."

"Gable?" she asked quietly.

"Not really," Grant answered truthfully. "I guess in some ways we were compatible, but in others…. He's not an easy man to live with, Izzie. Of course, I'm no prize either, so I don't want to use that excuse, but to answer your question, no, I don't believe in love ever after." Grant set a determined pace, feeling uncomfortable talking about his private life with anyone, let alone a woman. On the one hand, it felt good to actually talk about Gable with her; on the other hand, he still didn't know whether he could really trust her. After all, he was working for her family, and she could easily get him fired, although he was pretty sure that Izzie knew about his sexual preference. He'd been without a steady job for a while, though, and right now he needed the fixed income, so he didn't want to run the risk of losing it again.

They were nearly back at the stable when Izzie briefly took Grant's hand and squeezed it. "Thanks for taking my side with Delco."

"I didn't take sides," Grant answered. "I just don't bother with guys who have slightly inflated egos."

"Slightly?" Izzie's snort was very unladylike. "You're right, you know. I should cut him loose. I just like giving guys a second chance." She moved a little closer. "And thanks for not losing your temper. Hugh has in the past, and it only made things worse."

"Hugh lost his temper?" Grant asked, although he now knew from experience it took a lot of self-control not to when Delco was involved.

Izzie nodded amusedly.

They finished their work with the horses, and once they were all back in the stables, the troop parted ways. The Krause family returned to the big house, and the wranglers and stable boys who lived on the ranch returned to their own quarters, where a hearty meal—prepared by Lisa and Beth—and a free evening was waiting for them.

Although after dinner most of the men ended up in the living room in front of the TV, Grant preferred to stay by himself. He didn't really fit into the group, which had clearly been living together for a while, and he could frankly do without the usual questions that were posed to the new guy.

The other wranglers had tried to find out more about Grant, but he had ignored their questions or given them some smart-ass answer, especially when they probed deeper into his personal life, asking him whether he'd ever been married or if he had kids. He really didn't feel like sharing the answers to those questions with anyone he barely knew. In any case, some of his answers wouldn't have been too well received, so he preferred to stay vague.

The place that housed the crew quarters was like a big ranch house, complete with a kitchen, shower block, and a porch all around. Grant liked sitting at the back, where he missed the sunset but could read his book in silence without anyone bothering him. Looking out over the field to where the earth and the sky met meant more to him than catching the late evening sun. The nice view was one thing, but from time to time, he'd catch Hunter taking his unruly horse out for a late ride. Although he knew better than to let the sight of Hunter on horseback entice him, he couldn't help looking up from the pages of his book whenever he heard the tall man mutter and curse at his horse.

Grant had often thought that if he and Hunter had a more amicable relationship, he'd offer to show Davenport who was boss, but Grant feared this wouldn't be taken with much of a sense of humor, the way they stood now. He had no idea why Hunter behaved so sternly around him. It wasn't the way he remembered him from the times Hunter had visited Gable's ranch. Whenever Hunter had come around there to buy horses, he was always jovial and smiling, nothing like the cantankerous bastard he appeared to be now.

As the light started fading, Grant closed his book and got up from the old weatherworn chair he usually occupied. He'd have to get up at the crack of dawn to start his chores if he hoped to beat the heat for some of them, at least. He just wished he was tired enough for sleep to overtake him quickly, and prayed that his dreams wouldn't leave him frustrated.

# —4—

THE next time all the men from the Blue River Ranch went out for a night on the town, Grant joined them, although it had taken a lot of coaxing from Tim and Hugh. Finally, it was Hunter who made him cave.

"Come with us," Hunter had said. "It's a lot of fun to see Hugh make an ass of himself behind a microphone."

Silently, Hunter thought it would be good for Grant to see Miranda, so Grant would stop eyeing him. They hadn't worked together that much—Izzie had made sure of that—but it was still hard not to bump into each other if your horses occupied adjoining stalls in the stables. Hunter had assured himself it would be one step too far to move Raven to the other side of the stable block just to make sure he saw even less of the striking cowboy.

He couldn't shake the feeling that Grant looked at him differently, though. With the others, he joked and played around, but around Hunter, Grant seemed overly polite and gentle. Then again, although Hunter made sure Grant knew he wasn't his boss, Hunter *did* own the ranch, so he was sure Grant knew he could fire his ass if he wanted. Hunter was smart enough to know a good employee when he saw one, so he had no intention of actually throwing Grant out, even though every few weeks, Grant asked Hugh for a few days of unpaid leave, which was a little unconventional.

At the bar, Grant stayed in the background, quietly drinking a beer.

Although that was usually what Hunter did as well, he couldn't stay close to the bar now, afraid that he'd have to talk to Grant, so he walked around in search of Miranda. When he couldn't find her, he asked one of her friends when she would be arriving.

"Miranda's gone to the city tonight," the petite blonde answered. "I think she said she was meeting a friend."

Hunter couldn't help thinking the blonde was flirting with him. For a moment he thought about taking her up on it, but then he figured she'd be on the phone to Miranda as soon as he went home, so he decided against it. He nodded in thanks and left her with her friends.

"Girls not interested?" Grant asked when Hunter returned to the bar.

"They're friends of Miranda," he answered. "She's sort of my girlfriend."

"Ah," Grant nodded. "Only sort of?"

"We're not engaged or anything," Hunter replied. He didn't feel like elaborating, especially not if it meant that he had to tell Grant, of all people, that he and Miranda had sex and very little else. It wouldn't look good for Miranda to get that reputation.

"Have you ever seen Jack perform?" Hunter asked Grant, eager to change the topic of conversation.

"I've only seen him with his hand down a horse's throat," Grant admitted with a chuckle. "If he's as good a singer as he is a horse dentist, we should be in for quite a show."

Hunter nodded, saluting a guy at the other side of the bar with his beer bottle. "Best show in town. We're grateful he still comes here regularly, because he's on stage with his band almost every Friday and Saturday. I think he makes almost as much money now he's touring the other counties as he does doing his day job."

At that moment, Izzie walked in.

"Hey, sis," Hunter greeted her.

"Hunter," she said. "Grant."

The way she said Grant's name, with that teasing, amused smile of hers, worried Hunter, especially after all the innuendo that had been creeping into every conversation he'd had with Izzie these past weeks. Did Izzie think that he and Grant were here together?

"I hear Miranda went to see the Chippendales in the city," Izzie told Hunter. "Guess you're going to be able to get up at the crack of dawn tomorrow."

Hunter swatted the back of her head. "Hey, watch your mouth," he told his sister, making sure she understood he wasn't serious. He did want her to stop, though. Hunter knew she wasn't shy around Grant, and he didn't want her to say anything to make Grant think he was interested in him.

Instead of continuing her banter, Izzie's face suddenly went dark. "Oh, shit," she mumbled.

"What's wrong?" Hunter asked.

Izzie pointed across the curved bar at the entrance. "Delco and I just broke up. I'd hoped he would just get in his truck and drive off, but I guess he's not done with me."

The two men watched Delco look around and finally settle far enough away from Izzie so she could stay out of his range of vision.

"Do you want me to take you home?" Hunter asked.

Izzie shook her head. "I promised myself that I was going to have fun tonight. I've finally worked up the courage to get that pest out of my life. I'm not going to let him ruin my evening."

Hunter could see the determination in her face, but he could also see her trying to keep an eye on Delco's movements. He couldn't blame her.

"We'll protect you, sis," Hunter assured her.

"Yeah," Grant agreed. "Come stand between us. A shrimp like him wouldn't touch you with two butch guys like us standing by you."

Izzie chuckled and bumped Grant's hip with her ass as she moved to sit between them. "You're right," she said, flirting more than she usually did with Grant. "Maybe it's time we piss him off just a little."

The band had finished getting ready, and Jack took the mic. "Good evening, ladies and gentlemen. Especially the lovely ladies here tonight. Let's start off getting some of you on the dance floor! This is 'Shake a Tail Feather'."

Jack and his band started playing a country rock song, and the dance floor filled up fast. Most of the patrons knew Jack and the band, so the tone was set from the first chords that were played. Izzie, Hunter, and Grant watched from the bar, losing sight of Delco.

It wasn't until Hunter saw Hugh crossing the dance floor, making a beeline for where they were standing, that he noticed Delco wasn't sitting where he'd last seen him. He looked at his two companions, both mesmerized by the band on stage, Grant's arms hanging loosely on the bar behind Izzie without touching her. Hunter didn't have time to react when he suddenly saw a fist whiz past him and land squarely against Grant's jaw.

The big guy wavered a bit but recovered, a stunned expression on his face.

"Delco!" Izzie shouted.

Delco hesitated, unsure why Grant didn't retaliate, but then he turned to Izzie. "You whore. You couldn't wait to get rid of me so you could get into his pants! Well, I ain't leavin'." He was pointing at Grant, who was rubbing his jaw but otherwise seemed the epitome of calm.

Hunter knew he needed to intervene. "If you think she's such a whore, maybe you should just leave her alone?"

"Nobody calls Izzie a whore," Hugh said from behind Delco, grabbing him by the shoulder and twisting him around before slugging him with his fist. Hugh, being almost a head taller than Delco, packed a mean left hook, and Delco fell back against Izzie and Grant, who immediately pushed him up again, so Hugh grabbed Delco by his shirt and hauled him outside.

Not everyone in the bar followed the altercation, but those who did saw Hugh walk outside, closely followed by most of the wranglers from the Blue River Ranch. Once outside, it took three men to drag Hugh away from Delco, but not until Delco's nose was bleeding and his lip was split.

One of the men following them to the parking lot was the county sheriff. "Break it up, guys. Enough is enough."

"Arrest him, Sheriff," Delco cried out. "He's a bully. Look at what he did to me!"

"He started it," Grant interjected calmly, pointing at Delco. "He slugged me first."

The sheriff, assessing the situation and likely understanding there was a mob here that was ready to defend Izzie's honor, defused the situation. "Let's go back to the station and sort this out. Hunter, I trust you'll bring the men who were a part of this with you? I'm taking this one with me now."

Hunter nodded.


ABOUT an hour later at the sheriff's station, Delco was in one room, Izzie and Hugh in another, and Hunter and Grant were sitting in the waiting room up front.

"You're good at staying calm," Hunter sighed.

Grant shrugged. "He's a shrimp. Ten years ago I would have reacted, but now I've learned my lesson. Ten years ago I almost killed a guy. I'm not letting that happen again."

"You almost killed a guy?" Hunter parroted.

Grant nodded. "Long story."

Hunter smiled. It wasn't any of his business. He felt good about Grant's self-restraint, though. If he'd reacted like Hugh had, they'd all be in trouble.

Grant leaned forward and looked at the opposite wall. "Izzie told me this wasn't the first time Hugh's defended her against Delco?"

"Delco never treated her right," Hunter answered. "He always acted like she was his possession and nobody could look at, let alone touch her. Hugh's a gentleman all the way. He thinks a woman is something to treasure."

"He's got the right idea," Grant agreed. "Especially Izzie. She's everything a man could want in a woman. Knows how to saddle a horse, muck out a stable, and still look good on a night out on the town."

Hunter chuckled and shook his head. He felt relaxed around Grant now, which surprised him. "So do you have your eye on Izzie?"

Grant shook his head. "Naah, she's a great girl and a good friend, but you know me. She needs a guy who loves her for her. I can't give her that."

Hunter looked at Grant but averted his eyes as soon as Grant met his gaze. Grant's statement suddenly awoke the tension between them again.

Then the sheriff came into the waiting room with Hugh. "Grant, can I talk to you now?"

Hugh took Grant's place.

"You okay?" Hunter asked.

Hugh rested his elbows on his knees and sighed. "I can't do this anymore, Hunter."

"Can't do what?" Hunter felt uneasy all of a sudden. He had no idea what to expect, and he didn't like that feeling.

"Lisa and I are getting a divorce."

"You're *what*?"

Hugh looked at Hunter, and there was no doubt in Hunter's mind that his brother-in-law wasn't kidding.

"All this because of a bar brawl?"

Hugh rolled his eyes and smiled a little uneasily. "We've been talking about it for a while and always said we'd wait until Danny was older, but I can't do this anymore."

Hunter was stunned into silence. He kept looking at Hugh and back at the door through which Grant had disappeared and then back at Hugh.

"You know I only married Lisa because I got her pregnant, right?"

Hunter nodded. "Yeah, but I thought you loved her too?"

Hugh shook his head. "The girl I was in love with was Izzie. Only she was way too young. She was fourteen then, so I couldn't even get close to her. And by the time she was eighteen, she had other boyfriends and Lisa had taken a liking to me. I figured Izzie wasn't interested in me, so I took what I could get. But I never really loved Lisa, although I swear I tried."

The men sat next to each other, mimicking each other's posture and not saying anything for long, tense moments.

"I told Izzie I loved her when we were sitting together in the other room."

Hunter looked up at Hugh. "You mean she never knew?"

"Oh, course not!" Hugh answered. "I've been married to her big sister for ten years, Hunter."

"And how did she react?"

Hugh shrugged. "She was nice about it but made it pretty clear she didn't think we had a future."

Hunter cocked his head in understanding.

"So you see I can't stay. I'm sorry, man, but you're going to have to find another foreman. Talk to Grant. He's a good guy."

Hunter didn't know what to say. Sure, they were shorthanded all the time and he was going to miss having someone he trusted completely to run the day-to-day stuff around the ranch, but it was more than that. Hugh leaving meant Danny was going to miss his father and Hunter was losing his best friend. He and Hugh had been as close as two guys could be since they were in elementary school, yet he'd never known about Hugh's feelings for Izzie.

They sat together in silence until the sheriff came into the waiting room with Grant and Izzie.

"Okay, everything is settled. Delco wanted to press assault charges against Hugh, but Izzie countered by telling him that if he did that, she'd file charges against him herself, and there are plenty of witnesses who'll testify that Delco slugged Grant without provocation, so I think he's got nowhere to go. Wouldn't put it past him to try other ways to give you a hard time, though, so be careful out there. I can't really hold him, but we know he's tried stuff like this before, so I'm afraid we might not get rid of him this easily."

All of them nodded in accord as the sheriff showed them out.

"Since I'm the only one who didn't even get a drink tonight, I guess I'm driving," Izzie stated as she held out her hand to Hunter to get his keys. "Saddle up, boys!"

# —5—

HUNTER didn't enjoy being in the house now that Hugh had packed his things and driven off. He often wished his sisters were more like other women and would just have a good cry from time to time, but they never did. Instead, Lisa ordered everyone around, and their mother seemed like she had lost the ability to smile. Not that she was much of a jovial woman at the best of times, but right now, Hunter could barely be in the same room with his mother and sister. Izzie seemed to feel the same, since she always found excuses not to join the rest of the family for dinner. At night, in the kitchen, Hunter and Izzie shared late-night leftovers for at least half of the days of the week.

It was true they were busy. Izzie had taken on quite a few of Hugh's foreman tasks, and Hunter had found the need to spend more time getting his hands dirty as well. Hugh's were big boots to fill, after all. But they both knew anything was better than hanging around the house.

They tried to keep Danny busy as well. He seemed to be the only one shedding a tear now and then. They both knew he missed his dad tremendously, and nobody was going to be able to fill those boots.

On top of everything, another foal had disappeared, and the rain, which had been pouring down day after day, had erased all tracks. Hunter and Grant had done a quick survey of the fences around the lower fields and had found one hidden corner where the fence had been flattened, adding credence to the cougar theory, but they had yet to find a carcass or half-eaten remains. They fixed the fence and talked about posting all-night vigils but abandoned the idea because they just didn't have the manpower.

Now that he was being forced to work together with Grant all the time, Hunter managed to relax more when they were together. Grant hadn't made a move toward him, and Hunter found he actually liked the man quite a bit. Of course, Izzie couldn't resist teasing him about it, but it did make everyday life a bit easier.

One evening, Hunter took Davenport out to teach him a lesson and the stubborn horse threw him off. When he got up, wiping the mud off his jeans, Hunter noticed Grant sitting on the back porch of the crew quarters. He was holding a book and smiling as he looked at him.

"What's so funny?" Hunter asked once he'd approached the porch.

"My book," Grant lied.

"You're laughing because I fell off my horse."

"I wouldn't dare." Grant smiled cheekily. "You have to admit, for a guy who was practically born in the saddle, that horse is taking you for a ride, and you have absolutely no say in where you're going."

Hunter shrugged.

"I think he's as stubborn as his rider," Grant added.

"Yeah, you might be right," Hunter reluctantly admitted, sinking down on the top step of the porch with his back toward Grant.

"Weather's nice tonight," Grant said.

"Mmmh," Hunter agreed. "It's going to rain again, though. Look at those ominous clouds in the sky over there." He pointed toward the top of the tree line.

"Could just be getting dark," Grant replied.

"Nope. It's rain," Hunter replied determinedly. "I love the view here, though. This is one of the few places where you can see the earth touch the sky."

When Hunter looked to the side, he saw Grant give him a curious look that he couldn't quite read. "Well, most places have trees or hills obscuring the view, but here you just see the horizon."

"Yeah, I noticed that too," Grant said quietly.

Hunter had no idea where this conversation was going, but he had to admit he enjoyed it. He'd had this type of conversation many times with Hugh as they talked about their day, and he missed the totally useless small talk about horses and the weather almost as much as he missed having his trusted friend around. Maybe he should consider Grant his friend too. After all, it couldn't be easy for Grant either, being the new guy and hiding his true self from everyone around. Except, of course, from Hunter and Izzie. Although they never talked about it, Hunter was sure that Grant knew that he and Izzie knew about his sexual orientation, and that it seemingly didn't matter.

Maybe they should strike up a friendship?

"I better catch Davenport and take him inside before he's soaked and I have twice as much work with him," Hunter said, getting up from the step.

"Good luck with that," Grant said, a teasing smile playing around the corners of his mouth. "I'll enjoy the show." He paused for a moment and then added, "On second thought, I better help you out. That bastard will no doubt run away, and in that case, two is better than one."

They walked toward the high grass, where Davenport was peacefully grazing, but as soon as they came close, he bolted.

"Sssh, don't go after him. He'll think it's a game," Grant said softly. "Hang on."

Hunter stopped and watched Grant walk around the horse in a large circle to a clearing in the grass. There he turned around and crouched down as if he was looking for something. He then got up again and repeated his action a little bit farther out.

From the corner of his eye, Hunter could see Davenport raise his head and look at Grant. His ears pointed forward and he took a tentative step toward Grant, stopping as soon as Grant got up and moved a little farther away from him. This time, when Grant crouched down, Davenport took another few steps. Clearly, the horse was curious about what exactly Grant was looking at on the ground. It took some time, but eventually Davenport was so close to Grant, as soon as the horse lowered his head to investigate with him, all Grant had to do was raise his hand to grab hold of Davenport's halter.

"Bingo," Grant said triumphantly, walking Davenport to where Hunter was standing.

"You're good at this," Hunter said, hoping it would be enough of a compliment.

"Nah, Gable's the master. He would have gotten hold of this lug a lot faster, but he did teach me a thing or two."

"I think he taught all of us a thing or two," Hunter confessed. "If it hadn't been for his support, I don't think this ranch would have survived."

They started walking toward the stables.

"He told me a few things about the time your dad died," Grant said tentatively.

Hunter sighed. "I was way too young to take on the responsibility, but Mom had never worked the ranch. She was a housewife and a mother and, frankly, had her hands full with all of us. Bernie was still a baby, and although Izzie and I were good riders, we didn't know the first thing about the business side of things. Lisa was a lot like Mom. She barely knew the front end of a horse from the back. All she wanted to do was finish school and get married. Hugh's dad was a good foreman, but he didn't have a head for figures, so in the beginning, when we let him run things, we worked at a loss. If it hadn't been for Gable showing me the ropes, helping me to do the buying and selling and not just the horses, this ranch wouldn't exist anymore. We would have gone belly-up before I turned eighteen."

It felt good to tell someone about that, especially someone who knew Gable.

"But now you're the boss," Grant replied. "You have this big, prosperous ranch."

Hunter sighed. "Gable never wanted a big business. He was never interested in making money. He wanted perfectly trained horses that handled like a dream. That's why he never bred them himself."

"No patience to wait two years before he could start training them," Grant chuckled, and Hunter laughed along.

"He had an eye for picking the best foals, though."

"Oh yes," Grant agreed.

They had almost reached the stable block when suddenly the skies opened up, and with a big flash and a loud bang, it started pouring down. A spooked Davenport ran straight inside, and both men followed in an attempt to stay dry. It was to no avail. When Hunter turned toward Grant, he couldn't miss the other man's shirt clinging to his chest, and it left nothing to the imagination.

"Think it'll be over as fast as it started?" Grant asked, turning around and looking outside.

"'Fraid not," Hunter answered, unable to take his eyes off the wet jeans clinging to Grant's buttocks and long legs. He shook himself out of his reverie and took Davenport's saddle off, placing it on the saddle rack and taking a cloth to wipe it down.

"I'll rub him down," Grant volunteered, taking Davenport into his stable and taking his tack off.

Hunter was surprised at how little grief Davenport gave Grant. Grant had a no-nonsense approach that was both gentle and swift, and he was done in no time.

"Guess I better make a run for it," Grant said by way of good-bye just before he ran out of the stable.


LATER that night, Hunter was just about to go to bed when there was a knocking loud enough to be heard over the sound of the storm. He opened the front door and saw Tim standing on the porch, soaked to the bone despite his heavy weather gear.

"Grant asked me to come get you. Danny's in trouble!" Tim shouted. "Since Davenport's useless in this weather, I brought Raven so you could ride out with me."

Hunter ran into the mudroom to get his oilskin duster and his hat and followed his wrangler outside.

It was pitch-black and very cold for the time of year, and the ground was totally waterlogged. At first they could make good time, letting the horses gallop, but Hunter halted when they came to a lopsided fence.

"We don't have time," Tim shouted at him. "We have to take these ropes to Grant. We'll come back and fix the fence later."

Hunter nodded and spurred Raven on so he could catch up with Tim, who by now was making his way through the brush. The horses slipped every few steps, and Hunter was glad Tim hadn't saddled Davenport. Raven handled like a dream, unperturbed by the slippery ground and the fact that his hoofs sank into the mud. Every once in a while, Tim took his handheld GPS out of his coat and checked it. Hunter was glad they'd bought those gadgets a few months ago, although he'd never understood their power until tonight.

"Almost there," Tim assured him.

Hunter could hear the river, and even over the rattling rain, he could tell it was roaring louder than it usually would this far into the year. Melting water from the mountains always made it swell in early spring, but by this time of year it was usually a soft, flowing stream—only this didn't sound like that.

They came to a clearing, and Hunter immediately saw what the problem was. The swell of the river had caused it to find another way of running, forming a small island in the middle of the torrential flood. On that island was a big amber mare with a frightened young boy sitting on top of her.

Grant was standing on the shore of the river, shouting at Danny to stay calm, that help was on the way.

Hunter understood why both horses were carrying ropes now. They were going to have to rescue his godson.

"You're a sight for sore eyes," Grant said as he came closer to Hunter. "There's what looks like a pretty sturdy tree on the other side." He pointed at the island. "We'll tie a rope around the tree here, and I'll wade across on Raven. Then I'll secure the rope around that tree and bring Danny back."

Hunter nodded, glad for Grant's self-assuredness. "I'll go."

"Are you crazy? This is dangerous stuff. I'll go," Grant replied sternly.

"He's my godson," Hunter protested.

"And he doesn't have his dad here right now, so he needs you. I'm going, end of discussion."

Grant took the rope from Hunter, tied one end around the western saddle and the other around the tree, and exchanged places with Hunter before turning Raven toward the river. It took him some persuading to get the animal to step into the water, but eventually they were on their way.

Hunter was holding his breath, almost as afraid something would happen to Grant as he was about Danny. The stream on this side of the island wasn't very wide or deep, but the water was flowing very quickly, and more than once, Raven misstepped and almost toppled Grant off. Tim had his hands full trying to feed Grant the rope, but all Hunter could do was watch.

Eventually Grant made it to the other side, Raven clambering out of the rolling stream before Grant helped Danny down from his horse. Hunter could see how Grant took a quick look at Danny to see if he was in one piece before letting him go to secure the rope to the other tree. Grant then tied a rope around Danny, trailing it over the guide rope before he let him mount the dark horse. He took Belle's reins and got on in front of the kid, tying the rope around his own waist before slowly letting Raven step back into the river. It was bit of a balancing act—controlling both horses and making sure Danny held on to him firmly—but Grant seemed in total control.

Hunter counted every step Raven took, hissing every time the horse lost its footing, breathing whenever the steps seemed to be easier. Little by little, they came closer to the shore and eventually made it up on dryer land. Grant untied the ropes and let Danny dismount into Hunter's waiting arms.

Hunter knew he couldn't have felt better if Danny were his own son. He would never have forgiven himself if something had happened to the boy, and he nodded his appreciation at Grant and Tim.

Grant patted Hunter's back. "Go on, ride home on Belle and take Danny to his mother. Tim and I will see if we can fix the gate, and then Tim'll pick Belle up at the house. We'll make sure the horses are well taken care of."

Hunter tried to convey his thanks to the other two men as they helped Danny onto the horse behind him, and then he urged the mare to bring them home safely.

## —6—

IT WAS still raining when Hunter walked into the shower block more than an hour later. Automatically, he shook the wet off his oilskin duster and took off his hat, a stream of water running off that as well. He was so nervous he could barely breathe, yet he had to do this. He remembered feeling like this when he'd come home from school with bad grades one term and his mother had made him wait in the mudroom for his dad to come in from the ranch. Only this time, he wasn't going to be scolded. He simply wanted to convey his thanks to Grant, and that was that. Yes, knowing that the wrangler was washing the rain off his skin, standing under the shower butt-naked, was making Hunter sweat. Part of him hoped that Grant hadn't shut the stall door all the way so he could catch a glimpse of him and could let his eyes wander over those broad shoulders and narrow hips, but another part of him knew that if that happened, he'd never be able to get the image out of his mind.

So he paced the small corridor that led to the shower cubicles, hat in hand and incessantly dripping, until he heard the shower being turned off. He knew Grant had to pass through the corridor on the way to the main house, so it was simply a matter of being patient and Grant would come to him. Hunter couldn't stand still, though, so he paced. He had just turned around when he heard Grant's voice behind him.

"Hunter. What an unexpected pleasure."

Straightening his back, Hunter turned to face him. "Grant," he nodded. Hunter couldn't look him straight in the eye, afraid he wouldn't be able to hide his appreciation of the long limbs, the slightly rough skin, still wet with moisture, the fact Grant wasn't wearing anything but a towel slung low on his hips. Suddenly Hunter was grateful Grant was carrying his wet clothes, otherwise he would have seen the dusting of chest hair or the washboard stomach he knew Grant possessed. Damn, there was a reason Hunter never went into the men's shower block, and it was because it would awaken feelings he tried every day to hide.

Grant was still staring at him, clearly expecting him to say something.

"I wanted… I wanted to say thank you."

"My pleasure." Grant nodded. "I didn't think twice, to be honest. I saw Danny leave and I thought he might get into trouble, so I followed him out. He's too young to be out in this sort of weather on his own and on a horse he's barely old enough to manage, so it was obviously without permission. I knew you'd never let him go out like that."

"With his dad gone, he's a bit messed up," Hunter said, by way of apologizing for Danny's behavior. "He seemed to be okay about it, but I guess he misses him."

"Yeah, we all do," Grant mused. "So he's okay now?"

"Yeah," Hunter said, still not looking directly at Grant. "He was shivering like mad, and he'll get an earful from Lisa as soon as she's sure he'll live, but other than a cold and a big scolding, he won't take anything away from it."

"That's good to hear," Grant replied. "He's a good kid."

"Yeah, he is," Hunter agreed, fiddling with his hat. "So, what happened to that gate?" He knew he should let Grant get on with it, but he somehow had a hard time leaving.

"The storm dislodged it. Looked pretty bad and we couldn't fix it, so we tied it up. We'll have to repair it for good tomorrow."

Hunter nodded, stealing looks from time to time but not daring to feast his eyes. "Listen, I better let you run upstairs so you can get dressed, otherwise I'll be responsible for you getting a cold as well."

Grant smiled, so Hunter turned around to leave.

"I had the feeling you didn't mind seeing me naked," Grant added just before Hunter rounded the door.

Hunter stopped. He had to prevent himself from turning around and shouting something about Grant being an insolent prick, so instead, he started walking again. With every step he took away from the crew house, he walked faster. Every step away made him realize that it was good that he hadn't shouted at Grant, because he knew that the words would have only served to push Grant away; he hoped that, if his resolve not to kiss the man faltered, Grant *would* move away from him, preventing the inevitable from happening.

There it was. He'd admitted to himself that he wanted to kiss the man, push his body against Grant's, and feel those hard muscles under his hands.

It was still raining when Hunter reached the mudroom at the side of the main house, but he didn't walk in. Instead, he smashed his fist against the worn wood. There was no reason to think that Grant would push him away if he returned to the crew quarters. He'd seen the way Grant had looked at him. He'd seen the unashamed lust in the man's eyes, felt the stolen touches, the way Grant always sought him out, despite the fact Hunter hadn't been very welcoming toward him. He'd only now allowed himself to understand them. The adrenaline of rescuing Danny was just ebbing away, but his heart was still beating fast. He was tired and wet to the bone, but all he could think of was that he needed to release the tension, and his own hand wasn't going to do. Not anymore.

Hunter turned around and paced back to the crew house. He had to get it out of his system, had to taste the forbidden fruit, just this once, and then maybe he would never again wonder, "What if?"

Hunter entered the house through the same door he'd left it earlier and almost ran up the stairs. Then he realized he had no idea which room was Grant's. He had no other course of action than to call out his name. He hoped the other guys would either not recognize his voice or simply think that the boss was here to give Grant a hard time.

At the end of the corridor, a door opened and Grant stuck his head out. As soon as he saw Hunter, he gestured for him to come inside his room.

"You're back quick," Grant said as soon as he closed the door behind Hunter. His voice was subdued, as if he knew noises carried too far through the house.

Hunter didn't answer. What could he say?

"Guess I don't have to ask you if it's still raining."

Hunter looked up and gazed straight into Grant's dark eyes. Grant's smile was teasing and seductive and, coupled with the fact that the towel that had only barely clung to Grant's hips had been replaced by a pair of boxer briefs and nothing else, made Hunter avert his eyes again.

"Why don't you take your coat off?" Grant suggested. "You're dripping all over my floor."

Hunter hesitated, but Grant moved away, opening a closet and taking out a bottle of whiskey.

"Drink?" Grant offered.

Hunter nodded and placed his duster over the chair standing next to the near wall while Grant took out two glasses and added about an inch of amber liquid to both of them.

"Here," he said, offering one of the tumblers to Hunter. "It'll help warm you up, because you must be cold by now, and we can't have the boss catching a cold, being as understaffed as we are."

Hunter accepted the glass and downed the entire contents in one swallow. The liquid burned, but Hunter welcomed the feeling. He gave Grant just enough time to take one sip and then took a step toward him.

GRANT noticed the overture and put his glass down on the table. He was still smiling as he reached for Hunter's glass, and just managed to bring that to safety before Hunter launched himself forward. Grant was roughly pushed against the window, and as he spread his legs slightly, Hunter pushed even closer. Hunter's kiss was rough and aggressive, but Grant could easily hold his own, even when his ass was pushed onto the windowsill. He scooted back as far as he could and pulled Hunter to him. Hunter didn't resist. In fact, he pushed his groin against Grant's and Grant felt Hunter's arousal, which made him smile into the kiss.

"What's so funny?" Hunter murmured.

"You are," Grant answered as he put his hand on the back of Hunter's neck to pull him back in for a kiss. This time Grant took the lead, pushing his tongue into Hunter's mouth. Grant let go of Hunter's hip to attempt to find his way into Hunter's jeans. As they kissed, they fought for dominance until Grant found his prize and unzipped Hunter, inserting his hand into Hunter's boxers and enveloping his swollen cock.

Hunter pulled back slightly, but didn't move away. He stopped fighting Grant, his movements seeming automatic, slipping from Hunter's control. The way Hunter was moaning against his mouth turned Grant on so much, he was rock-hard inside his boxers as well. He resisted touching himself, not wanting to scare Hunter off. Instead, he rubbed the hard shaft in his hands as Hunter was thrusting against the friction until, without warning, Hunter came with a loud moan. To Grant's surprise, Hunter did pull away this time, hurriedly zipping up his wet jeans and not looking at Grant before grabbing his coat and hat and running out before he'd had time to put them on.

Grant was left sitting on the windowsill, rock-hard and unsatisfied. He eventually got up to close his door and wash his sticky hand at the small sink in his room. His groin was aching and he took his cock in hand to finish himself off, simply to kill the dull ache, but it did little more than that. He let himself drop to his bed and rubbed his fingers through his short, curly hair, trying to get over his frustration. Why had Hunter done that? Why hadn't Hunter reciprocated? Grant couldn't find an explanation that satisfied him. He hadn't made a direct move toward Hunter before because he knew that Hunter was one of the few men who knew about his sexual preference. He imagined he wouldn't need to advertise. If Hunter wanted him, he'd come to him; but now that he had, Grant was even more confused.

The other reason had been that he needed the job. He'd been sent packing for far less than coming on to the boss. For some foremen, the knowledge that Grant was gay was enough. And news traveled. So all his life, Grant had played it like the others, by either staying vague about his sexual encounters or, in groups where it was commonplace to brag, he'd boast about his Saturday night conquests. It was surprisingly easy to lie about taking home some big-bosomed barfly. After all, Grant had had his fair share of women, just not lately. These past few years, he'd only slept with men, most of them nameless and faceless one-night stands, with one exception: Gable.

Grant had arrived on Gable's ranch looking for a job. Although the pay was low—much lower than what Hunter was paying him now—Grant had taken the job. It hadn't taken long for Grant to figure out Gable's preferences for a companion and to realize just how lonely Gable was. Their transition to sexual partners had been virtually seamless, yet Grant had always thought Gable was holding back, not showing himself completely. Somehow, they never became more than convenient fuck buddies. Grant didn't even feel like they were friends, so he'd wandered, often going into town to drown his sorrows.

Grant turned to his side and tried to get comfortable in his bed. He was going to have to get rid of his demons if he wanted to catch any sleep tonight. Tomorrow was another working day, and with Hugh gone, he was going to have to work with Hunter again. Part of him hoped that Hunter would simply ignore what had happened tonight, but on the other hand, Grant wanted some answers too. In any case, Grant wanted to secure his job, so he was going to have to give Hunter a reason to keep him on staff.

Grant licked his lips, hoping to still be able to taste the other man, but he couldn't.

# —7—

WHEN Hunter woke up, it was still raining cats and dogs. There was no use fretting over it, though. They'd tied the broken gate up the night before, but if they actually wanted to use it again, it would need extensive work, and there was no use postponing it.

As soon as Hunter made it to the workers' office, he knew he'd have to do the mending himself; the storm had dislodged several trees, and the men were already out clearing them and making sure the breaches in the fences were fixed as well.

"You sent them out?" Hunter asked Grant, who had clearly gotten up before him.

"Izzie did, actually, although she made it clear that she'd rather die than become the next foreman... woman... or whatever, around here," Grant chuckled.

"Which leaves the two of us to fix the gate, I suppose," Hunter answered. On any other day he would probably have laughed along with Grant, but right now he wasn't sure how to behave around the big guy, the memory of what had happened the night before all too vivid in his mind. He knew he'd overstepped more than a few boundaries, and he didn't want to give Grant the impression that it was going to happen again anytime soon, if ever.

"If you prefer, I can stay busy and find someone else to help me this afternoon. I'm sure the storm damage won't be that bad."

Hunter looked at Grant to gauge his expression, but he didn't know how to interpret it. Did Grant not want to work with him? Or did Grant sense his unease and want to give him an easy way out? "Hugh told me you had two right hands, so why don't we get it over with so when the workers return, they don't have to drive the long way around?"

"Sure," Grant answered evasively, leaving Hunter with all his questions unanswered. "I'll go get some tools if you have a new spring lock?"

Hunter nodded as he watched Grant leave.

Just over ten minutes later they were on horseback, making their way over to the broken gate. The ground was saturated with water, and although it didn't seem to bother Raven, it made Davenport even more skittish than other days.

"You know, it's none of my business," Grant started a little hesitantly, "but I would have given up on that horse of yours eons ago. He's a stubborn, annoying animal with an attitude problem, and he makes you look bad."

Hunter threw Grant a sideways look but didn't say anything.

"Like I said, it's none of my business," Grant added with a shrug.

"There are no badly behaved animals, just riders who don't know how to handle them," Hunter murmured.

"Makes you look even worse," Grant laughed. "And you sound just like Gable."

Hunter smiled as he realized Grant was right. "I know, but this was the first horse I ever bought for myself at auction, so I can't give up on him."

Grant raised an eyebrow as Davenport skidded off a wet patch and whinnied, giving Hunter one hell of a time to get him under control again. "You don't have to sell him. Just put him with the herd for a few months. They'll put him right. I'll ride him for you a few times. We might need to give him some stern training, though."

Hunter sighed. He knew Grant was right but didn't want to admit it. It was too close to admitting defeat, and he wasn't about to turn over for anyone, least of all Grant. "I suppose I could buy another horse from Gable. As a backup."

"Yeah," Grant replied, stifling a chuckle, "merely as a backup, of course."

Although he realized Grant was mocking him, deep down, Hunter was glad of the banter. Grant didn't seem to be fazed by what had happened the night before, which made it easier for Hunter to relax around him. Maybe they could do this. Maybe they could just work together and become friends.

Grant dismounted, and water splashed up as his feet landed in the mud. It was only now, in the full light of day, that it was clear how damaged the gate really was. Hunter jumped down as well and tied up the two horses while Grant surveyed the wood they'd hurriedly patched up the night before.

"Looks like we'll need a new side post. This one is pretty rotten," Grant evaluated. "The lock is broken, which we knew, and the top beam needs replacing too."

"We can measure the size of wood we need and use the truck to bring it over here when the workers bring it back this afternoon," Hunter agreed. "You're good at this," he added, sounding surprised as he watched Grant take the measurements.

Grant shrugged. "I didn't work on ranches all my life. Started out making furniture when I lived in the city. School was never really my thing. I wanted to go out and make money, but with barely a high school education, my options were either a life of crime or becoming a carpentry assistant. Lucky for me, the second option was the most appealing."

Hunter was more than a little surprised to hear Grant talk about himself. This was the most he'd ever learned about the guy. "You're definitely good with your hands."

Grant threw Hunter a teasing look that made him blush.

Hunter wished he could take back his words, or at least make them less open for interpretation. He was happy Grant didn't say anything, but there was no doubt about what he was thinking. Hunter thought it too: that Grant had shown just how talented his hands were when he'd made Hunter come the night before. Hunter's pants were growing tight just remembering those hands.

Grant broke the tension by purposely bumping into Hunter and handing him one side of a folding measure. "Hold that so we can get accurate measurements."

Although Hunter was usually the organized one, now he was glad Grant knew what he was doing too.

Grant pulled out a piece of paper and a pencil and jotted down the numbers. "I think I saw a few pieces of wood in the worker's shed that will do nicely for this."

Hunter shook his head to stop daydreaming and looked up at Grant. "Yeah, I suppose. You're the man. I trust your judgment." He was going to have to pull himself together and start acting like the boss again, before Grant started taking advantage of him. For now, the big guy just gave him an understanding look, and that was good, but Grant was still staff.

Hunter knew he was going to have to make a decision on a new foreman soon. Although Grant had only been with them for a short time, Hunter knew that Grant had all the qualities to make a good foreman. The only problem was that he'd been the last one hired, and the other wranglers might object to seeing Grant rise through the ranks. And then there was the obvious attraction, of course. Were these feelings Hunter had for Grant clouding his judgment? Not to mention they'd have to work pretty closely together. With Hugh, that had never been a problem. Hugh was his brother-in-law and one of his best friends since childhood. They could pretty much read each other's minds. But now, with Hugh gone, was Grant really his best choice?

"Okay, I'm all done. Do we need to ride anywhere else before I go get the wood for this?"

Hunter shook his head. Grant was smiling at him, and Hunter felt his knees go weak. He was really going to have to stop acting like a girl.

"Okay, let's go. I'll race you home."

Hunter turned around, hoping to find Davenport waiting for him, but the only horse peacefully grazing nearby was Raven, Grant's mount.

"Guess you're walking!" Grant laughed as he mounted his horse and turned it around. "I'll go see where he is."

Hunter leaned against the gatepost that was least rotten and waited, shaking his head. He was going to have to stop Davenport from embarrassing him even more.

It took Grant forever to return and Hunter eventually sat down on a tree trunk. "Guess he gave you a hard time?"

Grant nodded and then shrugged. "I still think he needs to learn who's boss around here, and it isn't him."

"Well, you can make it your pet project. I'm taking Hugh's horse, starting this afternoon."

Grant chuckled. "Best decision you've made all day, if you ask me."

They rode back to the house, handed their horses to the stable boys, and walked to the workers' shed to get the wood. As Grant had predicted, they found what they needed, and Hunter felt like a ranch hand as he took instruction from Grant on how to hold what where. Grant cranked up the big circular saw to cut a rather large beam to size. Despite the storm the night before, the temperature outside was picking up and with the high humidity, they were both sweating in no time.

After the large pieces were sawn to size, Grant used a handsaw to cut a few smaller support planks. Since he didn't seem to need an extra hand, Hunter walked outside to get them some water to drink. When he returned, Grant had taken his shirt off, and Hunter swallowed away the lump in his throat the sight caused.

"That looks heavenly," Grant said, straightening his back and holding out his hand toward the cup Hunter was holding. Hunter handed it to him and watched Grant gulp it down, his Adam's apple bobbing up and down as he swallowed. Just like the night before, lust boiled up inside Hunter, and he realized he wanted to kiss Grant's neck. He couldn't, though. Not again.

"Are you going to drink yours? Because the cool water felt really good," Grant asked, pointing at the other cup. When Hunter didn't immediately answer, Grant came closer. "Or shall I wrestle you for it?"

Hunter swallowed hard as he saw Grant approaching. Although his instincts told him to run, his feet wouldn't move. As Grant invaded his personal space, Hunter could smell his sweat, and to his surprise, it turned him on even more.

"You should really drink that yourself, you know," Grant drawled. "Wouldn't want you to get dehydrated."

Hunter's breathing quickened. Grant wasn't cornering him. He could just step aside and walk out if he wanted to. Only, he didn't want to. He wanted Grant to move even closer.

"I guess I should," Hunter managed to squeeze out of his voice box.

Grant nodded. He took Hunter's wrist and raised it. "So drink." When Hunter hesitated, Grant took the cup from Hunter's hand and lifted it to Hunter's mouth.

Their gazes locked, and Hunter swallowed the cool liquid until he couldn't quite follow the speed with which Grant was pouring it into him and it drizzled down his chin. Before Hunter could react, Grant lapped up the drops, and Hunter moaned at the contact of the hot mouth against his even hotter skin. The cup fell to the floor as Grant enveloped Hunter's head with his hands and moved his mouth to Hunter's lips, devouring him in one movement.

Hunter couldn't prevent himself from giving in. Despite all his reluctance, it felt so good, so right, and he dared to let his hands ghost over Grant's long back muscles and broad shoulders, holding back, almost afraid to actually touch him. As Grant pushed him against a supporting beam, Hunter felt a rapidly growing hardness against his groin, and in that moment it dawned on him that he wasn't the only one in lust right now. Their interaction felt even more passionate than the night before, but this time, Hunter wanted to repay the favor. He grabbed the back of Grant's jeans and pulled him closer, grinding his groin against Grant's and eliciting moans from the other man.

Grant moved his lips to Hunter's temple, clearly struggling for breath.

"We shouldn't be doing this," Hunter sighed as soon as his mouth was released.

"I know," Grant answered. "But damned if I don't want to." They didn't move away from each other, though, as Hunter saw his own mixed feelings mirrored in Grant's expression.

Suddenly they heard the large entrance door swing open, and they pulled apart.

"Put the small branches there and use the trailer loader to bring the big tree trunks in. There's space here to put them. We can always use the wood."

It was Izzie's voice, instructing the workers in what to do with the wood they'd recovered from the fallen trees they had taken down. When she saw the two men, she stopped.

"We're getting wood to fix the fence," Grant told her. She was looking admiringly at Grant's naked chest, smiling knowingly.

"Grant measured it and we found what we needed. We just needed to saw it to length," Hunter added, more for the men than for Izzie, who no doubt had deduced that they had been doing more than sawing planks.

Izzie's gaze traveled to Hunter, and although there was no longer lust in her eyes, Hunter definitely felt caught.

"So you'll be needing the truck to take the beams and planks out to the gate?"

Both men nodded.

"Don't suppose you need an extra pair of hands?"

"No," Grant was quick to answer. "We can manage."

"Mmmh, thought so," she said, before turning on her heels and walking out. Hunter could swear he heard her giggle.

"Last thing we need is for her to know," Hunter whispered at Grant. "She can't find out."

"I think it might be too late for that," Grant replied.

Hunter gave Grant a sideways look. "Well, if she asks you anything, we were just sawing planks!"

"Sure thing, boss," Grant answered, tipping his absent hat.

—8—

GRANT enjoyed the carpentry work around the ranch and silently hoped there'd be more of it. Sadly, Hunter was still blowing hot and cold around him. One moment he seemed to seek his company, and other times he was nowhere to be found. Grant had the distinct feeling that Hunter was avoiding him whenever he could. When circumstances threw them together, though, and there were no other wranglers or workers around, there was definitely electricity in the air. The way that man kissed didn't leave any doubt: Hunter wanted this.

It stroked Grant's ego that Hunter was in lust with him, and he certainly wasn't averse to taking it further, but he was still afraid to take those steps. Hunter obviously wasn't comfortable with the attraction, and Grant couldn't afford to see it turn sour. This was the best-paying job he'd had in a long time, and he promised himself he would do everything to keep it. If that meant keeping his dick inside his pants, then so be it. Unless Hunter took it out, of course.

Grant bagged his tools and smiled as he checked that the barn door closed like it should. He spent way too much time thinking about his boss.

"Do you have time to come with me and look at a gate that needs some work?"

Grant turned around and stared straight into Hunter's face. As soon as their eyes locked, Hunter became uncomfortable.

"There's a rotten post, like the gate we fixed last week, and I measured it like you did, so I figured you could saw it to length and we wouldn't need to drive over there twice. It's near Gable's property."

Grant let Hunter ramble and tried not to smile too much lest Hunter think he was mocking him. "Let me see your sketch?"

Hunter handed over the crumpled piece of paper.

"I think we have something close to that in the woodshed."

"I'll get the truck so we can load it," Hunter replied, turning on his heel and walking away.

Grant shook his head and made his way over to the woodshed. Like he thought, there was a beam that was pretty close to the size Hunter had jotted down, and it wouldn't take a lot of sawing to get it to fit. If Hunter's numbers were accurate, of course. Grant smiled. How could he suspect Hunter, who was a stickler for details, might get something like that wrong?

He bent his knees enough that he could hug the post and lift it. It was really too heavy for one man, but since Hunter wasn't here yet, he tried to get it a bit closer to the door.

He'd almost made it when he heard the sound of a truck engine being shut off. A few more steps and then…. The shed door opened and Grant stumbled, buckling under the weight of the beam.

"Whoa!" Hunter shouted. "Don't hurt yourself." He put his hands against Grant's shoulders, preventing Grant from toppling over, trapping the beam between them. As soon as Grant seemed stable, he let go and moved his hands to the post. "Let's get this in the truck. The sooner that gate is fixed, the better."

They loaded the beam in the back of the pickup truck and got in front, Hunter in the driver's seat. The ground was still soggy from all the rain they'd had, and Hunter had to swerve around a few potholes in the unpaved road to prevent them from being covered in mud. They didn't speak, and although Grant wasn't the greatest talker, he knew it was because of the tension between them. He wondered why Hunter hadn't simply told him where the gate was and sent him with one of the manual laborers. Surely Hunter had enough to do without coming out to help him mend a gate.

Hunter stopped the truck in one of the most remote corners of the ranch, at a point where the road became too hard to drive even for the sturdy pickup truck. Grant followed Hunter outside and looked up at the menacing clouds in the sky, thinking they were going to get wet before they were done, but he didn't say anything. Not when Hunter was clearly not in a talking mood.

They unloaded the beam, and Grant threw his bag of tools over his shoulder before they started off toward the gate, balancing the heavy beam between them. Grant recognized the gate as being one on the border of Gable's property, separating his land from the Blue River Ranch. The lock was facing the other way, so Grant wondered why they were mending his fence. He didn't want to state a fact that was as clear as day to Hunter, so he simply threw the younger man a look and set to work.

Hunter's measurements were pretty accurate, and like Grant had predicted, it didn't take a lot of sawing to get the beam to the right size. They worked together well, the only conversation being Grant asking Hunter to hand him a certain tool or to hold a particular part of the gate in place so Grant could screw the bolts into the new beam to hold the gate up. They were just standing back, testing to see whether the gate fell nicely into the lock when they threw it shut, when all hell broke loose and rain started pouring down. The truck was a fair walk away, but there was no other shelter nearby. It didn't take more than a look for them to decide to make a run for it, laughing when, in their haste, they couldn't get the door to open on the first go. By the time they sank down on the worn seats of the truck, they were soaked to the bone.

"I should have known this would happen," Hunter panted, still laughing.

"It's done nothing but rain for weeks, and the clouds were pretty dark when we arrived," Grant agreed.

"Yeah, but it was warmer today, so I hoped we'd get at least one dry day," Hunter said, by now sounding more pensive.

Grant tried to look out over the meadows, but the windows had steamed up all around them. When he looked at Hunter, he caught him staring.

"It's going to take forever to get these clothes dry." Grant wiped the wetness off his shirt, which made it cling even more to his nicely chiseled chest.

"Unless we take them off," Hunter said, barely audible. With some hesitation, Hunter leaned closer to Grant, as if he wanted to kiss him, but he didn't quite make it close enough. Grant knew he'd need to close the gap, so he leaned closer until their lips touched. Raising his hand to grab Hunter's neck, he could feel Hunter's racing pulse.

"It's okay," Grant said to soothe the other man. The kiss, hesitant at first, slowly became more passionate as their tongues came into play, teasing, tasting each other's lips and mouth. One of Hunter's hands came to rest on Grant's thigh, and Grant felt the heat emanating from it rise up to his groin, making his jeans grow tight.

"I'm not gay," Hunter said without looking at Grant as they broke for air. "I've never even kissed a guy before, let alone...." He didn't finish his sentence.

Grant didn't want to respond to what Hunter had said. He'd been in denial himself for years, even after he'd had his first encounter with a man. Even while he was living with Gable, he still told himself he wasn't gay, that women still interested him, that he just liked sex with anything that moved. But deep down, he knew. Hunter would know too, one day, when he was ready. In the meantime, Grant enjoyed Hunter's kisses and most certainly conveyed that by kissing him back. They were moving toward each other, the cramped confines of the truck their only constraint, and as the kisses became more passionate, Hunter hooked his knee over Grant's leg, forcing him to spread his knees wider. It gave Grant access to the nicely filled package between Hunter's legs, and when he placed his hand over it, Hunter moaned into his mouth. Hunter ground against Grant's hand, and Grant obliged by gently squeezing.

"Sit back," Grant said softly as they stopped kissing for a moment.

A little startled, Hunter complied and sat back down behind the wheel. His eyes grew big when Grant turned toward him and started unbuttoning his Levi's.

"Grant," Hunter sighed.

Grant looked up at Hunter with a teasing smile on his face. "Want me to stop?"

# —9—

HUNTER didn't need to answer, and Grant didn't stop. Instead, he cupped Hunter's bulge over the boxers he was still wearing, making Hunter moan even more. "I think we need to let the bird out, don't you think?" Grant lowered the elastic on the boxers and let Hunter's impressive cock spring free. Slowly, he wrapped his hand around it and moved the skin up and down until a shiny bead of precome gathered at the slit. "I bet you want me to lick that off?" Grant's voice sounded teasing, but also seductive. Again, he didn't wait for confirmation but simply bent down and licked at the head of Hunter's cock.

A loud groan escaped Hunter's mouth. It was a next-to-impossible task for him to keep his hands on the truck seat, so eventually he gave in and put his hand on the back of Grant's head, feeling it bob up and down, adding to the sensation of the hot mouth around his erection. He'd had blow jobs before, of course, but this felt different. Grant made all the right moves, taking Hunter's cock deep into his throat and swallowing around it, then moving up and letting his tongue graze over the large vein at the bottom, right up to the crown. Grant's tongue played with the sensitive underside leading to the slit, and Hunter could easily be convinced that Grant really enjoyed doing this to him. He also had to admit it was the best blow job he'd ever had, and he hadn't even come yet.

Hunter was moaning. He couldn't stop himself. His hand was guiding Grant's movements, and he was trying to get him to speed up a bit as the tension in his groin rose. Frustrated with Grant's teasing ministrations, he started rolling his hips, pushing his cock into Grant's delicious mouth in an attempt to gain more friction. Grant's hand was inside Hunter's jeans, and it felt good to grind his sac against it, so good that he didn't know where he wanted to feel what first. His senses were flooded with need. He desperately wanted to come, but he wasn't quite there yet. Then Grant pushed his fingers up as he cupped Hunter's balls and applied pressure behind his sac. Electricity shot through Hunter, and he could just call out, "Coming!" He reflexively thrust up into Grant's mouth and pushed his hand down, making Grant take him deeper, when he felt his orgasm hit him hard, harder than ever before.

Still twitching and overly sensitive to touch, Hunter slumped down against the worn leather of the truck seat. When he opened his eyes, he looked straight into Grant's, which were black with lust. Grant didn't give him a lot of time to come down. Instead Grant kissed him passionately, and the taste of Grant's mouth was strangely salty and tangy. Then Hunter realized he was tasting himself, his own come, in Grant's mouth. If he'd had even a smidgen of coherent thought left, he might have pulled away, but he didn't. He'd never felt so accepted before. Grant had let him come in his mouth and hadn't spit it out. Then Hunter realized he hadn't given Grant a lot of choice in the matter. He pulled away.

"I was a little late. Didn't give you a lot of warning," Hunter said by way of apology.

Grant smiled widely. "Even if you had, I still would have wanted to taste you."

"Seriously?"

Grant nodded. "Yeah. I like it. I like to feel you surrender to me."

Hunter swallowed hard. Grant was back on his side of the truck, and Hunter's eyes wandered down Grant's frame to the clear bulge in his wet jeans, which were clinging to his thighs. Could he do this? Could he help Grant out like Grant had helped him out? Could he take Grant in his mouth and make him come?

"I've never…," Hunter started. "You know…."

"Given a blow job?" Grant helped.

Hunter sighed and nodded reluctantly.

"You don't have to," Grant shrugged, shifting his seat.

"But you wouldn't mind?"

Grant laughed. "I don't think I've ever met a man who would refuse a blow job. I don't think I need to explain to you how good it feels."

"I wouldn't know where to begin," Hunter admitted.

"Just do what you know feels good," Grant instructed. "You're a guy. You know how the equipment works, and we all have the same equipment. In that respect, we're a lot easier to figure out than women."

Hunter couldn't keep his eyes off Grant's groin. Grant was right. What could go wrong? He knew what felt good, and as a reminder, Grant had just shown him. Then why did he feel so insecure unzipping Grant's jeans? It felt awkward, although he knew he wanted it.

As soon as Grant's pants were opened, his briefs pushed out, aided by the thick flesh that had been confined underneath the fabric for way too long. Grant groaned at the release, shifting his hips to get more comfortable as Hunter let his fingers trace the ridges of the hard cock underneath the straining cotton. Hunter could easily pull the fabric down enough to bring Grant's cock into view, but he hesitated, torn between wanting to and being afraid to fail the more experienced man. Curiosity overtook his shyness, though, and he placed his hand over it, rolling it until it felt heavy in his palm. He'd only ever felt his own, and although Hunter judged they were roughly the same size, Grant's cock still felt very different. As he started moving his hand up and down, he felt the pulsations of Grant's rapid heartbeat.

"Feels good, Hunter," Grant moaned, keeping his eyes on what Hunter was doing to him. "Feels really good. Don't stop."

Grant's words were all the encouragement Hunter needed. He wanted to touch so much, wanted to run his fingers through Grant's dark, curly pubic hair and kiss the fine hairs leading to his belly button. Hunter pushed Grant's wet shirt higher up his stomach and let his mouth ghost over the soft skin near Grant's hip, all the while slowly moving his hand up and down Grant's erection.

Never in a million years would Hunter have guessed that actually being here, he'd still be so turned on by a man. In the back of his mind he'd always known about his attraction to men, of course, but he'd told himself that if he ever got the chance to get close enough to do the things he'd only dreamed of, it would feel so wrong, so unnatural that nothing much would happen. He never contemplated that the musky smell and tight, muscled body would make him hard again just minutes after coming, that it would make him bold enough to want more and act to get what he wanted. Never could he have imagined that it would feel so right.

He looked up at Grant to see him smile invitingly. Grant touched Hunter's hair, nodding his approval as Hunter opened his mouth just enough to take in the head of Grant's erection. It tasted like nothing he'd ever tasted before and was smooth and soft against his tongue. Surprisingly enough, it seemed to fit as well, and Hunter let it slide a little deeper. He wished he could look up to see Grant's reaction, but the confines of the truck cabin made that impossible.

Grant let his head fall back. "You know," he said, his voice a little forced, "for a virgin, you have a great mouth. Just a little less teeth, please."

"I'm sorry," Hunter said, pulling back.

Grant looked back at him and gently stroked Hunter's short-cropped hair again. "Keep going. You're doing great." He moved his hand to Hunter's chin so he could pull him closer and kiss him. "Don't stop."

Hunter smiled, still not feeling totally at ease with what he was doing to Grant but trying not to think about how he never knew how tender the man could be. How he had almost let his dislike of him, because of his history with Gable, stand between them.

Moving his hand up and down Grant's rigid shaft, Hunter continued where he'd left off, taking the head of Grant's erection in his mouth. He was a little wary about taking Grant as deep into his mouth as Grant had taken him, but remembered how glorious it felt when Grant swallowed, so he tried letting it slide further. His saliva flowed copiously, and Grant's cock felt slick as it slipped into his throat. Suddenly he felt his stomach turn and he gagged, pulling back as he retched against the feeling of something at the back of his throat.

"Wow, easy," Grant soothed him, his hand caressing his cheek. "That takes practice. Something you don't have this first time. You don't need to go so deep. Your mouth feels good around the head too."

Hunter nodded, swallowing the excess saliva and trying to make his heartbeat calm down. He wiped away the tears that had shot into his eyes and tried to hide it from Grant, feeling very much like a wimp.

Grant bent down and caught his mouth in a soft kiss. "It's okay. Maybe this is enough for today. You can make me come with your hand if you like."

Hunter shook his head. "You made it good for me. I want to make you come in my mouth too."

Grant smiled. "It's not a competition." He didn't stop kissing Hunter, possessively cupping Hunter's head in his hand, effectively preventing him from bending down again.

Hunter couldn't help grinding his hips against Grant's leg. The cock in his hand felt heavy, and it was easy to imagine how what he was doing felt to Grant. He'd done it to himself enough times, after all. Although the angle was slightly different, he tried to twist his wrist in a motion he knew felt good. His reward was Grant moaning into their kiss and thrusting his straining erection up into Hunter's hand. Hunter tried to think straight, but Grant's kisses were clouding his mind, not to mention the fact he felt like he hadn't just come, like he still wanted more. Would they go further? Would Grant possibly let him fuck him? Or would Grant want to fuck him?

Hunter pulled back, his breathing heavy. Grant let his head fall back over the edge of the truck seat. His hand was tucked into his jeans, cupping his balls, while Hunter continued fisting him.

"Hand feels good," Grant murmured. "Told you it was easy. Not much longer now...." Grant was rolling his hips, following his body's instincts.

Hunter licked his lips. He wanted to taste Grant again, wanted to taste the need, the desire in the other man. The friction he was getting from grinding his still-exposed cock against the coarseness of Grant's wet jeans was hard to abandon, though, and he knew he would have to put his mouth over Grant's erection. Then he remembered Grant's confession, that he wanted Hunter to come in his mouth, and the shiny bead of precome that had gathered at the tip of Grant's cock suddenly became irresistible. He continued fisting Grant while he bent down and licked the head.

Grant groaned loudly and convulsively thrust up, pushing his cock into Hunter's mouth. This time Hunter didn't gag. He simply pulled back reflexively when he felt the rush of hot, salty fluid hit his taste buds. Almost immediately he plunged back in, not wanting to give up this time, and swallowed around Grant's thick cock. It tasted different from what he'd tasted in Grant's mouth, and wasn't altogether unpleasant, but he couldn't say he loved it right off the bat. Maybe it was an acquired taste? He didn't want to spit it out, though, like Miranda had on the one occasion Hunter had come in her mouth. Maybe it meant something to him? Feeling Grant lose control, seeing how Grant came just because he felt Hunter's mouth on him, was enough for Hunter to feel powerful, and more than a little proud.

Hunter licked the last bead of come off Grant's cock and smiled smugly, looking at how Grant was lying back, a look of bliss on his face. He didn't have to wait long for Grant to open his eyes and look at him.

"Come here," Grant gestured, his voice still a little unsteady.

Hunter straightened his back so he could align his body with Grant.

"Can't believe you're hard again," Grant said, grinning widely at Hunter's exposed erection and shaking his head. "It's a dead giveaway, you know." He pulled Hunter's head closer so they could kiss and then let his hand trail down Hunter's wet shirt until he could insert it into Hunter's jeans.

"Dead giveaway for what?" Hunter asked innocently.

"You're so eager for it. So hungry," Grant answered in between teasing pecks at Hunter's mouth. "Bet you've never been thoroughly fucked by a guy either, right?"

Hunter's breath hitched when he felt Grant push his finger between his ass cheeks and find his rear entrance, stealing any chance for a witty answer. He kissed Grant back, avoiding having to tell him he didn't feel ready to be fucked and didn't know if he ever would. Still, it felt good to kiss the other man and grind against his hard body. What Grant was doing with his finger felt good too, and although Hunter couldn't exactly think straight, he realized this was unexpected. Grant slipped his finger past the tight ring of muscle that guarded Hunter's rear entrance and made him come again. The sudden rush of his second orgasm toppled Hunter's world, because the few fantasies of being with a man he had ever allowed himself had all centered around him fucking that man, not the other way around. The fantasies were too sketchy, too much a part of a jacking-off image, all too soon concluded by a strong orgasm—but Hunter was always the one on top. Now all he could think of was Grant entering him. Although Grant was definitely Hunter's type, he'd never before imagined himself in the arms of a man, a hand slowly stroking his back and lips languidly kissing him while he came down off his high, yet here he was. Grant's ministrations felt good, and Hunter had a hard time pulling away from the tender caresses.

As Hunter sat back behind the wheel, Grant grew silent.

"So what's going to happen now?" Grant asked after a few tense moments.

"Our work is done here," Hunter answered flatly. "By the time we get back to the homestead, it'll be about dinner time."

Grant nodded and Hunter could see the movement from the corner of his eye. He couldn't look at Grant, though. No matter how good this had felt, he couldn't get carried away. He'd let his dick speak too much already today. In the end, he still had to go home and face his family, and if they ever found out what he'd done with Grant here, they might never want to speak to him again.

All he could hope for was that Grant understood. It wasn't like he could ask him.

Hunter started the engine, and Grant leaned forward to wipe the steamy windows with his hand. It had stopped raining, and with one more look at the fixed gate, Hunter turned the truck around and drove home.

# —10—

THE incessant rain had finally stopped, clearing the way for a surprisingly strong summer sun, which cleared up all the remaining puddles and muddy bogs in record time.

Grant's heated encounter with Hunter was just a memory, one he fervently hoped he'd get to repeat, but his hopes were dashed by the fact that Hunter never seemed to run out of excuses to avoid him. While at first Grant had blamed Hugh for standing between him and Hunter, now that Hugh was gone, Grant had to find a better reason. He had to admit that Hunter didn't want to see him.

He tried not to pine too much. After all, Hunter was his boss, and since Grant was just here to work and make some money, sleeping with the boss was a bad idea anyway.

The work was the one thing that went well for him. Although Blue River was a well-run ranch, it was clear that maintaining the infrastructure—from stables to fences and gates to parts of the houses—hadn't been a priority for a long time. When Grant had started working there, Hugh had told him they sometimes paid a carpenter from town to do some of the mending, but that the man was usually too busy to come for the small stuff, like replacing a leaky gutter or a step up to a porch. Feeling like the fifth wheel on the wagon around the wranglers anyway, Grant had stepped up and volunteered his expertise. Now it seemed like everyone brought their wood jobs to him to fix. Grant didn't mind. It brought him a lot of respect, not in the least from the women around the ranch, and he still got plenty of time in the saddle, which he wouldn't give up for the world. In fact, it was the perfect balance, and Grant was starting to feel at home on the ranch.

Hunter still hadn't picked a new foreman, but Grant and Izzie pretty much shared the extra duties Hugh had always taken on. Izzie had a casual way of seeking Grant out whenever she had something to discuss or if she wanted his advice, and they still understood each other with half a sentence or a sideways glance. The consequence was that gossip was going around that Grant had replaced Delco in Izzie's bed, but neither commented on it. Grant had always assumed Izzie knew how his cards were stacked, and that was at least part of the reason they got along so well.

"Want to saddle a horse and race me around some of the outer fences?" Izzie asked, dashing around the corner of the woodshed just as Grant was taking his toolbox inside.

"Sure," Grant answered. "Give me five minutes."

It took him about twenty in the end, since he'd found Davenport looking a little lost in the herd of working horses standing in the near paddock and decided he wanted to test his theory to see whether he could whip the stubborn steed into shape.

Izzie gave him a teasing smirk as she watched him ride over to her. "You're a glutton for punishment, just like Hunter," she snorted, turning her own eager bay around and looking behind her in a gesture that was pure provocation.

Grant spurred Davenport on, and to his surprise, the horse seemed in the mood to give his rider a good chance at catching up with Izzie. Izzie didn't give in easily, though. As soon as Grant caught up with her, she kicked her heels into her gelding's flank and sped off, leaving him to chase after her. After he spent about twenty minutes following her, jumping where the fences were low, Izzie pulled on the reins and turned her horse around. She was panting but seemed elated.

"Wow, I don't think I've done this in at least three years! Hunter and I used to race from time to time, but he's no fun anymore and, well, the other guys just aren't the same."

Grant grinned. "But I'm good enough?"

"You look like you could use some fun too," Izzie answered smugly. "Never thought Davenport had it in him, but I guess Hugh was right. You have a way with that bastard of a horse."

"He's just stubborn and not at all compatible with Hunter, I think."

Izzie shot a teasing look at Grant. "Hunter doesn't seem compatible with anyone these days. For a while there, I thought you and him were hitting it off, but I rarely see you together anymore. He's back to being his cantankerous self." Izzie dismounted and let her horse graze a bit. "Did you two have a fight?"

Although he was a little startled by her question, Grant followed suit, walking toward her with a surprisingly complacent Davenport trailing him. "Why do you think that?" he asked her, testing the waters.

"Oh, I dunno. For a while there you didn't seem to get along, then after that little altercation at the bar and Hugh leaving, you and he were doing everything together, and then all of a sudden, the love seemed to have cooled again."

Grant knew Izzie well enough to know she was an incredible tease, but her face was serious now, and her use of the word "love" in relation to his friendship with her brother made Grant extra careful. Had he and Hunter been that transparent, or was this Izzie's way of luring him out of hiding?

"I don't know what you're talking about," Grant replied, walking next to her and looking out over the wide, grassy plains so she couldn't see his expression.

Izzie stopped, forcing Grant to turn around as soon as he noticed she was no longer walking next to him. "What?"

Izzie shook her head. "I keep forgetting how dense men are. You'd think I'd know better by now." An understanding look spread over her face as Grant didn't take the bait. "Hunter screws around with Miranda," she explained. "He's never had a girlfriend, though. Don't think he's ever been out on a date. At least not the kind where you take a girl out to dinner and have an actual conversation with her."

"So?" Grant replied, hoping she'd change the subject.

Izzie sighed. "Just between you and me... I know what kind of relationship you had with Gable. I know it was more than that he was the boss and you were his ranch hand. I know, Grant, and it doesn't matter to me." She left an uncomfortable pause. "I think Hunter wants it to be like that between you and him too."

"And what makes you think that…." Grant found he couldn't finish the sentence. He knew what Izzie meant, but actually saying it aloud was another thing altogether. Especially because Izzie was speculating about something he wasn't sure about, and as far as he could read her brother, neither was Hunter.

"… Hunter is gay?" she filled in Grant's missing words. "I'm his sister, and sisters know. Of course, he'll never admit it to us."

"I don't think he even admits it to himself," Grant replied thoughtfully. "If it is true, of course," he added quickly, hoping it wouldn't give too much away.

Izzie gave him a sideways look, making sure Grant knew just how dense she thought he was. Then she sighed again. "Listen. I don't care if Hunter is gay or straight, as long as he's happy and stops being so cantankerous. I think Lisa and Mom and Bernie are actually glad he rarely joins them for breakfast or lunch and are only subjected to his temper at dinner."

"I hear you don't join them that much anymore either these days?" Grant interjected, hoping to sway the conversation away from Hunter's sexual preference for a moment.

Izzie shrugged. "I don't like the tension when we're all together. I try to pretend I'm late for dinner because of all the work around the ranch so that I can eat alone in the kitchen afterward. Much more peaceful there."

"You can always come and eat at the crew house," Grant suggested. "We're a pretty friendly bunch."

"Maybe I should do that," Izzie answered. "But I'd prefer it if Hunter was a little happier. I wish you two would kiss and make up. So to speak."

Grant smiled. On the one hand, he wanted to confide in Izzie, but he knew Hunter would never forgive him if he did. "It's not that easy, Izz."

Izzie flung her arm around Grant's shoulders and gave him a squeeze. She didn't say anything and Grant was glad.

"So, are you over Delco?" Grant asked, hoping they could leave their earlier train of conversation alone now.

"You can't imagine how happy I am to be rid of him," Izzie confessed. "I always knew he was trouble, but when we were alone, he was a really nice guy. Considerate, even."

Grant eyed her suspiciously and Izzie noticed.

"Honestly!"

"He's a psycho, Izzie."

She shrugged. "I know. I'm just glad he's leaving me alone for now." They walked along, in between the horses, Izzie hanging on Grant, her head on his shoulder. "Hugh's confession was a bit of a shock, though."

"To say the least," Grant agreed. "I thought he and Lisa were a good couple."

Izzie let go of Grant's shoulders and grabbed his arm instead, hooking her hand around his elbow. "I knew it wasn't all smooth sailing there. Lisa used to shout at him, and you know Hugh. I don't think I'd ever heard him raise his voice before that first time he confronted Delco. He certainly never shouted back at Lisa."

"Don't think I'd shout back at Lisa either," Grant quipped.

Izzie laughed; then she turned serious. "Hugh deserved better than her."

"You like him, don't you?"

Izzie sighed. "I'm not supposed to like him, Grant. He's my brother-in-law. He's Danny's dad and I'm Danny's aunt. Lisa and Mom would throw me out of the house if I chose Hugh's side."

"Too bad we have to choose sides, hey?" Grant saw the parallel between Izzie and Hunter. They had more reason to get along than just being brother and sister.

They mounted their horses and rode back to the homestead. Neither said anything more about riding fences, but Grant figured it was just an excuse to talk anyway. He knew he wanted to talk to Hunter, if for no other reason than to warn Hunter that he wasn't fooling Izzie, but he had no idea how to go about it.

LESS than a week after his conversation with Izzie, the opportunity presented itself. It was actually Hunter who approached him.

"I'm going over to Gable's ranch to buy some horses," Hunter told Grant one evening in the stable block. One of the wrangler's horses had gone lame, and Grant had suggested he take a look at it before they called the vet.

"Going to buy a replacement for Davenport too?" Grant asked without looking up from the hoof he was inspecting.

"Possibly," Hunter answered evasively. "I would have asked you along, but I didn't think putting you and Gable in the same place was a good idea."

Grant looked up at Hunter and saw the insecurity in his face. "Very considerate of you. Does he know I work here?"

Hunter shook his head. "I'd like you to give me your opinion on the horses when we unload them, though."

"Okay, I will," Grant assured him. "You taking Tim with you?"

"Yeah, probably," Hunter answered.

Grant nodded. "He's got a good eye, just like his big brother." He could tell how much Hunter still missed Hugh.

Hunter lingered for a while as Grant continued examining the horse's hind leg, and then started walking out. Just as he rounded the barn door, Grant called him back. "Hunter?"

"Yes."

Grant stood by the horse, looking at Hunter with the midday sun behind his back. For a moment he didn't speak, simply enjoying the view of a very angelic-looking Hunter; then he broke out of his reverie. "I wanted to say 'give my regards to Gable', but I guess you better not. Just let me know how he's doing, okay?"

Hunter tipped his hat before walking out.

# —11—

HUNTER loved going to Gable's ranch. It was so different from his own that it was like walking into a different world. While Hunter had horses of various ages, from newborn foals to horses reaching retirement age, Gable's horses were all between two and four years old. Gable usually bought them at auction shortly after they were weaned off their mothers and then spent two years turning them into good, sturdy working horses that took excellent guidance from even the most inexperienced riders.

There was nothing fancy about Gable's horses, no Thoroughbreds or fickle riding ponies. Most of the stock he bought were quarter horses. Occasionally he couldn't resist a half-breed Appaloosa or a paint, but every single horse he bought he managed to turn into a reliable steed for a rancher or wrangler.

Gable's ranch was a two-man operation, but Hunter knew how hard it was to get good help. In the past, whenever Gable was without a ranch hand, the place would look a little dilapidated. The horses were always well taken care of, but the barn could usually use a coat of paint, and the ranch house would have weeds growing in the garden.

That wasn't the case now. Hunter had heard that Gable had found a helping hand, which was good news, since Gable had injured his leg quite badly in an accident the year before. For a while, Hunter had ordered his men to take some work off Gable's hands while he recuperated, but that hadn't lasted long. Gable was still limping quite badly, but he'd refused any more help all too soon.

Now a young man who'd introduced himself as Flynn was clearly helping out quite a bit around Gable's ranch. Everything was neatly stashed away inside the barn, and the house looked like it got some regular maintenance too. Even Gable's beat-up truck looked washed.

"Gable around?" Hunter asked Flynn.

"Yeah, he'll be here soon. He's out in the range. Anything I can help you with?"

Hunter smiled at the dashing young man, thinking for a moment that Gable had hired him for more than horse wrangling. "I have an appointment with him to buy some of his horses, but I'm sure you can give me a tour?"

Flynn smiled, his eyes squinting against the bright sunlight. "Gable will be right back, I'm sure. I only work here. He handles the sale of his horses."

Hunter watched Flynn move away and grab a bucket, filling it with water from a garden hose. Although Flynn wasn't his type, he caught himself eyeing the ranch hand's jeans-clad ass anyway. "Gable's a good friend of mine," Hunter said, trying to make small talk. "We go way back. I'm sure he wouldn't mind if I took a look around."

Flynn looked up. "I'd rather you wait here, sir. Gable will be right back, and then he can show you around."

As if by command, a horse skidded to a stop near them, and Gable jumped down from it, wincing momentarily as if the jump hurt his injured leg. He walked over to Hunter, extending his hand. "Hey, buddy! How have you been? Here to look at some horses?" He turned to Flynn. "Can you saddle TJ so Hunter can ride with me?"

Hunter could tell Flynn wasn't entirely happy with Gable's demand, but Gable was carting Hunter off toward the house, so he didn't say anything.

"So what are you looking for?" Gable asked, seeming in good spirits.

"Some horses I can sell on, a few I can keep, and a horse for me," Hunter replied, taking off his hat as soon as they entered the kitchen. Gable gestured for him to sit down and poured them each a cup of coffee. He unceremoniously plunked down the sugar bowl in front of Hunter, while Hunter tried to inconspicuously look around the usually messy kitchen, which was now spotless.

"You finally ready to ditch that mongrel you usually ride?" Gable was sporting a smile from ear to ear.

"Yeah, yeah," Hunter answered in a tone that conveyed that he was tired of the relentless teasing.

"You have to admit that was probably the worst buy you ever made."

"Just 'cause I didn't buy him from you," Hunter rebutted.

"I would never have sold you an animal like that. In fact, I would never have bought an animal like that. He's good for nothing, except maybe a glue factory."

"Gable!" Hunter said with clear disgust in his voice, making Gable laugh out loud. Hunter enjoyed the friendly banter between them. He and Gable had been friends since he was fourteen, and it didn't matter that Gable was more than ten years older than him. Gable had lost his father the same year that Hunter's dad had unexpectedly died, and they'd had to take on running their ranches on their own after that. Gable had been a big support, since Hunter had really been too young for such responsibility. Now they pretty much did their own thing, but Gable's ranch was still the first port of call whenever Hunter was looking for new horses.

"So you want something for yourself as well?"

Hunter nodded.

"Mare, stallion, or gelding?"

Hunter shrugged. "Something that does what I tell it to do."

Gable took a big gulp from his coffee mug. "For that you need to get yourself a wife, Hunter."

"No thanks," Hunter replied, thinking to himself how true that felt right now. He couldn't say anything about Grant, though, feeling it would be too hard on Gable. Instead he nodded to the front of the house. "Looks like you found yourself one?"

Gable almost choked on his coffee. "You mean Flynn? He knows his way around the ranch, and he's a damn fine cook."

"Knowing you, he's more than that, right?"

Gable threw him a mock glare that didn't deny or acknowledge Hunter's suspicions. "Let's go look at some horses, okay?"

They rode out to the higher meadows, Gable pointing out the horses that were ready to be sold and Hunter giving them a first cursory look. Most of them looked good enough to try out, so Gable marked them with a yellow ribbon, and they agreed Hunter would return later that afternoon with an extra wrangler and two horses so they could round them up.

With Tim and Flynn to help them out, they easily rounded up about twenty horses and steered them toward a small holding pen next to the corral. Hunter couldn't resist watching the way Gable and Flynn behaved around each other. Although that morning their relationship had seemed strained, this afternoon the sun was shining and they seemed to be quite comfortable around each other. Hunter even thought they were flirting and eyeing each other. Was this what it could be like? Sometimes Hunter wished he had a ranch like Gable's, where there were rarely others around and he had all the privacy he could want. At home, it wasn't just his mother and sisters scrutinizing his every move; he was also subjected to the pressure of being the boss to quite a few employees. He would never be able to flirt with Grant there.

"Flynn's going to show the horses, if that's okay with you," Gable said, shaking Hunter out of his reverie when he came to ride next to him. "That way we can talk about him behind his back," he added, winking at Hunter.

Hunter smiled, suspecting this was as close as Gable was ever going to get to confessing to Hunter how he felt about Flynn. He hoped that one day he'd be able to admit to Gable that he'd hired Grant to work for him. Telling Gable he had the hots for his ex was something Hunter didn't even dare to contemplate. Then again, Hunter had never come out to Gable either. "Sounds like a plan," Hunter said eventually, feeling he still owed Gable an answer.

Almost every horse Flynn showed them met with Hunter's approval. Strictly speaking, he didn't need twenty horses, but he knew he could sell them to his clients with confidence because Gable had trained them, and he also knew he was doing Gable a big financial favor. Both of them would benefit from the transaction.

"Now this little girl looks like you could handle her," Gable joked as he nudged Hunter with his shoulder.

Hunter shook his head, clearing away his daydreams. He really had to pay better attention. For a second time, he was late responding to Gable's taunt. "I was born in the saddle, Gabe. I can handle any horse."

"Any horse *I* pick out for you. You're a horrible judge of horses yourself, if I may say so."

Gable was probably the only man who could get away with taunting Hunter like that, and the way Tim stared at the two of them after Gable's last statement was a good indication that he agreed. It was a battle Hunter knew he couldn't win.

"So what makes this one so special?"

"She's gentle and docile and the first horse I broke in after my accident. She was no trouble at all and very eager to please. After seeing you ride Davenport, I think she's just what the doctor ordered."

"She looks like a little girl's pony," Tim intervened. "But you're the boss."

Hunter directed his look from Tim to Gable and saw Gable cock his head. "She's a mixed breed, and that's why she's a bit smaller than the rest, but she's got great stamina and determination without giving you attitude."

"I agree, you could do without the attitude," Tim concurred.

Hunter yanked off his hat and swatted Tim with it, making him jump down off the fence they were all sitting on, but he had to agree with both men: he was due a good horse. "Can I ride her?"

Gable waved his arm in a welcoming gesture. "By all means."

Flynn dismounted and held the horse so Hunter could get on. She was smaller than he was used to but could easily take Hunter's weight without sacrificing her mobility. Hunter trotted her around a bit and then gestured at Flynn to open the corral so he could give her some space to gallop. As Gable had promised, she handled like a dream. Hunter enjoyed letting his mind wander while he rode her at a surprising speed through the meadows.

"Sold," he told Gable after returning to the corral.

"She's called Honeybee, by the way," Gable said after they shook hands. It wasn't lost on Hunter that Gable was trying hard not to laugh, but Flynn and Tim had no such restraint.

# —12—

"SO HOW is Gable doing?" Grant asked, his hat in hand, fingering the brim as if he was nervous.

"He seems okay," Hunter answered as he patted the docile little honey-colored mare he'd just unloaded from the truck. "I think his leg still hurts a fair bit, but the ranch looks great. His help is called Flynn. Looks like a kid with two right hands."

"Are they…?" Grant didn't finish his sentence.

"I don't know, Grant," Hunter replied sternly, sighing after a tense pause. He knew what Grant was asking, and he realized it made him jealous. Not just Grant's words, but his composure, the way the big guy looked small all of a sudden, his shoulders slumped and his gaze dropped to his feet, where he was kicking around some stalks of wayward straw. He knew he couldn't hold it against him, so he smiled, more for himself than anyone else. "Bought a nice little mare off him, though." He turned her around to face Grant. "I'd like you to meet Honeybee."

Grant stifled a chuckle, then laughed out loud. "I'm sorry," he apologized, his spirits clearly lifted. "This is Davenport's replacement?"

"What's wrong with that?" Hunter asked, not ready to admit he knew it looked funny.

"I suggested you find an easier-to-handle horse, not a little girl's pony," Grant answered, still laughing.

"She's not a pony!" Hunter replied.

"No, she isn't," Grant replied with another chuckle. "But I bet your feet can almost touch the ground when you're in the saddle."

For a moment, he didn't know how to take Grant's comment. He looked at Grant's teasing face, then at the docile creature with the long eyelashes next to him, and decided it had gone far enough for now, so he took his hat off and used it to swipe at Grant. He missed him by the smallest of margins, but only because Grant moved aside and back. Hunter only had to step forward to corner Grant inside the stable. They both noticed the sudden added privacy, and Grant's face turned serious. It only took an almost imperceptible nod from Grant before Hunter launched himself at Grant's mouth and kissed him.

Hunter felt his control slipping as Grant kissed him back, a strong hand at the back of his head. His arousal grew as he felt the bulge in Grant's jeans grow more defined as well. He was about to slip his hand into Grant's pants when the noise of footsteps invaded his blissful cloud. They stopped kissing but didn't dare move, only looked over the opened half-door of the stall toward the rest of the barn. One of the stable hands walked right into view, looked around as if he'd lost something, noticed the open door, and kicked it closed before walking out again without spotting them. It wasn't until the sound of the footsteps had died away that they both exhaled loudly.

"That was fucking close," Hunter said, leaning a little closer to Grant again.

Grant gave him a quick peck on the mouth and ruffled his hair. "What would happen if he'd actually registered us being here?"

"I don't want to think about it," Hunter answered sternly before pulling away.

"Would it be so bad?"

"Asks the guy who never admitted being gay to anyone," Hunter was quick to add.

"You're not exactly out of the closet either."

"That's because I'm not…." Hunter didn't finish his sentence, because all of a sudden he couldn't deny it, at least not to Grant. He turned around and started fiddling with Honeybee's halter just to occupy his hands. He knew what they'd been doing to each other was enough to prove he *was* gay, although it had less to do with their actions than with the feelings those actions caused in him. The attraction to men had always been there, he'd just never acted on it before, because sex with women was easier. He didn't have to hide, and since he wasn't a bad looker and he owned a flourishing business, he practically had to swat the women off anyway. It wasn't until Grant came along that he'd realized he could take his secret fantasies further and not be turned off. Quite the contrary. Whenever they were in the same room, sparks were flying, and Hunter found himself avoiding Grant because he was afraid everyone would be able to see it. After a few days it became unbearable, though, and he had to seek him out.

"I've had relationships with women too, Hunter," Grant admitted. "It makes it confusing, but I know what gives me the satisfaction I crave."

Hunter swallowed hard. Was it really that easy? Jeez, they hadn't even gone all the way. All they'd done was some kissing and groping— and yes, of course, how could he forget those blow jobs in the truck during the downpour? One side of him was glad that Grant was giving him time to explore these new sensations and didn't push him, but another side wanted more.

"We have nowhere to go. I can't bring you inside the house. Not with four women living there. I swear they have eyes in the back of their heads and better hearing than bats! And we can't do anything in the crew quarters because I'm the boss and I shouldn't even come there. If one of the men finds me there, I wouldn't be able to explain why I was on their territory."

Grant's hands snaked around Hunter's sides and across his stomach. Leaning slightly into the touch, Hunter felt Grant's chin rest on his shoulder and his hot breath next to his ear. He felt warm and cradled between Grant's strong body and the horse's warm flank. It felt so good he never wanted to leave.

"We could drive to the next county and check into a hotel," Grant suggested.

"We'd have to drive almost to the city before I can be sure they won't recognize me. My family's been in this region for generations, Grant."

"So come to the city with me next time?"

"I can't," Hunter said, making a weak effort to pull away from Grant. But Grant wouldn't let him. He tightened his grip and pulled Hunter even closer.

"Can't, or won't?"

"Can't," Hunter whispered, hoping Grant would understand it for what it was: his way of saying he definitely wished he could.

Grant's hand slowly traveled south, and Hunter sucked in his stomach to allow Grant to dip below his belt. Grant couldn't do much more than rub a little, so Hunter loosened his belt a notch and opened the top button of his jeans.

"Fuck, you're hard," Grant growled in Hunter's ear. "Guess you really do want me."

Hunter couldn't do much more than nod, because by now Grant's hand was firmly gripping his shaft, and all he could do to stay upright was hold onto the docile mare in front of him. Grant was grinding his crotch against Hunter's ass, and Hunter was sure it wasn't just his imagination that Grant's erection fit nicely between his ass cheeks. He let go of Honeybee with one hand to loosen his belt buckle even more and open his jeans all the way so Grant could pull his cock out. As soon as he felt the cool air, he reached back to touch Grant.

"Fuck me," Hunter heard himself say. He couldn't believe his own ears, but then realized that he would do anything Grant asked of him right now, and that included letting Grant fuck him.

Grant let go of Hunter's erection to open his own pants and slip Hunter's down to expose his ass. He gently stroked the curve of Hunter's backside and purred an appreciative, "Nice."

Hunter had no idea how this would go, but he knew he trusted Grant to guide him. He tried to spread his legs a bit more but found he couldn't because his jeans were still halfway up his thighs. He tried to pull them down some more, but Grant stopped him.

"'S okay. In case we need to make a quick getaway."

Hunter swallowed, torn between ending things right now for fear of exposure and continuing because it was all he could think about.

Grant broke the stalemate by slipping his thick erection between Hunter's thighs.

"Shit, that's tight," Grant groaned. Hunter tried spreading his legs again. "Don't. Feels good," Grant assured him, thrusting forward.

Hunter felt his groin tingle. It was a curious sensation when Grant's cock hit the back of his sac and rubbed across the sensitive area behind it, like Grant had done with his fingers when he'd given him the blow job in the truck. Grant cupped Hunter's balls, and Hunter couldn't resist fisting his own cock. Grant picked up the pace, and Hunter felt himself spiraling out of control so fast it made him dizzy. He wanted more, wanted Grant to truly fuck him, but Grant was thrusting frantically between his legs until he pushed Hunter so hard against Honeybee that the animal stepped to the side. Luckily, she wasn't easily spooked, because Grant didn't let up until he groaned loudly and Hunter felt the hot stickiness of Grant's release between his legs. Grant was panting hard, and it didn't take more than the feeling of Grant's hand on his cock to send Hunter over as well.

"You didn't fuck me," Hunter said once he'd regained some of his breath.

Grant was still clinging to him, panting equally hard. "We didn't have a condom or lube, and I'm not hurting you your first time."

"I wouldn't have minded," Hunter said.

"Trust me, for the first time you want privacy, time, and a lot of lubrication."

Grant reluctantly let go of Hunter, and Hunter let go of Honeybee with an appreciative pat. He was going to have to clean up not only himself but also the horse's flank, which he'd sprayed with his release. He was still a little shaky on his feet but wanted to bridge the awkward moment between disconnecting from Grant and getting on with their work by giving himself something to do.

They both washed their hands underneath the faucet at the back of the stable block. Grant tucked himself in and wiped his hands on his jeans, while Hunter needed more extensive washing.

"The offer of going somewhere stands as long as you want," Grant told him, giving Hunter's semi-naked form the once-over before picking up his hat and walking outside.

Hunter hastily continued cleaning up, worried about getting caught with his pants down, literally. He knew Grant would be good for it, and that somehow worried him. The ball was in his court now. It was up to him to find a place for them to enjoy a little privacy. He was going to have to lie to his family and possibly some of his employees too. Was it worth it? Was it worth lying for a few moments of ecstasy? For sexual gratification?

While he was wiping off Honeybee's flank, the alternative came into his mind. He was sure that if he wanted to keep up appearances, Miranda would marry him and bear his children. Was that what he wanted? A loveless marriage of convenience? All they were good at was fucking, and even for that he usually liquored up at the bar first. Whenever Miranda tried striking up a conversation, they ended up arguing, mostly about meaningless little things. Maybe that told him they weren't meant to be. Then again, it wasn't like Grant and he were moving toward happy-ever-after either. They were friends, at best, but Hunter barely knew more about Grant than that he'd been Gable's lover and that he'd abandoned Gable after his accident. He knew nothing more about what kind of man Grant was, and when he thought about it, Grant might just as well be a serial killer. On several occasions he'd asked for personal days off without giving anyone a reason. He'd disappear for days on end, only to return to work looking tired and worn out. Hunter had no idea what Grant did during those weekends, and he was afraid to ask. He wasn't about to antagonize one of the best horse wranglers he'd ever hired, not to mention a man who'd shown him ecstasy every time he laid his hands on him. On the other hand, he wasn't about to sacrifice everything he held dear for a man he barely knew. He was going to have to be patient and play it by ear for now.

Satisfied that he'd set the stable, his new horse, and himself to rights, Hunter walked out into the afternoon sun.

# —13—

"I'LL see what I can do and let you know," Grant said before closing his cell phone. He sighed deeply and walked in the direction of the main house. They were fairly busy at the ranch, rounding up the horses for the yearly worming, but sometimes things in his private life took precedence, and this was one of these days.

He was just about to ring the doorbell when Bernie walked out. "Hi! You're here to see Hunter?" she asked with much youthful enthusiasm.

Grant nodded.

"He's round the back. Why don't you come with me? Can I get you some lemonade? I just made a fresh pitcher."

Grant wasn't much of a lemonade drinker, but Bernice was a sweetheart, and he simply couldn't say no to her. "Sure thing. Sounds perfect." He rounded the corner while she disappeared into the kitchen, and found Hunter sitting on a bench in the shade, going over a stack of papers full of figures.

"Books giving you grief?"

Hunter smiled and looked up when he heard Grant's voice. "We're doing okay. Times are tough, but somehow we always manage to keep our head above water."

"That's good management," Grant said, sitting down next to Grant. "Although it must be tough with Hugh gone."

"Yeah, it was a lot easier when I just had my own work to worry about. You and Izzie pick up a lot of Hugh's work, though. Thanks for that."

"Suppose it was easier between you and Hugh?"

"Yeah, I'll admit to that. After all these years, we barely needed to say anything to each other. Now I need to remind myself to communicate more with you and Izzie. Plus, I have to decide on whether I'm going to choose a new foreman from the hands already here, or whether I need to hire an outsider. Don't really like that last option, to be honest."

Grant had heard the rumors going around that Hunter was going to ask him to become foreman, and he'd picked up that he had clear supporters and strong protesters. He was pretty sure he could do the job, despite how hard it would be to fill Hugh's boots, but in light of what he needed to ask Hunter, he knew he couldn't claim the position. The money would be welcome, but his private life didn't allow for the sacrifices it would take right now. Not to mention that if anyone ever found out about the relationship that was growing between him and Hunter, he'd lose all credibility with the men. He didn't want to lead Hunter's decision, though. He preferred playing it by ear.

Hunter was silently making notes, and Grant's eye fell on Hunter's full glass of lemonade. "Bernie's?"

Hunter swallowed with a grimace. "Yes, and it's way too sweet. You didn't say yes too, I hope?"

Grant chuckled. "Couldn't resist."

"Couldn't resist what?" Bernie asked, handing over a large glass of yellow liquid.

"Couldn't resist your delicious offer of lemonade," Grant was quick to answer, taking the glass from Bernie and downing at least half of it in one gulp. Tears shot into his eyes as soon as the sourness hit him, but he swallowed anyway, hoping the taste would soon dissipate.

"Needs more sugar, right?" Bernie asked with an unsure expression.

"Maybe a bit," Grant answered. "But it's good!"

"You think so?" Bernie asked, wide-eyed.

"Sure, honey," Grant assured her.

She smiled widely and twirled around. "Best leave you two to talk business then." And with that she practically skipped inside.

"Thanks for making her feel good," Hunter said with half a smile, his face still buried in papers.

"Thanks for warning me," Grant replied, nudging Hunter with his shoulder. "Too sweet? Damn thing was sour enough to burn through metal. I felt it all the way down to my stomach."

Hunter laughed. "Sorry. She's crap in the kitchen, but Mom keeps telling her that if she doesn't learn, she'll never find a man."

"She's probably like you and Izzie. Better at working the ranch than the house."

Hunter nodded. "Yeah, but Izzie was always a tomboy. Bernie's all girl. She's a good rider, but she'd rather braid her horse's mane than actually get her hands dirty."

"Well, maybe she'll meet some show jumper and take off on the circuit?"

"Yeah, maybe," Hunter said, sounding melancholic all of a sudden.

Grant wondered if this was the right time to spring Hunter with the news that he needed a few days off. Maybe not. Maybe a little more empathy was needed right now. "Sounds like you wanted to get away too?"

Hunter eyed him suspiciously, but his shy smile returned. "This is my land. I want to be buried here, like my father and his father before him. I get homesick when I drive to the next county."

Grant nodded. He was a gypsy and had never really had a feeling of home, but on an intellectual level, he could understand Hunter.

"I miss having a place of my own, though," Hunter said after a long pause. "I mean, it's great to be able to come home and shove my feet under a table full of great food, but on the other hand, I'd love to be able to do something without four pairs of eyes watching my every move."

Grant nodded in understanding, watching how Hunter's hand seemed to casually brush against the side of his thigh. The sensations sent shivers up his leg, making his cock swell. He knew they wouldn't be able to do anything about it here. Not with Bernie inside and

Hunter's mother and sister no doubt somewhere in the house as well. Just as casually, Hunter put his hand on Grant's knee as he bent down to pick up a large, rolled-up document.

"I always fancied building my own house," Hunter said, unrolling the plans to what looked like a moderate version of the large ranch house they were sitting in front of.

Hunter had clearly been thinking about this a lot longer than their conversation about finding more privacy. Grant gave the plans a quick once-over. "Where do you want to build this?"

"Right there," Hunter said, pointing at the large stretch of land in front of them.

Grant turned the blueprint. "I'd suggest facing the master bedroom away from the main house, then. And the entrance maybe to the side or facing the same way. That way they won't see everything that goes on."

Hunter gave him an amused smile. "You have a point there. I'll have the plans changed."

Seeing Hunter's mood lighten gave Grant the courage to ask what he needed. "I was actually here to ask for some days off, starting tomorrow."

The smile on Hunter's face disappeared. "It's kind of the wrong time of year, Grant. We need you here."

"I know." Grant sighed. "I wouldn't ask you if it wasn't important."

"Can you tell me why it's so urgent that you do whatever it is this weekend? Can't it wait?"

Grant stared out to the open plains before them. "Like I said, if I could have it any other way…." He couldn't tell Hunter why he needed to leave. Not without going into a lengthy explanation.

Hunter bit the inside of his lip. Grant could tell he was weighing his decision. "When will you be back?"

"Tuesday at the latest."

Hunter nodded, silently giving his not-entirely-wholehearted permission.

Grant got up, knowing he wasn't in Hunter's best books after asking him for yet another favor. After a few moments of hesitation, he started walking away.

"One day I want to know what you do when you run off like this, Grant."

Hunter's voice sounded loud on the abandoned porch, and Grant looked around to see if anyone else had heard him. Maybe that was the point? Maybe Hunter felt he'd given in too easily and needed to appear to be the boss by asking him for an explanation.

"I will," Grant said before walking off the porch. He meant it too. One day, when he and Hunter were a little further along into their relationship, he'd explain where he went. He just hoped Hunter would understand.

# —14—

IT WAS raining cats and dogs when they arrived back at the stables. Izzie looked exhausted, and Tim didn't say much either while they took care of their horses and wiped the mud off them. Danny had been out to help them, and Hunter's priority was to get the youngster inside and into a hot bath before his mother could give Hunter any grief.

"I'll take care of Belle and Honeybee," Izzie offered.

"Maybe you should take Danny inside?" Hunter suggested.

"No way, José," Izzie replied with a teasing smile. "I may be a woman, but I'd much rather muck out a whole stable block than argue with Lisa about why we took her precious boy out in this horrid weather."

"She knows we're a hand short. In fact, we're two hands short." Hunter handed the reins to his mare over to Izzie and noticed Danny standing in the doorway, looking forlorn. He instantly realized he'd heard their conversation.

"Come here, cowboy," he said, wrapping his arm around the boy and marching him out the door. "Let's go tell your mom who the new foreman is going to be."

Danny's eyes lit up. "Who? Is Grant going to be the new foreman?"

"Nah, I think I should hire you," Hunter said, squeezing the kid as they walked off toward the house.

"I'm too little," Danny replied, sounding sad again.

"You are now, but you'll grow up. And you did one hell of a job today. I'm telling your mom how proud I am of you."

Danny smiled. "Are you sure I can keep Honeybee? She's really sweet, and I'm not so afraid of falling off her. Belle's kinda big," he admitted.

"Why don't I hang onto Belle until you're a bit taller, and in the meanwhile, you can ride that little tan mare. She's quick on her feet, isn't she?"

Danny nodded fervently. "Think I could train her to barrel race?"

"You know, I think she'd be perfect for that."

While they were walking toward the house, Hunter smiled. After Grant's taunts about the size of the horse, Hunter had sung her praises to Danny. Hunter knew Danny was putting on a brave face every time he rode out on the back of Belle, who was a huge mare even for a grown rider, so he'd suggested switching horses. Danny had leapt at the opportunity, and Hunter had observed Danny riding Honeybee all morning. The two of them seemed to move together quite naturally, and it hadn't escaped Hunter that Danny was a quick study, making the horse ride fast and turn sharply whenever one of the horses they were rounding up strayed from the pack. He could easily see them competing in the junior barrel races when the rodeo came to town. He also had to admit that Belle suited him just fine as well. She was a calm, easy-to-manage horse who seemed very attuned to her rider. Hunter could easily direct her with his thighs, something he knew Gable taught all his horses, leaving his hands free. All in all, it was a very good swap.

"You know Mom's going to eat you alive, don't you?" Danny asked cheekily just before Hunter opened the door to the mudroom.

"Let's get you into a hot bath really quickly, before she sees you, okay?"

Danny hastily stepped out of his boots while he hung up his mud-covered oilskin. "I really enjoyed today, though."

Hunter winked at him. "Just be sure to tell her that!"

They ran up the stairs, and Danny disappeared into his bedroom while Hunter ran the bath. Danny was barely in it when Lisa came up the stairs.

"Everything okay?" she asked gruffly.

"He's fine," Hunter answered. "We got all the horses moved, and Danny worked like a grown-up."

"That's what I was afraid of," Lisa said, not smiling. "He's a kid, Hunter. You can't let him work that hard just because his father abandoned us."

Hunter threw her a warning stare and closed the door, taking Lisa out in the hallway.

"Listen, I know Hugh hurt you, but don't take it out on Danny. He's a great kid and he enjoyed himself a lot out there today. He's got a way with horses and he loves the work. It's not like I'm a slave driver, Lise."

"He shouldn't be working. He should be playing with his friends."

Hunter sighed. "All I'm asking for is one day a week. When I was his age, I worked the ranch every day after school, and I didn't turn out so bad, now, did I? In fact, I was glad of it, because after Dad died someone had to take over here."

Lisa still wasn't smiling. She wasn't giving Hunter one of her angry stares either. Hunter was about to turn around and knock on the bathroom door when he saw Lisa try to tell him something, but she hesitated.

"What's wrong, sis?"

"Could you…. Are you going to the Barrel Run with us tonight?"

Hunter thought about it. He didn't feel like going and bumping into Miranda, since it was Saturday and she was sure to be there. "Hadn't really thought about it," Hunter admitted. "Wasn't planning on it, truthfully."

Lisa finally smiled. "I'm going and I was wondering if you could look after Danny? That way I can go out to dinner with my friends first."

Although Hunter was a little puzzled by Lisa's new partying ways, he was also kind of glad that she wasn't hiding there at the ranch. She deserved to have some fun now and again. Since staying at home was pretty much all she'd done since she'd married Hugh, he didn't know where she'd found friends so quickly, but he saw the upside of telling her he'd take care of his nephew. It was as good an excuse as any not to go out until later, in the hope that Miranda would have given up on him ever showing.

"You can count on me, sis," he said, smiling at her. She smiled back, and for the first time in years, Hunter saw the shy but fun-loving Lisa he'd grown up with. "You go out and have some fun."

After she nodded, Hunter went back inside the bathroom, where he found Danny in the tub with bubbles up to his ears and spilling over the side.

"Went a bit overboard with the bubble bath?" he asked lightheartedly.

Danny nodded cheekily. "It wouldn't foam much, so I added some more."

"You're going to smell like a girl," Hunter teased. He held up the bottle, which said "lilac scent."

"Oh, man!" Danny cried out, quickly getting up.

Hunter laughed. "You might as well stay in there. You'll never get the scent off now."

Danny started playing with the bubbles, trying to get them to disappear. Hunter helped out, playfully swatting at them. They finally gave up and Hunter held up the shampoo bottle, asking Danny whether he wanted him to wash his hair.

"So are you going to ask Grant to become foreman?" Danny asked, settling down in the hot water again while he clearly enjoyed the pampering Hunter was giving him.

"I don't know. What do you think?" Hunter asked, genuinely wanting Danny's opinion. He wanted more than that, though. He wanted Danny's opinion of Grant as a man; he realized he couldn't explain the nature of his relationship with Grant to Danny, but he wanted his silent approval anyway.

Danny shrugged. "I like him. He's nice."

"'Nice' is not what I'm looking for in a foreman," Hunter said, quietly happy that Danny liked him. "Do you think he could do the work?"

"What work is it exactly?"

Hunter took the showerhead to rinse the suds out of Danny's hair. "You know, what your dad did."

Danny grew quiet. "He's never coming back, is he?"

Hunter wiped the water off Danny's head and put his hand on the slim shoulder of the youngster. "I don't know, Danny. I'd love him to come back, but I don't think he can live with your mom anymore."

Danny nodded. He looked sad, but Hunter thought he understood.

"But I think if anyone can do what Dad did, it would be Grant," Danny said suddenly. Hunter squeezed Danny's shoulder by way of thank you.

"I'll talk to Grant as soon as he returns."

"Where is he, anyway?" Danny asked.

Hunter shrugged. "He said he needed some time. And he'd be back on Tuesday."

To Hunter's surprise, Danny took his hand and squeezed it. "You miss him, don't you?"

Hunter felt caught, wondering if he was so transparent a nine-year-old kid could see what was going on between him and Grant. He shrugged, not really knowing what to say.

"I miss my friends when school is out too. They all live on the other side of town, and it's too far to ride there on my bike. Anyway, Mom won't let me go that far on my own anyway, so when I'm not in school, I don't have any friends. I guess you don't either, since you're not in school anymore."

Hunter had to laugh at Danny's simple way of looking at things. It was also a great relief to hear the kid's explanation. "You're right, cowboy. Grant's my friend, and I miss him when he's not around." It was very close to the truth, and Hunter enjoyed the fact he could tell Danny how he felt about Grant.

"I like Grant too. He's really good with the horses, and he said he was going to make me a doghouse if I could persuade Mom to get me a dog."

Hunter smiled conspiratorially. "I think you deserve a dog. You're old enough to take care of one now."

"You think so?"

Hunter nodded. "You're working really hard here, and that deserves a reward."

Danny's eyes grew sad, though. "Mom won't let me. She says dogs aren't supposed to live in the house. They should live outside and work with the horses, not live with us, where they spread disease." He said that last word like he didn't really know what it meant, but was just copying what his mother had said.

"Why don't you leave your mom to me?" Hunter said determinedly, winking at Danny. "Now let's get you out of the water and dried off before you wrinkle like a prune. Then we can go downstairs for dinner." He held out the large bath towel, remembering how embarrassed he always was when he was Danny's age with someone looking at his scrawny body, so he turned away as Danny got out of the tub. After wrapping the towel around Danny and giving him a last squeeze, he moved away. "Can you manage? Dry behind your ears and between your toes, okay?"

Danny smiled and nodded. "Yes, Dad," he said, and then rolled his eyes.

When Hunter walked out of the bathroom, he suddenly felt sad, realizing he'd probably never have children of his own. He and Danny had always been close, but as long as Hugh was around, Danny was definitely Hugh's son. Now Hugh was gone, Hunter realized that Danny was looking at him to take on the father role, and although he felt he could never fill Hugh's shoes, he certainly enjoyed taking care of the youngster.

Still deep in thought, Hunter rounded a corner and promptly walked into Izzie.

"Hey, big boy. Watch where you're going!"

Hunter looked at his sister, her long, dark hair braided into one long strand on her back, but around her head some strands had broken loose and were clinging to her face, telling him she was still soaking wet. It was only then he realized he was still wet as well.

"Danny's in the bathroom, but he's about done. Why don't you go in there next, and I'll run to the shower block in the crew house. That way we'll both be clean by dinner time."

Izzie gave him a curious look. "Grant said he wouldn't be back until Tuesday."

Hunter narrowed his eyes at her. "I know that. I just figured that if we all had to take turns, we'd never be ready in time, and you know how Mom hates us being late for dinner."

"Oh yes," Izzie replied with a mocking look on her face.

"Well, if you prefer going out there to take a shower, be my guest."

"Nope," Izzie replied. "Your arrangement suits me fine." She nudged him with her shoulder. "Don't be so cross with me just because I mentioned Grant. I know you hate it when he leaves with very little notice and no real reason, but I can't help that. We both know if it weren't for his absences, you would have made him foreman almost as soon as Hugh left."

Hunter shook his head. "It's not easy appointing a virtual stranger and passing over Tim and some of the others."

"They all know Grant can do it. He's an all-around guy. Good with the horses, two right hands when it comes to woodwork, and a gentle way with the other wranglers and the stable crew. I'm sure if you give him the job, he'll be firm with them as well. Nobody messes with the big guy. And I'm sure if you talk to Tim, he'll tell you he feels fine handling the job he has and doesn't really want the added responsibility." She winked when she told him that, silently asking him to keep it a secret.

Hunter was glad of Izzie's approval, but he knew it was more than that. There was the fact that Grant had a personal relationship with him, his boss. "But what about…."

"What's going on between him and you?"

Hunter nodded almost imperceptibly.

"Unless you're going to scream it off the rooftops anytime soon, I don't think it matters."

Hunter liked his baby sister's levelheadedness, but he knew not everyone would be so forgiving.

She gave him her most compassionate smile. "Honey, as long as the two of you stay discreet, nobody will notice. It's not written all over your face, you know."

Hunter bit his lip. "You were pretty quick catching on."

"None of these guys went to college and lived with two male roommates who couldn't keep their hands off each other," Izzie deadpanned.

"You lived with…?"

Izzie nodded, amusement in her face.

"Those two guys who helped you move out when I drove up there to pick you up after graduation?"

Izzie nodded again, smiling even more broadly.

"I never…."

"You didn't live with them. In front of strangers they looked pretty ordinarily frat-boy straight, but when it was just me…." She smiled as if she remembered better times.

"Mom never knew this, right?" Hunter just had to ask.

"Are you kidding? She'd have had me out of there so fast my head would be spinning. There was a reason I liked the fact she wasn't the travelling sort, and I was more than happy that it was you and Hugh who helped me move out of there in the end. Mom or Lisa would have shit bricks if they'd known I had male roommates, and gay male roommates at that."

Izzie lovingly caressed Hunter's face. "You're going to have to break it to them gently."

Hunter determinedly shook his head. "I'm never telling them."

She let her hand rest on the side of his neck. "You can't keep this hidden, Hunter. It's a part of you. Like those mysterious amber eyes of yours and that scar over your brow. It's inherent."

"I'm not so sure of that," Hunter answered, his voice filled with emotions he was trying to keep at bay.

Izzie raised herself on the tips of her toes to tenderly kiss her brother. "I'm perfectly fine with having a gay brother, and I'm sure Lisa and Mom will warm up to it eventually. Bernie will be the easiest. I'm sure she'll love knowing that Grant's here to stay."

"I don't know if that's true," Hunter replied.

"Bernie's naïve and sweet, you know that. She worships the ground you walk on and adores Grant, who flirts with her every chance he gets but has made it more than clear to her that's all she'll get."

"I don't know if Grant's here to stay," Hunter elaborated.

"Well, make it worth his while, then. Tell him you want him to stay. Start by giving him the foreman job, but tell him *you* want him to stay for more than the ranch."

Hunter pulled Izzie into a tight hug and didn't let go until she pushed him away. "Let go of me, you big lug." She took his face in her hands. "You know I love you, right? I'll love you even more if you find happiness with Grant."

"I don't even know Grant."

"And you're worried about what Gable will think." It wasn't a question.

Hunter nodded. "Grant left Gable after his accident. Disappeared without a trace."

"Have you asked him about what happened?"

"No," Hunter admitted. "But whenever the subject comes up, you know, indirectly, Grant shuts down. He doesn't want to explain it to me."

"Give him time. He probably feels guilty. I would."

"But who would leave his…."

"Lover?" Izzie aided Hunter.

"Yeah…. What kind of man would do that to a loved one who was hurt?"

"We don't know what happened between them before the accident, Hunter."

"Ten minutes to dinnertime, folks!" Lisa's voice calling upstairs disturbed their intense conversation.

"I better run to the showers," Hunter said.

Izzie nodded. "Yeah, me too." She gave him an intense stare. "Think about it, Hunter. Don't wait for Grant to make the first move. Talk to him."

She didn't give Hunter any chance to protest as she turned around and disappeared into her room. Hunter quickly grabbed a towel and a bar of soap and retrieved a clean pair of jeans and a shirt from his room before running out to the crew quarters. He was grateful that the shower block was deserted, with most of the men at dinner, and was quick to strip and get under the hot water. He knew he didn't have a lot of time, so he lathered up and ran his hands over his wet skin to wipe off the grime.

It felt good to get clean, but he couldn't shake the images of Grant, the way he'd looked just before they'd kissed for the first time. Hunter tried to ignore his cock, which was quickly growing heavy, but the memories of Grant wearing nothing but a towel in this dimly lit shower block, and then afterward in his room upstairs, made him horny as hell. Hunter wrapped his hand around his heavy erection and tugged at it a few times. He knew what he wanted was Grant's hand on him, his mouth around his cock, sucking him, teasing him with his tongue. He wiped his free hand over his ass, letting a finger slip between his ass cheeks. He swallowed when he circled his hole and felt the muscle contract involuntarily. Could he let Grant inside him there? He pushed his finger against the scrunched-up muscle and felt resistance. Surely Grant would never fit. Hunter had had enough trouble getting his mouth around Grant's more than ample erection. There was no way Hunter could accommodate that. Then why did he suddenly crave it? Why did Hunter feel that if Grant suggested it next time, he'd agree to give it a try?

Then he remembered the encounter in the stables and how horny and eager he'd been. He'd asked Grant to fuck him, and he'd meant it. It was just when he was alone that he doubted he could handle it. When they had enough time and privacy, Grant had said. Izzie was right. Hunter was going to have to make the first move: organize a way for them to be together, away from the prying eyes of his family and the ranch crew.

Hunter felt the heat rise as he fisted himself, his cock now rock-hard from the idea of letting Grant inside him. He looked up, letting the hot water stream over his face as he imagined feeling Grant against his back, pushing against him, into him, going further than the last time they'd been together in the barn. Just as he realized he could no longer hold back and bright lights flashed behind his closed eyes, his finger slipped through his tight guardian muscle and he bucked into his hand, shooting white ribbons of come against the wall.

Feeling his legs go weak, he let his head fall forward against the separating wall, finding some sort of support. Panting hard to catch his breath, he understood there was no denying it. He could say he wasn't gay—at least he didn't *feel* gay—but he couldn't say he didn't lust after Grant, didn't grow hard at the mere thought of the big guy's hands on his naked skin. He couldn't deny that. And Izzie understood.

"SORRY I'm late," Hunter apologized as he sat down behind his plate, his hair still wet and tousled, since he's forgotten to pack his comb. Lisa and his mother looked at him sternly, but Bernie and Izzie smiled, as usual. Hunter couldn't help smiling too as he handed his empty plate to his mother so she could put food on it. That was the way it was at their house. Mother was boss.

Hunter was still flying high and hoped his mom and sisters wouldn't catch on exactly why he was feeling so elated. He even had to prevent himself from announcing that he was going to take a weekend off in the near future. Of course he couldn't tell them he was going to spend it with Grant, but he was certainly going to arrange something. As soon as Grant was back, he'd asked him about it and figure out a place to go.

# —15—

GRANT sat on the bench, trying to stay awake. He'd had to ride his motorbike all night and most of the day to get here, and now the door he was staring at remained closed. Not that this was anything unusual, but he had come running as soon as he was asked, so he felt betrayed again. He looked up at the window. The light was on and the curtains were still open, but he couldn't see what was going on inside.

It was dinnertime, so they'd probably be getting ready to eat, all of them sitting around the large table, sharing food. Grant felt his stomach growl, but he ignored it, knowing he couldn't leave yet. Not while there was still a chance the door would be opened to let him in, just to say hello. He'd stopped expecting more a long time ago, but there was no way he was going to squander his chances. A few more hours and then it would be too late for today. He'd be back early the next morning, sitting on the bench where he couldn't be seen from the window but where he could spot any movement inside or see them leave the house.

Wrapping his coat tighter around himself, he tried to stay warm, hoping, wanting desperately to see them, not knowing whether he'd get a chance this time.

His nights in the cheap motel were restless, filled with longing— not just for what he'd come all this way for, but also for Hunter. He'd never met a man who was his equal: tall and strong and fairly self-assured. Although he knew Hunter was still full of self-doubt about what he wanted in a partner, there was no doubt in Grant's mind that Hunter would grow into the feelings, just like he had, after years of insecurity. Grant knew he had Gable to thank for helping him make up his mind. Not that Gable had been the love of his life. Far from. Gable was too quiet, too introspective, and way too closed off for Grant, but they'd worked together well, and for the first time in his life Grant had understood that although their relationship was far from ideal, he did see himself building a life with another man. One of the few things he'd learned from Gable was that it was possible, even without compromise.

After a frustrating weekend of missed chances, Grant started on his way back to Hunter's ranch. After several hours of driving, he finally stopped for gas and found a missed call on his cell phone. After returning it, he knew Hunter would have to wait a little longer for his return.

It wasn't much of a detour; in fact, it was practically on his way. He hated hospitals, though, had hated them with a passion ever since he'd had to say good-bye to his mother at the tender age of eight. Being left an orphan after his mom had promised she wouldn't leave him was something he'd never been able to shake. This hatred of hospitals had cost him a lover. When he'd found out Gable had been hurt, he hadn't been able to get over his dislike of the whiteness and the smell and had left town instead of being there for Gable. He'd lulled himself into believing Gable would be home in a few days, but when he didn't recover, Grant had been so ashamed he'd left. It wasn't until much later that Calley had told him the truth about Gable's injury and how hard they'd have to work to keep Gable's ranch afloat.

Now was his chance to make amends of some sort. He knew Gable wouldn't want to see him, and he couldn't blame him, but Gable was back in the hospital, and Calley had told him it was touch and go.

With sweaty palms and shivering with irrational fear, Grant walked into the overly bright white environment. He had to ask for directions and eventually found the waiting room outside the ICU where Calley had said Gable was being taken care of. It was deserted, and on the plaque outside, it said visiting hours were short and didn't start for a while yet. He took a deep breath to calm his nerves and glanced around the waiting room. Although he was usually very perceptive, it took him a few moments to recognize the tall, thin woman sitting in the corner.

"Calley?"

She looked up at him and her face started to shine. She looked tired, though, as if she hadn't slept much.

"Grant, darling." She got up from the uncomfortable-looking PVC seat and walked toward him, pulling him into a hug before he could react. Her touch was soothing, and to Grant's surprise, it helped calm his nerves.

"How bad is it?"

Her smile disappeared. "They still don't know whether he'll make it. Flynn and I had to make the decision to have his foot amputated, and now we don't know whether it was all worth it. Luckily, he doesn't know yet."

"He's not awake?" Grant asked. Despite everything that had happened, he still worried about Gable.

She shook her head. "He had blood poisoning and his organs started shutting down. He's on a ventilator. They're trying to wean him off it, but it isn't easy after all this time."

Grant sighed. He needed to see Gable, although he knew he wasn't welcome. "Is... Flynn with him?"

"Yes," Calley acknowledged. "They let him stay in there as long as he wants."

"They know he's Gable's... lover?"

Calley smiled a little. "Flynn's not the type to hide that. He's pretty straightforward, so to speak."

"Good," Grant said. He was still holding her hand, hanging on to it like a security blanket. He was glad Gable had found someone who was secure in his feelings. "I'm glad Gable has someone like Flynn. He deserves that."

Calley squeezed his hand. "Don't put yourself down, Grant. You just made one wrong choice."

"A choice for which everyone is all too eager to crucify me."

Calley cocked her head. "Can't really blame those who don't know the full story, but I know what happened, and I won't crucify you."

Grant smiled. "You're easy. You've always been on my side." He looked around to assure they were alone and then pulled her into a tight hug. She didn't fight him, and they stood like that for a while. When they parted, she looked a little flushed.

"Why don't I go get us something to drink?" she offered.

"I can—"

She shook her head. "I need to take a walk. I've been sitting here way too long."

She left Grant alone in the waiting room, so he sat down. There were some magazines on a table nearby, but they all looked like women's magazines, and Grant didn't think he would be able to focus enough to read anyway, so he just sat quietly, looking at the speckled floor. A door to the side opened and Grant saw it led to the ward, so he got up and caught it just before it closed. He knew Gable was somewhere in the corridor, and he wanted to see him one more time, before it was too late.

No one paid much attention to him as he walked along the corridor, peering through the floor-to-ceiling windows that separated the rooms.

"Can I help you, sir?" a young man in white scrubs asked him.

Grant figured he was a nurse. "I'm looking for Gable Sutton."

"Are you family?"

Grant shrugged. "Sort of. We're not related by blood."

"I see," the man said with a soft smile. "I'll have to ask his friend." He pointed at one of the rooms, and Grant saw a young man with short, curly hair sitting in a chair next to a bed. He was holding the hand of the man lying down. The man's eyes were open, and suddenly Grant realized the gaunt-looking and emaciated man in the bed was Gable. He almost hadn't recognized him. From the corner of his eye, Grant saw the young man get up, an annoyed look on his face, but Grant's gaze was pinned to Gable as the recognition in Gable's eyes suddenly hit. He couldn't mistake that look for anything else but panic, and alarms started going off.

Grant felt his heart suddenly speed up and he knew he had to get away. He turned around and walked back down the corridor toward the door he'd entered through. He couldn't get it to open, and kicked it. Then he noticed a large knob on the wall, and when he thumped that, the door opened. He burst into the waiting area.

"I lost you," Calley said, concern in her face. "I thought you'd left and I tried calling you on your phone, but I figured it was still turned off from being inside the hospital—"

"I was... I saw Gable," Grant interrupted.

She stroked his arm to soothe him. "He doesn't look very well."

"I know. And he saw me. He panicked."

The wrinkle in her forehead deepened. "You two need to talk it out, Grant."

"That's not very likely now, is it? Gable's too sick for anything, and I don't know if I want to incur Flynn's wrath."

"He *is* very protective of Gable," Calley agreed. At that moment the door between the waiting room and the ICU opened and Flynn stormed through.

"Grant, I believe?"

Grant didn't have time to react. Although Flynn was shorter than him, his fist was surprisingly powerful, and Grant felt something crack as Flynn slugged him. He staggered back and only just kept himself on his feet.

Flynn's eyes were on fire. "I don't ever want to see you anywhere near Gable."

Grant shook his head. "I didn't mean to upset him. I just...." He didn't finish his sentence. Instead he rubbed his jaw and felt around inside his mouth with his tongue after tasting blood.

Flynn seemed to calm down as he rubbed his own knuckles and spotted Calley. "He's okay," he told Calley. "He's breathing on his own now."

"I'm sorry," Grant apologized again.

Flynn turned back toward Grant. "Gable's not ready for you right now, Grant. He may never be. Please don't try this again. At least not until he has a choice on whether or not he *wants* to see you."

"Fair enough," Grant agreed. "I'm working at Hunter's ranch if he ever wants to see me. I understand if he doesn't."

Flynn nodded. "I have to go back inside," he said, more to Calley than Grant.

"Take care of him, darling," Calley said as they watched Flynn leave.

Grant took a deep breath and felt the adrenaline leave his system. "He's a bigger man than I could ever be."

"Told you Gable hit the jackpot." Calley was looking at him with a face full of concern. "So you're working at Hunter's place?"

Grant nodded. "Hunter and I are...." He stopped because he couldn't believe he was divulging his best-kept secret to her.

"I never knew Hunter was gay," Calley said quietly, but in her usual no-holds-barred way.

"He's figuring out he is," Grant replied. "But don't tell anyone, okay? Nobody knows yet."

She winked at him. "I may have the reputation of being the town gossip because my shop is a central meeting point for so many people, but I know how to keep a secret too."

Grant nodded. He knew that. Calley had kept more than a few of his secrets in the past. Maybe that was the reason he was so eager to tell her his new one. It felt good to tell someone. It made it more real somehow, although he still wasn't sure Hunter was not going to bolt on him.

"We're not... it's nothing steady or committed yet. Hunter is still getting used to the idea," Grant elaborated.

"Seems you're getting more comfortable admitting you like men too?"

Grant nodded. "Was always stupid to deny it, I suppose. I just never saw myself having an actual relationship with a guy before either. Not even when I was living with Gable. That wasn't a real relationship, Calley."

She hugged his arm and nodded. "I know."

"But with Hunter I find myself wanting more than just...."

"Sex?"

Grant smiled at how easily she said the word. He shook his head at how uncomfortable it still made him to say it out loud. Years of prejudice weren't easily wiped out. "Of course, the moment I meet someone I want to spend the rest of my life with, he's the one who can't imagine such a thing."

Calley gave Grant's arm another squeeze. "He'll come around. You'll just have to be patient."

# —16—

HUNTER was working late. Although he enjoyed doing the ranch work when Grant was gone, he'd known there were stock papers waiting for him in his office, and since he hated spending entire days in there to catch up, he went there after a whole day in the saddle just to avoid falling behind.

The office was downstairs in the big house, just off the mudroom, and Hunter had to turn on his desk lamp to see what he was doing. It was already quiet in the main house, so when Hunter heard an urgent knock on the door, he startled.

"Come in," he answered, after a brief pause to figure out whether he'd dreamed the sound or not.

"Hey there," Grant saluted him.

Hunter couldn't hold back a smile. Grant looked dead tired, but he was still a sight to behold. "You're back early."

"Thought I'd check in with you before I turned in to make sure I could start work first thing in the morning."

Hunter nodded and got up from behind his desk, trying to stall for time so he could think of a way to keep Grant with him a bit longer, but it made him feel selfish to see the dark circles around the other man's eyes. He really should let the man go to bed. Then Hunter remembered something.

"We're missing another horse. I was going to take Tim out to ride fences in the morning so we could check for signs of cougar, but he's pretty busy with some of the mares going into heat, so if you don't mind, maybe you and I can go?"

Grant took a few steps closer to Hunter as Hunter sat down on the corner of his desk. "Sure. Sounds like a fun day."

"So how was your time off?"

Grant shrugged. "Tiring. I better turn in because we'll be leaving early, right?"

Hunter nodded slowly and Grant lingered, reluctant to leave.

"I swapped horses with Danny," Hunter said in an effort to keep Grant with him. "Danny rode Honeybee on Saturday, and I rode Belle."

Grant took another step closer to where Hunter was sitting. "Belle's much more your size than Honeybee. Danny didn't mind?"

It wasn't lost on Hunter that Grant's voice was becoming softer, more seductive, although the topic of their conversation was fairly neutral. "No, I think he's happy with the trade. He looked a lot more at ease on the smaller horse." Hunter had to prevent himself from leaning toward Grant, because Grant was so close he could smell the musky, slightly sweaty scent of a man who'd been on the road for a few days, and it was making his jeans grow tight. He wanted to pull Grant closer, kiss him, feel that hard body under his hands. He wanted to ravish the other man, but he didn't dare, so he simply looked into Grant's dark eyes.

Grant put his hands lightly on Hunter's thighs, and almost without thinking Hunter moved them to his hips, spreading his thighs a bit more so Grant could fit between them. Grant pulled him closer, and as soon as Hunter looked up at him again, he found his lips captured by Grant's mouth. Hunter didn't even think before kissing him back, hoping to convey to Grant that he'd missed him. Within moments their kiss became fiercely passionate as Grant ground his bulge against Hunter's and moaned into his mouth.

"Fuck, you feel good," Grant groaned when they pulled apart for air.

"I missed you," Hunter replied.

Grant's forehead was still touching Hunter's. He acknowledged Hunter's statement with a longing moan and a short kiss.

"Let's go away next weekend," Hunter said softly. "To a hotel room somewhere. Somewhere they don't know us."

Grant nodded and kissed Hunter again. Hunter was surprised at the tenderness and care he felt from Grant, and for just a moment, he simply wanted to feel Grant close to him, his hands possessively on his hips and his mouth claiming him, but then Grant moved his hand to the middle, cupping Hunter's bulge and palming his erection through his jeans, and the lust boiled up again with a vengeance. Every time they came close, Hunter felt red heat like he'd never before felt for anyone, least of all a woman. His mind boggled when he tried to figure out what it was about Grant that made his legs turn to putty and his heart race a mile a minute. Surely it had everything to do with Grant's skilled hands and take-charge attitude when it came to their encounters, but Hunter failed to understand why he was eager to give up control when he'd always imagined himself being quite dominant.

"Want you to fuck me," Hunter whispered, feeling he couldn't give up control completely.

"Told you I want to do it right, 'cause it's your first time. You can't rush these things, Hunter."

Hunter knew Grant meant well, but he was desperate for contact, desperate to consummate their union. He didn't like postponing things, especially things he dreaded. He knew it would hurt and wanted to get it over with as soon as possible, and as horny as he was now, he knew he'd be able to do it.

"What if they catch us?" Grant asked as he pulled back just enough to look Hunter in the eye.

"We can't do it here," Hunter said determinedly. "This is an old house, and sounds carry."

"I want you comfortable on a bed, not bent over a desk," Grant agreed. "Crew house isn't much better. Walls are paper-thin there too."

Then Grant smiled as if he'd found a solution. He pushed himself away from Hunter, grabbed his hand, and pulled Hunter onto his feet. "Trust me?"

Hunter nodded and followed Grant outside, his jeans more than a little uncomfortable because of the tightness around his distended groin.

"Keys?" Grant asked when they walked up to Hunter's truck. Hunter threw them and Grant caught them neatly in his hand before getting behind the wheel.

"Where are we going?"

Grant didn't answer as he pulled up right next to the crew house door. "Be right back."

When Grant returned moments later, he was carrying two blankets and a plastic bag. Hunter didn't dare ask what was inside, but he had a pretty good idea.

"It's a little cold to sleep outside," Hunter protested weakly.

"We're not going to be outside," Grant stated curtly.

It didn't take long for Hunter to figure out they were driving toward Gable's ranch. "We'll get caught there as well."

Grant smiled. "They're not home." Grant parked the car under a tree out of sight of the main house and got out. Hunter figured he wanted him to follow, so he did.

"Up there," Grant said as he pointed at a ladder in the darkened barn.

Hunter could hear horses in their stalls and the movement of hoofs, but other than that there wasn't a sound anywhere. "An old-fashioned hayloft?"

Grant nodded mischievously. "It's private and has plenty of straw to make for fairly soft bedding. And I know you're not allergic."

For a moment Hunter felt a pang of jealousy as he imagined *how* Grant knew this was such a good place to fuck, but lust won after only a few moments of hesitation. He'd dreamed about this, imagined what would happen and how, and since they were both horsemen, this was as good a place as any.

Neither stood on ceremony, and as Grant rolled out the blankets over the thick covering of straw, Hunter stripped off his clothes.

Although his erection had died down some on the drive over, seeing Grant follow suit, a teasing smile all over his face, made little Hunter stand at attention quickly enough.

Hunter didn't have time to react when he saw Grant fall to his knees in front of his feet. "Fuck, you look good enough to eat." Grant didn't wait and pulled Hunter's erection toward his mouth, swallowing it whole.

Hunter practically came right there and then. "Fuck! Grant!" he cried out. "Don't make me come yet."

Grant didn't flinch. He simply continued his ministrations, licking Hunter's rock-hard erection with the fervor of a starving man. Hunter couldn't continue looking at the too-enticing sight, so he backed up slightly until he could lean against a support beam.

"Spread your legs," Grant asked, as if he didn't expect Hunter to object.

Thanks to the support, Hunter managed to comply, and Grant abandoned the blow job just long enough to coat his fingers with saliva. Grant dove right back in while he fondled Hunter's balls and let his wet fingers slide further until he encountered Hunter's opening. Grant fingering Hunter's entrance was enough to make him jump for a moment, but then Hunter remembered how he'd come so violently the night he'd tried it on himself in the crew shower, and he relaxed. He could sense Grant's experience and flinched a lot less when he felt the tip of Grant's big, manly finger slip inside.

"Tight like a virgin," Grant said, smiling seductively.

"Don't laugh," Hunter managed to squeeze out.

"I'm not laughing. I'm just thinking of how much I'm going to enjoy that tight, pulsating heat around my dick when I'm fucking you into our improvised mattress." At the moment the sexually explicit words dripped from Grant's mouth, he pushed deeper into Hunter and found his trigger.

"Shit! Fuck! What was that?"

Grant just smiled and made Hunter writhe by brushing over the spot again until Hunter felt his legs about to give way. He was so close to coming and had the feeling he'd been there for a while, but something was holding him back. Was it the curious sensation of what Grant was doing inside him? It was certainly something he'd never felt before, and every time Grant moved his finger, he felt the urge to come. Yet something was preventing him. Then suddenly, Hunter felt empty again as Grant withdrew the digit. He almost cried out "no" but settled for moaning in protest. Hoping Grant would blow him again, he rolled his hips, making his cock flop in the direction of Grant's face.

"Trying to poke my eye out?" Grant teased. "Or do you want to fuck my mouth?"

"Fuck," Hunter muttered. It was more a curse than an indication of what he wanted to do, because he didn't think Grant would want to get a cock thrust into his throat, nor did he think he'd have enough self-control to move gently, but Grant took it as a preference and wrapped his lips around Hunter's now-leaking member anyway.

Grant was driving Hunter crazy, but he couldn't say anything. His mind simply couldn't manage to tell his mouth to form the words. When Hunter didn't move, Grant gently eased two fingers into Hunter's entrance, and although it felt good, it also burned, and Hunter's muscles involuntarily tried to expel the intrusion.

"Relax," Grant soothed him, momentarily interrupting the blow job. "Roll your hips and fuck my mouth. That'll take your mind off my fingers."

"Don't want to take… my mind off… your fingers."

Grant teased Hunter by opening his mouth around Hunter's bobbing erection but not actually sucking on it, forcing Hunter to move forward.

"Yeah," Grant urged him on. He moved his fingers in sync with Hunter's movements, slowly opening his lover up while Hunter needed all his restraint not to ram his cock down Grant's throat. For extra support, Hunter let his hand rest on Grant's head. When Grant smiled around Hunter's cock, Hunter actually grabbed a handful of Grant's hair and pushed his cock in deeper, provoking a moan from Grant. Hunter could just see Grant move one hand to his own cock, fisting it in time with Hunter's thrusts, and the next time Grant curled his fingers inside Hunter, Hunter shuddered and came down Grant's throat with such sudden violence he couldn't even moan a warning.

Grant didn't seem to have a problem with it. He simply swallowed a few times around the head, making Hunter spasm even more. Both of Grant's hands had returned to steady Hunter's hips, and it was only then that Hunter felt the emptiness.

"Didn't want to come yet," Hunter sighed more than said as Grant slowly lowered him to the ground.

"I meant to make you come," Grant replied, gently wiping the hair away from Hunter's face. "If you still want me inside you, it will be easier because you'll be more relaxed."

Hunter nodded, unable to speak and feeling very relaxed in Grant's embrace after Grant snuggled closer to him on the soft blanket covering their makeshift bed.

"You're one heck of a moaner," Grant said softly. "I'm glad we're all alone here. I'll have to remember that when I find us a hotel room next weekend."

"I was going to," Hunter replied. "I asked you to meet me somewhere."

"Taking the upper hand again?" Grant teased.

"I'm your boss," Hunter said matter-of-factly.

"Tonight you're not my boss. You didn't pay me for today, remember?"

Hunter, feeling his energy return, ran his hand up and down Grant's still-rigid shaft.

Grant kissed him again, this time exploring Hunter's mouth. "So when did you decide you wanted me to fuck you?"

"Somewhere between what we did in the truck during the storm and a particularly hot shower in the crew house," Hunter answered.

"You showered in the crew house? Should I be jealous and ask who with?"

Hunter could see the mix of smugness and slight apprehension on Grant's face. "Just me and my hand," he answered shyly. "Izzie was in the shower at the house and I was soaking wet from working in the rain, and we had ten minutes before dinner."

"And heaven forbid you should be late."

"Well, needless to say, I *was* late that night."

"Oh, I'd love to hear the details."

Hunter could never resist Grant's smile, although it always made him cautious. He wanted to tell him, though, wanted to admit what the crew showers did to him. "Every time I go in there I remember the way you brought me off that night. I get hard just thinking about you, and I try to imagine what you would do to me if you caught me with my dick in my hand under the spray."

"And you thought I'd fuck that little virgin hole of yours?"

"I couldn't imagine you bending over for me, so yes."

Grant flashed his always-teasing smile. "Play your cards right and I just might." He didn't wait for Hunter's response beyond his surprised expression and kissed him violently. It made the heat rise between them, and Hunter felt himself growing hard again. Grant's hand between his legs certainly helped in that department too, and Hunter wantonly spread his knees to allow Grant more access. Suddenly Grant pulled away, and Hunter felt the chill of the night air. Grant didn't stay away long, rolling back against Hunter, holding the lube and a condom, which he rolled onto his erection before slicking himself up.

"Turn on your side," Grant instructed softly.

"I want to see you," Hunter protested.

"I know. Next time." Grant kissed Hunter's shoulder tenderly. "It'll hurt less this way, and if it feels good we can still change position, okay?"

Hunter nodded, feeling terribly nervous right now. He was used to having the upper hand in bed, being the one in charge, being the one doing the fucking. It wasn't that he didn't trust Grant, but it wasn't easy being the passive one, especially not because he anticipated it being fairly uncomfortable.

"Relax," Grant purred in his ear. "You're coiled tighter than a spring, and that's not a good thing right now."

Grant gently caressed Hunter's stomach muscles, but instead of making him feel relaxed, Hunter felt ripples of anticipation run across his skin. It was finally going to happen. He was finally going to find out what it was like to be fucked by a man. Hunter had a hard time focusing, though. With Grant's hand playing with his nipples—which were suddenly a lot more sensitive than he'd ever realized—and that gentle, soothing voice in his ear interspersed with a sloppy wet tongue licking his earlobe, it almost made him forget that there was something cold and slippery rubbing over his hole. Hunter felt the pressure, though.

"Push back," Grant ordered. "Push yourself over my cock."

Hunter did just that and felt the burn increase, so he retreated, but not completely.

"That's it, rock back and forth a bit."

Hunter did, grabbing his waning erection and fisting himself. He didn't think Grant would fit, so he tried to forget how big and heavy Grant's cock had felt in his hand. Instead, Hunter tried to focus on the feelings he'd experienced earlier, when Grant had his fingers inside him and was touching that spot that sent electricity through his spine. It would feel so good when Grant thrust against it with the head of his cock. Hunter pushed back again, and it felt like something gave.

"Yeah, that's it. Easy now. Just get used to feeling me inside. Just feel how good it is to be filled by my cock."

Hunter groaned, not so much from the burning pain as from how full he felt and how this was so foreign, yet felt so right at the same time. Grant was inside him and the burn was slowly subsiding. He wanted to feel that surge of electricity again.

"Move," Hunter managed to utter.

"Are you sure? Why don't you fuck yourself on my cock first? See what it feels like."

"I'm not fucking doing all the work myself here," Hunter hissed through gritted teeth. He didn't mean it to sound so brutal, but he couldn't take back his words.

Grant pulled Hunter's head back and kissed him. "I thought you liked being in charge."

Hunter was glad Grant hadn't taken it the wrong way, so he smiled. "I do," he admitted, a little sheepishly.

"So meet me halfway?"

Grant pushed his cock a little deeper, and Hunter pushed back. It helped somewhat with the burn, but he still couldn't say it felt comfortable. It didn't take them long to find an easy rhythm, though, Grant covering Hunter's hand so they could stroke Hunter's slowly refilling cock together.

"Does it feel good yet?"

Hunter nodded and Grant thrust in a little more forcibly, making Hunter whimper. Some nagging voice in the back of his mind told him it sounded silly, like a girl, but Hunter didn't care. He felt right about not entirely trusting his voice. Every time Grant thrust into him, it was like he pushed air out through Hunter's vocal cords and made him moan. It was no longer something Hunter had any control over, especially now it was starting to feel better. The sensation of being filled by Grant's red-hot poker was like nothing Hunter had ever experienced, but he didn't want it to stop. His hand was wet and slippery with the fluid that was oozing out of the slit of his cock, though, signaling it would all be over soon.

"You're so tight, baby," Grant panted in his ear. "Feels so good. Are you enjoying it yet?"

Instead of answering, Hunter arched his back and twisted his neck so he could kiss Grant. It changed the angle of Grant's thrust, and suddenly Hunter felt sparks shoot up his spine again. He groaned loudly, making Grant stop.

"Everything okay?" Grant asked, concern all through his voice.

"Don't stop. Don't fucking stop doing that," Hunter grunted.

Grant picked up the pace again, and Hunter resumed his synchronous moaning. He couldn't believe how this strange sensation could bring him so close to coming less than half an hour after he'd had a mind-numbing orgasm, but he knew that if Grant kept up this rhythm he'd be shooting ribbons any time now.

"Fucking make me come," Hunter chanted. "So close. Fuck me, Grant."

Grant didn't need Hunter to repeat himself. He tried to aim for the spot that made Hunter react most loudly and sped up the movements of his hand over Hunter's cock. Hunter had long since abandoned trying to jack himself off with any sort of rhythm and was simply letting the sensation flow over him, until he clawed at Grant's hip, gripping it and pulling it closer, and then wailed. Thick white strands shot out of Hunter's cock and through Grant's fingers onto his belly, and the spasms of his back passage proved too much for Grant too.

After a few moments of panting, Grant reached between their sweat-covered bodies to hold onto the condom as he pulled out.

"Don't!" Hunter shouted with all of his remaining breath, his otherwise spent body tensing up again.

Grant shushed him. "What's wrong? I'll be gentle. I won't hurt you, trust me."

Hunter could only groan with the feeling that Grant was mocking him, so he let his face sink into the blanket.

Grant smiled against Hunter's neck. "Not going anywhere, baby." He grabbed his T-shirt and rubbed it over Hunter's cum-stained belly. "Just going to clean us up a bit and grab a blanket so we don't get cold."

Hunter looked up and shivered, both from the feel of the night air on his damp skin and from feeling empty after Grant pulled out of him. Although it wasn't altogether painless, he wanted to do it again as soon as Grant was ready. Was he being too demanding? Would it be too much too soon? He let himself fall to his back and tried not to look at Grant too expectantly.

Grant returned to their makeshift bed and got down next to Hunter, wrapping them both in a fleece all-weather blanket.

Hunter felt tired and lethargic, but when Grant kissed him tenderly, he realized they'd turned a corner. He ran his hands appreciatively over Grant's tight frame and cupped his ass, squeezing it playfully. It felt so much more right than he could ever have imagined.

"So was it as bad as you thought it would be?" Grant asked.

"It was nothing like I'd imagined," Hunter answered. "It hurt some, but it felt so good."

"I could tell," Grant chuckled.

"Can we do it again?"

Grant laughed. "I created a monster, didn't I?"

Hunter looked into Grant's dark eyes and nodded seriously. "I never imagined…." He looked up, away from Grant. "I've always had feelings for other men, but I could never understand the mechanics of the sex. Couldn't understand that they actually wanted to take it up the ass, and since I always go for the butch ones, the clear tops, I never took it any further, afraid they'd want to fuck me."

"But you let me?"

Hunter nodded, daring to look at Grant again, although only fleetingly. "I didn't want to lose you."

"And you thought I wouldn't have taken this further if you'd refused?"

Hunter shrugged. "I don't know. How would we have done it if neither of us had wanted to take it up the ass?"

"I've been known to bottom for the right guy," Grant replied, looking a lot less smug all of a sudden. "Not that I've met a lot of right guys so far, but I'm willing to be more versatile than I usually am, for you."

"I think I like having you fuck me," Hunter admitted, this time not turning away from Grant's gaze.

Grant playfully growled at Hunter and pushed himself on top of the other man. "Good, 'cause it will be really hard to keep my hands off you, baby."

"Just don't call me baby, okay? I still sign your paychecks, remember?"

Grant laughed. "Don't remind me!"

# —17—

GRANT didn't mind riding behind his boss—especially not because that boss was having clear difficulties getting comfortable in his saddle. He looked good on top of the tall brown mare named Belle, and Grant still smiled when he imagined Hunter on top of Honeybee, the diminutive filly he'd bought from Gable a few weeks earlier.

They were riding out together to check for breaks in the fence and evidence of cougars, since they'd lost another colt, this one slightly older than the last two.

If the sight of Hunter sitting on horseback, thighs spread wide and ass flexing whenever he directed his horse to change direction, wasn't enough to make his cock wake up, the memories of their night in Gable's hayloft were certainly enticing enough.

They'd slept for a little while, both of them exhausted, but Hunter had woken Grant up for round two a while before daybreak. This time they'd made love face to face, and it was even better than the first time, which had been a lot less smooth because of Hunter's inexperience. They'd fallen asleep again, legs and arms entangled, and had been awakened by the horses growing restless from the burgeoning morning. Afraid of being caught by Flynn, in case he came in to feed the horses, they'd dressed quickly and had driven off to the crew house, where they said their good-byes amidst fears of being discovered, while still having a hard time keeping their hands off each other.

It was certainly going to be a challenge to keep their relationship a secret. Not that Grant was the type to shout it from the rooftops. Even though the feelings he had for Hunter were fairly new to him, he was anything but indiscreet, remembering all too well what it felt like to have to hide his taste for men. In fact, he had never been very forthcoming with personal matters. Most of his fellow wranglers still didn't know about his sexual preferences, and he preferred to keep it that way. At least until Hunter was ready to tell his family. Which could be never.

Grant nudged his horse to walk alongside Belle. "Sore?" he asked casually.

Hunter gave him a sideways look, but he didn't speak.

"It gets better after a while, you know, with practice," Grant replied, still having a hard time not seeing the funny side of this.

"And how would you know?" Hunter asked gruffly.

Grant put his hand on Belle's backside, which made the horse slow down. "Okay, it's not exactly from personal experience, but Gable…." He didn't finish when he saw a look on Hunter's face that he thought was a "don't go there" look, so he simply shut up.

"What about Gable?" Hunter asked when Grant didn't continue.

"You probably don't want to hear about him, so I'd better not say anything. I understand." Grant felt uncomfortable all of a sudden. It wasn't right to talk about his relationship with Gable, especially not with his new lover and a friend of Gable's to boot.

Hunter stopped his horse and turned it around. "It's okay. I'd like to talk about Gable, actually."

"You would?"

Hunter nodded his head determinedly. "It's the one thing I can't understand." He sighed, which made Grant feel even less at ease. "Before you came here, I didn't really know you. Then when I heard how you'd abandoned Gable after his accident, I really didn't like you. In fact, I didn't want Hugh to hire you, and if we'd had nearly enough wranglers, I would have fired you that first morning. But we were desperately short of workers, so Hugh persuaded me to keep you. I'm glad we did, because I got to know you," Hunter said with an absent smile. Then he looked straight at Grant with those light brown eyes of his and Grant felt a different kind of rush. "I have a hard time marrying the Grant I heard about before I got to know you to the one I know now."

"Who said anything about marriage?" Grant joked, because he really had no idea how to answer Hunter's question.

"Grant," Hunter said with a pleading tone.

Grant sighed and stopped trying to turn it into a joke. "I wasn't the same man I am now," was the best he could come up with.

Hunter directed Belle to come alongside Raven so he could face Grant. He put his hand on Grant's thigh. "I can live with that. I hope you'll tell me what changed you, though. You know, one day?"

Grant nodded. There was so much he still had to tell Hunter, but that would have to wait until they were a little more advanced in their relationship. Right now, everything was still new and exciting, but he knew from experience there was also a big chance they wouldn't make it to anything long-term, so he preferred to keep his cards close to his chest.

Hunter turned Belle around and gently kicked her side to speed her up. They were still taking it quite leisurely, mostly because Hunter still winced with every sudden movement, but they both knew that despite their need to spend time together, they also had to get some work done, and taking all day to ride along the fence line would look a bit suspicious to anyone taking notice.

They rode in silence for a while, dismounting a few times to check on things a little closer up, but it wasn't until they found an obvious break in the fence and were wiring it back together that Grant finally found the courage to speak again.

"I went to see Gable in the hospital last weekend."

"Oh?" Hunter reacted, clearly trying to be casual about it.

"There was a message on my voicemail saying he was admitted again and doing quite badly, so I had to go see and make sure he wasn't going to die or something." They weren't looking at each other, and Grant didn't dare to check Hunter's reaction.

"Is that where you were for four days?"

"No," Grant said definitely. "I went there on the way back home. Back here," he corrected himself. He couldn't think of Hunter's ranch as home yet. That would be way too forward.

"I heard from Flynn that they had to rush Gable back to the hospital, but that was a while ago. How's he doing?"

Grant shrugged. "Still in intensive care."

"Wow," Hunter replied, taking off his hat to scratch his hair. "We keep an eye on his horses, but I didn't think he was in such bad shape."

"Flynn seems to think he'll be okay eventually, but he's still pretty worried."

"You two talked?" Hunter said, clearly surprised, since he stopped what he was doing to stare at Grant.

"He planted his fist against my jaw first. Can't say I blame him," Grant said with a serious face, and rubbed his jaw at the memory. "I bet Gable's told him some horror stories about me."

Hunter went to his saddlebag and took out a thermos of coffee. He sat down on a fallen tree trunk and poured a cup. He gestured for Grant to join him. "So what happened between Gable and you?" Hunter asked, a little hesitantly.

Grant shrugged. "We didn't have some sort of torrid love affair, Hunter."

"I know," Hunter replied.

"We were both lonely and sex was easy, but we weren't in love. At least I thought we weren't. I guess I was wrong about him."

"Judging from how miserable he was, I think he loved you," Hunter said softly.

Grant noticed there wasn't any sort of reproach in Hunter's voice, and he had to admit he was glad of it. "He was very closed off. Didn't share his feelings. I swear I never knew how he felt about me. I never knew he felt more than lust."

Hunter handed Grant the cup of coffee and then put his warm hand on Grant's thigh. It was a comforting touch, and Hunter didn't speak. They just sat there and shared the coffee. They sat for a long time without speaking, but Grant had to admit it wasn't entirely uncomfortable.

After all the coffee was finished, Hunter got up. "I guess us country boys aren't very good at sharing our feelings, hey?"

Grant looked at Hunter and then surveyed their surroundings. When he was satisfied they were completely alone and nobody could see them, he took a step toward Hunter, and when Hunter didn't step away from him, he put his hand on the back of Hunter's head and pulled him into a kiss. There was nothing hesitant about their exchange. By the time they pulled apart, Grant was so turned on he was about ready to rip the shirt off Hunter's back. In fact, he noticed he'd dislodged one corner of it from Hunter's jeans already, so he pointed at it and smiled.

Hunter returned the smile and tucked it back into place.

"We really need to get away this weekend," Grant said quietly.

"I'd like that," Hunter admitted before reluctantly turning around and mounting his horse again.

They rode back in silence, and after taking care of their horses, they went their separate ways. Hunter had books to do, and Grant needed to help bring in the hay from the meadows so they'd have food for the horses during the winter.

He didn't see Hunter again until Friday evening, when everyone picked up their paychecks. He'd been looking forward to Friday all week, anticipating the weekend to come and remembering Hunter's promise that they'd take Saturday off to go somewhere together. When he came face to face with Hunter, his handsome boss didn't say anything, though, so Grant lingered around the office.

"Do we need to do Saturday chores before we leave tomorrow, or is someone covering that?" Grant asked in a subdued voice once all the other guys had left.

"Yeah, we'll need to pull our weight tomorrow. It will look less suspicious, but I think we can leave by two," Hunter replied with a soft smile.

Grant felt his heartbeat pick up. "I know a place we can go. Can we take your truck? My bike's a bit—"

Hunter chuckled. "I'm not climbing on the back of your bike and clinging to you like a girl, thank you."

Grant cocked his head and smiled. "They're talking about rainstorms again anyway, so we'd be more comfortable with some sort of roof over our heads."

Hunter nodded in agreement, and Grant thought he saw anticipation in Hunter's face as well. Or maybe it was the memory of the last time they'd been in a truck together during a lightning storm. Hell, the memory made him grow hard as well. He took a step toward Hunter, but Hunter moved away.

"Tomorrow," Hunter said quietly.

"Yeah," Grant acknowledged. He was a little disappointed that, after several days apart, he didn't even get as much as a kiss, but then, being inside the big house intimidated him as well, so he didn't push for it. They'd have tomorrow night in a motel room somewhere, and then there would be no chance of anyone looking over their shoulders or of someone overhearing the sounds they made. They'd be able to spend their passion on each other and have time afterward to talk.

On his way out, Grant encountered a very agitated Tim. "Need to talk to Hunter."

"He's in the office," Grant said, pointing at the still-open door. Worried about what caused Tim's agitation, he followed the wrangler inside.

"It's two horses this time, Hunter. One of last spring's foals and one a year older."

"Any signs of that cougar?" Hunter asked, getting up from behind his desk.

Tim frantically shook his head. "Dave thinks he saw her yesterday, but he wasn't sure."

"Any signs of a struggle near the fields where the horses are?" Hunter asked.

Grant saw the concern in Hunter's eyes but also saw how calm he stayed, despite Tim's agitation. It was obvious Hunter was thinking through all the possibilities in his head before deciding on his best option.

"I'm riding out there now," Tim replied. "I thought you needed to know first, boss."

Hunter patted the younger cowboy's back with his big hand. "I'll come with you."

"Me too," Grant said. He saw both men turn their gaze in his direction. "If there's a hungry cougar on the loose, there's safety in numbers."

Tim ran out to the stables, and Hunter and Grant followed more slowly.

"You really think it's a cougar?" Grant asked.

Hunter shook his head. "If it was just one or two foals, then yes, I'd bet on a hungry mama cougar with a litter of cubs, but two horses at once? And a one-year-old? Cougars are big cats, but I don't see one tackling an almost full-sized horse *and* dragging it off into the woods. Now, if we find a half-eaten carcass, then my bet's on the cat again."

Grant nodded in agreement as they turned the corner to the stable block that housed Raven and Belle. In record time they saddled their horses and rode out to the south range, a rifle in Hunter's saddlebag.

Grant knew their weekend away was in jeopardy unless they found clear evidence of either a cougar or horse thieves.

# —18—

AFTER another fruitless search, Hunter sank down onto his bed. It was past midnight, and he was dead tired. Of course he hadn't slept much since his virtually sleepless night in the barn, and that was the reason for his extreme fatigue, but he still smiled when he thought about the reason for staying up all night. It didn't take a lot of imagination to remember Grant's rough, calloused hands all over him, the rasp of Grant's beard against his neck, the hot, wet mouth latching on to his nipples, his stomach, his cock and balls. As he crawled under the covers, he couldn't resist stroking himself, touching his erection, and imagining it was Grant touching him.

Fuck! Who would have ever imagined that the things that turned him on in his imagination and that he'd always found impossible to understand were even better when he experienced them in real life? Now he'd had time to mull over the happenings of the last few days, some things had become clear. Hunter's occasional girlfriends had always been small and delicate; even Miranda, although quite a vixen in bed, was your typical run-of-the-mill Midwest girl. Nothing special, but above all, very... girly. They were the opposite of what Hunter knew turned him on but had always avoided like the plague. Giving in to his urges would only end up with him being ostracized and humiliated, he'd always been sure of that. Until he'd met Grant.

Now the memories of touching that tight body, feeling those bulging muscles ripple underneath his hands while tasting the sweat on Grant's skin and feeling that amazing cock ramming into his body, were once again bringing Hunter to the brink of orgasm. Oh, why did it have to feel so good? Why couldn't it have hurt more or felt more uncomfortable? Hunter knew there was no turning back now. For a moment that afternoon, while he was writing his workers' paychecks,

Hunter had tried to conjure up enticing memories of frolicking around with Miranda. And failed miserably. All he could remember was that he'd never had a problem getting an erection, but he'd always had some sort of liquor before ending up in the sack with a girl. His first time with Grant, he'd been stone-cold sober, and he remembered every single thing about it. It couldn't have been more different than his very first sexual experience.

Hunter had lost his virginity with a working girl. For his eighteenth birthday, Hugh's father—then the ranch foreman—had taken him to the Bunny Ranch, a whorehouse about twenty miles outside the county line. Hunter had been given a choice of girls and had picked an angelic-looking blonde who had played her innocent-school-girl act all the way to the end. He'd been passive and shy, and she had smuggled him in some alcohol, making him promise not to breathe a word to anyone outside the room. The act itself had been over almost before it started, but at least afterward Hunter was "a real man."

All his other conquests had been girls just like his first one. Nice, plain, not-bad-looking petite girls who cooed and seduced and often got him drunk before dragging him to their bed. They had scratched his itch, but they'd barely been able to scratch the surface. All Hunter could say was that they were a good alternative to his own hand, but certainly no more than that.

Now his hand brought back memories of Grant's hand but took him back even more.

Hunter remembered the first time the touch of a man had made him grow hard. He'd only been fourteen and overcome with grief after suddenly losing his father. He'd fled into Gable's barn, running away from the responsibility that had been thrust upon him after his dad's funeral. Now he was the man of the house, and he was going to have to make the decisions that kept a two-thousand-acre horse-breeding ranch afloat. He was too young for that and he knew it, so he'd fled to the one place that had always been safe.

Gable had been twice his age at the time, but Hunter knew he could count on him. Gable had been a quiet presence at his dad's funeral and had offered his calm, soothing support to Hunter, his mother, and his sisters. Hunter knew that Gable and his dad had been friends, like Gable's father and his dad had been friends before the older Sutton had died earlier that year.

That night, after Hunter had fled into Gable's barn, Gable had held him, caressed his hair while he cried. Hunter had kept a brave face until then, but he broke down that night and poured his heart out to Gable, who'd simply been there for him, not offering solutions or instant gratification. Gable had simply assured him that everything would work out in the end.

Hunter had believed him, had wanted to believe him, and being held by the strong, sinewy man had indeed calmed him down. Feeling the sturdy arms around his shoulders, the soft flannel of Gable's shirt against his cheek and the hand on his hair, and smelling the mix of leather and sweat and horses had done other things to Hunter as well. As the panic and intense grief had abated, he'd felt his body react to the curious mix of tenderness and strength. Feeling his pants grow tight had raised a different sort of panic and a feeling of betrayal, of being betrayed by his own body. Although he didn't understand what was going on, Hunter knew he couldn't have those feelings, not now, not in the presence of another man. He'd pulled himself away from Gable's grasp as if Gable's hands had been on fire, and Gable had let him leave without stopping him.

When Hunter was fourteen, he hadn't known about Gable's sexual preference. Those things weren't talked about, but they'd stayed in contact, as Gable was still the closest thing he had to a father figure and Hunter often turned to Gable for advice. He'd noticed the ever-changing ranch hands Gable employed, and as time passed, Hunter began to notice how Gable treated some of them differently from others. It wasn't until Grant started working at Gable's ranch that Hunter's suspicions had been confirmed. He'd caught them pulling apart one day when he'd arrived at Gable's unexpectedly and had seen them frolicking naked under Gable's outside shower, back when the bushes around the shower were newly planted and not nearly as thick as they were now. He'd been too embarrassed to watch, but it had confirmed to him that Gable was gay and Grant was his lover. For a while he'd felt awkward around Gable and Grant, but then he'd realized that Gable was still the same man he'd always been.

And now Grant was Hunter's lover.

Hunter rolled to his back on the bed. He was still achingly hard and couldn't stop thinking about how he felt about Grant. For more than a year he'd been mad at Grant, angry because he'd left Gable at a time when a partner was more important to Gable than anything else in the world. Even now, Hunter still felt a lingering sense of recrimination. Grant's weak excuse that he and Gable had been bed partners, but never lovers with everything that entailed, didn't sit right with him. Even if they'd broken up just before the accident, Hunter felt that Grant had run away from his responsibility, which was to take care of the ranch. He could just as easily have left after Gable came back from the hospital.

Rolling to his side and into a fetal position, Hunter stuck his hand between his legs and touched himself, more to get rid of the ache than to find satisfaction, but it didn't work. "Fuck!" he cursed to himself. He couldn't even get himself off tonight. Why was it so easy to love Grant when he was in the same room with him? What was it that made the wrangler so seductive? Hunter couldn't get a handle on it, because whenever he was alone, the doubts returned. Maybe they shouldn't go away tomorrow? Maybe it was best to stay at home in case there was another attack on the herd. Then he wouldn't need to face his doubts. Then again, Hunter knew he had to get Grant away from the ranch and on neutral ground, because he wanted answers. Even if demanding those answers meant Grant would turn away from him. He owed that much to Gable.

# —19—

GRANT didn't mind getting up early. Seeing the sun come up was almost as magical as seeing it set, and a lot easier to stomach when you had nobody to share it with. He also liked the quiet of the morning, with no banter from the stable boys, just the occasional snorting from the horses. That and a good, honest morning's work helped him clear his head.

By the time Hunter walked into the stables, most of the Saturday morning chores were done. Grant's heart lifted when he saw the dark-haired cowboy stroll toward Davenport's stable.

"Think he's learned his lesson?" Grant asked from near Raven's box.

Hunter startled slightly and turned around with a wry smile. "Are you suggesting I start riding him again?"

Grant shrugged. "He seems to have lost some of his attitude. Tim rides him from time to time, and he says he behaves almost impeccably."

"Yeah, but Tim's got a way with horses, just like his big brother Hugh."

Grant smiled. This was an argument he wasn't going to win. "In any case, it's a good thing that Davenport is getting some exercise other than being put on the treadmill."

Hunter nodded.

Grant couldn't help feeling something was off. Yesterday Hunter had been passionate and eager, and today he seemed standoffish and cold. He moved a little closer to Hunter. There was nobody else in the stable block, but it paid to be careful about people overhearing their more intimate conversations. "Are you having second thoughts?"

Hunter shook his head. "No, but maybe we should postpone another week. What if another horse goes missing while I'm gone?"

"You're not indispensable, Hunter. I know you're the boss and the man of the house and everything, but Izzie can take on the day-to-day operation for one night. You deserve a vacation, and it's not like you're jetting off to Las Vegas for a week. It'll be just like going to an auction or to the county fair." Grant paused to check Hunter's reaction, but Hunter's face remained impassive. "Unless you don't want to go and spend time with me?"

A doubtful smile broke on Hunter's face as he seemed to think of something. "I'll go. On one condition."

"Shoot," Grant said, feeling apprehensive.

"I want some straight answers."

"Sure," Grant shrugged. "What do you want to know?"

"I want to know what happened that day Gable had his accident and you left him. And I want the truth this time."

"You think I was lying?"

Hunter shook his head and shrugged. "I don't know. I just don't know if I can be with someone who leaves his lover at the first hurdle. What if something happened to me, Grant? What if I fell off a tractor or got thrown by a horse and landed on one of the troughs? What if I got so hurt I'd need someone to take care of me? Would it be you?"

Grant felt anger boiling inside him. He'd tried to explain it to Hunter, but it clearly wasn't enough. How could he explain everything that had happened when he didn't even know it all himself?

"You don't trust me? Well, I can't exactly make you," Grant replied, raising his hands in defeat. He had to get away from Hunter before his anger became impossible to hide, so he walked outside into the early fall sunshine. There were clouds on the horizon, and Grant was afraid of roaring thunder of more than one kind.

He'd been looking forward to spending some time with Hunter away from the ranch, both because screwing your boss was a little hard when he was playing boss all the time and because the sneaking around was getting to him. Being discreet was one thing, but not having a place to share some private time was harder than he'd thought.

Once outside the stable block, he felt a little lost. All the work was done, and taking one of the horses out for a run wasn't an option, since all the riding horses were back in the stables and he didn't want to see Hunter right now. His second option was the wood shop. He could start on what he'd intended to do once he had the time: sort all the scrap wood into piles of useful and not-too-useful wood.

Usually working hard was what cleared his head, but this time it wasn't enough. Was it time to leave and find another job? Maybe he could move closer to where he'd come from, so he wouldn't need to drive through the night every few weekends. It would certainly help him sleep more, and maybe he would be able to make it for visits more often too.

Grant wiped the sweat off his brow and pulled his fleece sweater over his head.

"Need a hand?"

Grant looked up at Hunter standing in the doorway. Hunter didn't look too sure of himself, and Grant checked his watch just to tear his eyes away from the man he knew he loved. He was surprised to see that more than an hour had passed.

"Or do you need breakfast first?"

Grant smiled. Hunter was right. He was hungry enough to eat a horse, which was no surprise, since he'd pretty much worked for four hours straight.

"Give me a few minutes to clean up and I'll take you out to Barnaby's."

The smile spreading on Hunter's face was the reason he'd asked to go out. Grant would do anything for that smile. He picked up his sweater and skirted around Hunter, who smiled even wider as he turned to keep watching as Grant made his way to the crew house.

He didn't have time for a shower, but in between taking his dusty clothes off and exchanging them for another pair of jeans and a clean shirt, he threw some water on his face and washed his armpits and his neck. It would have to do. He couldn't waste time on frivolities in case Hunter changed his mind again.

Once outside, he found Hunter leaning against his truck, a faraway smile on his face. "I told Bernie I was taking you to go look at some breeding mares in Billings. And I told her I didn't know whether we'd be back before tomorrow."

Grant smiled broadly. "I should have packed some extra clothes."

Hunter leaned toward Grant as he passed him. "I don't intend to keep you in these clothes for long, so they'll keep for tomorrow."

Grant raised his eyebrows. "I'm hungry."

Hunter smiled some more. "Well, you better eat your fill at breakfast then. Should we warn Barnaby's to stock up before we get there?"

"If we're driving all the way to Billings, we should get carryout."

Hunter's eyes started glinting. "I like the way your mind works, but I'm serious when I say we'll need a decent breakfast."

Grant held onto the side of the truck cabin as Hunter floored the gas pedal and made the truck spit up gravel as they turned off the ranch driveway.

Just over an hour later and after wolfing down a full breakfast along the way, Grant realized that they were driving in the wrong direction for Billings, Montana. He didn't care, though. Where they were going didn't really matter.

It didn't take them long to check into a motel just outside of Idaho Falls. Grant had been hard since Hunter had kissed him violently in the restaurant restroom, and he was having a hard time fitting the key card into the motel door slot.

"Shit!" he cursed loudly.

"Gimme," Hunter suggested, snaking his arms around Grant to relieve him of the card. With that movement, he pinned Grant to the door.

"And you think this'll work better?" Grant asked. "Fuck, I can feel your cock right through your jeans." He put both hands on the door. "You can't fuck me out here, Cowboy. At least let me get us inside first." Grant looked down and plucked the card from between Hunter's fingers. He had a hard time ignoring the way Hunter was grinding against him, but he managed to get the lock to flash green on the third go, letting them burst inside.

"Will you let me fuck you here?" Hunter asked, still tightly holding onto Grant as they stepped inside.

Grant threw his head back onto Hunter's shoulder as Hunter kissed his neck. He hadn't bottomed in a long time. In fact, he could barely remember what it felt like to have a cock up his ass, but he knew that if Hunter insisted, he wouldn't have the heart to say no. He decided to grunt noncommittally, postponing his answer, and simply enjoyed Hunter's mouth on his skin and the vice-like grip Hunter was holding him in. He decided he liked this take-charge side of Hunter. This was the type of man who could run a successful business, one who didn't let anyone walk over him and didn't take no for an answer. This was the type of man who could give him a run for his money.

Grant unbuttoned his jeans, helping Hunter, who'd been trying to get his hand down his pants while continuing to kiss his neck.

"Fuck, you're hard," Hunter murmured.

"That shouldn't surprise you. You're hard too," Grant answered.

"You feel good," Hunter continued as he gently kneaded Grant's sac, then gripped his cock and fisted it inside his underwear. "Please tell me you'll let me fuck you? Want to give back to you what you gave to me."

Grant nodded. With Gable there had never been any question, but it didn't surprise Grant that Hunter wanted both to be fucked and to fuck. And if he was really honest with himself, he was looking forward to letting Hunter hold the reins.

"Did you bring supplies?" Grant asked, suddenly remembering he hadn't packed anything, and it wasn't like he walked around with lube and condoms in the pockets of his jeans.

Hunter pulled back just enough to take a plastic bag out of his jacket pocket. "This should last us until tomorrow."

Hunter spilled the contents on the bed, and Grant saw at least ten condoms and a bottle of lube. He couldn't stifle a chuckle. "Please don't tell me Calley sells Astroglide?"

"Calley doesn't even stock condoms," Hunter answered.

"Yes, she does," Grant replied with another chuckle. "But you have to ask for them. They're behind the counter."

Hunter stopped his kissing to look at Grant's expression, turning him around until they were standing face to face.

"She has some, because some of her customers don't have Internet and can't order them online. They don't even have to ask her, she says. Their flushed expressions are enough, apparently."

Hunter eyed him with amusement. "And you know this, how?"

"Sometimes you need condoms in a hurry," Grant answered enigmatically.

"I didn't know you knew Calley that well."

Grant shrugged. "Calley and I go way back." He didn't feel like elaborating. Calley and her grocery shop, the only one for miles, was one of those secrets he preferred to keep to himself for now. Grant knew Hunter would keep asking him, and he was sure he'd divulge it one day, but right now he was alone with Hunter in the privacy of their rented motel room and his hands were aching to touch the other man, so he grabbed the back of Hunter's head and pulled him into a searing kiss. At the same time he started tugging at Hunter's flannel shirt, hitching it up so he could get to bare skin. Discovering more fabric, he pulled the T-shirt up and out of Hunter's jeans.

Their movements were uncoordinated, rushed, clumsy as they tried to get each other out of their clothes. Hunter managed to sneak his hands down the back of Grant's pants and was kneading Grant's buttocks, at the same time pulling him so close their groins were undulating against one another. Although it felt heavenly, it complicated the disrobing, because Grant couldn't slide Hunter's shirt down all the way off his shoulders. Instead, he focused on running his hand over Hunter's back under the soft cotton T-shirt Hunter was wearing beneath his shirt. His other hand was busy steadying Hunter's head while they continued to battle for dominance with their tongues.

Eventually Hunter pulled back, lips red and swollen, to rip his shirt off and pull the T-shirt over his head. Grant followed suit and also managed to push his jeans down, together with his tight white underwear. Grant caught Hunter's appreciative stare.

"What?" he asked Hunter.

"I thought everyone wore boxers these days."

Grant shrugged, feeling self-conscious all of a sudden. "Too much freedom." He chuckled to release the tension. As Hunter moved closer again, he felt himself relax. "This isn't the first time you've watched me take my pants off."

"I know," Hunter murmured. "Just never allowed myself to look at you."

They kissed again, this time slower, but no less passionate.

"Were you serious when you said you'd let me fuck you?"

Grant nodded. "'S been a while though. You'll have to prep me well."

Hunter gently pushed Grant in the direction of the bed, never breaking the kiss. As soon as Grant felt the mattress against the back of his legs, he turned around and leaned forward, resting his hands on the bed.

"Shit, you look amazing," Hunter exclaimed.

Grant looked over his shoulder and saw Hunter standing behind him, jeans unbuttoned, head slightly tilted, and touching himself. If he hadn't been hard already, this image certainly would have made his cock stand to attention. He realized that he enjoyed seeing Hunter without his usual glimmer of uncertainty. This look only seemed to invade his features when they were alone, and it always rubbed off on Grant. Now all he could see in Hunter's eyes was lust, and that, too, influenced Grant.

"Stop staring and get me ready before you pop your lid," Grant replied with a teasing smile, grabbing the lube from the bed and tossing it to Hunter.

Hunter only just caught it, and the uncertainty reappeared.

"Just do it, Cowboy," Grant urged Hunter on, using the new nickname that Hunter seemed to like better than the last one. "Want you, right now." Grant reveled in how easily he could change Hunter's mood with a few carefully chosen words. The fact they were all true was a bonus.

Grant hissed when Hunter rubbed his slicked-up fingers over his exposed entrance.

"Sorry," Hunter apologized. "Should have warmed up the lube."

Grant reached back for Hunter. "Just don't stop. Need you, Cowboy." He knew he was hamming it up a bit just to keep Hunter's confidence up, but he did want it, now that he'd convinced himself he could do it.

Although a little unpolished, Hunter's movements continued, and Grant tried to relax, accepting the invasion of Hunter's finger. "Remember how I prepared you?" he murmured. "Now's your chance to reciprocate. Make me nice and open for you, and then when you push inside me, you'll still be amazed how tight I am around your cock."

Hunter let out a surprisingly raunchy grunt, and Grant pushed back on the finger, driving it deeper. Hunter curled it and the tip hit Grant's prostate, making him groan too.

"Fuck, yeah. That's the best feeling. Don't make me wait too long."

"You're nowhere near ready. You're so tight, I'll never be able to fit my cock in," Hunter said, and Grant heard a hint of amusement, possibly mixed with some apprehension, in Hunter's voice.

"Don't flatter yourself too much, Cowboy," Grant replied, his voice soft and slightly strained as Hunter added another finger. Grant reveled in the burn, which subsided quickly as Hunter upped the speed of his movements. Grant guessed he hadn't lost his appetite for it after all. He almost couldn't wait to feel that heavy cock of Hunter's push inside him. He could just imagine the sounds Hunter would make when he entered that tight heat, and that thought turned Grant on even more. Suddenly he realized the sounds he imagined weren't just in his mind. He was making them himself, and Hunter was leaning close to him, purring in his ear.

"God, I love the way you moan."

"Just do it. Put on a condom and fuck me, Cowboy." Grant was rock-hard. He didn't need to reach between his legs to verify that fact. His senses were on edge and zoned in around his groin area and that spot on his hip that Hunter was using to grind his erection against. With a hurried movement, he pushed the string of condom packets in Hunter's direction, hoping he'd catch the hint.

To his disappointment, Hunter pulled away his fingers to roll on a condom. Grant could see how nervous Hunter was, because he fumbled a bit, but as Hunter succeeded and started coating the condom with extra lube, the anticipation won and Grant moved a bit so he was leaning over the corner of the bed instead of the back. "Just do it, Cowboy."

Without much of a transition, Hunter grabbed Grant's hips and pushed his cock against Grant's entrance. The circular muscle almost instantly gave way, and Grant felt the intense burn making him groan.

Hunter almost immediately pulled back. "Sorry. Lost control."

"Don't—" Grant was quick to grunt. "Don't move for a minute." He knew that if Hunter pulled out completely, he might never have the nerve to let him do it again, because he knew it would burn at least as badly then. He just needed some time to adjust to feeling so full.

"Feels like you're sucking me inside," Hunter replied, his words clipped by the effort of holding back. "You're so fucking tight."

"Yeah," was all Grant managed to mutter as he slowly rocked back and forth. The burn was subsiding and slowly being replaced by the amazing, filled-up tingling he hadn't felt in a long time. "Move," he commanded. "Gently," he added quickly.

Hunter chuckled, and Grant could feel it right through his own body. The connection was growing in more than just a physical way, especially when Hunter leaned over him and wrapped his arm around his chest.

Their exchange was becoming more passionate too.

"You okay?" Hunter asked. "Can't hold back anymore."

"Then don't," Grant replied. "You feel good."

With a low grunt, Hunter started pushing in and out. "You're so tight, so hot. Can't stop," Hunter almost chanted in between thrusts.

Grant could easily take it now, and he found he was enjoying it almost as much as when he was the one sinking into the tight heat. The harder Hunter pushed, the more Grant's knees slid apart, and when he suddenly felt his cock brush over the coarse bedspread, he realized he didn't even have the need to touch himself. The intensity of Hunter's thrusts was picking up, and every time he hit rock bottom, Grant felt the surge of electricity he associated with having his prostate stroked. He wasn't going to last much longer, he knew that for sure, and as Hunter's rhythm started to falter, Grant figured Hunter was pretty close as well.

"Just fuck me, Cowboy," he urged Hunter on. "Don't hold back. Ride it out."

Hunter licked him on his neck, then behind his ear, and Grant leaned into the touch. This changed the angle of Hunter's thrusts, and suddenly Grant realized he wasn't going to be able to hold back his own orgasm.

"Fuck! Don't stop, Cowboy." He desperately wanted to touch himself, throw himself over the edge, but he couldn't. Hunter's strong movements made it impossible for him to stop bracing himself, so he sank just a little deeper onto the mattress and let the surge of his racing orgasm hit him hard. He was still twitching when Hunter collapsed on top of him.

"Fuck, that was amazing. Almost as good as when you fucked me." Hunter was still catching his breath and pushing himself off Grant. He held onto the condom as he pulled his waning erection out of Grant's body and got up to toss it away.

Grant rolled onto his back, still panting hard. As he watched Hunter walk to the bathroom, jeans still clinging to his thighs, he realized how bad he had it for the other guy. His Cowboy.

By the time Hunter returned from the bathroom, Grant had crawled under the covers.

Hunter smiled when he saw Grant lying in bed. "It's the middle of the day," Hunter stated matter-of-factly.

"I know," Grant replied. "Just take off those jeans and come here." He didn't say anything more, just pushed the covers back.

Hunter slowly pulled down his jeans and boxers and stepped into bed, practically curling himself around Grant.

"Do you feel guilty about lying in bed at this time of day?"

Hunter shrugged. "Never did it before. Feels weird." He snuggled closer, though, then looked straight at Grant again. "Thanks for letting me…."

"Fuck me?" Grant finished when Hunter didn't show any intent himself.

Hunter nodded. "Although now I don't know which I like best."

Grant chuckled. "I don't mind doing both."

# —20—

THEY stayed in bed, kissing and cuddling, licking and playfully biting each other, simply enjoying each other's company and bodies, for a few more hours, and then got up and dressed to drive to the local diner for some food.

Hunter was surprised how easy it was, how good it felt to just spend time with Grant, and it pushed aside some of his doubts. He'd find a way to figure out the truth about the questions that still nagged him at some point, but right now, he knew he'd never felt this comfortable around a lover.

He couldn't stop looking around the diner from time to time, checking whether the other patrons were looking at them funny, because he was afraid everyone within a mile radius would know they'd just fucked the stuffing out of each other. But nobody treated them differently from the other patrons. On the one hand, he hoped that all the other people just saw them as two horse wranglers having dinner together, but part of him also wanted people to see it. He knew he'd never be able to shout it off the rooftops, though. His love for Grant would always be shrouded in secrecy.

Suddenly Hunter felt a shoe rubbing up the inside of his leg.

"What's wrong?" Grant asked.

Hunter shrugged. "Nothing."

Grant gave him a doubtful look. "You're brooding."

Grant's foot was traveling up his leg, and Hunter felt his groin area tighten.

Hunter sighed. Suddenly he wanted privacy and time alone with Grant to talk and maybe do some other things as well. Wasn't this why they'd driven away from the ranch? "Do you want dessert? Because I want to get out of here."

"We can get a couple of pieces of pie to go," Grant suggested.

"Sounds good."

On the way back to the motel, it started to rain. Hunter wanted to drive back to their room to ravish Grant some more, but he knew the somber mood would return as soon as he had some time to think. He wanted to talk to Grant first, and he knew he wouldn't be able to do that in the room, so he pulled off the road into a deserted parking lot near a vista point. From there they could see the fields below and the sheets of rain coming down over them. For some reason this was a soothing sight for Hunter, so he killed the engine and turned toward Grant. He didn't need to read Grant's mind to see he wasn't sure what was going on.

After a few moments of silence, Hunter sighed. "I want to clear a few things up."

Grant was still holding the cardboard box with the pies, and he turned his gaze to the rain-swept scenery outside without speaking.

Hunter felt his heart plummet, but he knew he couldn't back down now. He put his hand on Grant's thigh. "I was mad at you this morning because I felt you were keeping so many secrets from me. You might be a serial killer and I'd never know it."

Grant glared at him briefly but then returned his gaze outside.

"I'm diving in at the deep end here, Grant. I'm so far out of my comfort zone it's making me really anxious, but at the same time, I finally know what I'm all about." He squeezed Grant's leg. "You opened my eyes and I can't deny that I only want more. I feel so greedy." He paused to gather his thoughts. "When we first got together, all I could think was that, whatever happened, we'd have to keep it a secret. And now I'm trying to figure out ways of telling my sisters and my mom, because I'm never going to be able to live a lie for the rest of my life. I know that now."

This time when Grant turned toward him, his eyes were dark and sad. The look made something crack inside Hunter, and he scooted closer to put his arms around Grant's broad shoulders. He heard the pie box slide to the floor as Grant returned the hug, burying his face in the crook of Hunter's neck.

"What do you want to know?" Grant asked quietly when they finally let go of each other.

The rain was pummeling the roof of the truck, making it hard for Hunter to think. There were so many things he wanted to ask, but his questions had driven a wedge between them before, so he knew he'd have to weigh his words carefully.

"I've already asked you where you go when you take time off, and you didn't want to answer me then, so I'm not going to ask you again. Just tell me one thing." Hunter stopped to take a deep breath. "Is there someone else in your life?"

Grant sighed. "If you're asking me whether I have another lover, then the answer is no. There's been nobody in my life since Gable."

Although it was only a partial answer and Hunter was dying to know why the hell Grant needed so many weekends away, he knew not to go there. He treasured the nose he had and didn't want it bitten off again.

"Did it feel like this in the beginning with Gable too?" As soon as the question crossed Hunter's lips and he saw Grant inhale to answer it, he held up his hand to stop him. "I can't believe I just asked you that. I sound like Miranda. She always wanted to know if she was better than so-and-so."

Grant smiled shyly. "That's okay. I told you we weren't in love. It was just sex. And companionship, I suppose. It gets pretty lonely on a small ranch like Gable's, and before I came along, he hadn't had anyone in his life for a while. He was in need of someone else's hand, I suppose. We didn't talk like you and I do. Whenever we talked, it was about what needed to be done around the house or with the horses. Outside of his bed, I was just the ranch hand."

Hunter nodded that he understood. He still wanted to know more, though.

"We'd had an argument and I drove off, thinking I was never coming back."

"What did you argue about?"

Grant shrugged. "I don't even remember. Probably something trivial. We never argued about the important stuff. Probably because we never talked about the important stuff."

"So you didn't even know about the accident?"

Grant shook his head. "Calley finally got a hold of me after about a week, and she told me. She talked about the gossip around town, that I'd had something to do with the accident and that was why I had fled, so I couldn't really return unless I wanted to be lynched."

Hunter's eyes grew big. "She said that?"

"No," Grant chuckled. "That was the image it conjured up for me. In any case, I tried going to the hospital, but I hate hospitals, and it just stifled me so much walking in there that I turned around and walked out again. It wasn't until Calley told me Gable was doing okay that I dared to return here."

"Yet you went to see him when he was in the hospital this time?"

Grant nodded. "Guess I still want to make amends." They sat in silence for a while. "I have pretty bad memories of hospitals, you know," Grant continued. "My mom spent her last six months in and out of one."

"I'm sorry," Hunter said, squeezing Grant's thigh for comfort.

"You see, we have something in common. She died when I was eight, and she was all I had. She'd left my stepfather because he was slapping me around, and we didn't have a penny to our name or a roof over our heads, but she worked three jobs getting us out of that slump. Then, just as we were doing better, she got sick. It took them a while to figure it out, but she died anyway. They called Child Services for me, and I was in and out of foster homes until I was fifteen, but they were all pretty crappy, so eventually I ran off. Every time I walk inside a hospital I get all clammy and anxious, because all I remember is that my mom died and they dragged me off to live at some stranger's place."

"You've been on your own since you were fifteen?"

"Yeah, pretty much," Grant acknowledged. "I lived on the streets for a while, but it was rough. I met up with a friend of my mother's who taught me to build furniture and work with wood. He let me stay in his spare room as well, so I wasn't completely alone."

"So how did you meet Calley?" Hunter asked a little tentatively, feeling they were on a roll but still worried about asking the wrong questions. Grant smiled, though, which made Hunter worry a little less.

"For about three years I drove a delivery truck, and I delivered fruit and produce to her shop. One day I was complaining that I wanted to go back to working on a ranch like I had when I first moved away from the city, and she suggested I go talk to Gable, since he needed help around his place."

"You've really worked all kinds of jobs, haven't you?"

"I suppose," Grant answered. "Guess I get bored easily. Love working on a ranch, though. No boredom there. So much to do, and there's rarely a day that pans out like the previous one."

"You're very good with the woodwork and brilliant with the horses. That certainly makes you an asset," Hunter agreed. He was happy they could talk about real life in a relaxed way now. He'd learned quite a bit about his lover, and although he was sure Grant hadn't given up all his secrets yet, he did feel more relaxed. Leaning a little closer, Hunter waited for Grant to turn his head so he could kiss him. They lingered, kissing softly, both of them reluctant to deepen the kiss or pull away. It felt very intimate and loving.

"It's dark," Grant stated, leaning forward to wipe the steamy windows.

"Guess we better think about going home."

"Home?" Grant asked, sounding surprised.

"Well, our room for now. We'll have to go home to the ranch tomorrow, but tonight I want you all to myself for a while."

Grant smiled and pulled Hunter closer.

Suddenly a quick rap on the side window made them both jump. Hunter scooted back to his side of the bench, and Grant straightened his shirt before rolling the window down.

"Officer." Hunter nodded at the policeman standing outside in his rain gear.

"No loitering, sir. I should write you a ticket, since it's clearly posted."

Grant opened the door and stepped outside, spooking the cop enough to make him draw his weapon. "You're not supposed to get out of the car!"

Grant raised his arms and walked away from the man. "Easy, I just wanted to talk to you. I didn't mean to make it worse."

"Turn around and place your hands on the roof of the car," the anxious cop ordered.

Grant complied and spread his legs for good measure. Although it was a tense situation, Hunter couldn't help smiling. Seeing Grant stand there, leaning against the truck, reminded him of what Grant looked like before he'd fucked him that afternoon. It made Hunter's jeans grow tight. He looked at the cop and decided the man didn't see the humor, which was just as well. It wouldn't do to get caught necking in a public place.

"Listen, man," Grant said in a surprisingly calm voice. "That guy behind the wheel is my boss. We drove out here to talk, and I think he might tell me I'm fired, so humor me and don't give him a ticket. I was trying to persuade him to keep me on the payroll, and if you give us a ticket, I'm sure to be out of a job. So, please, cut us some slack?"

The cop seemed to think about it. For a brief moment he looked at Hunter and then back at Grant. "Okay, fair enough. But I'm going to have to ask you to leave right now."

Grant stretched his back as he stood up and saluted the man. "I'm in your debt. Thanks, man." He gingerly stepped into the truck cabin as Hunter started the engine. "Let's get out of here," he murmured at Hunter.

While they were driving out of the parking lot, they were already laughing.

"Please, sir, he's going to fire my ass if you give us a ticket, sir," Hunter mocked Grant's voice.

Grant punched him in the ribs. "I had to say something. I couldn't tell him we'd steamed up the windows because my boyfriend is so hot we couldn't keep our hands off each other."

"Boyfriend?" Hunter repeated, still laughing.

"Do you prefer 'lover'?"

Hunter snorted. "I'd be happier if you didn't call me anything. At least not when you're trying to seduce a cop out of giving us a ticket."

Grant leaned closer so he could whisper into Hunter's ear. "And what shall I call you when we're alone?"

Hunter smiled coyly. "I kinda like it when you call me Cowboy."

Grant smiled as he put his hand over Hunter's groin and squeezed it.

"Will you fuck me when we get back?" Hunter asked, not even blinking. "I want to feel you inside me again." He reached for Grant's groin to reciprocate Grant's earlier actions and felt Grant's hard length right through his jeans.

"Does it feel like I'll be able to wait until we get to our room?"

Hunter laughed. "Well, you'd better, because I don't want to run the risk of a ticket again by doing it at the side of the road. Besides, I want you naked and spread out on the bed so I can ride you like a real cowboy would."

"Fuck, Hunter!" Grant shouted, laughing. "I should have known that even when you bottom you like being in charge."

# —21—

HUNTER had a spring in his step when he walked into his office Monday morning. The weekend had left him sore to the point that he didn't feel like climbing onto a horse first thing, and he was both tired and still pretty high from his little getaway. He didn't mind locking himself into his office for a few hours so he could check stock and send out feed orders.

"Hey, bro," Izzie said, walking into the office without knocking. Like most people who came in, she was in full working gear: oilskin duster, jeans, chaps, boots, and a hat.

"Still raining out?"

"Yup." She nodded. "Horses are all huddled together on the drier patches. Ground is soggy as hell. So how was the weekend?"

The lack of transition didn't faze Hunter. He could tell from Izzie's expression she pretty much knew what he'd done. Okay, maybe not the details. He hoped.

"Weekend was good," he answered evasively. He expected her to lay into him, ribbing him for leaving the ranch for her to take care of by herself, but she didn't. She simply turned to the notice board, where everyone left little notes for Hunter about the goings-on at the ranch and which items needed to be ordered from the suppliers.

Hunter got up from behind his desk and stood next to her. "Looks like I'm not the only one who's happy this morning?"

"Looks that way, doesn't it?" she answered. He recognized her enigmatic look, thinking they were alike, he and his middle sister.

"Did you get lucky this weekend too?" he asked, quite happy that the focus had moved away from his activities.

"You could say that," she answered.

Hunter reached for the door and closed it, leaning against it to prevent others from barging in. "Come on, 'fess up!"

She smiled, uncharacteristically shy. "Let's just say I didn't sleep at home on Saturday night."

"That makes two of us," Hunter confessed. Not that it was much of a confession. He was admitting to more than just not sleeping in his own bed, though. He'd asked Izzie to cover for him over the weekend and had to tell her he'd be away. She hadn't asked questions, which was just as well, since Hunter was pretty sure he wouldn't have given her a straight answer anyway. This morning he was dying to tell someone, though, and Izzie was possibly the only one he trusted with the news, since she'd sussed him out anyway.

"I know," she replied softly. She leaned a little closer, invading his personal space, and he put a brotherly arm around her, ignoring the wetness of her coat. Suddenly she looked up at him. "Was it nice? With… Grant?" She seemed a little hesitant to give him the opening, but he smiled at her anyway.

"It was more than I could have ever hoped for."

Izzie smiled back at him, giving him one of her genuinely warm smiles. "I'm so happy for you."

"You look like I should be happy for you too. Did you meet someone?"

She shrugged, but the corners of her mouth remained curled up, and her eyes shone. "More like a repeat offender."

"Please don't tell me it's Delco?"

She laughed. "Hell, no! The farther that man stays away from me, the better!"

Hunter let out a breath. "Phew, I'm glad."

She turned serious. "I can't tell you who it is yet, so please don't ask. He makes me very happy, though."

Hunter nodded in understanding. "I hope one day you will be able to bring him home."

She shrugged. "Well, either the four of us should run away together, or we'll all have to come out of the closet."

"Depends," Hunter quipped.

"On?"

"On whether I get along with him."

She pulled away from him and pushed him away from the door. "Oh, you like him all right." And with that, she walked out, leaving Hunter to wonder what she meant.

He didn't have time to ponder it, since his cell phone rang. Hunter recognized Calley's number. "Hi, Calley."

"It's… Flynn," a hesitant male voice answered. "From Gable's ranch?"

"Of course," Hunter replied, taking a moment to get his thoughts in order. What was Flynn doing at Calley's? And why was he calling him? "How's Gable doing?" he asked. He almost added, "Grant told me he was getting better," but at the last moment, he bit his tongue, remembering that mentioning Grant's name was something best avoided around Gable, and probably Flynn too. Hunter vaguely remembered Grant telling him he'd had a rogue encounter with Flynn's fist, putting to rest the question whether Gable had ever divulged anything about his relationship with Grant to Flynn.

"He's…." Flynn sighed deeply. "Listen, I can't do this on the phone. Can I come by your place?"

"Sure," Hunter answered. "You know how to find us?"

"Yeah, Calley's given me directions."

Flynn's hesitant voice worried Hunter. Had Gable taken a turn for the worse and Flynn been saddled with the responsibility to inform his friends?

"Is everything okay, Flynn?"

"Yes and no," Flynn replied. "I'll explain it to you when I get there."

Flynn terminated the call after that, leaving Hunter with a queasy feeling in the pit of his stomach. Flynn said he'd be right over, so he'd know soon enough, but it still made him feel more than a little uneasy. What if something bad had happened to Gable? All this fooling around with Grant had left Hunter with very little time to think of other things, and he suddenly felt guilty that he hadn't even taken the time to go visit Gable in the hospital. What kind of friend was he, anyway?

"I thought you'd be all smiles, and here I find you brooding."

Hunter looked up to see Grant standing in the doorway. The smile returned instantly to his face. He got up and walked toward Grant, at the same time closing the door and pinning Grant to the wall next to it, kissing him fervently.

"Good morning to you too, Cowboy," Grant said after being released from the kiss.

Hunter nuzzled him, loudly inhaling Grant's scent. "I missed you and I wish we had more time, but I'm going to have to ask you to leave."

"I'm hurt," Grant replied with a mock indignant look.

Hunter smiled shyly, his body still pressing Grant against the wall. "Flynn's coming over. He didn't sound too good. I'm afraid he might have bad news about Gable, so maybe it's not such a good idea for you to hang around here."

Grant entangled his hand in Hunter's hair and kissed him quickly before pushing him off. "You're probably right." He looked uncomfortable all of a sudden, as if he had some bad news too. "You will keep me posted, though?"

Hunter nodded. "Of course. As soon as he leaves, I'll come looking for you."

Grant smiled. "I'll be in the woodshed, finishing what I started on Saturday. I was mucking it out when you dragged me—kicking and screaming, I might add—off to that motel in the middle of nowhere, remember?"

"You put up a weak fight for such a big guy," Hunter teased, quickly kissing Grant before letting him leave.

When Grant opened the door to walk out, Flynn was standing just outside of it. Hunter could see his startled face, but Grant just nodded, tipped his nonexistent hat at him, and walked around him out into the hall.

"Come in." Hunter gestured at Flynn, hoping it would take away the tension. "Can I get you anything to drink?"

"No, I'm fine," Flynn answered. "I won't take up much of your time."

"Sit down," Hunter said, resisting the urge to pour himself a cup of coffee from the coffeemaker in his office. He didn't really know how to get Flynn to put him out of his misery quickly, but he knew his nerves would be on edge if Flynn stalled. He couldn't crawl behind his desk again, so he sat down on the edge of it. "What did you want to see me about?"

Flynn took a deep breath. "I have a business proposition."

Hunter raised his eyebrows. Business? "Go on."

"Gable told me you'd always had your eye on Brenner, his stallion?"

Hunter smiled. "It's a magnificent animal and very easy to handle to boot. That's a rare combination."

Flynn nodded, but he didn't smile. He seemed to have a hard time forming the words he needed to say.

"You're offering to sell him to me?" Hunter offered.

"Oh, no!" Flynn was quick to respond. "Gable would skin me alive if I did that."

"Not to mention you don't have his power of attorney either, I presume?"

Flynn shook his head. "My offer is a little different."

Hunter nodded, trying hard not to tell him to get to the point.

"We have a few young mares, and I thought about having Brenner sire a few foals."

It wasn't lost on Hunter that Flynn wasn't looking at him, as if he was afraid of Hunter's reaction.

"And you want to sell me Brenner's foals?"

Flynn nodded.

"How will I know they'll have Brenner's good qualities?" Hunter asked, not wanting to put Flynn's idea down but being a cautious businessman first, before letting his emotions take over. In all honesty, he'd kill to get his hands on Brenner, but since that wasn't going to happen, he'd easily settle for the next best thing: his offspring.

"There's no guarantee," Flynn answered honestly. "I just know that the mares are hard-working, easily trained, docile horses, and that I'll sell you the foals for fifteen thousand each."

Hunter laughed. It was a lot of money, but he suspected Flynn wasn't in it for personal gain. "Gable's ranch isn't a horse-breeding operation, Flynn. Gable's always told me it was too much hassle and too risky, not to mention the vet bills had the potential to skyrocket quickly if anything was wrong with the little ones."

"Bill, Calley's husband, is our vet and he assured me I could always call on him in an emergency. He said it was his way of helping Gable out."

Hunter thought about it for a moment. Was this everyone chipping in for Gable like they'd done when Gable first had his accident? That time, Gable's ranch had been on the verge of bankruptcy, and he knew Calley and Bill had done a lot for Gable then too. Everyone had. Hunter had sent a ranch hand over every day to take care of the horses. He hadn't done that this time, thinking Flynn would be able to manage, but last time Gable hadn't been in the hospital for very long. Now it seemed his health was a lot worse.

"Gable needs the money?" Hunter asked. "Obviously," he added under his breath.

Flynn raised his head, straightening his back with innate pride. "I'm not here to beg. I'm here to sell something."

"You're asking for a loan with the foals as collateral."

Flynn shook his head. "It's true that we need the money now, but if you give it to us, then the foals are yours. No discussion. So it's a sale, not a loan."

"From my point of view, it's a very risky loan. I don't know if you'll be able to pay me next year, and if you do, there are still no guarantees the payment is what I want."

Flynn sighed deeply and got up from the chair he was sitting in. "Listen. Forget it." He started to turn around, but Hunter was quicker, grabbing his arm.

"Stay, Flynn." Hunter let go as soon as Flynn stopped walking away. "I'm more than willing to help out. Financially or logistically or both. I'd give you the money even without the collateral, but—"

"But Gable would never accept charity," Flynn interrupted.

"Exactly," Hunter agreed, smiling along with Flynn as he realized they were definitely on the same page. "I'm willing to take the risk on the foals if that's what it takes for Gable to accept this money."

"He doesn't know," Flynn confessed. "Calley and I agreed not to tell him how deep in debt he is."

Hunter raised an eyebrow.

"I almost lost him, Hunter. He's still not well, and the doctors don't know if he'll recover fully. The ranch is his life. Even if he can never work it again, I want it to survive."

Hunter took a moment to look at Flynn. "That's quite a sacrifice you're making, tying yourself to the ranch that way." Hunter knew more or less how long Flynn had worked at Gable's, and it wasn't even a full six months. Could Flynn have come to care for Gable that much in such a short time? He'd never seen this sort of dedication between two men. Then again, until recently he hadn't really paid much attention to that sort of relationship anyway, trying very hard *not* to see things like that.

"I'll give you fifty thousand," Hunter said suddenly.

Flynn looked up at him, startled. "That's—"

"That's thirty for the two foals and twenty for boarding them."

"They're not even born yet and we're feeding the mares anyway," Flynn protested weakly.

"You'll need extra oats and pellets for the mares once they are sired, and vaccinations," Hunter lectured.

"They're already pregnant. Brenner got out and had his way with three mares, and Bill confirmed that two of them are with foal," Flynn confessed.

Hunter smiled. "I would have liked to have seen that."

Flynn gave him a look like he wanted to call him a pervert but didn't. Instead, he just nodded.

"I'll have a contract drawn up. Can you get Gable to sign it?"

Flynn shook his head. "No, but Calley can sign it. She's got Gable's power of attorney."

Hunter nodded in agreement. "Okay, I'll let Calley know, then. She's in on this big secret, I hope?"

"Yeah," Flynn admitted. "In fact, it's partly her idea." Flynn started to turn toward the door.

"Will this give you enough money to get through the winter? I know you haven't had the time to train any of the horses, and since I bought all Gable's fit ones, there's nothing more to sell right now."

"We didn't buy any new ones either, so the herd is smaller. I think we'll manage."

Hunter watched Flynn leave. "If you need anything, I'll gladly help out. Just holler."

With one more nod in Hunter's direction, Flynn walked out.

Hunter followed after a few moments, walking out in search of Grant.

# —22—

AS IZZIE had warned him, it was still raining, although it was more of a drizzle now. Hunter wanted time to talk to Grant, preferably alone, and although the thought of climbing into the saddle didn't feel very appealing at the moment, he knew it would be a sure way to get Grant to himself for an hour or so.

After saddling Raven and Belle, he trotted over to the woodshed. He dismounted, loosely tied up the horses outside, and couldn't prevent himself from leaning against the entrance, admiring the sight.

The woodshed was a dusty place, illuminated by a dirty skylight. There were stacks of sawed wood to one side and whole tree trunks on the other. All around were mounds of sawdust and shorter, leftover planks. And in the middle of it was Grant, wearing just jeans and boots, no shirt or hat. His dark hair was flaked with woodchips, and his skin had a yellowish sheen from the sawdust.

The shed, like a few other places around the ranch, brought back sensual memories, and combined with the sight in front of him, it made Hunter instantly grow hard. He knew he had to keep hold of himself, though. "So, are you about done?"

Grant looked up and smiled. "Looks better already, doesn't it?"

Hunter couldn't really tell. It still looked like a mess, but then, this was a place of work and not designed to look neat and tidy. "Want to go out for a ride?"

Grant scratched his hair. "Still a lot to do in here, I'm afraid."

Hunter saw the tuft of armpit hair when Grant raised his hand and found himself practically salivating. He couldn't believe how his self-control slipped every time he was around the man. "So finish it later. I'm coming to rescue you from death by dust inhalation." Grant didn't budge immediately, although he did look like he was thinking about it. "I saddled Raven for you."

Grant smiled and seemed to give in. "All right, but let me clean up a bit. I'll end up with chafing wounds from all this dust if I don't."

Hunter wanted to say he'd prefer Grant to have chafing wounds from rutting him against a tree, but he bit his tongue, which was just as well, as Tim walked into the woodshed just then to see Grant.

"Hey Grant, do you have a leftover plank about this long to patch up one of the lean-tos in the north range?" He held his hands about two feet apart. "I'll ride up there this afternoon to fix it. One of the cross beams rotted through, and in this weather, the horses up there don't have enough shelter."

Grant looked briefly at Hunter and then back at Tim. "Hunter and I were riding up there anyway. We'll take a plank and some nails and do the job."

Although Hunter couldn't see Tim's expression, it was obviously a puzzled one, because Grant added, "We're going to check out cougars. Didn't you say last week that Dave had spotted one up there?"

Tim nodded.

"So we'll take the shotgun and check it out. That way, you can ride to the west range with Dave to check whether the horses there still have dry grass, and you can move them if need be."

"Sure thing, boss," Tim said, tipping his hat at Grant before turning around and realizing his real boss was there as well. "If you agree as well, Hunter?"

Hunter smiled. "As long as he's making sense, I agree. We'll take care of the lean-to on our way over to the north side."

Hunter waited for Tim to leave and then paused before walking over to Grant so that Tim would certainly be unable to hear them. "I like the way your mind works. Maybe I should make you foreman? The men obviously think you are anyway."

Grant shrugged. "Sorry. I didn't mean to—"

Hunter put his hand on the back of Grant's neck and pulled him closer but stopped himself from kissing him at the last minute. "Don't apologize." He let go. "I'll meet you at the crew block in ten minutes?"

It was still drizzling when they rode out, but neither man cared. After riding full speed for a good twenty minutes, Hunter slowed down and Grant waited for him to catch up.

"So how did your talk with Flynn go?"

Hunter laughed. "You certainly held back long enough to ask."

Grant smiled coyly. "I thought about it while I was working, but then you walked into the shed and all my thinking went out the door."

They walked their horses alongside each other.

"Gable's got massive hospital bills to pay, and Calley and Flynn are trying to figure out a way to keep his ranch afloat."

Grant nodded pensively.

"Gable won't accept charity, and they don't have any more sellable horses, so it's not easy."

"And they'll need oats and hay for the winter," Grant added. "Gable doesn't have enough land for grazing to last them through the winter. I suppose you could let his horses graze on your land and give him some of your spare hay?"

"Or I could buy two of Brenner's foals," Hunter said cheekily.

"Brenner? Foals?" Grant asked, raising his voice as the rain suddenly started cascading down in such a torrent that the men couldn't hear themselves think. They both jumped off their horses and ran into a nearby lean-to, which became even more crowded than it already was. Luckily, the horses were accommodating and scooted even closer together, allowing them to enter with Raven and Belle in tow.

Hunter took off his hat and wiped the water off his face. "Apparently Brenner got in with the mares and there's proof he's in full working order because two of them are pregnant."

Grant laughed. "You mean there's actually a straight male creature on Gable's property?"

"Apparently so," Hunter agreed.

"Gable doesn't breed horses, Hunter," Grant added a little less merrily. "Does he know his precious Brenner's going to be a father?"

They both sat down on a bale of hay that Tim had left when he'd spotted the damage to the old shack. When one of the horses nuzzled Hunter because he was keeping him from his food source, Hunter and Grant both plucked some hay out of the bale and offered it to the horse. The animal munched on it contently.

"Nope, Flynn and Calley are keeping Gable in the dark about his dire finances."

"Bad move," Grant said. "There's going to be hell to pay once Gable finds out they hid things from him."

Hunter nodded in agreement. They sat in silence for a while, watching the horses and listening to the rain still pouring down in buckets outside.

"How is Gable, by the way? Did Flynn say anything?" Grant eventually said.

Hunter thought Grant sounded insecure, so he took his hand and squeezed it, trying to convey that he was okay with Grant wanting to know. "He says the doctors aren't sure if he'll make a full recovery. Flynn seemed pretty sure that he'd survive, but he wasn't sure whether he'd be able to work the ranch again."

"Ah, hell," Grant muttered. "It would kill him if he couldn't be with his horses anymore."

Although Hunter did feel some jealousy, he assured himself that Grant's relationship with Gable was over, and that even if Grant wanted Gable back, there was always Flynn to stand in their way.

"Flynn said something about wanting to do everything to keep the ranch from going bankrupt, so even if Gable couldn't work anymore, he'd still be able to live among the horses."

Grant leaned closer to Hunter. "I'm glad Gable's got Flynn."

"Yeah, they seem very much in love."

Grant shrugged and sat up, pulling away from Hunter. "That depends on your definition of love."

Hunter raised an eyebrow and looked at Grant, but Grant was staring straight ahead at the meadow, or as much as he could see of it between the horses. Hunter couldn't read Grant right now, and if he didn't know any better, he'd think Grant was still in love with Gable. The green-eyed devil was back, and it was wreaking havoc inside Hunter's gut.

Grant got up. "Let's fix this shack so we can ride back to the house." It wasn't a question.

Hunter decided to shake his uneasy feelings and help Grant out. At least he knew they worked well together. Grant didn't say much, and Hunter definitely felt the cold shoulder. After securing all the loose planks against the new piece of wood Grant had picked out, and checking it was secure, they didn't wait for the rain to abate and simply ran the horses at full speed back to the main house.

After wiping down their horses and making sure they had food and water in their stables, they each returned to their own space: Hunter to the main house and Grant to the crew quarters.

Hunter hid in his office, hoping at least his family would leave him alone there. If he'd known that talking about Gable would put his lover in this sort of mood, he'd have shut up about it. Now it was too late.

*Lover.*

Hunter let the word play in his head. He even whispered it once, to hear it. The weekend had been pretty amazing, better than he'd ever dared to imagine. Making love to Grant had felt like coming home, and he ached for Grant's touch, his hands all over him, his mouth, his lips. Hunter felt his groin stir just thinking about what he would do to Grant once they found time to be together again. Could he get away next weekend? How could he explain to his mother that he'd be gone for two days so soon after this weekend? There were only so many horse shows and auctions to go to in a year, and eventually it would surface that they didn't actually go to these events.

Hunter shook his head. He was running ahead of himself. How could he think of coming out to his mother and sisters when he wasn't even sure this thing with Grant was going to last? What if Grant saw him as a fling, something to pass the time? Something to scratch his itch and then move away from again. Hadn't Grant admitted that his relationship with Gable was only based on sex? What if that was all Grant was after?

No, it couldn't be. Not after last weekend. Grant had even called him his boyfriend, although it was definitely in jest.

"Dinner's ready!" Bernie shouted from upstairs.

Hunter looked around the empty office, put on his best smile, and walked upstairs to join the women.

# —23—

GRANT grabbed a quick plate of mashed potatoes and ribs and plonked himself in front of the football game to eat. The last thing he wanted was polite dinner conversation, so as soon as his hunger was sated, he dropped his plate in the bunkhouse kitchen and went upstairs to his room.

What a strange day it had been. He'd woken up missing Hunter, so after his morning chores, he'd gone to Hunter's office to say hello. They hadn't slept together—not because they didn't want to, but because here at the ranch they had no place to share. Even so, as soon as he saw Hunter, his hands were aching to touch him.

These feelings were foreign to him. He'd never felt for another man what he felt for Hunter. He was the whole picture. Not just brilliant sex, but stimulating conversation and a shared love of good food, horses, motorcycles, and football. What more could he want?

Grant knew he didn't deserve Hunter. Why would a successful business owner—a wealthy business owner to boot—want to take up with a drifter like him? Grant didn't have more to his name than he could pack onto his motorcycle. In fact, the only thing that had any value *was* that motorcycle. If he sold it, he'd maybe have five hundred dollars to his name. Hell, he didn't even have a bank account or a credit card. All he had was the money he kept in a sock. A few hundred, for rainy days or the times he was looking for another job.

Even if Hunter decided to come out to his family and introduce Grant as his lover, they'd think he was after their money. Not to mention he'd be accused of corrupting their precious boy, their closeted gay son who'd only ever shown interest in girls before.

Should he cut his losses?

Grant dropped down on the bed. Lying on his back, staring at the ceiling, all he could think of was their two days and one night spent ravishing each other, and how Hunter had changed from being shy and insecure to being an amazing lover. Grant had even bottomed for him. Not since he'd started exploring sex with men had he offered his ass to a guy. It still ached, but it had been so worth it. It had reminded him of why Gable was such an eager bottom and why Hunter, even after fucking him until he'd screamed, had chosen to be on the receiving end all the other times they'd gone all the way. How could he give that up? How could he never again lust after Hunter?

Even now, thinking about Hunter made Grant's erection almost painfully hard. He unbuckled his belt and freed it from his jeans before hurriedly stroking it. It wasn't enough. What he really wanted was Hunter's hands on it. And maybe his mouth around it. Yeah, that would be great. For an inexperienced guy, Hunter gave pretty good blow jobs. What he lacked in finesse he more than made up for in eagerness.

Grant rolled onto his stomach, rutting against the hand in his pants. Yeah, this felt good. It was a poor substitute for the tight, muscled frame he'd felt under his hands just twenty-four hours earlier, but it would have to do. Right then, the idea of giving Hunter up was something he couldn't think about. He simply had to have him again. They'd find a way. They'd have to hide, but then he'd always hidden his true feelings. He was used to not having anyone to confide in. It would simply mean having one more secret to stay mum about. No big deal.

Turning onto his back again, Grant gasped, exasperated. His orgasm was just out of reach. Was he thinking too much? Was he worrying? Damn. He let go of his cock and got up off the bed. Pulling down his damp jeans and boxer briefs, he took himself in hand again, this time getting on the bed on all fours. The memory of Hunter fucking him was a strong one, and he fisted himself frantically. Then it dawned on him that there was one thing missing. Leaning on his shoulders with his ass up in the air, he licked his fingers and brought them to his entrance. The muscle felt raw, but as he pushed his fingers against it, it felt so glorious his balls pulled tight. It wasn't hard to imagine they were Hunter's fingers or Hunter's cock. He wanted it to be him, his man, his Cowboy. "Fuck, Hunter." After circling the hole a few times, both fingers slipped inside, and he involuntarily bucked into his other hand, spraying thick white ribbons of come all over the bedspread.

As he lay panting after his orgasm, Grant knew for sure. He wouldn't be able to walk away from Hunter like he'd walked out on Gable and countless others. This was something more. And it scared the hell out of him.

# —24—

THE search for the cougar hadn't yielded any results, and although there were clear breaks in the fence whenever a foal went missing, they didn't look man-made, so the mystery remained unsolved.

After a few weeks of no missing horses, the men started alternating the herds between the meadows and slowly bringing them back down closer to the homestead, where they'd spend the winter. It was easier to feed them extra hay there, and the valley was warmer, so there was less chance of their water supply freezing during the cold winter nights.

The rain had held off as well, making it possible to harvest the hay for the winter, so everyone had been kept busy cutting the grass, letting it dry, and stacking it in the barns.

Hunter and Grant had continued to keep their relationship a secret from everyone but Izzie, who'd been discreetly teasing them every chance she got. Hunter had been often tempted to tease her back about the secret liaison she was carrying on, but he hadn't been able to figure out who her intended was, so he'd held his tongue.

From time to time, Hunter and Grant had found the opportunity to sneak off the ranch, but most of their encounters had been conducted in deserted barns around the ranch, and occasionally in Gable's hayloft when it was raining outside and they were sure that Bridget, Gable's dog, wouldn't be around to catch them. It was a less than perfect arrangement, but they made do, and it took the pressure off Hunter coming out to his family.

Grant had been working in the woodshed all day, sawing wood to make hurdles for Bernie, who was training her horse for jumping. He and Hunter had always agreed that Bernie wasn't a rodeo girl, being attracted to the more formal types of riding, and she'd taken up three-day eventing. Hunter had bought her a fine horse that could tackle all three events—the dressage, jumping, and cross-country—and she was training every day after school.

The work gave Grant time to think and come up with the nerve to ask Hunter for another few days off. He'd neglected going home for more weeks than he cared to think about, and despite his anxiety about asking Hunter for something he wasn't ready to explain, he knew he couldn't put it off any longer.

After finishing off the long beams and crossbeams for the jumps, he loaded them onto the pickup truck and drove out to the riding paddock that was cordoned off for Bernie to use. They'd marked out where he'd have to put which hurdles, so he unloaded what he needed in the right spots. It was hard work, but Grant was a strong guy, so he managed. Building up the circuit was another thing, though, and he knew he'd need one of the other men to help him out.

"Need a hand with that?" Hunter asked.

"I thought about asking some of the ranch hands to help me out later," Grant replied. He didn't want to confront Hunter here, knowing it would be a difficult conversation. The plan had been to talk to him in the office after he finished up in the paddock, so neither would lose their tempers in public, or say things that weren't meant for all ears.

"I can help," Hunter said happily. "I'm pretty much done with my week's work, and since it's Friday, I thought we could discuss what we're doing this weekend."

Grant looked around to see whether there was anyone within earshot who could hear them. Hunter was becoming careless, he thought, although none of the crew seemed to be around.

"Jack and his band are playing at the Barrel Run tomorrow, and tonight there's a big football game on. I heard some of the guys saying they were all going to watch it together at Dave's house, which means we'll have the crew house to ourselves for two evenings in a row," Hunter said, wiggling his eyebrows suggestively.

"Listen, Hunter," Grant started, righting his back so he stood his full height. "I was going to ask for a few days off next week. Possibly

Monday and Tuesday, and I need to leave tonight. I'll be back as soon as I can." Grant knew that having the crew house to themselves was rare. It meant they could spend time in Grant's room without worrying who could see or hear them. He was tempted to postpone his trip, but Hunter seemed to come up with enticing things to do every weekend, and every time it became harder to put him off, so Grant knew he had to stand his ground. Even if that meant seeing the disappointment in his Cowboy's face. "I'm sorry, Hunter."

"Still no explanation, I see?"

Grant shook his head. "Trust me when I say you can be sure I won't do anything you won't like."

Hunter pursed his lips. "It's a little hard to trust you when you disappear at a moment's notice because you have more important things to do than spend time with your *lover*." Hunter whispered that last word, as if he needed to make sure that this most incendiary term was only heard by Grant.

Before Grant could react, Hunter had turned on his heels and was determinedly walking out of the paddock.

Grant was tempted to follow him, take Hunter's arm and pull him back, but short of actually telling him where he was going and why, he didn't think Hunter could be persuaded to see his side. With a deep sigh and an ache in his stomach, he let his Cowboy walk away.

He had done all he could do for Bernie's jumping course, so he surveyed the dirt-covered paddock and hoped she would like what he'd done. He walked in the direction of the crew house, hoping somehow to meet Hunter along the way, but his Cowboy was nowhere to be found.

After a quick shower and donning his leathers, Grant packed his duffel bag with a change of clothes and strapped it to his motorcycle before speeding off the ranch. He'd stop somewhere along the way to eat and then continue his way west to Portland. Right now he wanted to put as much distance between himself and Hunter's ranch as he could. Hopefully what was waiting for him was worth it, and he'd be able to clear his mind and make the most of his time there.

The ride out west was boring and long, and Grant had driven it so many times in the past years he didn't even need to pay much attention.

He stopped along the way for a burger but didn't linger. If he made good time, he'd hit the outskirts of Portland by daybreak and catch forty winks in the park before heading out to the usual place. It wasn't that cold yet and it was fairly dry, so he knew he'd be able to sleep rough for a few hours.

After about six hours of driving, Grant left the Interstate feeling tired and weary. He also needed to pee, so when he saw the lights of a roadside bar in the distance, he decided to stop for a little rest. He resigned himself to drinking just one beer, so it wouldn't prevent him from riding on safely, but he knew the break would help him be more awake and alert for the remainder of the ride.

Although he'd taken the same route many times, Grant had never stopped at this particular bar. Inside was what looked like a pretty standard Friday night crowd: a few middle-aged, beer-bellied drinkers hanging out by the bar, an older guy with a younger woman sitting in one of the booths, and a few youngsters hanging around the pinball machines. Grant walked to the back to relieve himself and then returned to order a beer. He caught himself eyeing the ass of the long-haired, heavily tattooed bartender when he was accosted by a more-than-a-little-tipsy barfly.

"Hey there, stranger."

"Evening," Grant replied courteously. He didn't encourage her, though. She looked like she was jailbait, although at the same time she looked wasted, like she'd been drinking for years and hadn't seen a sober day in at least two of them. Grant was worried that she would try to hustle him into giving her money.

When the buff bartender dropped off Grant's beer, the man eyed her with concern. "I think you've had enough, Jewel."

"Aaaw, come on, Stevie!" She put her arm around Grant. "I'm sure this nice man will buy me a shot or two."

Grant gave Stevie a look to convey he would do no such thing, and to his surprise, the man understood.

"Come on, Jewel. I'll call your old man to come pick you up."

"No, Stevie! Please don't. I don't want to go home. All Al does is sit in front of the TV, and there's football on tonight," she whined.

"Fine," Stevie conceded. "But then you sit in a corner and leave my paying customers alone."

She drifted off and Grant took a swig of his beer, nodding a thank you to Stevie.

The young woman who'd been sitting by the older gentleman in the booth came to stand alongside Grant by the bar.

"Top us up again, Steve, will ya?" she asked the bartender before feasting her eyes on Grant. "We don't get your kind here very often."

Grant looked at her and smiled. She was a good-looking woman in her early thirties, he guessed, elegantly dressed, with a bit too much makeup and jewelry for his taste, but it didn't hurt to look at her anyway.

"And what is my kind?" Grant asked a little apprehensively. For a moment he wondered if he'd encountered a woman with exceptional gaydar.

She smiled seductively. "Handsome strangers."

"Ah," Grant replied. "I thought there'd be plenty of handsome men around here."

"Oh yes," she drawled. "But it's *always* the same men. You're not from around here, are you?"

"Nope," Grant answered, drinking more beer. He didn't really want to give her any more information. If he'd wanted to be seduced by her, he'd probably indulge her, but he just wanted to have a quiet drink. The last thing he needed was any sort of intimate encounter, least of all with a woman, and judging by the way she was invading his personal space, that was exactly what she was aiming for.

Grant looked around to gauge the reaction of her earlier paramour, but he was asleep in the corner. He completely missed the all-too-familiar face watching him from one of the other dimly lit booths.

# —25—

HUNTER didn't like the look of Grant sitting at the bar flirting with that woman. They seemed friendly enough, although it didn't appear to Hunter that she and Grant knew each other well. He was smiling, though, giving her a teasing, seductive look.

She leaned over the bar, winking at the bartender after nicking a fresh bowl of peanuts from where the guy had hidden them. She offered them to Grant and he accepted, grabbing a handful and eating them while he talked to her.

Hunter was tempted to walk over to Grant and possessively put his arm around his lover's shoulders, making it clear to the woman that Grant was off limits. The problem was that would have two effects he didn't really want. It would mean coming out of the closet, and outing Grant as well, in front of a bar full of strangers in the middle of nowhere; and it would mean admitting to Grant that he'd followed him all the way out from the ranch.

HUNTER had watched Grant leave the paddock and walk out to the crew house. He'd waited for him to come back out, determined to follow him and figure out where the hell Grant spent his days off. After seeing Grant take out his motorcycle, Hunter had jumped in his truck and driven out of the ranch, waiting around the corner of the one-way Grant would take to get to the Interstate. Once he'd seen him emerge from the driveway, Hunter had followed him.

It hadn't been easy. On the empty stretches, Hunter had had to keep his distance or Grant would have spotted him. Where the road was busier, Grant weaved in and out of traffic in such a way that Hunter had a hard time staying close, since his truck had no such mobility. A few times Hunter thought he'd lost Grant, but somehow he always caught his trail again. Hunter had spotted Grant leaving the Interstate but almost missed the bar. It wasn't until he'd driven past it and saw a long stretch of empty road ahead with no motorcycle in the distance that he turned his truck around and saw the bike next to the bar's entrance.

Hunter had snuck inside, trying to stay in the shadows and hoping neither Grant nor the bartender would see him.

Was this what Grant did? Go to a bar and pick up women? Hunter felt anger boiling up inside him. Anger and jealousy. He just couldn't reconcile the idea of Grant with a woman to all the times they'd spent together ravishing each other. Was it all just something to pass the time, a way for Grant to scratch an itch before he moved on and felt the need for a woman again?

Hunter knew what it felt like to have a woman's body under his hands. He also knew that now he'd discovered what it was like to make love to a man, he never saw himself returning to women again. What he'd experienced with Grant had blown his mind, and it'd felt like coming home. Finding out it was different for Grant was a rude wake-up call.

Just as Hunter was succeeding in telling himself to quietly sneak out again and drive back home, Grant extricated himself from the woman's grasp, threw a few dollars on the bar, and walked out.

Hunter had to talk to Grant. To hell with Grant finding out that he was stalking him. Hunter either wanted to have it out in the open with Grant or tell him not to bother coming back to the ranch.

It was dark out when he exited the bar, and Hunter saw Grant just riding off the gravel parking lot, continuing his journey. Hunter jumped in his truck and sped after him, not bothering to keep a safe distance but trying to stay as close as he could to avoid losing Grant again.

Grant seemed to notice something was up. He picked up speed until he was way over the speed limit, and Hunter had to push his truck to the edge to stay with him. Hunter knew neither of them would be able to keep this up for long, so he took a chance and tried to pull alongside Grant on a straight piece of road. Grant moved to ride more along the center where the road was more even, ignoring Hunter, until suddenly he threw an angry look in the direction of Hunter's truck. Hunter saw Grant's expression change to surprise as he looked straight into Hunter's eyes, but then they heard a sharp horn and their gazes turned to a large truck coming from the opposite direction.

It all happened in a split second, and at the same time, the moment seemed to stretch forever. Grant's motorcycle wavered and the long-haul truck nicked him, catapulting him against and over the bed of Hunter's truck. Hunter immediately hit the brakes and swerved to the side. The larger truck never stopped, but Hunter was out of his pickup without even cutting the engine. He ran over to where he thought Grant had landed and tried to look for him along the dark road. He eventually heard labored breathing.

"Fuck, Grant. I'm sorry," Hunter said, crouching down next to him in the dirt. It was too dark to see if he was hurt, let alone make out Grant's expression. All Hunter could do was frantically feel all along Grant's body, looking for signs of blood or broken bones. From time to time, Grant yelped when he squeezed a part of an arm or a leg.

"Tell me you're okay?" Hunter tried.

Grant just grunted, then swallowed hard.

"Oh, please, Grant. Please, love, be okay?"

When Grant still didn't answer, Hunter pulled Grant's helmet off his head and saw the dark splotches along the side of Grant's closed eyes. Without thinking, he pulled Grant's limp body into his arms.

"Talk to me, lover. Please tell me you're okay!" He rocked Grant back and forth, trying hard to support him. Hunter kissed Grant's face, heedless of the blood that was all over it. He didn't care. All he wanted to know was that Grant was alive and not hurt so badly he was going to die. He couldn't let Grant die.

"Everything okay, man?"

Hunter looked up into a flashlight.

"We saw a truck standing across the road, and then you and him." A young-looking guy pointed at Grant and then directed his flashlight over to him. "Holy shit, Sandy, call an ambulance!"

Hunter felt dazed, both by what had happened and by the sting of the bright light shining in his eyes.

"No ambulance," Grant murmured, and Hunter looked down. "No hospital, Cowboy."

Hunter didn't have the power to overrule him. On the one hand he wanted to listen to Grant; on the other hand, he knew his lover was badly hurt, and they would have to take him to see a doctor. He couldn't think, couldn't figure out what was best.

Everything happened in a daze. It took forever for the ambulance to arrive, and then the EMTs picked Grant up and put him inside before speeding off with sirens and lights all over. Hunter vaguely remembered a cop asking him whether the truck was his and then guiding him to it, letting him get in on the passenger side and getting behind the wheel himself.

When they finally arrived at the hospital, he heard the cop tell one of the nurses that he didn't think Hunter was involved in the accident, but that he seemed very confused and should be looked after as well.

Hunter had no idea how much time had passed, but he found himself being shown to the waiting area by a petite woman in a white uniform and handed a cup of coffee.

"Doctor says you're okay," she said, sitting down next to him. "You're worried about your friend, though, aren't you? Did you see it happen?"

"Lover," Hunter replied, ignoring her question.

"The man they brought in was your lover?"

Hunter found himself nodding his agreement.

"Hang on," she said.

Hunter watched her leave and return a few minutes later with a clipboard.

"Then I think you can give me some of his details, right?"

It dawned on Hunter that he'd just come out to a stranger and that she hadn't even blinked.

"What's his name?"

"Grant Jarreau," Hunter answered.

"Birthday?"

Hunter smiled, still feeling pretty confused. "I don't know." He really didn't. How warped was that? Grant was his lover and he didn't even know when his birthday was. Hugh had hired him and had taken care of the paperwork.

It didn't seem to bother her, though. "Why don't I give you the clipboard and you can fill out the questions you can? Is that okay?"

Hunter nodded.

She gently squeezed his arm. "I'll go see if the doctors are done with him so you can go in and see him."

Hunter's heart leapt. Yes, he wanted to see Grant. A split second later he realized that maybe Grant wouldn't want to see him. After all, he'd caused Grant's accident. If it hadn't been for him trying to drive alongside Grant's bike, Grant wouldn't have been startled and he would have noticed the massive truck sooner.

Hunter got up out of his seat, leaving the clipboard on the table beside him.

The girl returned with another cup of coffee, though. "Do you know whether Mr. Jarreau has insurance?"

"Yes," Hunter answered almost automatically. "Well, actually, no, I don't suppose he has insurance, but I'll pay the bill."

Her eyes went wide.

"He works for me. I own a stud farm outside of St. Anthony, Idaho, and he's one of my best wranglers. I was going to make him foreman when he returned." She gave him a compassionate smile, and Hunter realized she didn't really need to know that information. Then again, he'd already told her more than he'd ever told anyone else, so he supposed this wasn't too bad.

"I'm sure it'll be very reassuring for Mr. Jarreau to know that part is covered."

Hunter nodded. "Can I see him now?"

"The doctor will be right out to talk to you."

Hunter looked at her, but she didn't meet his eyes. His stomach clenched again. Before she'd left, she was talking about letting him in to see Grant, and now all he was going to see was the doctor? That didn't bode well.

She gave his arm another squeeze and then left him alone again.

Hunter's mind was a lot clearer now, although his anxiety had grown. He paced the waiting area, happy that there was no one else there to see his apprehension. As the nurse left, he saw a glimpse of another waiting area, where there were more people. Some of them looked sick or injured. Why had they separated him from the other people?

Hunter didn't have a lot of time to ponder as the door swung open again and a red-haired man in a long white coat walked in. "Mr. Krause? You came in with Mr. Jarreau?"

"Yes," Hunter answered, trying not to let his voice betray his anxiety but failing miserably.

"I'm sorry you had to wait this long, but Mr. Jarreau took quite a beating, and we had to make sure there was nothing life-threatening going on."

"Is he… okay?"

The man smiled. "He's bruised and battered, and we will need to keep him for one or two nights to make sure he's okay, but he seems to have escaped with only minor injuries."

"Minor…?"

"He has a little bleeding around his spleen, which is the reason we want to keep him for observation. Right now it doesn't look bad enough to operate, though. And he has a few hairline fractures in his pelvis and three broken ribs, but other than being immensely sore for the next few days, he looks like he'll live."

"Can I see him?" Hunter asked quietly.

"Your name is Hunter? He asked for you. Repeatedly."

Hunter swallowed away his fear.

"I should warn you he looks really bad, but I assure you we turned him inside out. They're transferring him to intensive care for the night, or I should say for the day, since it's morning already. Why don't I take you to see him?"

Hunter nodded and thought he was going to throw up.

# —26—

HUNTER thought his anxiety would drop when he walked into Grant's room, but it got even worse when he saw his lover.

Grant was lying on his back, his eyes closed. His short, almost black hair was sticking to his head where they'd tried to wash the blood out of it. He had several bruises along the side of his face, and his eyes were swollen to the point where Hunter almost didn't recognize him. One of his arms was in a splint, and the other had tubes sticking into it. His torso was bare but also fairly black and blue, and there were stickers on his chest and clips with wires leading to it. Grant was connected to a few machines, one of them making soft but annoying beeping noises that were significantly slower than the heartbeat Hunter felt in his throat.

When Hunter looked around, he realized the doctor had left him alone in the room. He didn't know what to do. He didn't want to startle Grant, so he stood by the foot of the bed for what seemed like a long time until Grant managed to open one eye.

"Will you come here and sit down? You're making me nervous standing there, hovering over the foot of my bed like the angel of death."

"Doctor says you're not dead yet," Hunter answered, feeling some of his fears flood away after hearing Grant's voice. "You look like shit, though."

"Thanks, Cowboy," Grant replied. "And here I thought you'd be able to lift my spirits."

Hunter walked a little closer so he could touch Grant. He brushed his knuckles over the back of Grant's hand and pulled a little stool closer so he could sit down. "Doctor says you need rest and then you'll be right as rain again in a few weeks."

Grant shrugged slightly, then winced as if it hurt.

"He says you got really lucky."

"Yeah," Grant said quietly. He took a deep and rather shaky breath in. "What were you doing on that road so far from home, Hunter?"

Hunter couldn't look straight at Grant, but he noticed Grant turning his hand until his palm was facing up and opening his fingers. Hunter hesitantly placed his hand over Grant's, and Grant closed his fingers, gently squeezing Hunter's hand. Hunter felt tears well up in his eyes, so he sniffed and quickly wiped his face.

"When I saw you lying there in the dirt, I thought I'd lost you."

"You won't get rid of me that easily."

When Grant's words sank in, Hunter felt the warmth return to his body. He lifted Grant's hand and squeezed it, kissing Grant's bruised knuckles.

Their intimate moment was interrupted by a nurse coming in to check on Grant. Hunter didn't let go of Grant's hand until the nurse walked around the bed to shine a light into Grant's eyes, but she didn't seem to be bothered by the two men holding hands.

"I'll get you a more comfortable chair to sit in," she said before leaving them alone again.

"We could both use some sleep," Grant said after she was gone.

"Are you tired?" Hunter asked.

"Aren't you?"

Hunter nodded. "We missed a night."

After the nurse returned with the chair and Hunter made himself comfortable, he took Grant's hand again.

"What happened, Cowboy?" Grant suddenly asked.

"You don't remember?"

Grant slowly shook his head. "I was riding west, and the next thing I remember was when I woke up and my whole body was sore."

Hunter swallowed. Grant not remembering anything meant Hunter had to think of what version of the truth he was going to give him. Should he reveal that he had been stalking him? Should he tell Grant that he'd been the cause of the accident?

"I followed you when you left," Hunter started. "I wanted to know where you went when you disappeared for days." He waited to see Grant's expression, but he could make nothing out. "I saw your bike parked outside a bar, and I followed you there."

"I remember that bar. There was a woman in there who wouldn't take no for an answer. I would have stayed longer if it hadn't been for her."

Hunter looked at Grant's face, but it was so swollen there was no way to read any sort of expression.

"You were there?" Grant asked. "Then you saw what a nuisance she was. I bet she was a working girl. Or a very bored housewife. Her husband, or her date, who knows, was asleep in the corner booth."

Hunter smiled. So Grant hadn't gone to the bar to pick up women. At least that was a relief. It sounded like Grant didn't remember the actual accident, though, so maybe it paid to stay a little vague.

"Well, I watched you walk out of there and speed off. I followed you again and saw how you got swept off by that immense truck. It catapulted you right off your motorcycle and into the ditch. That's when I thought I'd lost you."

Grant smiled as much as he could with his bruised face. "Those monster trucks are lethal." He exhaled deeply and went still, which worried Hunter until he realized the machine was still beeping at about the same rate as his own heart rate, so he figured Grant had drifted off to sleep.

Hunter realized he, too, must have fallen asleep when he startled a while later, sore from sitting in the chair. Grant was still asleep, and a different nurse from the one before was standing on the other side of the bed, checking on Grant.

"Everything okay?"

She nodded. "He's resting, which is what he needs right now. If you want, you can get something to eat and walk around for a bit. If he wakes, I'll tell him you'll be back in a few hours. With the painkillers we're giving him, he's going to be asleep for most of them anyway."

Hunter nodded and stretched some of his muscles to iron out the kinks. Her suggestion made sense. He was hungry, and a bit of fresh air would do him a lot of good. He was reluctant to leave Grant's side, but like she said, they were taking good care of him, and since he was determined to bring Grant home with him after his discharge, he knew he had to be rested so he could take care of Grant.

Hunter squeezed Grant's hand. "I'll be back later."

He left the ICU without looking back and tried to navigate his way through the hospital. He found a cafeteria that sold sandwiches and coffee and then walked outside to feel the afternoon sun on his face. He was an outdoors sort of guy anyway. Sitting outside, eating his sandwich, he realized he had to call home and tell the girls he was okay. He'd run out the day before without telling anyone where he was going, and it suddenly dawned on him that they would have realized he was missing by now.

His safest bet to call was Izzie. At least he could tell her the truth.

"Fucking man!" Izzie shouted as she answered the phone. "Where the blasted hell are you?"

"Hi, sis," Hunter answered, surprisingly calm.

"You better tell me you got laid last night."

Hunter chuckled as he realized she wasn't angry with him. "I didn't. The reason I left had to do with Grant, though."

"Everything all right, Hunter?" she asked.

Hunter could hear the concern in her voice. "Yes and no. Grant had an accident last night. He's in the hospital."

"Shit! What happened?"

Hunter sighed. How much should he tell Izzie? He had to tell someone, and he did trust her. "He asked for time off again but still refused to tell me what he needed it for, and I guess I got jealous." He winced at hearing himself say the words. "So I followed him, for six exhausting hours."

"Damn! And I know how he speeds around on that motorcycle of his. So what did you find out?"

Hunter sighed. "Nothing much. Just that he takes long trips. He got whacked by a monster truck and ended up in a ditch with a cracked pelvis and ribs and a really bruised body."

"Awww, honey," Izzie replied, concern in her words. "He'll be all right, though, right?"

"Yeah, doctors think he might be able to come home tomorrow or the day after."

Izzie chuckled. "Well, you've missed the pandemonium around here as well."

"Oh?" Hunter replied

"I'll tell you when you get back. And in the meantime I'll hold the fort here. Oh, and take care of Grant, okay? We're going to need him around here. Not to mention you'll need him, right?"

"Yeah, I do need him," Hunter said.

"So take care of him, get back when you can, and the ranch will still be here."

The line clicked off, and Hunter realized Izzie probably thought he and Grant had shacked up together somewhere, like they had the last time she'd covered for them. Then he shook his head, thinking Izzie would never believe he'd come up with such an elaborate lie.

The mention of pandemonium around the house did make him worry. Izzie didn't sound too upset about it, though, and Hunter knew that a house full of women meant hysteria was never far away anyway. All he could think was that Bernie had eloped, although she'd never shown any interest in boys her age and had only ever focused on riding her eventing horse. What else could cause trouble at the Blue River Ranch? He'd just have to curb his curiosity until Grant was healthy enough to travel back home.

When Hunter returned to Grant's room, Grant was not only awake but sitting up in the chair Hunter had slept in earlier. He didn't look entirely comfortable, but the swelling in his face had gone down enough for him to open his eyes.

"The nurse told me you went for a walk."

Hunter smiled. "You know me. Can't stay cooped up inside for long before I get all antsy."

"They said that if I can sit up for a while without any trouble, they'll transfer me to an ordinary room, and then maybe I can go home tomorrow."

Grant's face was soft and inviting, and despite all the swelling, there was a clear smile playing around his lips. Hunter felt a curious flutter in his stomach and an overwhelming urge to pull Grant into his arms. He knew that would have to wait, though.

"I'd love to take you home," Hunter said instead.

BY THE time Hunter was allowed to take Grant home with him, two more days had passed. Hunter had strapped what was left of Grant's motorcycle on the back of his truck and had been in touch with Izzie to give her an estimate of when to expect them back and to ask her how everything was going at the ranch. She'd been as vague as the first day, telling him she'd bring him up to date once he returned. It only worried Hunter for a moment. His attention was fully focused on Grant, whose face had finally started to look familiar again. He'd been declared out of danger of complications and was allowed to go home, despite the fact he could barely walk and was clearly still in considerable pain. Of course, he tried his best to keep a brave face.

"Stop fussing around me, okay?" Grant pleaded when Hunter tried to help him out of the obligatory wheelchair at the hospital exit. He sounded annoyed and his body language conveyed the same, but Hunter couldn't help himself. He hated seeing how much effort everything took out of Grant and only wanted to make things a little bit easier for him. Of course, that didn't take into account the fact that

Grant was used to fending for himself, and no lover could ever break that habit.

Even Hunter's concerned look before he started the truck's engine was almost met with a growl. Hunter knew it was going to be a long ride home.

Hunter had barely driven off the hospital grounds when Grant asked him to stop.

"Everything all right? Do you need something for the pain?"

Grant shook his head. "Can I ask you a favor?"

Hunter smiled. "Of course. Anything you want."

"Can we agree that I'm fine unless I tell you I'm not?"

Hunter nodded. "On one condition."

Grant raised his eyebrows.

"That you actually tell me and not try to keep a brave face. This is me, Grant—the man you've fucked on as regular a basis as we can manage. I don't need your brave face. You didn't keep a brave face when I had my dick up your ass, and I certainly don't need it when you're hurting."

Grant's eyebrows rose almost into his hairline, which Hunter found funny, given the fact Grant's face had a multitude of colors that would make an Indian brave jealous.

"If you promise that you'll tell me when you need something, then I promise I won't ask you if you're okay every five miles."

"Deal," Grant answered, amusement in his face. Then it turned serious. "I have another favor to ask."

"Shoot," Hunter said, looking over his shoulder to see whether he could pull into traffic again.

Grant put his hand on Hunter's arm. "Stay here for a second."

Hunter relaxed, turning to look at Grant.

"I was on my way somewhere, and I'd still like to go there, if you'll drive me."

Hunter felt the anxiety rise inside him, but he didn't know whether it was because he was afraid of what Grant was going to show him or because he was finally going to become privy to Grant's big, bad secret.

"It's probably another five-hour drive, so we'll have to stay there overnight and not return to the ranch before tomorrow."

Hunter took Grant's hand. "I'll have to phone Izzie and tell her our plans have changed, but yeah, let's do it."

## —27—

ASKING Hunter about driving him to Portland hadn't been a spur-of-the-moment decision. Grant had been fretting about what to do for days. He'd called ahead when Hunter had gone for a walk, and his window of opportunity hadn't closed completely, so he knew it was now or never. It had taken a lot of gritting teeth to persuade his doctor that he'd be able to cope with going home, although the doctor had told him he wasn't ready. He'd had a prescription filled at the pharmacy for more pain medication, so he figured he was all set to go. He'd been through worse. The last time he'd been in this state was after being beaten up, and he hadn't had anyone to take care of him afterward. He'd coped then too.

"So what's in Portland?"

Grant shrugged, then realized that wasn't a painless gesture. "You'll see. It's hard to explain but much easier to show." He hoped Hunter would understand. Very few people knew what was in Portland for him, and he thought he was ready to tell Hunter about it, only he had no idea how exactly to go about it. He wasn't kidding that it was easier to show him.

The truck ran over a pothole, and Grant grunted when pain shot through his body.

Hunter glanced at him sideways, and Grant was grateful it was only a concerned look. "I'm okay. I can just feel every bump in the road. I can't take another painkiller until lunchtime, so take it easy, okay?"

Hunter nodded and gave him a loving smile, which made Grant blush. He was suddenly grateful for the war stripes on his face masking his true feelings.

"What happened to the truck anyway?" Grant asked to change the subject. "You look like you were in an accident too."

Hunter looked straight at the road and didn't immediately answer.

"I was," Hunter eventually said. He took a deep breath and only continued after letting it out very slowly. "I was driving next to you when the truck hit you. You were looking at me, and the next moment you were catapulted into my truck and over it before you hit the dirt at the side of the road."

Grant could see the tears filling Hunter's eyes. "Pull over."

Hunter continued driving.

"Pull over this instant!"

With screeching tires, Hunter brought the truck to a stop by the side of the road. A few cars hooted their horns, but they could easily pass, so Grant didn't care.

"I understand if you're mad at me. It was my fault you had the accident."

Grant tried to gauge the honesty in Hunter's statement. "There was no other truck? This is the truck that hit me?"

"No!" Hunter replied immediately. "There *was* another truck. One of those huge long-haul trucks with a trailer. But you didn't know I was following you, and after you'd left the bar, you were driving so fast, I got worried. I didn't know how much you'd had to drink, and I thought you were maybe overestimating yourself or underestimating your speed. You were doing about eighty, and I took a chance trying to come alongside you to make you pull over, but then you saw me and you missed seeing that truck and then—"

Grant stopped Hunter's rambling by squeezing Hunter's hand. "It's okay, Cowboy."

"It's not okay. If it hadn't been for me, you wouldn't have gotten hurt."

Grant shook his head. "The doctors told me that I was saved because I got to the hospital quickly. If I'd been left in that ditch, I might have died, so the fact you were there to call an ambulance actually saved me. You saved me." *In more ways than one*, Grant wanted to add.

"I distracted you."

"You said I was speeding. I might have had the accident just because of that. Because of the combined speed of me and that truck traveling in the opposite direction, both above the speed limit. It was a deserted road in the middle of the night. What was a big truck like that doing on that two-lane road anyway? He probably never realized he'd hit me, or maybe he didn't even hit me at all. The force of him passing might have blown me into you."

"But you don't know that."

"And we probably never will. All I know is that I'm happy you were there. That's all that matters."

Hunter nodded, but Grant feared that he hadn't been able to convince his Cowboy completely. They sat next to each other, holding hands and not talking, for quite a while.

"Now you think you can drive some more?"

Hunter started the engine again and silently drove off, carefully maneuvering the truck to avoid as many of the bumps on the shoulder as he could until they were back on the Interstate.

All during the drive, Grant kept his hand resting lightly on Hunter's thigh. They didn't talk again until Grant had to give him directions near the end of their journey.

Hunter drove into an ordinary-looking suburban area of similar-looking houses with front yards and trees. Grant made him stop near a house that had three kids playing in the yard. One of them was raking up leaves, and the other two were putting them in a large sack, but doing it so playfully they were making more of a mess than the third one managed to clean up. The oldest boy was getting quite annoyed with it all.

Grant just smiled, even when he noticed Hunter giving him a questioning look.

"Are these your kids?" Hunter eventually asked in a subdued voice.

"Yes," Grant answered calmly. "Not legally, on their part not emotionally either, but biologically, yes. Except for the oldest one, but he thinks I'm his dad. It's complicated."

When Grant glanced sideways, he could see Hunter's confusion. Then a woman walked into the front yard, scolding the children for making a mess and sending the two youngest inside. She took the rake from the oldest boy and gave him instructions. It didn't take them long to finish, but before the woman went inside, she looked straight at Grant.

"Is that your wife?" Hunter asked softly.

"No," Grant answered. "I said I didn't have a wife, and I meant it. She was never my wife, but we used to be friends."

"But you had children with her?"

Grant sighed. He knew it wouldn't be easy to explain. He also knew he wanted to. He had to try to explain it to Hunter if he ever wanted their relationship to have a chance.

"I met Christy about ten years ago. I was driving a delivery truck and she worked in town, at a shop. She was a single mom with a little boy and having a hard time making ends meet. She had another job that started after the grocery shop closed, and I looked after her boy every evening so she could go to work. I've had relationships with women, but although I wasn't ready to admit to myself that I was gay back then, I didn't make a pass at her. She was a good friend, and I'd never been able to keep good friends after I slept with them, female or male. She told me once she appreciated the fact I didn't make a move on her, and she was probably the first person I ever admitted to that I was gay."

The two youngest children came back out to play.

"So how did you end up being the biological father of those two?"

Grant briefly looked at Hunter, expecting to find recrimination in his expression but seeing only genuine interest and maybe a little worry.

"Pretty soon after she realized I wasn't the man for her, she met someone else. He's my age and drives one of those monster trucks, you know?" Grant smiled and Hunter followed suit. "He's often gone for days on end, driving from one side of the States to the other. I never liked him, so after a first meeting where he made a few rude comments directed at me, she kept us as far apart as she could. But she said she loved him, and before I knew it, he'd married her and she was moving west and into his house."

"This one?"

"Yes." Grant nodded. "Her boy often asked for me, so whenever Frank was away, she'd let me spend time with him. Then she told me she and Frank had been trying to have a baby, but it didn't seem to be working, and she asked me whether I was willing to help her out."

Hunter raised his eyebrows. "Help her out?"

"She said she was desperate for a baby, but since Frank wouldn't go to see a doctor, she had gone alone, and the doctor had said there was no reason she couldn't conceive. She had no money for fancy stuff like artificial insemination, so we did it the old-fashioned way."

"You fucked her?" Hunter said blankly.

Grant closed his eyes. "That sounds very crude for what we did."

"Okay, fine," Hunter added in an annoyed tone. "You *made love* to her."

Grant sighed. He'd hoped Hunter would understand. "I loved her in my own way, Hunter. She's a great woman. It didn't take much. The first time she got pregnant after three or four tries. The second time we only did it twice. Making love to a woman isn't *that* hard. It was just never what I wanted for the rest of my life."

"I know," Hunter answered, all hurt gone from his voice. "But these children know you're their father?"

"No," Grant answered. "They know me. From time to time I call her, and sometimes she tells me that Frank will be away for a week, and then I drive up here and spend some time with her and the kids. They think I'm just a friend of their mom's. And I'm a secret. The kids play the game pretty well. Frank only found out once."

"And then what happened?"

"He slapped her around. She claims that it only happened once, but sometimes she gets sad and I think he's hit her again, but she'll never admit to it. So when she calls I run to her. I'm always scared that she'll need help getting away from him, but maybe I'm just imagining things. She was black and blue that time he hit her. I've never seen bruises on her any other time, so maybe he's good to her and it was just a lapse in judgment that once. At least he provides her with money for her kids and she doesn't need to work. They have food and clothes and nice things."

"Was that time he slapped her around the time you left Gable and he had his accident?"

Damn, the man was perceptive. Grant closed his eyes. Most of the truth was out anyway. "Yes. Gabe and I had a fight about me leaving, but Christy sounded so frantic on the phone, and I didn't have time to explain it to him. He never knew about her, and it would have taken a few hours to tell him the whole truth. When I didn't give him a sufficient explanation, he got mad as hell, but I figured he'd get over it once he'd gone riding for a few hours. I swear I didn't know he was hurt."

"I know," Hunter said. "I know." He scooted closer and put his arm around Grant, running his hand through Grant's hair in a gesture that felt so loving and intimate Grant couldn't prevent himself from leaning into it.

"I'm sorry I misjudged you, but I didn't know the full story," Hunter said, kissing Grant's temple. "I'm sorry I thought you didn't treat Gable very well and that you were cold and mean to him."

"I know what it looked like, but I couldn't defend myself without exposing everything. I know they live a long way away, but the last thing I wanted was for Frank to find out I was the father of his children and to give him a chance to take it out on them or Christy."

Hunter nodded. "Do you want to go in and say hi to them?"

"No," Grant said. "Christy saw me. She knows I'm around. I'll call her later tonight and ask her whether there's a chance I'll be able to see them. Then again, they might run away screaming, seeing the way I look."

Hunter pulled Grant closer, and Grant felt the pain shoot through him. He also felt incredibly tired. "Do you think we can find a place to stay and maybe sleep? I think I need a good dose of painkillers and a decent bed."

"Sure thing," Hunter replied softly, letting go of Grant to start the car.

# —28—

HUNTER had too much going on in his mind to be able to sleep, although Grant was lying next to him, softly snoring under the influence of a dose of strong painkillers. Hunter couldn't help but look at Grant's face, still swollen and dark in places. It was the face of the man he loved.

Grant's story had wiped away the last doubts Hunter still had. He now knew what he'd felt all along: that Grant was a good man and that he was worthy of his love. The more he thought about it, the more in awe he was. Grant had consistently done unselfish things that, on the surface, had seemed not at all altruistic. He'd risked being labeled as undependable because of his need for extra days off, while they were meant to serve the protection of innocent children who didn't even know he was their father. He'd unselfishly given a woman the children she craved without making any demands. Hunter was pretty sure that, given half a chance, Grant would make an amazing father to these children, yet he seemed content to be known as a friend of their mother's.

Grant stirred in his sleep and then woke with a start, rolling to his back and gasping for air.

Hunter gently placed his hand on Grant's chest. "Sssh, it's okay. I'm here."

Grant turned wide eyes in Hunter's direction and then seemed to realize where he was. "Hunter," he acknowledged, his eyes softening.

"I'll get you a drink," Hunter said after seeing Grant swallow with some difficulty. "Do you need more painkillers?"

Grant shook his head. "Too early. Wish I could, though."

When Hunter returned with a cold glass of water, Grant was sitting on the side of the bed, breathing with measured breaths.

"Here you go," Hunter offered, holding out the glass.

Grant drank a large gulp and then paused to catch his breath. "Thanks, Cowboy."

Hunter could tell even sitting down hurt his lover. He knew Grant hadn't wanted to admit it, but he'd seen the bruises around Grant's hips and could tell they gave him grief. All those hours sitting on the bench of the truck on the way to Christy's house couldn't have helped either.

"Why don't you lie down again?" Hunter suggested.

Grant shook his head. "I can't find a position that doesn't… that feels comfortable."

Hunter didn't want to tell him that it was okay to say it hurt. Grant's pride didn't need to be as bruised as his body was. He took the pillows from the other bed and placed them around Grant while Grant watched him with an amused look on his face. The room was semi-dark, but the reflection of the light from the bathroom gave Hunter a good look at Grant's expression.

"What's so funny?" Hunter asked as he gently helped Grant to lie down on the pillows.

"You'd make a good nurse. Although I hate hospitals, I could see you in one of those white uniforms."

Hunter chuckled and took the last pillow. "Can you spread your legs?"

"I'm flattered, but I don't think I can…," Grant replied a little hesitantly. "How did you know how to do this?" he continued after Hunter put the pillow between his legs and the tension immediately left Grant's body.

Hunter just smiled and tucked the blankets around Grant before walking around the bed and carefully crawling in behind Grant. When he put his arms around Grant's shoulders and gently pulled him back against his chest, Grant moaned quietly.

"How does that feel?" Hunter asked a little apprehensively.

"Like I've died and gone to heaven," Grant answered. "Only you've left the light on in the bathroom."

Hunter chuckled and started moving again.

"Don't you dare get out of bed to turn it off!" Grant insisted. "I haven't been this comfortable since before that truck hit me. Can you sleep like this?"

Hunter gently kissed Grant's hair. "I could sleep like this for the rest of my life." It felt so damn great to hold Grant, and it hit Hunter just how close he had been to losing his lover. "When we get back to the ranch, I'm going to tell my mom and the girls."

"Are you sure?" Grant asked quietly.

"Yes, I am. But if you don't want to, I suppose I can wait. I'm just sick and tired of hiding."

Grant nodded. "They may not react as well as Izzie, though."

"I know." Hunter sighed. He had to admit he was afraid of his mother's reaction. And Lisa's. Izzie knew about them, and he was pretty sure Bernie would take it well enough too, but the two older women had a tendency to be harder to read, and those two were the ones he feared. "I just want to go on with our lives and stop being careful how I look at you when they're around."

"There's still the crew to consider."

"I sign their paychecks. If they don't want to work for a gay boss, then it's their loss."

"Workers are hard to come by," Grant replied.

"You don't want this to get out, do you?"

Grant sighed. "This is as new to me as it is to you, Cowboy. When I worked for Gable, the rumors were everywhere, of course, because most people in the county know about him."

"But you always denied it then."

"It's scary, Hunter."

Hunter didn't miss that Grant used his real name and not his most-loved nickname. "Why don't we just tell my family and keep it quiet for the crew right now? That way we can get used to it first, and it gives them a little more time as well. Besides, I still have to sell it to the guys that I want to make you foreman, and I think that'll be easier if it doesn't look like I'm pushing my lover forward."

Grant nodded. "Are you sure?"

"About making you foreman? You pretty much do the work now anyway, and I trust you. That's what I need most. Someone I can trust implicitly." Hunter gently caressed Grant's chest, kissing the back of his head and, after Grant turned his way slightly, his temple and the side of his jaw. "Besides, Izzie already told me that she didn't want the job, and Tim said he was comfortable just doing what he did now and he didn't want the added responsibility. Also, he's a bachelor, so it's not like he needs the money."

Grant nodded.

That was how they fell asleep, and exactly the same position Hunter woke up in hours later. He was sore from not moving all night, and he didn't dare move now either, because Grant was still completely out of it. His soft snores comforted Hunter with the knowledge that Grant was still breathing steadily.

"I love you, my beautiful man. I love you so much, and I can't even tell you out loud."

"Mmm?" Grant murmured as he seemed to wake. "What did you say?"

"Nothing," Hunter answered. "Go back to sleep." He took the moment to retrieve his arm from underneath Grant and turned so he could sit on the side of the bed and stretch his muscles. He shivered slightly when he felt Grant's fingers ghost over his bare back. "Everything okay?" he asked, looking over his shoulder.

"Yeah," Grant answered. "Sore as hell, but I slept like a baby. Now I need to get up and pee."

Hunter walked around the bed so he could help Grant get up. As soon as Grant was on his feet, Hunter couldn't resist pulling him closer and kissing him. It never ceased to amaze him how well they fit together, being of similar height and build, although Grant was slightly broader. Hunter smiled into the kiss when he felt Grant's hard-on nudge his hip. Well aware of Grant's sore ribs, he couldn't do more than gently squeeze Grant's ass as he deepened their interaction.

"We better move, unless you want a golden shower," Grant teased as he pulled away.

Hunter guided Grant's good arm around his shoulder so he could support him, and they made their way to the tiny motel bathroom, where Hunter held Grant steady as he leaned over the toilet.

Grant shook his head.

"Pee-shy?" Hunter asked teasingly. He snaked his arms underneath Grant's so he could wrap them around Grant's broad chest.

Grant let his head fall back on Hunter's shoulder. "Not usually, Cowboy, but I could use a little privacy just so my boner gets a chance to cool off."

Hunter languidly kissed Grant neck's to the point that Grant moaned in exasperation, before teasingly pulling away and leaving Grant to his own devices.

"You're a devil, Cowboy," Grant called after him before Hunter heard the telltale sounds of water cascading into the toilet bowl.

An hour later they were on their way to a breakfast place Christy had suggested after Grant had called her. Hunter could tell Grant was nervous.

"Was she going to bring the kids?" Hunter asked.

Grant nodded. "It's just across from their school, so I'm sure we won't get a lot of time together, but at least I can wave them off. It's always good to see them."

"You spend a lot of time sitting across the street from their house when you come here?"

"Yeah," Grant answered, his voice not exactly devoid of emotion. Hoping to offer some silent support, Hunter quickly took Grant's hand to give it a squeeze before turning into the parking lot.

Christy was there with the kids, and Hunter and Grant spotted them immediately. Hunter was glad there was a parking space close to where they were waiting and just in front of the place Grant had pointed out as the diner he and Christy had agreed upon.

As soon as Grant opened his door, the three kids came bounding over.

Christy quickly followed. "Be careful! Grant's had an accident. Don't hurt him."

The kids halted as soon as their mother stopped shouting. Hunter walked around the car and saw Grant's eyes well up at the sad face of the little girl standing in front. With some difficulty, Grant managed to swing his legs out of the car, but he remained seated.

"Come here, princess," Grant said quietly, gesturing for her to come closer. She hesitated and looked at her mother. Hunter couldn't stop looking at Grant.

"It's okay," Christy said.

Hunter took a step forward and kneeled next to the little girl. "He looks funny right now, but he really wants to see you."

She looked up at him with wide eyes and then practically leapt onto Grant's lap. Hunter could see Grant wince, but she was all over him, hugging him tightly, and the two boys followed, albeit a little less eagerly. Grant looked like a proud dad, though, when he gave the oldest boy a fatherly squeeze and ran his hands through the youngest one's unruly black hair. Hunter could definitely see the resemblance.

"Let's get inside for a quick breakfast because it's almost time for school, kids," Christy said, breaking up the family reunion.

They went inside and found a large booth, Grant and the two boys squeezing into one side and Christy and her daughter joining Hunter in the other. They all ordered pancakes, and Hunter could see how the shy boys quickly warmed up to Grant again and started talking to him about school and about playing Little League. He couldn't keep his eyes off his lover, seeing how Grant was smiling and enjoying the company of his kids. He was constantly hugging them and running his hand over their hair to the point where Lindy, his little girl, pushed her plate further up the table and crawled underneath it to settle on Grant's lap.

Hunter wished he'd brought a camera to take a picture of the family scene, although he didn't know whether Grant would want to be reminded of how black and blue he looked. He did seem to have forgotten about how sore he was.

Christy suddenly got up from the table. "I hate to break this up, guys, but it's time for school."

"Aaaw, Mom!" Lewis, the oldest boy, whined.

"No complaining," she replied with a stern face. "I told you we could come see Grant but that I wouldn't let you skip school for it."

"When will you be back?" the youngest boy asked quietly.

Grant pulled him into a hug. "I don't know, Robby. In a few weeks, maybe?"

Robby nodded.

"Why don't I take them to school?" Hunter suggested. "It's just a matter of walking them across the road, right? That way you two can discuss the next meeting?"

Hunter looked at Christy, then at Grant, and saw the grateful look in Grant's eyes.

"Sure, if you don't mind," Christy answered, a little hesitantly.

Hunter helped the kids put on their jackets and get their school bags, realizing he felt very much out of place. He'd never done this sort of thing, not even when his baby sister was that age, but he wanted to give Grant some time with Christy, so he tried acting cheerful.

In any case, how hard could it be? The kids seemed very well behaved, and they could practically see the school's entrance from where they'd had breakfast.

# —29—

GRANT scooted back into the booth and took a swig from his now half-cold coffee in the hope it would help him relax and feel less of the pain. He was grateful that Hunter had given him this time with Christy, because he'd seen the bruise on her arm, and although he felt uneasy about pointing it out to her, he felt he had no choice.

Christy was sitting across from him, uncharacteristically avoiding his scrutiny.

"Everything okay, Chris?"

She nodded, staring at the table with the leftover pancakes. The waitress came to clear the plates and offer more coffee, but after she was gone, Grant knew he couldn't put it off any longer. He touched her arm, pushing the sleeve up to reveal the bruise. "Did he do this to you?"

She shrugged.

"Christy." Grant sighed. "This scares me, when I see you hurting."

"It doesn't hurt."

"Chris." Grant sighed. "It's bad enough that I'm so far away and I can't protect you and the kids from him."

"I don't need you to protect me."

"Stop protecting *him,* then!" Grant sighed once more. He hadn't realized how loud his voice had sounded until he shouted at her. This wasn't helping. People were staring at them, and Grant tried to calm himself down. And on top of everything, his painkillers were wearing off and his breathing was becoming painful again.

"He never does anything when the kids are around. It always happens when he comes home late at night and he's been driving for days and he's tired. The kids are all in bed by then."

Grant swallowed, trying to keep the rage from showing. "I'm glad he doesn't hurt the kids, but what happens if he loses it and hurts you so badly you can't take care of them anymore?" He didn't want to say, "What if he kills you, Christy?" but that was certainly what he was thinking. "Come with me, Chris. Pack the kids and come with me."

She shook her head. "I can't. He feels horrible about it when it happens. It's just when he's tired. When he's had a good night's sleep, he's really sweet to me and the kids. He takes us on trips and buys them stuff and plays catch with them in the yard. I swear he never lays a finger on them, Grant."

The pleading look on her face made Grant feel defeated. He knew there was nothing he could do.

Christy pulled down her sleeve so the bruise was covered and then put her hand over Grant's. "So is he your...?" She gestured outside.

"Yeah," Grant replied softly.

"I'm glad," she said. "He's cute."

Grant smiled wryly. Although he was still feeling uneasy about the situation Christy and the kids were in, he was happy to see his old friend reemerge. "Don't know if he'll appreciate being called cute, but he's special to me, Chris."

She squeezed his hand. "I know. I see the way he looks at you and how you look at him. You'd have to be blind to miss that."

"Didn't know we were that obvious."

Christy smiled. "I'm glad you found someone, Grant. Are you living with him?"

Grant shrugged. "He's my boss, actually. Owns a big-ass ranch out in South Idaho."

"You were living in Idaho a while ago too."

"Different ranch and different man," Grant admitted.

"So he's got money?"

"I suppose," Grant replied. "It's a family ranch, so it doesn't really matter."

"He's got a family?"

"Everyone has a family, Christy," Grant answered with a smile.

"You and I don't."

"True," Grant agreed. "We just have each other. And you have the kids."

"I do. And they mean the world to me, Grant. You know that, right?"

Grant nodded. He never doubted that. "Just keep them safe, okay? And if you need anything, I'm at the Blue River Ranch in Idaho, near St. Anthony. Everyone in town knows the ranch and Hunter's family."

"So you're thinking of staying there permanently?" she asked with a hint of amusement in her voice.

"If it were up to me, yes. Hunter's pretty hooked on the place. It used to be his father's, and now he runs it with his sisters and his mother."

"Sounds like they could use another man around the house."

Grant chuckled, getting a painful reminder of his injured ribs. "I think they're just fine without my interference."

"Does he need you? Hunter?"

Grant nodded. "I think so. I need him too. Especially right now."

"I can tell he's really protective of you," Christy said with a knowing smile.

Grant looked up and saw Hunter walk back into the diner. He couldn't take his eyes off the long, jeans-clad legs and broad shoulders encased in the sheepskin coat. This was the man he loved. "He says he loves me," Grant said, so quietly it was only really meant for his own ears. Christy had picked it up, though, and she was smiling brightly as Hunter arrived next to their table.

"Kids are inside. They were just in time for classes to start." Hunter didn't sit down and stood a little awkwardly, Grant thought.

"Good," Christy said, nodding a thank you in Hunter's direction.

"So have you discussed when we'll be back here?" Hunter asked.

Grant didn't miss the "we." "We haven't, actually. When *can* we make it back here?"

Hunter shrugged. "If we know it in advance, it's easy to take a few days off. And traveling in a truck is more comfortable than on a bike."

"Bike's wrecked anyway," Grant added, looking expectantly at Christy as he tried to get out of the booth with minimal effort.

"I wish I could make long-term plans, guys, but you know I can't. I'll call you, Grant," she added.

Grant hugged her good-bye, minding his ribs, and Hunter held out his hand, but Christy pulled him closer into a hug. "Take care of him for me, Hunter," she whispered in Hunter's ear before letting go of him.

Grant eyed her amusedly, and she swatted him. "You know I like the feel of a big guy, Grant. Don't read anything into it."

"Take care, Christy," Hunter replied. When he looked back at Grant, Grant felt his heart skip a beat.

After saying their good-byes, Grant couldn't help noticing how Hunter stuck close by him, and it wasn't just because of his concern for his physical well-being. Grant had the feeling Hunter was loaded with questions he wanted to ask. Grant didn't feel ready to answer them yet, so he was glad Hunter seemed to have a hard time finding the right words to put them in.

After getting settled in the truck and driving off toward the highway, it took Hunter almost half an hour to finally broach the subject.

"You and Christy are pretty close."

Grant nodded. "Wouldn't have had children with her if we weren't."

"Why didn't you stay around here?"

"It's a long story," Grant answered dismissively. Then he realized maybe Hunter wanted more of an explanation, and if he was honest with himself, he had to admit Hunter deserved one.

"Like me, Christy doesn't have a family. When we met, she was all alone in the world, except for this little boy she had. She never told me who his father was, and I never pressed her about it, because she didn't seem to want to have anything to do with him. When I made it clear to her that I had no intention to be more than a friend to her, she seemed okay with that. I played Dad to Lewis for a while, and she seemed to appreciate that, but then she met Frank and I was put on the back burner. In the beginning, she was afraid to even see me. Said Frank didn't believe a woman and a man could be just friends and that he was jealous of me, so we met in secret, whenever Frank was out with his truck."

"Sounds like not a lot has changed." Hunter sighed and kept his eyes on the road.

"I tried finding work around here, but Frank blew his top whenever he'd see me around town, so I had to put some distance between us."

"You think he beat her up every time you came close?"

"I don't know," Grant answered honestly. "I guess."

"So you wait for her phone call and then you drop everything and drive through the night, risking life and limb to spend a few hours with her and the kids?"

Grant nodded slightly. "You make it sound really stupid."

Hunter put his hand on Grant's knee, and Grant could feel the warmth of the touch seep through the fabric of his jeans. It felt very comforting, and as Hunter kept his hand there, the heat flooded into the rest of his body, relaxing him and somehow helping him deal with the pain.

"It's not stupid to run to her when she calls and you feel there's reason to worry about her or the kids. It's a little silly that you're so far away from her, though."

Grant put his hand over Hunter's. "Right now there's this guy where I live. He's sort of connected to the place, on account of his daddy being buried in that soil, and his grandma and grandpop," Grant said with an exaggerated Southern drawl. "And sometimes a man has to think of himself as well."

"Maybe that man could be talked into moving?"

"I wouldn't dream of asking him to do that. His job isn't the sort of job you can just start up somewhere else."

Hunter squeezed Grant's hand, and Grant felt his throat tighten. Damn, the pain was making him soft. He swallowed away the tears and didn't dare look at his lover sitting next to him, afraid he'd totally lose it if he did.

They sat together like that for a long time, with Hunter only letting go of Grant's hand to switch gears, which wasn't very often, since the traffic was light. Hunter pulled over every now and again to let Grant stretch his muscles. Sitting on the truck bench was torture, though, and Grant questioned his sanity more than once during the ride. Maybe he should have stayed in the hospital a while longer, but he couldn't keep Hunter from his ranch any longer than absolutely necessary, and Hunter didn't want to leave him behind. So Grant was bearing the pain and hoping they'd be home soon.

Home.

Hunter's ranch.

Would it ever really be home?

"Why are you stopping? We're almost there. I can last ten more minutes, Cowboy." Grant looked at Hunter as the truck stopped by the side of the road.

Hunter put the truck in neutral and turned toward Grant. He put his hand on the back of Grant's head and pulled him closer, gently kissing him. When he pulled back, he looked sad, and something dawned on Grant.

"I'll be fine in my room in the crew block, Cowboy. The last thing I want is to come between you and your family."

"Are you crazy?" Hunter smiled sweetly. "Last night you couldn't even find a comfortable position to sleep in until I helped you lie down."

"I must admit you did wonders." Grant couldn't resist smiling. "But you can't just show up after five days and spring your dirty little secret on them. Drop me off at the crew quarters and then find an appropriate time to break it to them gently."

Hunter shook his head and grabbed Grant's hand again. "I'm not saying it doesn't scare me, Grant, but if I wait to tell them, I'll lose my nerve. I'm not hiding you anymore. Right now, I'm not leaving you alone in a room. Unless it's my room."

"As long as your mother doesn't throw both of us out of the house."

"If she does, I'll move in with you at the crew house."

"Hunter...."

"Are you telling me you don't want me? Am I just your casual piece of ass?" Hunter pulled his hand away with a frown.

"Come on, Cowboy."

Hunter raised an eyebrow. "We're back to the nickname."

"You don't like it?"

"I love it, but you're not answering my question, Grant. I made up my mind when you were in the hospital. There's only one answer for me, and that's to be honest with my family and explain to them that I love you and that I want them to treat you like my partner, no different than if I brought a girl home."

Grant sighed. If it were only that simple. "It's not the same, now, is it?"

"Yes, it is. Mom might not like Miranda, but if I'd brought her home and told everyone she was the woman I wanted to marry, Mom would have had to get used to the idea and would have to treat her like a daughter."

"Right," Grant answered with a slight snort. "But then Miranda would have given your mother a few other things I'm sure she would have appreciated. Like a big white wedding and a litter of grandkids."

"In that case, do you have pictures of Christy's kids? I'm sure Mom will appreciate the fact you come with a family attached."

"I'm being serious here, Hunter."

"So am I. Grant, if you don't want to be with me, I need to know right now, because I can't keep lying to them. I can't keep sneaking around. I want you in my bed at night, not just in the truck when we're fixing fences around the ranch or in Gable's hayloft. Especially now you're hurt. I don't see you crawling up there any time soon."

Grant felt a tightness in his chest. No matter how much he loved Hunter, he wasn't sure if he could be as open about his sexuality as Hunter suggested. "I'm not a shout-it-off-the-rooftops type, Hunter."

"Neither am I, but I can't lie to the people who are important to me. Which is why I'm asking you to be honest with me now, so I can be honest with them."

"So you just want to tell your mom and your sisters?"

Hunter nodded. "I think that will be plenty for one night."

"Okay."

"Izzie knows, so she'll be on our side. Bernie'll be fine. She likes you. Lisa and Mom probably won't say much with you there, but I think they'll be okay as soon as they have some time to think about it."

"They want you to be happy."

"And they'll see I'm happy with you. Izzie says it's hard to miss that, and Christy agrees."

Hunter squeezed Grant's hand again and then leaned forward to kiss him. Although Grant savored the kiss, his apprehension about what was going to happen when they reached the house prevented him from actually kissing Hunter back. Grant could see the disappointment in Hunter's eyes when he sat back against the truck bench and stared out at the road outside.

"Maybe you should just talk to your mom alone."

Hunter shook his head. "I want you there. I want her to see I mean business. If you're not there, she'll just be able to deny everything. It won't be real. But if you're there…." He looked at Grant. "She won't be able to…." He shrugged as if he didn't need to find the right words.

Grant smiled. He understood. "Okay, I'll be there." He didn't think it was necessary to tell Hunter just how scared he was. He was going to have to get through seeing Hunter's mother eye him with the knowledge that he'd had sex with her son.

With a firm, supportive squeeze of Grant's hand, Hunter let go and put the truck in drive, turning it onto the road and toward his ranch.

# —30—

HUNTER was shaking like a leaf after parking the truck by the side of the house. He shook his hands and dried them on his jeans before walking around the truck to help Grant get out. He knew if he kept busy he'd be all right. *Just act casually*, he told himself. *Pretend it's business as usual and no big deal at all that you're taking a man up to your room and getting him settled in there. Oh yes, and on the way up, in case you encounter your mother, you're going to have to come out of the closet. Tell your mother that her only son isn't going to bring home a daughter-in-law. Explain to her that you love Grant and you're going to take care of him until he's all healed up. And you're not going to take any grief from her. Or let her throw Grant out once he's on his feet again.*

Hunter took the small bag of Grant's things out of the truck and realized that, before the confrontation, he'd better take a shower and change his clothes. He'd left without packing anything five days ago, and although he'd had a shower somewhere along the way, he knew his clothes smelled rank. He looked at his watch and figured he'd have time to clean up before dinner.

Deep in thought, making sure a very sore-looking Grant got out of the truck without injuring himself any further, he was too busy to notice the unfamiliar car in the driveway. They were on their way to the front door when Lisa stormed out, carrying a suitcase, closely followed by a guy carrying another large bag. It took Hunter a few moments to recognize Jack, Hugh's middle brother and star of Saturday nights at the bar, where he performed for the locals. He didn't think he'd ever seen the guy around the ranch for anything else than horse dentistry, so he was a little surprised to see him running after his oldest sister.

"Jack? What the…? Lisa? What's going on?" Hunter was thoroughly confused. Neither Lisa nor Jack answered him, though. They simply loaded their baggage in the car and drove off.

Hunter looked at Grant, who shrugged before walking up the porch to the front door. Once inside, they bumped into Izzie and Danny.

"I'm gone for a few days, and when I come back, it's pandemonium?" Hunter asked her in amusement. "What's gotten into Lisa? She looked like she was moving out."

Izzie pulled Danny into the hallway, and Hunter could see the kid had been crying.

"Danny boy, what's wrong?"

"Uncle Hunter!" the boy shouted before flinging himself into Hunter's arm so forcibly, Hunter had to let go of Grant, who luckily had the wall for support. Hunter hugged Danny tightly, then threw a questioning look at Izzie.

"Bernie?" Izzie shouted upstairs. "Come get Danny and take him to his room."

Almost immediately they heard a stampede coming down the stairway, and Bernie arrived, looking very pleased with herself, as usual. "Sure, sis. Come on, Danny."

Danny looked up at Hunter, pleading to let him stay, so Hunter rubbed his hand through Danny's hair. "I just got home, kid. Why don't you run upstairs so I can talk to Nan and Izzie, and I'll be right up, okay?"

That seemed to appease Danny, who let go of Hunter and, still rather reluctantly, followed his aunt Bernie up the stairs.

Hunter waited until Danny was out of sight. "So what's going on here?"

Izzie wasn't looking at Hunter, though. "Hell, Grant. Did you get beaten up as well?" Her eyes were full of worry.

Grant shook his head as he let her touch him rather intimately to assure herself he was okay. "I'm fine. Few broken ribs and a bruised pelvis. Got thrown off my bike by a monster truck."

"Hunter told me about the accident." Izzie turned her gaze to Hunter. "You didn't tell me he looked this bad!"

Hunter shrugged. He didn't want to tell her the whole truth just yet, at least not until he got to the heart of the matter first. "Never mind Grant," he told his sister. "What happened while I was gone?"

Izzie pulled Hunter into the living room. Hunter checked to make sure Grant followed and helped him get comfortable on the couch while Izzie closed the door and returned to them with a conspiratorial smile. Hunter could tell it wasn't all bad.

"Jack got a record deal for his band with a country and western label in Tennessee. Lisa apparently has been seeing Jack, and they're eloping."

Hunter was baffled. "Last thing I knew she was still married to Hugh."

Izzie smiled triumphantly.

"And you're happy because, with Lisa out of the way... Izzie! Our sister left her son behind to go off cavorting with his uncle?"

Hunter's heart sank when he saw his sister's mood deflate. "And his aunt is sleeping with his dad. Yeah, I know. They couldn't have written it any better if it were a soap opera."

Hunter scratched his hair. "So Lisa and Jack and you and Hugh? Nothing ever happens when I'm home, but I leave for a weekend and—"

Izzie's triumphant mood returned. "Hugh and I have been going on almost longer than you and Grant, Hunter. Bernie's usually pretty flaky, but she said you hadn't noticed yet, and I didn't believe her."

"Well, you said that you had a soft spot for Hugh but couldn't do anything about it because he was married to Lisa. That's all I knew!"

"I was trying to tell you about us, but I guess you being a guy and all, I should have given you clearer hints."

Hunter wrapped his arms around his sister and picked her up, twirling her around. He didn't let go once he set her back on the ground. Instead he gave her a tight hug. "I'm happy for you, sis. Are you happy?"

"If I'd known that you turning gay meant you'd become a hugger, you should have done it years ago!" she giggled.

"That's not what I meant," Hunter said, blushing like a girl and feeling mightily embarrassed about it.

"I know," she said calmly. "Yes, I'm very happy. And don't worry about Danny. He was crying when Lisa left without as much as a warning, but I called Hugh, and he's on his way here. I'm sure seeing his dad again will help Danny get over it."

"So is Hugh moving back here?"

Izzie bit her lip. "I haven't broken it to Mom yet. I want him here when we tell her. I have a feeling she'll be furious, so the more support I can rally the better. I'm glad you got here just in time."

Hunter looked over at Grant, who'd been sitting on the couch, watching all of the proceedings quietly. "We sort of have an announcement she won't be very happy about either."

"Oh, God!" Izzie exclaimed. "You're going to come out to Mom?" She covered her mouth with her hand.

"Grant needs some looking after in the next few days while he recuperates, and I'm not letting him sleep in the crew house where there's nobody to take care of him. It's only fair I explain to Mom why I'm letting him stay in my room."

"You rascal," Izzie teased. "I don't know if I want to ask you not to say anything right away or whether I'm going to let you divulge your dirty little secret first, just to take the heat off mine."

"Where is Mom, anyway?"

"Where she always is, I suppose. In the kitchen."

They didn't have time to plot more strategy before the rarely used doorbell rang.

"Hugh?" Hunter asked.

"No way." Izzie shook her head. "He knows the door isn't locked."

"Then who…?" Hunter stopped talking when he heard his mother's voice in the hallway.

"Miranda, what a pleasant surprise!"

Izzie looked at Hunter, and Hunter switched between gazing at Grant and Izzie. "Oh, crap. That's all we need."

"Let's go into the living room."

"Shit," Izzie muttered under her breath just as the door to the hallway opened. They could see the surprise in their mother's face when she noticed the living room was occupied.

"Hunter," his mother acknowledged. "You're back."

Hunter nodded at her but couldn't stop looking at Miranda, who seemed very nervous and was avoiding his gaze. He had no idea what she was doing there, but he knew it couldn't be good. Something in his gut told him to be on his guard.

"Izzie, darling, could you make us some tea?" Beth asked her daughter in the usual calm, take-charge sort of way she carried herself. "And bring the cookies I made yesterday." Her gaze briefly traveled to Grant and Hunter, and they could see her wondering what the wrangler was doing in her living room, but the look passed within moments, and her courteous smile returned for Miranda.

Hunter knew his mother was just being the perfect hostess and her pasted-on smile had nothing to do with any affection she might feel for Miranda. More than once his mother had spoken in less than affectionate terms about Hunter's ex-girlfriend over dinner, so there was no doubt in Hunter's mind about how his mother felt. It was one of the reasons he'd never brought Miranda home—the other being that he'd never had any inclination to marry her in the first place.

"So, darling," his mother continued. "What brings you here?"

Hunter quickly looked at Grant before listening to Miranda's answer with more than a little apprehension. Grant seemed calm, but then Grant didn't know what to expect, and although he was hotheaded, Hunter had never known Grant to worry about things he had no control over.

"I actually came here to speak to Hunter," Miranda replied softly. Hunter didn't miss the quiver in her voice. He also didn't miss the way she touched her belly with her hands before looking at him. His throat went dry.

"Hunter and I are going to have a baby."

At that moment, Izzie walked into the room and almost dropped the tray with the tea china. Hunter jumped up to help her, glad for the distraction. He took the tray from Izzie and put it on the table, occupying himself with setting the cups upright again.

Nobody spoke, and Hunter didn't dare look at Grant. His mother had turned white and, to Hunter's surprise, had lost the smile she only ever wore around company. Miranda had returned to gazing at her clasped hands, and Izzie sat down with her mouth in a very unladylike gape. Hunter saw Izzie look at Grant, but he didn't dare to follow her gaze.

The silence seemed to last forever, and it was Izzie who finally managed to break it. "When are you due? I'm calculated for March," she said calmly, as if this was a civilized afternoon tea party among casual friends.

"February," Miranda answered, not hiding how stunned she was at what Izzie had said. After all, this was a small town; news traveled, and everyone had heard how Izzie had dumped her rodeo boyfriend months earlier.

"You're pregnant?" their mother asked with a less-than-steady voice. She was looking at her daughter, not at Miranda.

"Yes, Mother," Izzie answered, surprisingly calm.

Her words were barely cold when they heard the front door bang shut, almost immediately followed by the hallway door opening and Hugh blazing in. "Is Danny okay?" He looked around the room at the assorted company and raised his eyebrows. "Izzie called to tell me Danny needed me," he said by way of apology. "I didn't realize—"

Hugh didn't finish his sentence, because Hunter's mother gasped and sagged down into her chair. Izzie immediately went to her side, looking immensely worried. "Mom, are you okay?"

From the corner of his eye, Hunter could see his mother nodding. This was the woman who hadn't even cried a single tear when she was told her husband had died. Hunter had never known her to be compassionate or even affectionate, especially not to her own children, so he was rather surprised about her fainting. He didn't have time to mull over it, though.

"I'd better leave," Miranda announced. "I'll call you later to talk, Hunter."

Hunter didn't even think about objecting. There were things that needed to be talked over, and despite her earlier announcement, Miranda was not part of this family. The sooner she left, the sooner the air could be cleared. He escorted her outside. "You have my number."

She nodded, and Hunter walked her to where a car was waiting with an older woman inside. He nodded at her before watching them drive off.

Hunter stayed on the porch until Miranda's car was out of sight. He'd just been delivered quite a bombshell, and he didn't look forward to the next conversation with her, but for now, there were other fires to put out. He wasn't eager to get back into the living room, worried about what he would find there, but his biggest reason to return was that Grant was still in there. It was growing dark outside, and he was hungry, but most of all, he was worried about the people inside, all of them people he loved dearly.

# —31—

GRANT stayed quietly on the couch, watching the pandemonium unfold before his eyes. Beside the fact he wasn't very fast on his feet right now, he really wasn't part of this family yet, although he did feel close to Izzie and he knew Hugh, who'd been nothing but kind in hiring him, despite the knowledge that Hunter would give him grief about it. Unbeknownst to most of the group, he was about to add to the turmoil, though Hunter hadn't seen the chance to throw his lightning bolt into the fireworks yet.

As soon as Miranda and Hunter had left the room, Hunter's mother seemed to recover, and she was soon sitting up, Izzie still hovering over her while Hugh nodded a hello to Grant and sat down next to him.

"You look like you were run over by a truck."

Grant chuckled, pain shooting into his chest almost immediately. "Funny you should notice. It was a close call. I'm lucky to be alive. If it hadn't been for Hunter following me on Friday, I could have been dead in a ditch along US-26."

Hugh shot him a pained expression, then leaned closer. "Izzie told me about you and Hunter." He was whispering, and they were far enough from Izzie and her mother not to be overheard. "Have to admit I was a little surprised."

"Oh?" Grant replied noncommittally.

"Well, I knew about you. From when you and Gable…."

Grant nodded to forgive Hugh for not finishing his sentence.

"But I always figured Hunter as a bit of a ladies' man. Not just Miranda—all the girls at the bar were lining up, and I know for a fact he didn't always turn them down."

Grant pursed his lips and didn't answer. What could he say? The last thing he wanted was for people to accuse him of "recruiting" Hunter.

Hugh softly patted him on the back. "Well, as long as you two are happy. Izzie says you are, so who am I to argue? I'm far from a saint, as you know by now."

Grant nodded. "Congratulations, by the way. Izzie told us you were expecting."

Hugh smiled, and Grant could tell he was proud, although still a little apprehensive about showing it. "I've loved Izzie for a long time. She's an amazing girl." He cleared his throat. "Woman. And I couldn't be prouder that she wants to have my child. Danny deserves a baby brother or sister. Although from what I gather, he's going to have a little niece or nephew to play with as well."

"Yeah, that was a bit of a shock," Grant admitted.

Hugh patted him on the shoulder again and gave him a sympathetic smile. "I'm sure it'll all work out. Sometimes it takes a lot of patience, though. Things are never easy in this family."

"So I gathered."

Hugh got up from the couch. "Better go see how Danny's doing. Mom seems better." He nodded in the direction of his mother-in-law and Izzie. "But it was him I came for. Haven't seen my boy in a while."

Grant knew all too well what that felt like. "He was pretty miserable when I saw him earlier. He's upstairs with Bernie."

Hugh nodded gratefully and quietly left the room just as Hunter walked back inside. The sight of Hunter made Grant's breathing speed up, but instead of Hunter joining him on the couch, he went to his mother's side.

"You okay, Mom?"

"Well, Hunter," she sighed. "What could possibly be wrong? You disappear without as much as a word, only to return five days later without any explanation."

"It's not like I've had much chance to explain, Mother," Hunter answered quietly, but his tone betrayed his annoyance at her accusations.

"Then I find out that you knocked up that little whore—"

"Mother!" Hunter and Izzie interrupted her at the same time, both raising their voices.

"If I'd used those words, you'd make me wash out my mouth with soap," Hunter continued, not without a certain amusement in his voice.

"Well, she's not exactly known around town for her chastity, despite the fact she teaches young children and dresses like a nun most of the time. I was told that's not how she dresses at the bar."

"Mother, you don't like it when people gossip. Now you're doing it yourself," Izzie said with a smile.

"I just need to get used to her becoming a part of this family, that's all."

"She won't become a part of this family, Mom," Hunter said as he sat down on the couch next to Grant. He didn't look at his lover, though.

Grant swallowed away his nerves. Was this the moment he was going to be outed? Was this the moment they'd talked about in the car on the way over here?

"But if she's carrying your baby, you need to take responsibility."

"And I will," Hunter said with a determination that made Grant feel proud. "If that baby is mine—and I'm not entirely sure about that yet—then I'll make sure they'll be well provided for. I won't relinquish my fatherly duties, but I won't marry Miranda."

"Why ever not?"

Hunter took a deep breath in. "I don't love her and I won't live a lie, Mother."

"But she's the mother of your child, and you're not denying you have a relationship with her."

Hunter leaned forward, elbows resting on his knees, and Grant had a hard time not reaching out to touch him and offer his support. Even if he discarded the presence of Hunter's mother, he knew Hunter well enough to realize that, although Hunter probably craved his support, it wouldn't be very welcome right now.

"I *had* a relationship with her. A very casual one."

"I'm an adult, Hunter. You can admit it was all about the sex," Beth stated matter-of-factly, making Izzie stare at Grant with wide eyes.

"Yes, it was, Mother," Hunter agreed. "And since it ended some time ago, it also means I have no intention of picking it up again."

It didn't take a mind reader to understand that Hunter's mother was not happy with the situation. "I may not like the girl, but that doesn't mean I should let you simply turn your back on her, Hunter. If that makes me old-fashioned, then so be it. I think you young people don't take sex seriously enough. You simply…." She gestured with her hands as if she couldn't possibly vocalize her feelings on the matter.

"I'm not turning my back on her, Mother. *If* this is my child, and it remains a big *if*, I will support her, but I won't let you do to me what you did to Lisa and Hugh. Lisa was smitten with Hugh, and he made the mistake of sleeping with her once and getting her pregnant. He never loved her, not like she deserves to be loved, and you know it. They were both miserable, and so was Danny."

Izzie sat up a bit straighter at the mention of Hugh's name, and she smiled shyly at Grant as Hunter continued.

"I'm sure Hugh would have accepted his responsibility even if they hadn't gotten married, because that's just the kind of guy he is, and I would have been happy to employ him so he could be close to his son. It would have made a lot more sense to allow Lisa to live the life she wanted and not just the life you made her live."

"She wanted to marry Hugh!"

"But did you ever stop to ask Hugh?"

This time his mother didn't say anything. She seemed to be mulling over all the possibilities, and the tension was almost unbearable.

Grant realized the feeling was probably different for him than for everyone else in the room, except maybe Hunter. Grant had no idea whether Hunter still intended to tell his mother he was gay, but Grant's heart hadn't calmed down since they'd walked into the house, and that seemed like hours ago. Fatigue was claiming him, not to mention hunger and a dire need for a strong painkiller. He couldn't wait for the torture to end.

"Are you saying I'm not considering your feelings in the matter?" she asked calmly.

"Yes, that is what I'm saying."

As Grant heard Hunter answer as softly as his mother had asked the question, it dawned on him where Hunter got his strength. He'd never noticed how much they were alike, and it somehow calmed him down.

"I still think you're dodging your responsibility."

Hunter exhaled loudly. "I'm doing anything but," he replied. "But my responsibility lies with the person I love, not with Miranda."

Grant felt his heart beat in his throat. This was the moment of truth.

"There's someone else in your life?" She seemed puzzled and, Grant felt, utterly clueless about her own son.

"Yes, Mother, there is. And what I feel for him, I haven't felt for anyone else in my life."

*BANG.*

Hunter's mother didn't immediately respond, but Grant didn't need to look more intensely at Izzie to notice the shift of the gender-neutral conversation about love to something undeniable.

"Him?" Hunter's mother eventually said. Her voice was calm, and she said the word as if she were tasting it.

Without looking, Hunter reached out for Grant's hand, and Grant took it without hesitation. "Yes, Mother, him. Grant."

For the first time in what felt like hours, Hunter looked at Grant. Right then, Grant knew that no matter what, no matter how horrible Hunter's mother's reaction was, he knew without a doubt that Hunter loved him. Of all the looks Hunter had given him over the last weeks, Grant hoped he would never forget this one.

"I drove after him on Friday without him knowing it, because I didn't want to let him go. This weekend, we finally found the time to talk things out."

"You're throwing this whole family into turmoil because of something you decided over the weekend?"

"No, Mother. This wasn't something I decided. It's something I've known all my life. I've just never allowed myself to accept it. Grant and I have been trying to figure things out for a number of weeks now, but there were too many questions still unanswered. This weekend, we answered them all."

All of a sudden, Hunter's mother got up from her chair. "I don't know about you, but I'm hungry. It's way past dinner time, and there's a very sad boy upstairs who's still growing and needs a good meal."

With that she left them behind in the living room, all of them stunned into silence.

# —32—

"WHAT just happened?" Izzie was the first to speak as she looked between her brother and his lover.

"At least she didn't throw me out," Grant said with a chuckle that immediately made him reach for his sides.

"Oh, she'd never do that," Hunter replied. "Above all, she's the perfect hostess. She doesn't know you well enough to throw you out yet. I, on the other hand, am glad I still have a roof over my head."

"Your redeeming feature is that you run this ranch, Hunter," Izzie stated matter-of-factly.

"Maybe it was just a little too much for her?" Grant offered. "I mean, how many days do you get told you're going to be a grandmother not once but twice, and that your only son is gay and that your oldest daughter is running off with her brother-in-law, leaving her son behind, and your middle daughter is in love with her sister's husband?"

The more Grant talked, the more Hunter started laughing, and Izzie followed close behind. Hunter couldn't stop himself. The absurdity of the whole situation made it impossible for him to take it seriously. "I told you, Izzie, if they were to write this into those soap operas Mom loves so much, she'd tell you it was unbelievable."

Izzie was doubled over laughing, but she managed to get up and sit down next to Hunter, wrapping her arm around his broad shoulders. "I'm glad it's all out in the open, though. It was hard to live with all those secrets."

Hunter put his hand on her stomach. "My little sister's pregnant. I can't believe it."

"Guess our kids can grow up together," Izzie added, now calmer.

"That'll depend on Miranda, sis. I'm not marrying her, so she may take her revenge, especially after she finds out about Grant." Hunter gave Grant a loving look to convey he was in no way inclined to change his mind.

"That's right. She doesn't know about you yet!"

Hunter saw Izzie's mind working and wanted to curb her enthusiasm. "And *I'm* telling her myself. I told her I'd call her, and I'll meet her somewhere private to tell her." Izzie smiled. "If you want to get chummy with her afterwards and talk babies, that's fine with me, but not before I talk to her." Hunter put his arm around Izzie's slender shoulders and squeezed, then noticed how beat Grant looked. He put his other hand on Grant's knee and squeezed that too. "But first I'm going to put this one to bed, so he can rest."

Grant gave him a grateful smile.

"I'll bring up some food later," Izzie suggested. She got up from the couch and sighed. "Guess I'll need to help Mom in the kitchen, now Lisa's gone." Izzie pouted demonstratively to show she didn't like that idea.

"I'll be down in a minute," Hunter said after getting up from the couch. He reached out to help Grant rise and led him to the hallway.

"Think you can make it up the stairs?" Hunter asked softly.

Grant nodded and slowly inched up one step at a time. By the time he made it to the second floor, he was about ready to drop onto a bed and never get up again. Hunter directed him to a room near the end of the hall. When they entered, they saw the bed was unmade and clothes covered every surface.

"Sorry about the mess." Hunter started gathering his things and putting them all on one chair. Then he pulled on the sheets to straighten them, but Grant stopped him by sitting down on the bed and grabbing Hunter's wrist.

"Easy, Cowboy. I'm too tired to care and if I wasn't... well, I've never been in your room before."

Hunter gave him a shy smile. "If I'd known...." He shrugged.

"So you're a slob. I can live with that. You might get annoyed with me tidying up all the time, though. I'm used to living out of my duffel bag in a cramped space, so it pays to keep everything organized."

Hunter stopped fussing and just looked at Grant. Had Grant just made plans for their future together? Hunter didn't want to jinx it by pointing it out to Grant, so he simply sat down next to him, their shoulders rubbing together.

"Do you need help? I can get you comfortable like I did last night."

Grant nodded. Hunter could tell he was too tired to put up a fight, even though he knew Grant was the independent type.

"Let me get you a T-shirt and some boxers to sleep in." Hunter got up and walked to his closet, which was almost in worse disarray than his room. He picked out a T-shirt and smelled it.

"It's clean," he added, hoping it would reassure Grant.

Grant smiled and watched Hunter as he moved in front of him. Hunter helped him pull his fleece jacket over his head and couldn't resist gently running his hand over Grant's bruised ribs. The skin was black and blue, and his face must have shown his compassion, because Grant lowered his hands and tried to cover them.

"It hurts, doesn't it? Let me get you your painkillers."

"Yeah," Grant replied curtly. "Listen, I'll be fine here. Why don't you go talk to your mom, hey?"

Hunter handed him the pills and a glass of water. "Just let me make sure you're comfortable. Then I'll go downstairs and get us something to eat."

Grant shook his head. "Talk to her, Hunter. You need to work this out with her."

Hunter nodded silently as he helped Grant into the T-shirt and out of his boots and jeans.

"And take a shower," Grant added teasingly. "You smell like you've been on the road for five days. She'll think you're doing it for me."

"Why would she—?" Hunter stopped when he realized Grant was teasing him. "Fine," Hunter conceded, secretly happy that they were secure enough to joke about something so intimate. He helped Grant to lie down and arranged the bedding so he was comfortable, even getting another pillow from the guestroom, before heading for the shower.

When he returned less than ten minutes later, Grant was sound asleep, and even Hunter's gentle caress of Grant's short dark curls didn't wake him.

As he walked down the stairs in clean clothes, his hair still damp, Hunter felt his nerves rise again. He'd felt so calm in his room with Grant, but now he had to face his mother again. He was still puzzled about her strange reaction, or rather, her lack of reaction to all the news. As he walked into the living room, Izzie was setting the table. She didn't say anything, simply gestured in the direction of the kitchen.

Hunter nodded and opened the door. His mother was standing at the stove, straining gravy. She was wearing an apron over her clothes and didn't react to Hunter entering.

"Mom." Hunter's voice was soft as he came to stand next to her.

"Hunter," she answered, equally softly.

"Anything I can do to help?"

"Will you carve the meat?"

Hunter nodded. This was usually the job of the man around the house, and he was glad his mother still considered him to be that. It gave him some confidence that she wasn't going to throw him out after dinner.

"Not too much, darling," she said. "There's only seven of us."

Hunter counted them out in his head. Mom and Bernie, Izzie and Hugh and Danny, he and... Grant. He smiled when he realized she'd counted on Grant coming down for dinner.

"Grant's asleep, Mom, so there's only six of us for dinner."

She didn't immediately reply and pretended to be busy fishing the bay leaf out of the gravy. "Carve him a piece anyway. You can heat it up for him once he wakes up."

Hunter eyed his mother. The expression on her face was still as cold as ice, business as usual when emotions came into play.

"He was hurt pretty badly and he's still in a lot of pain." As soon as the words left his mouth, he felt conscious of the fact he was apologizing for Grant. Why did he feel the need to do that? They were all grownups.

"Did you put him in the guestroom?" she asked casually while she dished out the mashed potatoes.

"No, Mother. He's asleep in my room." Hunter couldn't stop the annoyance seeping into his voice.

"Then I suppose you'll be staying in the guestroom until he's well enough to go back to the crew house."

It wasn't even a question, Hunter realized.

"He's my"—he wanted to say "lover," but knowing his mother's opinion about premarital sex, that wouldn't be a safe word—"partner, Mom."

Her eyes shot up, but she turned away only moments later, busying herself with her cooking. Hunter didn't know what to say or how easily he'd crack under the pressure. He wasn't ready to stop fighting, though. He loved his mother, but he loved Grant too, and he was too old to choose her over the man he wanted to spend the rest of his life with.

With a grunt, she moved the heavy pot containing the roast from the oven to the table in the middle of the kitchen. Hunter rushed to help her but forgot how hot the copper pot was and burned his fingers. She let go of the pot and grabbed Hunter's hand, pulling him toward the sink to cool it off under the spray of the cold water. Hunter hissed at the sting.

"Izzie and Hugh aren't sharing a bed under my roof either, Hunter," she said eventually.

"She's carrying his baby, Mom. I think that's enough proof that you can't prevent them from sleeping together."

She turned away from him and shot him an intense stare. "What they do away from this house, I have no power over, but I will not have those two cavorting under this roof. What's Danny supposed to think?"

"There's no doubt in my mind that Danny is happy to have his father back. You know how close those two are."

She nodded curtly.

"I don't think Danny's giving it a lot of thought, Mom. We know he adores Izzie, and he worships the ground his father walks on, so I don't see what this has to do with Izzie and Hugh sharing a room." *Or with Grant and me*, Hunter wanted to add. He knew they were avoiding *that* conversation altogether.

"Hugh is still married to Lisa!"

Hunter was startled by the fact she'd raised her voice. "And they've been miserable since about the week after their wedding, and you know it. Now Lisa's found someone else, and so has Hugh. I know how long he's been in love with Izzie, so I'm glad they finally got together. Plus, we both know Izzie's only ever had eyes for Hugh since she was a little girl."

If her shouting hadn't surprised him, the tears that welled in her eyes after his statement made him even more uncomfortable. This was the woman who hadn't even cried at her husband's funeral. "What have I done to my children? Why can't they be happy?"

Hunter pulled her into his arms. "Izzie *is* happy, Mom. And so am I."

"But how can you…?"

Hunter leaned back to look at her face. "Grant makes me happy, Mom. Happier than any girl has ever made me. Or could make me."

The expression on her face was a strange mix of disgust and worry.

"I fell in love with him weeks ago, but I wasn't sure. This weekend, I saw the kind of man he is, and that cemented it for me. I couldn't stop loving him if I tried."

For a moment he thought she was mellowing, but then she shook her head. "I'd still prefer it if you slept in the guestroom, Hunter."

Hunter knew he wouldn't win this battle, so he didn't say anything. He simply pulled her into his arms again and squeezed her tight. Eventually she struggled free of Hunter's strong grip, wiped her face, and proceeded to finish dinner. She took two plates out of the cupboard and filled them with a bit of everything.

"Take these upstairs and eat with Grant. And when you're up there, tell Bernie and Danny to come out of hiding. I'm sure Izzie knows where Hugh is."

Hunter nodded. "Hugh's upstairs with Danny. I'll ask all of them to come downstairs."

She nodded, straightening her back and raising her head. The pride was back.

"I'll check on you in the guestroom."

Hunter smiled as he picked up the plates. "Oh no, you won't! I'm not sixteen anymore, Mom. I'm a grown man."

He didn't wait for her answer and walked out, feeling the tension leave him as soon as the door shut behind his back. He walked straight into Izzie, who was smooching with Hugh between the table and the cupboard. Danny was on the couch, enthralled by a game he was playing on his Nintendo.

"Heard you were banished to the guestroom too?" Hunter told Hugh.

Hugh turned around, smiling shyly. "You too?"

"Yup," Hunter answered. "Better be careful, you two. She's on the warpath, and deadly afraid you'll shock Danny."

Izzie looked over at Danny and shrugged. "I'm sure he'll live." She looked at the plates Hunter was holding, grabbed two sets of cutlery, and stuck them underneath Hunter's arm. "Better go feed your man."

Hunter almost blushed. He wasn't used to being accepted yet, and Hugh's wink only added to that feeling, so he just nodded and walked upstairs. After some careful balancing of everything he was holding, he quietly slipped into his room and put the plates and flatware on the bedside table. Grant was still asleep, and Hunter watched him for a few long moments. Part of him wanted to quietly sit there and take in Grant's gorgeous shoulders and veined arms, which never ceased to turn him on. Then again, his mother was a supreme cook, and letting the food get cold would be a mortal sin, especially because he was dead hungry and he knew Grant was as well.

"Hey, Stud Muffin," he whispered as he ran his hands over Grant's hair.

"That my nickname now, Cowboy?" Grant asked without opening his eyes.

"It fits," Hunter chuckled. "I brought food."

"Mmm," Grant moaned appreciatively, taking a carefully measured breath before attempting to raise his torso off the bed. Hunter was quick to offer help, but Grant swatted him away.

"Sorry, didn't mean to…." Grant groaned. "It's just easier if I do it myself."

Hunter was too worried to take it badly. "Maybe I should call the doctor to come and take a look at you again?"

"Maybe you should call the vet and have me put down."

Hunter gave him a dismissing look.

"You'd do it for you favorite dog or your horse."

"If my horse kicked my dog and it couldn't walk, I'd take care of it until it healed," Hunter said calmly, although his patience was running thin. He loved Grant, but there was a lot of self-pity in what Grant was saying, and it was so far removed from the man he thought Grant was that he felt he needed to counteract it. "Now let's eat, and after that, you can take more medication and I'll help you fall asleep again." He carefully pulled the bedside table in front of Grant and moved the chair so he could sit opposite it.

"Sorry," Grant apologized. "I just hate feeling like an invalid."

"Let's look at it this way. Now I know what a grumpy bastard you can be when you don't feel well. I suppose it gives me a good indication of what you'll be like when you're old." Hunter cut his meat, and although he didn't look directly at Grant's face, he saw how Grant was holding his still-splinted arm in front of him. "Need me to cut that for you?"

"I'm not old yet," Grant replied grouchily.

"No, but you're in pain and more than a little incapacitated. I'm just offering. If you want to make it hard on yourself, be my guest."

Grant sighed and put down his fork, sliding his plate a little closer to Hunter. Hunter wasn't expecting Grant to actually ask him, but then he figured he'd already pushed him enough for one night, so he silently carved up some of the roast beef, using his own utensils. Although he wanted to tease Grant about his macho attitude, he figured he'd get more chances to do it once Grant was all healed up. And if he was honest with himself, he knew it would be more fun then, too, since it would be an equal fight.

During their meal Grant didn't say much, and Hunter tried to keep the conversation light, telling Grant about the history between Izzie and Hugh and how Izzie had never expected to actually be allowed to come near the man she'd been in love with for years.

Hunter was famished, and he finished his plate way before Grant was even halfway done.

"It's amazing food, it really is," Grant said by way of apology. "If you can put it in the fridge, it will keep for tomorrow. If your mother is anything like mine was, she'll hate seeing food go to waste."

Hunter squeezed Grant's hand. "I'll clean up, and then I'll come tuck you in for the night."

When Hunter returned from bringing the plates to the kitchen, Grant was still sitting on the side of the bed, as if he hadn't moved at all. Hunter put the side table and his chair back where they belonged and crouched in front of his lover.

"Either I take you into the bathroom for a nice hot bath, or I help you get comfortable on the bed so you can sleep. Tell me what you need."

"Would you think any less of me if I passed up the bath?" Grant asked tentatively.

Hunter squeezed Grant's knee. "I like sweaty men."

Grant threw Hunter a disgusted look.

"I'll live."

"Does that mean you're staying here tonight?"

"I'm not letting my mother dictate whether or not I sleep with my lover. Besides, you might need me during the night."

Like the night before, it took them a while to settle, but eventually they managed to find a comfortable configuration pretty much like in the motel room, with Hunter behind Grant, spooning him.

"Your mom really didn't want you to sleep in here tonight?"

"Nope," Hunter answered with a shrug. "She's doesn't want Hugh to sleep with Izzie either. But it would be a safe bet to say Hugh isn't sleeping in the guestroom."

"Izzie's carrying his baby, for crying out loud!" Grant said, a fair bit louder than he should have.

Hunter shushed him by kissing his neck. "Just because we're going against her wishes, we don't have to announce it to the entire county."

"Fuck, you turn me on when you do that to me," Grant said, a whole lot more quietly.

"What?" Hunter asked, knowing full well what Grant meant.

"Mumble against my neck. Kiss me there, even if we can't do a damn thing about it."

"That's what you think," Hunter said teasingly, reaching for Grant's fast-filling cock and grinding his own against Grant's ass. In a matter of seconds, he had Grant writhing under his hands, and he had to keep reminding him to keep quiet. Hunter was relentless, though, knowing that, for relaxation purposes, the next best thing to a hot bath was a roaring orgasm.

Mid-grunt, Grant buried his face into his pillow as he came hard into Hunter's hand. Hunter's orgasm was a quieter one, but no less satisfying as Grant reached behind to aid him. They fell asleep in sated bliss after Hunter's quick dash to the bathroom to clean them up.

## —33—

TO GRANT'S surprise, the pain from the broken ribs was something he got used to. He knew he needed to take measured breaths and not laugh, and after a while, as long as he stuck to that, he was fine. The bruised pelvis was another thing entirely. He could move around without too much trouble, and then, suddenly, something would shoot through his hip and he wouldn't be able to move at all. Although Hunter was careful never to treat him as if he was helpless, he was a bit of a mother hen, and Grant was starting to feel the walls crowding him.

Every morning, Hunter would get up early to get a few hours' work done in the stables before coming back to the house to help Grant take a shower and get dressed. Most of the time, Grant would take his painkillers and fall right back asleep. But on Saturday, less than a week after they came back to the ranch, Hunter had made an appointment to go talk to Miranda, so Grant had to fend for himself. He was nervous about what the result of that conversation was going to be, but he'd resolved himself to being a bystander and not interfering. That made him feel even more helpless than he had all week and gave him an urgent need to find a way to occupy his mind.

Part of why Grant liked working on a ranch was that he got to spend time outdoors, but he'd been cooped up inside for almost two weeks, if you didn't count the drive from the hospital to Hunter's house. He simply had to go downstairs and try to make his way to the porch so he could smell some fresh air.

By the time he'd showered and struggled into his clothes, he needed to rest on the bed for a few minutes, but then he decided to tackle the stairs. He'd cut down on his painkillers so he'd sleep less, but that meant he was far from pain-free. After walking down the stairs, he realized he'd never make it to the porch in one go, so he slipped into the kitchen and onto one of the chairs there before registering that Hunter's mother was also there, preparing dinner.

"Ma'am," he greeted her after she'd given him an intense look.

"Grant," she replied, acknowledging his presence in a completely neutral voice while she continued cleaning leeks.

Grant didn't know what to say. He'd only ever met her with lots of other people present, and usually Hunter functioned as a buffer, but now he had no one to rely on. She didn't seem to be the most talkative person, either. Grant started wondering why Izzie and Bernie never seemed to run out of things to say and concluded they must take after their father.

"Is there anything I can help you with?" was the best Grant could come up with.

She looked up and scrutinized him, as if she wanted to assure herself he wasn't joking with her. "You're a guest in this house," she simply stated and continued to work.

"Yes, ma'am," Grant agreed in a quiet voice. He wanted to speak up and tell her that it was her attitude that made him feel like an unwanted stranger, but the last thing he wanted was to antagonize her even more. Although his mother had died before he was an adult, he did remember her teaching him about politeness and respect for elders. Hunter's mother was right, though. In her eyes he was a guest, and if that meant she was polite around him, then all he could be was thankful, because he had the distinct impression that it was her own good upbringing that prevented her from throwing him out on his ass.

Since he had no intention of stealing Hunter from the ranch, and he didn't need to ask anyone to know that Hunter's mother would live here until she died if she had any say in it, that meant that if Grant wanted to spend his life with Hunter—and he had every intention of it—he had to find a way to get into her good books. But, damn it, being forward about his affections was a hard thing to do. Grant was certain she'd never approve of her son's choice of mate, but he simply had to find a way to get her to at least tolerate him around the ranch.

"Your bruises seem to be clearing up, but Hunter tells me you're still in a lot of pain."

Grant looked up at her. She was standing at the same table he was sitting at, cutting the leeks with a dangerous-looking knife.

"I'm slowly getting there. The doctor said it would take time, but I suppose it's getting better. I hope I can get back to work soon, because all this lazing around is getting on my nerves."

That seemed to strike a chord with her. Maybe Grant was imagining things, but he thought he saw the merest glimmer of a smile playing around her lips. "Izzie says you're one of the best wranglers we've ever employed."

Grant shrugged. "I like working with horses. I love being outdoors. And I'm pretty good with wood too."

"Good," she said, turning around to grab a pot to put her vegetables in. "I hope you'll be joining us for dinner downstairs tonight?"

She didn't even turn around to ask him, so he allowed himself to smile, feeling like he'd won a small victory.

"Yes, ma'am, I'd like that. I was thinking of sitting out on the porch to rest there. Take in some fresh air."

Just as he was struggling to get up, she said, "Wear a warm coat. It's a bit chilly out. And take a mug of coffee and some sandwiches in case you get hungry."

Grant couldn't help feeling that was her way of mothering. Hunter had told him he never got a lot of physical affection from his mother, but that he always knew she loved him, in her own way. Maybe that love had spread just a little bit toward him.

About two hours later, with half his food still on his plate but his coffee long consumed, Grant watched Hunter's truck turn into the driveway toward the house. He was huddled warmly into a thick winter coat, but his feet were freezing. His eyes followed Hunter as he parked the truck by the side of the house and walked toward it. There were deep worry lines in Hunter's forehead and around his eyes, and Grant felt they didn't spell much good.

As soon as Hunter spotted Grant sitting there, his eyes lit up. "Hey, Stud Muffin."

"Sssh," Grant said, shaking his head. "Your mother is just inside."

"I know," Hunter said, sitting down next to Grant on the long bench that stood against the outside wall. He put his arm around Grant's shoulders and nuzzled his ear, taking in his scent. "But I'm so glad to be back home and to be close to you again."

"That bad, hey?" Grant said, pulling back a bit so he could see the expression on Hunter's face.

Hunter shrugged without letting go of Grant.

Grant didn't know if he should push Hunter to talk. They weren't that good with sharing, especially the emotional stuff, but he felt this was important, so he wanted to somehow offer his support. He brushed his nose over Hunter's eyebrows and kissed his forehead. "Want to talk about it?"

Hunter shrugged again. "She got really mad at me. Told me I was a pervert."

"Well, she's right, of course," Grant deadpanned.

Hunter looked up with a start but then seemed to recover. "About getting mad at me or about me being a pervert?"

"Both," Grant replied, trying to keep a straight face.

Hunter thumped him with his shoulder.

"Aaaah," Grant complained. "I'm an injured man, dammit."

"Sorry."

"So what else did she scream at you?" Grant asked tentatively.

"She assured me it was my baby. That she hadn't been with anyone else. She actually figured I would marry her, but I stuck to my guns."

"You think she intentionally got pregnant?"

"Who knows?" Hunter sighed.

"I can't blame her for being mad, Cowboy. It's not like she saw this one coming."

Hunter chuckled. "Hell, I didn't even see this one coming."

"Any regrets?"

"Not a single one. Should have done this ages ago."

The determination in Hunter's voice gave solace to Grant. He wished he were as sure of his case as Hunter was, though. Not that he didn't believe Hunter loved him, and he knew for certain he loved his Cowboy right back, but this was just such a leap for him that it took some time to adjust to it. He was still mulling it over when he noticed Hunter's hand disappearing underneath the hem of the sheepskin coat he was wearing. Grant could feel the warmth of Hunter's hand through the sweater he had on underneath, and he slowly turned his head in Hunter's direction.

"What are you doing?" Grant whispered.

"My hand's cold."

"No it isn't. I can feel just how warm it is," Grant answered with a slight smile.

"You're wearing my coat," Hunter said cheekily.

"Don't change the subject. We're sitting on the porch of your house, in full view of half the world, and you're feeling me up?"

Hunter gave him a mock-serious stare. "If I were trying to feel you up, I'd be way off course."

"That depends on where you're heading," Grant replied, jumping slightly when Hunter's hand found a nipple.

"You're not wearing a lot of clothes under my coat."

Grant cocked his head. "I took my shower alone, and it takes a lot out of me to put clothes on by myself."

"Pain getting any better?"

"Sometimes," Grant said. "You're distracting me quite well from it right now." Their faces were very close together, but they weren't really kissing. Grant had the feeling it wouldn't take much, though. Maybe what was stopping Hunter was the same thing holding Grant back: the fact his mother and sisters were inside and any of the ranch hands or wranglers looking over at the house would see them sitting there, smooching.

Suddenly the door to the house opened and Hunter pulled away slightly. To Grant's surprise, he didn't remove his hand from inside Grant's coat.

"Hunter? I thought I heard your truck pull up," Hunter's mother said. "How did your talk with Miranda go?"

"I was just telling Grant about it," Hunter answered as if they were just having a casual conversation. "I made it clear to her I would support her in any decision she made, but that I wouldn't marry her. Ever."

His mother nodded with a serious look on her face. "No matter what your plans are, Hunter, you need to take up your responsibility."

"And I will."

She left the two without once looking at Grant.

Grant put his hand over Hunter's, the coat separating them. "I don't think she was comfortable with our closeness, Cowboy."

"She wasn't or you weren't?" Hunter asked, not hiding his annoyance as he pulled his hand back and sat up, creating distance between him and Grant.

"I don't mind having you close, but we do share this house with your mother, and rubbing her the wrong way isn't the best way to make that more comfortable." Grant sat up slowly and put his hand on Hunter's back.

"Then let's move out. Let's move to your room at the crew house. I want to have sex with you without thinking she might hear me."

Grant raised his eyebrows. "We have an audience at the crew house as well. The walls are even thinner there."

Hunter sighed loudly. "Remember when I told you about what I wanted to do with that patch of land?" He pointed at the large empty space between the main house and the stables.

Grant nodded.

"Let's build that house."

Grant chuckled and grabbed for his ribs. "That will take at least a year, Hunter. What do we do in the meantime?"

Hunter sat back and leaned against Grant. "I thought telling everyone would make it easier, would mean we could stop hiding and sneaking around."

"And here I thought you liked sneaking around."

Hunter smiled. "It wears off quickly. Fuck, Grant, you're excitement enough for me."

"I know, Cowboy. Same here." How could he tell Hunter that, for the first time in his life, he looked forward to just being with someone? How could he explain that he lusted after Hunter but went all fuzzy warm inside from just a casual touch, or from the way Hunter looked at him across a room, and how could he do it without sounding like a woman?

"What 'no'?" Hunter asked.

"Did I say no?"

"You were shaking your head."

Grant shrugged. "Thinking too much. So tell me what Miranda said that bothered you so much."

"Something about her always knowing I was gay because I didn't like her tits."

"Hey, you like my tits," Grant joked.

"I like your nipples, because you like it when I lick them." Hunter wasn't shy to admit it.

"Guess who taught me that?"

Hunter pushed himself even closer to Grant, and Grant nuzzled Hunter's temple. "She's just yanking your chain, Cowboy. If I recall, she's not exactly big-busted herself."

"She is now. She grew real knockers," Hunter said, his mood clearly lifting.

"Are you turning straight again?" Grant asked, not really too worried.

"Nah," Hunter assured him. "But you've been with women, right?"

"Yes," Grant replied, none too enthusiastically.

"Have there been other women after Christy?"

Grant smiled. When had Hunter become so preoccupied with which women Grant had slept with? "Yes," he drawled.

"I'm not being nosy or anything, I'd just like to know."

"Calley, actually," Grant replied softly.

Hunter left Grant's embrace and turned to look him in the eye. "Do I know a Calley? Hang on. Not Calley who's married to our vet and who runs the grocery shop?"

"The very same."

"You sly fox. A married woman?"

Grant shrugged. "Long story."

"Your stories always are," Hunter laughed, settling his back against Grant before easing away as he realized it might hurt him.

Grant didn't flinch. "Good side."

Hunter snuggled closer again, signaling he understood what Grant had meant with that short statement. "Come on. Spill," Hunter said calmly without looking at Grant.

Grant took a slightly deeper breath. It didn't hurt as much as it did two weeks ago. "She was lonely and miserable and Bill hadn't touched her in ages, because they'd been through all these fertility treatments and she told me that fucking on demand had turned Bill off. He was practically living in his car. Didn't come home most nights, with the excuse that it was birthing season and he needed to work nonstop. I was avoiding Gable, although I lived there at the time, and had complained to her about driving back and forth to see Christy. In the course of everything, I'd explained to her what I'd done for Christy, and she figured I could do the same for her. She thought I could get her pregnant and then she'd tell Bill a miracle had happened and she'd conceived, carefully omitting that it wasn't exactly Bill's child. We went into the city a few times for an insemination, but they didn't take, and she couldn't explain the cost of it to Bill, so we stopped after two tries."

"Is that when you ended up sleeping with her?" Hunter looked up at Grant.

"One Christmas I was at her house with all the gifts for my kids. I'd gotten a message from Christy that it wasn't safe for me to drive up because Frank had unexpectedly gotten a few days off, so I was pretty miserable. Calley was more than a little tipsy because Bill had decided to officially move out of their house, and one thing led to another. I don't know who seduced who. I'd had a few glasses of wine with her, so I guess I'm just as much to blame. I also probably thought that if I could help her, it would make me feel good about myself."

Hunter chuckled, but didn't laugh. "But it didn't take?"

"It did, actually," Grant admitted. "Took more than a few tries. In fact, it took me almost a year to get her pregnant. She lost the baby when she was about five months along. Don't know if Bill knew it was mine, because I'd moved out of Gable's house by then."

Hunter sat up and smiled at him. "You *are* a stud."

Grant chuckled. "'S why I feel right at home on a stud farm."

Hunter settled against him again. "I just want to live with you, share a bedroom like any other couple would. Is that too much to ask?"

"We're sharing a bedroom now," Grant stated, although it was obvious. "I like falling asleep close to you and still feeling you when I wake up in the morning." There. He'd said it. That was as close as he could get to a declaration of love for now. Maybe one day he'd feel confident enough to actually say the words.

"I want that for the rest of our lives, Grant," Hunter said, so quietly that for a moment Grant wondered if he'd imagined it.

# —34—

GRANT'S bruises had faded, and he'd started doing some work around the ranch again. He still hadn't managed to get on a horse again, and Hunter knew why that was. He saw Grant flinch sometimes. It always happened when he wasn't paying attention and was just moving around without a care in the world, and suddenly he'd freeze and limp to a fence or a tree stump to lean against or sit on.

"We should take that hip of yours to a doctor, Grant," Hunter said one morning after they'd driven to the far side of the property, near Gable's ranch, to fix a broken strip of wire.

"Sure," Grant answered. "Why don't you take it tomorrow while I oil the saddles?"

It took Hunter a few moments to realize Grant was taking him literally, so his laugh came a little late. "I meant—"

"I know, Cowboy," Grant brushed away his concern. "It's getting better. Doesn't happen nearly as often as it used to." To stress the point, he got up and walked a few steps toward Hunter. "See?"

Hunter eyed him suspiciously, and Grant closed the gap between them with amazing speed, just to wipe that look off Hunter's face. As soon as Hunter smiled again, Grant grabbed the back of Hunter's head to kiss him. He lingered for just a moment before turning around and picking up the wire he'd dropped as if nothing had happened.

His pants uncomfortably tight all of a sudden, Hunter exhaled loudly. Grant showing him his jeans-clad ass didn't help calm down his arousal. He watched Grant rise to his full height again and turn around. It felt like time was moving in slow-motion; he didn't even notice himself moving closer until he felt Grant's muscled chest against his own, his hand on the back of Grant's neck and his mouth softly caressing his man's. He and Grant had kissed a lot in these past few weeks. In fact, with a few exceptions, kissing was all they did.

"Need you," Hunter murmured against Grant's lips. "Need your hands on me. Need you inside of me."

Grant chuckled. "You're gonna be loud. We have no place to go. Except maybe the truck."

"We're closer to Gable's barn than anyplace else," Hunter suggested, only taking his lips off Grant's long enough to finish his sentence. Grant didn't get a chance to respond until Hunter pulled away, panting.

"The hayloft?" Grant said, sounding amused.

"If you think you can make it up there? It's a bit of a rickety ladder to climb up."

Grant ground against him, and Hunter thought that if they didn't stop soon, he'd come in his jeans.

Grant moaned against his mouth. "For you, I'll do anything," he murmured.

They broke apart reluctantly to head for the truck. Hunter drove through the gate of the fence they'd fixed weeks earlier and parked at the back of the barn, where trees obscured the view of the truck. They didn't speak. They had a hard time keeping their eyes off each other and an even harder time keeping their hands to themselves. They had to move stealthily, though, afraid they might get caught.

"We can always say we came to look at the pregnant mares," Grant said, as if he was reading Hunter's mind. "You know, to check on your investment."

"They won't catch us," Hunter replied. He pointed at the horses' troughs. "They've been fed and they have water."

"And Bridget isn't much of a guard dog, luckily."

Hunter nodded, then moved toward Grant to kiss him quickly. He tangled his hand into Grant's hair. "Your hair's growing long."

"I thought you liked it?" Grant said, self-consciously smiling.

Hunter caressed it. "I do. Gives me sordid ideas."

"Oh?" Grant asked.

"Walk upstairs and I'll show you." Hunter waited to make sure Grant could manage the ladder, but he did fine. The hayloft pretty much looked like they'd left it last time. In fact, it looked like nobody had been up here since then. Hunter rushed to help Grant shake out the blanket they'd left in disarray the last time. They stretched it out over the hay before Grant reached into his jeans pocket.

"Damn."

"What's wrong?"

"I've been walking around with condoms and lube in my pocket for weeks." Grant chuckled. "I put on a fresh pair of jeans this morning and forgot to transfer them."

"We'll manage," Hunter said, zeroing in on Grant and aligning his body with Grant's. "I don't care. I want you anyway."

Grant hooked his fingers into the loops of Hunter's belt and forcibly pulled him even closer.

"Your arm is all healed too?" Hunter asked.

"You know exactly what parts of me still hurt, Cowboy. We've been sharing a bed for weeks. And being very good boys, all for Mommy's sake."

"At least she's not staring at us as if we have two heads anymore."

Grant chuckled. "I think she's actually starting to like me."

Hunter ground his excited groin against Grant's. "She adores you. In her own way. Now can we stop talking about my mother?"

"Sure thing, Cowboy," Grant said, pulling Hunter down with him.

Although Hunter was so hungry for Grant he thought he would burst, Grant took it slow, caressing Hunter's lean back and kneading his ass cheeks but making no attempt to get Hunter out of his clothes. They'd gone much further than this at home, in Hunter's bed. More often than not they brought each other off at night before falling asleep in each other's arms, and sometimes, if Grant woke up at the time Hunter got out of bed to start his chores, he'd drag Hunter back into bed for more intense kissing, but everything had to happen very quietly. They knew they were sleeping together against the wishes of Hunter's mother and had no intention of helping her find an excuse to split them up. Although Hunter had developed a taste for feeling Grant's hand over his mouth, stifling his moans of ecstasy, he knew he could pull out all the stops now. Their only audience tonight would be a barn full of horses. The nearest human beings were two guys just as much into each other as he and Grant were. And one of them was Grant's ex-lover.

Hunter pulled back, breaking their intense kiss.

"What's wrong?"

Hunter shook his head. "Did you ever do it here with—"

Grant took Hunter's jaw in his hand and forced him to look at him. "Don't be like this. I've told you before that what Gable and I had was nothing like what you and I have."

Hunter nodded. Grant had told him before. Grant's relationship with Gable had been purely sexual. What they shared was more, so much more. Hunter knew that. It was just that sometimes, he felt he didn't deserve Grant.

"Come here, Cowboy. Do that thing you do to me."

"That thing… I do to you?" Hunter asked, astounded.

Grant pulled Hunter's shirt out of his jeans and inserted his hand, running his fingers lightly over Hunter's almost-washboard stomach until Hunter felt his muscles contract involuntarily. Even before Grant let his hand slip underneath his belted jeans, Hunter was uncomfortably hard. Grant's kisses had made his blood run south, but the anticipation of what was going to happen, together with the memory of how he'd lost his virginity here, canceled out the knowledge that they had no supplies today, so there would be no repeat of what they'd done that night.

"I'm sorry," Hunter said softly.

"For what?" Grant asked, stopping his teasing movements.

"I could have thought about bringing supplies. Damn, I could have snuck some in here and hid them, since this is our secret place."

Grant smiled, and then something seemed to dawn on him. He got up and Hunter followed him with his eyes. Grant walked to the back of the loft, where the roof sloped down to the ground. There was a bundle of what looked like old horse blankets, and Grant, quite triumphantly, unearthed a few things from beneath them.

"Ta-da!" he exclaimed.

Hunter took the small bottle of lubricant from Grant with a smile, while Grant tried to read the small package he was holding in the dim light.

Grant's mood faltered. "Way past their expiration date, I'm afraid. We usually remember to bring our own, and these weren't exactly fresh when I put them there." He tossed the strip of condoms aside.

"This isn't much use either," Hunter said, shaking the bottle. "Besides being nearly empty, what little was in here dried out."

Grant chuckled as he sat down next to Hunter. "I'm not much help, am I?"

"We could just forget about the condoms. I trust you," Hunter said quietly.

Grant shook his head. "Yeah, but I don't trust myself. I know I haven't always been safe—picking up guys in bars after I've had a few drinks too many."

"Did you and Gable…?"

"No, we didn't use condoms. It was always a spur of the moment thing with him."

"But you and Calley must have…." Again Hunter didn't finish his sentence.

Grant thought it was funny and laughed. "I got tested for Calley, but I haven't exactly been a monk since then, Cowboy." He leaned over Hunter, making him lie down as he kissed him deeply. "I'll get tested again and then we can do it without the rubbers. Until then, we'll just have to be a little more creative. I'm not risking you for a five-minute romp in the hay."

Hunter looked up at Grant and how his longer dark curls framed his face. "I was sort of hoping for something longer than five minutes."

Grant grabbed Hunter's sides and tickled him, making Hunter double up and laugh. Within no time, Hunter was half on top of Grant and they were kissing again, grinding against each other.

"Still want to feel your skin," Hunter murmured as he tried to undress Grant further.

Grant helped him along by letting Hunter push his shirt over his shoulders and then shaking his hands to let the loose cuffs fall over them. While Hunter alternated worshiping his lover's body and kissing him passionately, Grant had wormed his way back into Hunter's pants and enveloped Hunter's erection until Hunter pushed him away.

"Want more," Hunter panted, the expression on Grant's face demanding an explanation for the brush-off. "I can get a hand job or a blow job every night, but I want more." He got up and pulled down his jeans and boxers in one go.

"Stop," Grant commanded as Hunter stood in front of him in just an opened plaid shirt. He was sitting on the blanket and pulled Hunter's hips closer so Hunter's swaying erection was right in Grant's line of sight. He didn't say anything else but took Hunter's cock in his mouth. Hunter moaned and couldn't prevent himself from bucking forward, but Grant took it easily, smiling teasingly around the intrusion. As they settled on a rhythm, Grant moved his right hand from Hunter's hip to his own groin, pulling his rock-hard cock from the confinement of his jeans.

"Shit, that looks good," Hunter groaned, watching the view that was obscured every time he thrust into Grant's mouth. "Want to—"

"No, you don't," Grant interrupted after pulling back. He returned his hand to Hunter's hip to prevent him from sitting down. "I have other plans for you."

Hunter swallowed as he watched Grant lick his fingers, coating them with ample saliva.

"Spread your legs a bit," Grant ordered in such a way that it didn't even cross Hunter's mind to disagree.

Grant was still smiling when he pushed his hand between Hunter's legs, leaving no doubt in Hunter's mind what his goal was. Hunter rolled his hips in an attempt to guide Grant's fingers, but Grant didn't need it. He slid his slick fingers behind Hunter's sac and pushed against the sensitive skin behind it. Hunter arched forward, and Grant came into contact with the circular guardian muscle, which opened like a flower.

"Somebody's hot and bothered and very ready for this, isn't he?" Grant teased.

"Fuck, it's been too long," Hunter panted, still undulating his hips in an attempt to get Grant to push his fingers inside. He didn't have to wait long. Both fingertips slipped in, and it burned, but Hunter couldn't get enough. When Grant took his cock in his mouth again, Hunter thought he was going to come right then, but he didn't want it to end. He threw back his head, hoping that blocking out the visual would help him hold on. Grant was pushing deeper inside him, though, and suddenly Hunter saw flashing lights behind his closed eyelids. Reflexively, he pulled back and was instantly sorry for the loss, but he knew it was the only thing that prevented him from losing his footing. Pulling his hips back, he leaned down to kiss Grant's enticing mouth, distracting him enough to be able to crouch down and sit on Grant's lap.

"I want more. Want you inside me," Hunter said softly after kissing Grant. "I'm serious," he added.

"I know. Lie down."

Hunter slid off Grant's thighs and reclined on the blanket, letting his shirt fall open. Grant pushed it off his shoulders but made no attempt to disrobe Hunter further. Instead, he admiringly caressed Hunter's chest, occasionally flicking a nipple or touching a bit of hairless skin as he moved down. He licked his fingers again before reinserting them, making Hunter rear up. He wanted more, wanted to be filled with Grant's magnificent cock, but he knew in what little coherent thought he had left that he wouldn't be able to persuade Grant. After licking Hunter's cock some more, Grant moved higher to kiss him, still pumping his fingers in and out of Hunter's body.

"Touch yourself," Grant said, his voice not entirely steady anymore.

"I want to touch you," Hunter replied.

"Later. Show me now how you touch yourself," Grant repeated.

Hunter did, although it was hard to focus. He was terribly close, so his movements weren't the most coordinated. He felt like he'd been close to coming since they started, but his orgasm hovered just out of reach. Grant's movements were deliberate and accurate, stroking Hunter's prostate over and over again. Hunter rubbed his own straining shaft. He wanted more, though, wanted to reciprocate, to touch Grant the way he was touching himself, but any attempt he made toward Grant was swatted away until he finally gave up.

"Fuck yourself," Grant urged. "Make yourself come. Shout out. Show me how much you want this."

Grant's words were enough for Hunter to reach the point of no return. A twist from his hand combined with Grant's fingers deep inside him, touching him in the special spot, were enough to send him over with more wailing than he'd ever dared to voice before. He repeatedly convulsed into his own hand, spraying white ribbons all over his chest and Grant's as Grant leaned over him to kiss his neck.

Hunter was panting hard and still twitching when he remembered that what he really wanted was to do to Grant what he'd done to him. He pushed him down on his back and kissed him passionately, leaving no doubt in Grant's mind that he was up for the task.

"My turn."

Grant chuckled. "I think you just had yours."

Hunter shook his head. "My turn to make you come so hard you see stars."

Grant relaxed under Hunter's touch, and although Hunter's powerful orgasm had made him feel more like a good cuddle than frantic lovemaking, he knew he owed Grant. He grabbed the base of Grant's shaft and enveloped his sac along with the rigid member, clearing the way to touch the sensitive flesh underneath. As Hunter leaned down, Grant spread his legs, and Hunter saw a chance to lick the area around Grant's entrance.

"Fucking hell!" Grant exclaimed, pulling his knees up further.

Hunter smelled the strong, masculine musk and felt his own cock stir again, despite his earlier release. He didn't know what he wanted in his mouth first. Should he rim Grant? Roll his balls around in his mouth? Blow him and suck the spunk out of him? He eventually decided to go for Grant's sac and fist his erection with his hand. When he nuzzled behind Grant's balls, Hunter could feel the tension in Grant's body and the feeble attempt Grant was making to relax, and knew it would be futile. His tongue was refused entrance as he tried to push it against Grant's guardian muscle, so he didn't insist. He crawled up Grant's body without letting go of his cock and hovered over Grant while leaning on his free arm. He nuzzled Grant's face, enticing him to open his eyes, and then kissed him.

"You're as tight as a virgin."

Grant smiled coyly. "I'm not always like that. You know, because you've fucked me."

"Once," Hunter stated superfluously but without reproach in his voice.

"That's one more time than most men I've slept with."

"I wasn't your first?"

Grant shook his head. "Years ago, when I was a lot younger, I had an older lover who didn't dream of bottoming, but other than that—"

"You've always been the alpha male, the boss in bed, the big macho man," Hunter interrupted with a chuckle.

"I'm not the boss when we have sex. You can never resist taking over."

Hunter kissed him almost violently. "And you love every minute of it!"

"I do," Grant replied, looking Hunter straight in the eye.

"So will you come for me, then?"

Grant threw back his head as Hunter upped the tempo of fisting Grant's cock; then he grabbed Hunter's face to continue kissing. His pushed his groin in the direction of Hunter's hand, so Hunter stopped his movements and just let Grant fuck his fist until Grant pulled away from the kiss, groaned loudly, and came all over Hunter's stomach and hand in repeated convulsions.

Hunter wiped his hand on his thigh before pulling Grant into his embrace.

"We need to find a place of our own," Hunter lamented. "I want to be able to cry your name when you make me come. I want to scream and shout and moan as loudly as I want and not hold back."

Grant just nodded as he caught his breath, their bodies as close and entangled as physically possible.

Their heart rates were still fairly high when they heard a voice downstairs.

"Wait here, girl."

"Flynn?" Hunter mouthed silently.

Grant nodded.

Hunter looked up at Grant's suddenly wide eyes when they heard a shotgun being cocked.

# —35—

GRANT had felt uncomfortable for weeks after getting caught in Gable's hayloft. He thought the unease had settled a little until they got an invitation for a dinner party at Calley and Bill's, where Gable and Flynn would be present.

He clearly remembered Flynn's stern face as first Hunter and then he had climbed down from the hayloft. Then Gable had arrived as well and given them quite an amused grin. There was no doubt in Grant's mind that Gable knew exactly what had transpired between him and Hunter. Remembering Gable's warped sense of humor, Grant could only imagine how much fun he'd have knowing he and Hunter were getting it on in his hayloft.

There were no more feelings between him and Gable, so why was being in the man's presence still creeping him out? Was he feeling that guilty? If he'd had to do it all again, he wouldn't change a thing. He'd still choose his children over his lover, although the choice had been a lot easier when he was with Gable than it would be now that he was living with Hunter. He hoped the fact that Hunter knew about Christy and the kids would assure he'd never had to make that choice again. He was pretty sure that, once Miranda gave birth to Hunter's baby, Hunter would understand the power a child had over a man.

This feeling of responsibility carried through during the dinner conversation with Calley and Bill.

Calley and Bill were amicable people, even though Grant and Bill had had an altercation at the birth of Brenner's foals, when Grant had defended Calley's honor and Bill had clearly taken that the wrong way. They'd had a chance to talk it out, and although they would never be best friends, Grant wasn't worried about being in the same room with Bill anymore. He admitted to some residual tension, though. He couldn't erase the past or the fact he'd had an affair with Calley, so it only stood to reason that he wouldn't be Bill's favorite person, but they'd reached a stalemate and now managed to be civil to each other.

Calley had been fairly vague about the reason for the sudden dinner invitation. Hunter and Grant had never been invited to their house before, and certainly not with Gable and Flynn as dinner companions. Calley, being the no-nonsense type, dropped her bombshell during the appetizers: she wanted to try for a child again. Although Bill was clearly in on the matter, he stayed quiet. The other four men simply stared at each other. It took some time to let her words sink in.

Grant was the first to say something. The proposal for them to become sperm donors wasn't foreign to him, after all.

"You basically only need one of us, Calley," Grant said softly, looking at Calley while she was rearranging the lettuce leaves on her plate with her fork.

"I know," she said, smiling lightly and reaching out for Bill's hand. "But it's taken me a long time to persuade Bill, and he doesn't really want to know who fathered the child, so this is our compromise."

"There is such a thing as an anonymous sperm donor," Flynn said. "I'm sure they can hook you up with some at the hospital?"

Calley nodded. "We talked about that too, but Bill feels we should be able to tell the child who his real father is at some point. When he's older."

"Or she," Hunter cut her off.

"Or she," Calley agreed. "You never know when it might be necessary to know."

Grant looked around the table at the one man besides Bill who remained quiet. Gable's gaze was miles away, and Grant knew what that meant. He was thinking things over, taking his time. Grant also caught Flynn lovingly gazing at Gable, though Gable was oblivious to it.

When Calley got up to gather the dirty plates, Grant helped and followed her into the kitchen.

"Well, I suppose it's the best sort of response I could expect," Calley said, taking the plates from Grant once they'd put some distance between them and the rest of the group.

"It's a big thing to ask." Grant put his hand on the small of her back but pulled away when the door opened. Bill walked in to pick up a bottle of wine before walking out again.

"I know," Calley replied once Bill was gone. "Don't suppose you'll put me out of my misery and volunteer again?"

Grant sighed. "I'm sorry, Calley. You'd be afraid all through your pregnancy."

"Who says the miscarriage wasn't my fault? I'll be afraid no matter what. It might happen again, Grant."

"I know." Grant placed a soothing hand on her arm, not daring to come much closer in case Bill walked in on them again. "But I think I have enough of my offspring running around for now. If nobody wants to help, I will. I won't let you down, but let's let the others decide first, okay?"

She nodded. "How about Hunter?"

"You'll have to talk to him yourself, I'm afraid." Grant inhaled deeply. "But he's pretty preoccupied with Miranda right now—"

"And one baby on the way is enough for him, I suppose," Calley said, finishing Grant's sentence. "I understand."

"Maybe Gable will say yes this time?"

Calley smiled sadly. "His arguments were pretty convincing last time. He wants to raise his child. I can't give him that."

"He hasn't said no yet. He was thinking about it, Calley."

Calley turned to face Grant and pulled him into a tight hug. "Thanks for giving me hope." She let go of him, turned around to grab the oven mitts, and handed them to Grant. "Will you carry out the roast for me? Bill will carve, I'm sure."

The rest of the dinner was delicious, and they spent it with lots of small talk and gossip about the goings-on at the nearby ranches and things that had happened around town. It was as if the evening hadn't started with such a loaded question.

Just before midnight, Hunter drove them home, and he and Grant were silent in the car most of the way.

"She's really desperate, isn't she?" Hunter eventually said as they drove up the driveway toward the house.

"Yes. She's been desperate for a long time. I'm just glad Bill has finally conceded to getting outside help."

"Must be very difficult for him. Does he know about your kids?"

Grant shrugged. "He probably does. I'm sure Calley told him."

"And they know I knocked up Miranda."

"Guess we've both proven our fertility."

Hunter chuckled as he parked the car. He didn't get out immediately, though, but turned to face Grant. "I really want to help her, but I can't. I'm already gonna be a dad, Grant. That's more than enough stress for me right now."

"I know, Cowboy. I told her you might say no."

Hunter leaned over to him and rested his head against Grant's. "If it hadn't been for Miranda, I might have considered it, since the chance of me having any sort of offspring would have been slim, but now…."

"She understands, Cowboy." Grant turned his head and gently kissed Hunter. Hunter responded like he expected, nuzzling him and creating intimacy without upping the ante.

"Let's sleep at the crew house tonight," Hunter suggested. "It's Saturday. Most of the guys will be still out at the bar. You have condoms there?"

"Does a bear shit in the woods?"

Hunter started the car again, driving it over to the other large house on the property. Like they'd predicted, it was shrouded in darkness; no lights were visible in any of the windows. Grant knew that the only one still inside the house would be old Mackenzie, and he would be asleep already. He was one of the ranch hands, and despite being older than time, he was always up at the crack of dawn, even on a

Sunday. Luckily he had a room downstairs and on the opposite side from Grant's. He wouldn't be disturbed by a little noise.

They didn't dawdle but quickly made their way upstairs and into Grant's room. It took them no time at all to get naked, and the lovemaking was frantic. They were used to muffling their moans and groans, but their movements were a lot more passionate than usual.

"Will you build me a house, Stud?" Hunter whispered in Grant's ear as soon as he had enough breath to speak. They were still entangled, Hunter behind Grant with his arms wrapped tightly around the older man's frame.

"I'd love to, but you're going to have to help. Especially if you want thick, sturdy walls that block out sound."

"I thought of something else," Hunter said in an even softer tone of voice than before. "Calley said we'd need to get tested for the donation. Just to keep up the pretense that we're still in the race."

Grant nodded.

"That means we'll know if we're both given the all-clear."

Grant knew where Hunter was going, and warmth spread inside him. "You want to get rid of the condoms?"

"I'm not going back to women, and I'm not likely to find another guy around here."

Grant chuckled. "So you're with me out of default?"

Hunter kissed his neck, and Grant pushed even closer to his lover. Grant expected him to get mad or to retreat, but Hunter didn't. "I'm with you because I love you. Because I've never felt for anyone what I feel for you. Because I never want to be with anyone else ever again."

Grant swallowed hard. The warmth inside him had turned to a big, fat knot in the pit of his stomach. Hunter had said the L word. No man had ever said it to him and meant it, and now he didn't know how to answer it. Saying it back would sound cheesy and cheap. Not saying anything would make him seem cold and distant. After a few moments of reflection, he turned around in Hunter's embrace and, taking Hunter's face in his hand, tried to convey everything with a searing kiss.

They fell asleep like that, kissing and cuddling. They wouldn't need to get up in the morning. Old Mac would make sure the riding horses were fed and watered.

It was still dark outside when they were awakened by someone banging on their door. It took a second salvo for Grant to wake up and disentangle himself from Hunter's death grip.

"Easy!" Grant called out. "Leave the door on its hinges!" He pulled on the corduroy pants he'd discarded near the door and made sure Hunter was pretty much covered before opening the door only slightly. He squinted against the bright light coming from the hallway and could just make out Hugh. "What's wrong?"

Hugh bit his lip before answering. "Do you know a woman called Christy?"

"I do," Grant admitted, not immediately connecting the dots.

"You'd better come to the house then," Hugh said curtly before turning around. Almost immediately he retraced his steps back to Grant's door. "And bring Hunter. He needs to be there for this too."

Grant didn't get the chance to ask questions. Hugh had donned his hat again and was rounding the corner toward the stairs before Grant moved.

"What's wrong? Was that Hugh? What time is it?"

Although Grant thought Hunter looked adorable sitting up among the ruffled sheets, scratching his chest and with his hair all over the place, he didn't take the time to admire the view.

"There's something wrong with Christy."

Hunter woke up completely. "Are you sure?"

"Hugh looked worried." He threw Hunter's shirt on the bed. "Get dressed. He told us to come to the house."

Less than ten minutes later, they were walking up the porch. Despite the fact it was about four a.m., all the downstairs lights were on, and Grant could see Izzie walking from the living room to the hallway in her dressing gown, her distended belly clearly showing her blessed state and her long dark hair in a braid over her shoulder. She opened the door as soon as they approached it.

Grant could barely contain his nerves. If something had happened to Christy, then something might have happened to the kids as well. He hoped it was nothing serious. Then again, if she'd sent word across two states in the middle of the night, it wouldn't be to tell him one of the kids had gotten a good report card.

"Come in, guys. It's freezing outside," Izzie said as she opened the door.

Grant hadn't even noticed. All he saw was the concerned look on Izzie's face.

"She's in the living room."

Grant walked around Izzie, leaving her and Hunter in the hallway. When he spotted Christy sitting on the couch with the three kids around her, he exhaled so loudly it made him realize he'd been holding his breath. Three pairs of scared eyes looked up at him, and he nodded, letting them flood over to him. He sank down to the floor and tried to fit them all into one embrace, pulling them closer.

"It's okay. You're safe. You're here now." After a while he started noticing the scrutiny from the others, especially Hunter's mother. "Let's sit down on the couch," Grant suggested to the kids. "We'll be more comfortable."

The kids wouldn't let go of him, but he managed to get all of them comfortable between him and Christy. He could tell the kids were exhausted, but they were struggling to stay awake. He pulled Lindy on his lap and let the two boys settle on either side of him. Clearly this was all they wanted, and within minutes they were sound asleep.

"We should take them upstairs to sleep in a proper bed," Hunter's mother said. Her expression was stern, but Grant heard genuine concern in her voice.

"Give them just a minute, ma'am," Grant said. "Then we'll carry them upstairs."

"Why don't we get their beds ready, Mom?" Hugh suggested. "I'm sure Christy and Grant have a lot to talk about."

Hunter's mother looked from Christy to Grant, to the kids, and then to Hunter. Her gaze lingered so long Grant could tell it made Hunter uncomfortable.

"I'll help carry them upstairs in a sec, Mom," Hunter said, clearly trying to get her out of the room. "You go on to bed. We'll talk about this in the morning."

Hugh put his arm around the small of Izzie's back as the three of them left the room.

There was silence until everyone was sure they were out of earshot. During the pause, Grant took his first good look at Christy. He could tell she'd been crying. A lot. And there were faint marks around her mouth and eyes that looked like faded bruises. "Did he hit you again?"

She nodded silently, her gaze downcast.

"In front of the kids?"

She didn't answer. Grant looked at Hunter, who threw him a concerned look.

"They're frightened, Chris, and from the look of them, they've been frightened for a long time."

Christy looked up. "I couldn't leave until he'd gone back to work. As soon as he left, I started packing and I came here. You need to take care of them for me, Grant. At least for a while. Until I can get back on my feet. Until I can save some money so I can take care of them."

"Or until he finds you and promises you everything will be better next time."

She shook her head. "No next time."

"That's what you said before!" Anger boiled up inside Grant, but he knew he couldn't shout. The last thing he wanted was to wake up the kids. They'd been through enough. He looked at them, and Robby stirred but soon stopped moving. "Where will you be?" he asked her, trying hard to make his voice sound calm.

"I have a friend who works for a big hotel in Vegas. She says she can get me a job cleaning rooms."

Grant sighed but moved his hand just a bit so he could touch hers in support. He didn't know what to say. Christy was too good for this.

"She says the tips are good, and I can get affordable housing there too, but I can't do it with the kids in tow." She looked at the children, who were draped all over Grant. "I'll have to work odd hours at first, and Lindy's not in school yet, so I'll need to find her daycare, and I don't think I can afford that."

"I'll take care of them, Chris," Grant said softly. "*We* will." Grant looked up at Hunter, and Hunter nodded without hesitation. It made Grant smile just a little. Knowing Hunter had his back was invaluable right now. "Just let me know where you are. And tell them what you're planning to do." He nodded toward the kids. "They need to know you didn't abandon them."

"They know I need to leave. I told them they were going to stay with you, and that's the first time I saw them smile in a long time." Her look was a strange mixture of hope and desperation.

Grant wanted to tell her everything would work itself out, but at the same time, he was desperately happy she'd escaped her violent husband and brought the kids to him. He hoped the kids would be safe here and was looking forward to playing dad and showing them that not all men were bullies. He knew he was getting ahead of himself, but he was already making plans to do things with them to make them smile and let them leave all their worries behind.

When he felt a hand on his knee, he looked up into Hunter's hazel eyes.

"Let's get them into bed and get some sleep ourselves, okay? It's been a long day."

Grant nodded and looked at Christy.

"Should I carry this one?" Hunter suggested, pointing at Robby, who was between Grant and Christy. He didn't wait for an answer and easily scooped Robby up.

"You look like you've done this before," Christy said lovingly.

"Maybe once or twice, but it's easier than carrying a dog," Hunter replied with a chuckle. This woke Robby up, but all he did was briefly look at Hunter and drape an arm around his neck before settling his head on Hunter's shoulder. "At least this one doesn't struggle."

"I'll take Lindy," Christy suggested.

With a child each in their arms, they walked up the stairs, where Hugh met them. He was carrying two pillows. "Mom's instructions were clear. The two boys in Danny's room, Christy and Lindy in the back guestroom, and—" he sighed theatrically and mimicked his mother-in-law like a pro "—I suppose I'll need to tolerate Grant staying in Hunter's room."

Grant's eyes went wide as he looked from Hugh to Hunter. "That'll be a hardship."

"I figured that much," Hugh replied with a chuckle. He nodded toward his son's room. "Danny's awake. We put up two camping beds in there, and I told him not to wake them. Christy? Izzie's in there, getting the guestroom ready. She'll help you settle Lindy. We brought your bags in from the car."

"Thanks," Christy said. She kissed both her boys on the head and then headed for the guestroom.

It didn't take Hunter and Grant long to get Robby and Lewis in their makeshift beds, and after saying goodnight to Danny, they retreated to Hunter's room. While Grant undressed, Hunter walked back out to go to the bathroom, and when he returned, Grant was lying facedown on the bed.

"You still awake?" Hunter asked softly.

Grant nodded and turned just in time to see Hunter slip under the covers. He was wearing only his boxers, and Grant enjoyed feeling him snuggle closer.

"You okay?"

Grant nodded again. He was once more at a loss for words. He loved this man so much, but to burden him with this new complication in his life and at this stage of their relationship wasn't going to be easy.

"I'm sorry," Grant murmured.

"Did you just apologize? What for?"

"This isn't what you signed up for."

Hunter was lying on his side, as close to Grant as he could manage, but he moved even closer by putting his chin on Grant's shoulder.

Grant could feel the warmth of Hunter's skin and the ghost of his breath against his ear.

"Hey, I'm the one who got his ex-girlfriend pregnant, remember? Your boyfriend's going to be a dad. Don't suppose you saw that one coming either."

"True," Grant admitted.

"Come here," Hunter gestured. He put his arms around Grant as Grant turned into them, and pulled him tight. "It's almost morning, and although it's Sunday, I get the feeling we're not going to get the chance to lie in."

Grant kissed Hunter's temple. "But you do know we're sleeping together with your mother's permission, right?"

Hunter snorted. "As if that ever made a difference."

"It does to me," Grant confessed. "I mean, we still have to be quiet, but now she can't delude herself anymore and pretend we're just friends."

"Sleep," Hunter commanded, stressing his point with a wide yawn.

—36—

HUNTER had slept for maybe an hour. Dawn was only just creeping up the horizon, but something had awakened him, and now he was lying there, listening to the sounds of a cold morning on the ranch. Lying close to Grant was always a treat. Grant snored a little, but not enough to wake Hunter up, and Hunter simply enjoyed the warmth and proximity of the tall, well-built man in his arms. He was pretty much a morning person and was usually awake before Grant, although Grant was no slouch by any means. He liked these quiet minutes. It gave him time to think. Sometimes too much time. Before Grant had become his bed partner, he'd never lingered. As soon as his eyes were more than halfway open, he used to be up and on his way to the bathroom. It would take him ten minutes tops to get ready for morning chores, and sometimes that even included making his bed.

Now he liked to linger. He liked waking up with Grant, teasing his lover into a quick round of morning sex before they got up to work. They made the bed every morning, because they'd been freaked out one day when someone had made their bed behind their backs. There was no telling what they'd found. Hunter was sure most people in the house were fine about him being with Grant, though. He was even pretty sure that his mother would get used to the idea eventually. Still, he knew they'd feel better having a place of their own.

Last night Christy and her kids had toppled their world, though. What was going to happen? Was she going to stay for a while? What was it going to do to Grant to have his kids around all the time? Hunter hoped it would bring good things, but he knew it wouldn't be smooth sailing all the way. To the children, Grant wasn't their father. Their father was a bully who beat his wife.

Hunter startled from his daydream when he heard a discreet knock on his door. He listened for another one but heard a weak voice instead. "Hunter?"

It was his sister Bernice. "Bernie? I'll be right there." Hunter tried to slide from under Grant without waking him but only partially succeeded.

"Hurry up. I hear a baby crying."

It dawned on Hunter that she'd missed most of the commotion last night. He slipped into his jeans and hurried to the door.

"What's going on?" Hunter asked his sister. Bernie was standing in the hallway in her nightgown, her hair in pigtails despite the fact she was seventeen. When she didn't answer, Hunter saw her eyes wander past him to the prone figure on the bed, and then realized he hadn't checked whether Grant was decent. He quickly turned around and covered up most of his lover's visible skin with the bedsheet.

"So where is this crying child?"

She pointed toward the guestroom, but her gaze was still locked on Grant. Hunter snapped his fingers in front of her eyes. "Distressed child?"

Bernie giggled shyly. "He's gorgeous, Hunter, even without clothes on."

Hunter nodded, sure that he was blushing crimson but not about to let his kid sister ogle his lover gratuitously. Bernie finally walked with him to the end of the hallway, letting him settle somewhat. The crying got louder, and Hunter started to worry. It could only be Lindy, but Christy was supposed to be inside with her and should be there to soothe her. Maybe she was in the bathroom or the shower.

Hunter carefully opened the door to find what he'd expected: Lindy sitting up in the middle of the big bed, crying her eyes out. Unaccustomed to consoling little children, he sat down on the bed and held out his hand. At first, this made her cry even more.

"Do something, Hunter," Bernie demanded.

Hunter shot her a look of desperation. "Do I look like I know what to do?"

"Hold her or something. You used to hold me when I cried. When I was little."

Lindy was still sobbing, so Hunter figured it couldn't get much worse. He'd simply lift the little girl up and carry her to Grant. She weighed next to nothing when he picked her up off the bed. To his surprise, she wrapped her arms so tightly around his neck he thought he was going to choke.

"Talk to her or something, Hunter," Bernie urged him.

"Sssh, 's okay, Lindy," Hunter spoke, gently patting her long, curly hair. He couldn't help noticing how her hair felt just like Grant's, soft and silky. Her sobbing was becoming quieter now, although she'd hiccup from time to time. "'S okay," Hunter repeated.

"You look good, Daddy."

Hunter looked up and saw Grant standing in the doorway. "She was upset. I don't know where Christy is."

Grant turned on the bedside lamp and sat down next to Hunter and Lindy, pretty much ignoring Bernie's unashamed stare at his naked torso.

"She's gone," Grant said despondently. He held up a handwritten note he'd picked up from the nightstand.

"*I hereby allow Mr. Grant Jarreau to make all necessary decisions about the well-being of the children Lewis, Robert, and Lindy Marshall from this day forward,*" Grant read. "It's signed 'Christy Marshall'."

"I'm sure that's not legal."

Grant looked at Hunter. "I don't care. I'm holding onto this."

"If her husband comes for them, this won't stand up in court."

"Don't you think I know that? *His* name is on the birth certificate of *my* children. Even if I push for anything, I might get the youngest two with a paternity test, but they still won't give me Lewis. And he has to be part of the package."

"Calm down," Hunter said. He understood why his lover was upset. They'd been through this before. Lindy was practically asleep in his arms now, so he couldn't move, but he wanted to touch Grant to soothe him and make him understand he wasn't alone. "Grant, sit here. We'll talk about this with our lawyer on Monday. Right now we need to take care of these kids, show them they're not alone, and try to make them see she didn't abandon them. Make them understand that she'll be back."

Hunter's words seemed to calm Grant down, and Hunter was glad of that. Hunter dared to let go of Lindy enough to reach out and put his hand on the back of Grant's neck. He pulled him closer until their foreheads were touching. "I love you. We'll pull through this."

Grant kissed him until Bernie's chuckle reminded them that she was still in the room.

"You two are really cute together," she said with an amused grin.

Hunter pulled away from Grant and shot her a mock-threatening stare. "Oh, grow up, Bernie."

"I'm serious," she said, bouncing on the balls of her feet. "You're really cute together. I don't know why Mom can't see that."

Hunter shook his head and rolled his eyes. Bernie wasn't too bad. He wanted to send her off to college next year so she'd gain some maturity, but he knew it would break her heart to be ripped away from her horses. Not to mention he'd lose one of his most avid supporters. "Go on downstairs and start some coffee, Bern. We'll be right there."

"Just don't do anything you'll regret. Lindy looks like a light sleeper, and she's only little! A little too young for your antics, I think."

Hunter narrowed his eyes at her. "And you'd prefer to stay and watch, I suppose? Fat chance, sis. We can maintain some self-control, you know."

Giggling, she left the room.

"Let's go see if the others are up?" Hunter suggested.

ABOUT an hour later, most of the household was sitting in the huge family kitchen. Grant was fully dressed in jeans and a checkered shirt and flipping pancakes on the large cast-iron stove that occupied most of the side wall of the room. Izzie was sitting with Hunter at the table, trying to get the four children organized, while Hugh was setting the table for breakfast. Bernie was hovering around Grant when Hunter's mother arrived.

She was greeted by a chorus of "Morning" from everyone while she checked out what Grant was doing on "her" stove. "Looks good," she eventually admitted.

Grant couldn't be sure, but he thought he heard several relieved sighs from around the room.

"Smells even better!" Bernie exclaimed in her always-enthusiastic voice.

"Hope you don't mind, ma'am," Grant told the matriarch. "Bernie showed me where everything was, and I thought pancakes would be a good breakfast for a Sunday morning."

"Need some help?" Beth asked in her usual stoic manner.

Grant couldn't prevent a smile spreading over his face. Although she hadn't explicitly shown her approval, the fact she hadn't told him off or left the room was enough for him.

"No thanks," Grant answered casually. "Bacon and eggs are just about finished, and I have a stack of pancakes down here in the slow cooker to keep them warm, so we're about ready to dig in."

"Bernie, go get the syrup from the pantry. Let's show these kids what a family breakfast tastes like."

When Grant looked around, he saw encouraging smiles from Hugh and Izzie and a look on Hunter's face he could only interpret as pride. They clearly all felt the same. It looked like he was now accepted into the family.

The idyllic breakfast was a little tense at first, with quite a few people exchanging looks across the table and the kids being quiet among the more rowdy grown-ups. Hunter was glad to have Hugh back, and now that Grant was healed enough to rejoin the group, he felt the balance was tipping over to his side again. After everyone had stuffed themselves and Hunter's mother had retreated to the living room, they excused the children and sent them outside to play.

"Izzie tells me Christy left," Hugh said casually after downing his last gulp of coffee.

"Yeah," Grant answered. He didn't elaborate, and Hunter wasn't sure how much Grant wanted Izzie and Hugh to know.

"She'll be back once she's settled, I think," Hunter eventually said, after trying to exchange a look with Grant and getting nothing. "She said something about finding a job in Las Vegas, right, Grant?"

Grant nodded, his thoughts still miles away.

"In the meanwhile, we'll just make them feel welcome here, I suppose. We'll need to turn the two guestrooms into children's rooms so Danny can have his room back," Hunter added. "And then once my house is built, we can move everyone across the yard."

"House?" Izzie said, almost choking on her coffee.

Hunter looked at Grant, but instead of finding approval, he saw his lover still staring at the remnants of breakfast.

"We don't know how long they'll be here for," Grant said pensively.

Hunter squeezed Grant's thigh under the table. "Even if Christy comes to get them, we'll make sure they have a room in the house, Grant. That way they can spend vacations here."

Grant nodded.

"So you're building a house?" Hugh asked, obviously nudged on by Izzie.

"Yeah," Hunter replied. "Been thinking it over for a while. The plans have changed a couple of times. Never thought we'd need that many bedrooms, for one, but if I build it here in the stretch of land between this house and the barns, we'd have our independence without having to move away. Wouldn't be very practical for me to live outside the property."

"And this house is getting a bit crowded, with all the extra additions," Hugh concurred. "Well, I'm not much of a carpenter, but if you need another set of hands, I'll gladly help."

Izzie playfully punched Hugh. "We're not even married yet and you're already trying to get away from me?"

Hugh wrapped his arm around her and pulled her closer, gently patting her bulging stomach.

Although Hunter was very happy for his sister and his best friend, he also felt a little jealous. Hugh was going to see his child grow up; Hunter didn't know if he would ever get that chance. Not that this was going to change his mind about not marrying Miranda, but it did bring it home to him that his choices had consequences, not just for him but for his unborn child. He looked at Grant, who was still brooding, and then realized it wasn't a choice. His hand was still resting on Grant's thigh, and that was where it belonged.

Just as he was leaning toward Grant to whisper a quiet "I love you" in his ear, he felt something tug at his sleeve. He glanced away from Grant and saw Lindy standing next to him, looking infinitely shy, as if she was afraid of the reaction she'd get for drawing his attention.

Hunter smiled at her and bent down. "What's the matter, sweetie?"

"The boys are playing rough. Can I sit here with you?"

"Sure, honey," Hunter answered, pulling her onto his lap. She settled easily, leaning against Hunter's chest and snuggling into his embrace. Grant looked at them, and for the first time since Christy's leaving became an issue, Hunter saw his lover smile again. Grant ran his fingers through Lindy's curls and smiled at her too. "So you found another cuddle bear, didn't you?"

Lindy looked up at Hunter and then back at Grant and nodded fervently before squeezing Hunter tightly—as much as she could, since she couldn't exactly reach around him.

It took all of two minutes for Lindy to fall sound asleep in Hunter's embrace.

"They didn't get a lot of sleep last night," Grant said. "Maybe we should put her back to bed."

"And have her wake up alone in a strange room like this morning?" Hunter shook his head. "I'm comfortable. She can sleep like this for a while longer."

# —37—

GRANT could watch them together for hours.

Lindy clung to Hunter like gum to a shoe. Now that the boys went to school with Danny, she was the only one left, so early in the morning Hunter would bring her out to the stables for morning chores and let her help with watering the horses and mucking out the stables. Although at first the large animals scared her a bit, Hunter had explained to her what to do and, more importantly, what not to do. Lindy had taken to it like a duck to water. Grant's heart stopped every time he saw her dash in and out of the stables, but he'd also noticed that the horses were very gentle around her and watched her every move.

Grant had sawed half the handle off a rake so she could help without poking anyone's eye out, and although it was a funny sight to see a four-year-old mucking out stables, she certainly gave it her best effort. What she lacked in strength, she certainly made up in eagerness, but seeing her bend over a patch of horse manure with her nose scrunched up never ceased to make him laugh out loud.

Although it warmed Grant's heart to see Hunter taking to parenting so easily, it surprised him even more that he enjoyed it so much as well, although he gravitated more toward the boys. None of the kids were used to living in the great outdoors, but all of them seemed to blossom, and Grant was silently glad they hadn't heard much from Christy. There was no doubt in his mind that she missed her kids, but at night, after they'd tucked them all in to bed, Grant sometimes despaired when he thought of the day that Christy would show up again to claim them back.

"What are you brooding about now, Stud?" Hunter asked after sitting down next to him on the bed. Hunter's hand lay possessively on Grant's thigh, and Grant enjoyed its warmth.

"I was wondering whether your mom would be able to work with Christy."

Hunter raised his eyebrows but didn't answer.

"I know I'm being very forward here, but with Lisa gone, your mother does the cooking for the crew, and I know it's a lot of work. She's not as young as she thinks she is, so I thought maybe we could try to find Christy and offer her the position of crew cook. That way she could come live here with us and the kids."

"You're just worried that she's going to come back and take the kids away," Hunter said empathically.

"I know you'd miss them too," Grant said.

Hunter nodded. "Very much."

"So you think…?"

"We'll have to square it with Mom first, and you know how she is with strangers working in her kitchen."

Grant sighed. "We could bring the crew kitchen into the twenty-first century, and that way Christy would have her own territory."

As Grant put his hand over Hunter's, Hunter twisted it and took Grant's hand in his. "We'll just have to explain it to her. Find the right moment. Do you know where Christy is?"

Grant shook his head. "But we have the postcard she sent us, and I know her friend's name, so we have two leads to work with. We'll need to spend a weekend or so in Vegas, though."

"And leave the kids here? Just you and me?"

Grant nodded. He could tell Hunter saw the potential of the two of them getting away.

"Let me talk to Mom first. No need to go out there if she thinks it's a bad idea."

Grant could tell from Hunter's smile that he figured he could persuade his mother to say yes. He also knew Hunter liked the idea of spending a few days in a hotel room with no family or kids to distract them, so there was no doubt in his mind that Hunter would make the time to talk with his mother as soon as possible.

As HUNTER predicted, it took a little persuading for his mother to say yes, and she had conditions. In the end, she, too, understood that it was all for the benefit of the children, whom she'd grown quite fond of as well, so Hunter and Grant packed an overnight bag and drove the truck to Las Vegas.

Deciding to splurge a bit, they took a modest room in the Bellagio, where Christy's postcard had come from, hoping to find her actually working there. After checking in, they walked around the hotel, talking to anyone from the housekeeping staff they ran into and asking whether they knew Christy or her friend Danielle. They had no luck, so after a few hours of fruitless searching, they ended up in a sports bar, where they decided to have dinner.

Their server was a buff jock-type young man, and Grant felt a twitch of jealousy as he saw Hunter check out the guy's ass. Hunter must have noticed, because when they were both scrutinizing the menu, Grant felt a smooth boot slide up his leg. Suddenly it stopped.

"Don't look behind you, but Delco's here."

Although it was hard not to look, Grant leaned closer so they wouldn't be overheard. "Izzie's Delco? The shrimp with the attitude?"

"The very same," Hunter replied. "He's at the bar with some friends, and he's telling tall stories by the looks of it."

"Can you hear what he's saying?"

Hunter shook his head.

Grant scooted out of the booth. "Order me a steak, medium rare with all the trimmings."

Hunter grabbed his wrist. "What are you doing? He knows what you look like, remember?"

Grant cocked his head. "I know. I'll be careful. I'm just curious."

Grant knew he was making Hunter nervous, but he had a debt to settle with the kid, and although he hoped it wouldn't come to a confrontation, his fists ached to prove he wasn't a pushover. Maybe he'd get his chance, maybe not. He discreetly walked past them, making sure Delco was in full performance mode, boasting to his friends. Grant pretended to study a menu as he lingered near the back of the bar, within earshot of Delco and his gang.

It didn't take Grant long to catch what he needed, and he took the long way back to the booth, where Hunter was sitting, watching out for him.

"Don't ever do that to me again," Hunter snarled.

"Did you order for us?"

"Yes, I did, but I'm not kidding. I nearly popped an artery seeing you come that close to him. What if he'd looked up at the moment you passed them?"

Grant chuckled. "He was boasting about stealing horses. Telling his mates how to do it."

"Stealing horses?" Hunter asked, his eyebrows reaching almost into his hairline.

"Yup," Grant replied calmly. "He said the trick was making it look like a cougar did it by not cutting the fence but putting a blanket over it to crush it down, and he talked about using a truck with threadbare tires that wouldn't leave tire tracks."

"We've been fixing those kinds of fences since the spring!" Hunter said, having a hard time keeping his voice lower than a whisper. "He's got some nerve."

"Exactly. He told his goons that the ranchers were a little puzzled that they stole young, untrained horses, but apparently, Delco has a buyer for them. And it makes it easier to disguise it as a predator rather than a horse thief. My vote goes to following Delco, dragging him into a dark alley, and beating the crap out of him."

"Grant!" Hunter admonished him. "You can't just go around beating people up!"

"Have a better idea?"

"We have to catch him in the act. Did it sound like he was planning to try it again?"

"Oh, yes," Grant replied, sure of himself. "He was saying it was so easy he could easily make a living at it, and it was less work than the rodeo circuit."

"So let's find Christy and then go home and set a trap for him."

They didn't sleep much in their luxurious hotel room, both because they were alone for the first time in weeks and because they were excited about their plans to catch Delco in the act of trying to steal horses. Eventually, after two bouts of lovemaking, one hurried and one more languid, they fell asleep, entangled, as they'd slept for the past months. Despite their short night, habit made them get up at the crack of dawn.

Another round of talking to housekeeping led nowhere, and they decided to stake out a few other hotels on the Strip. Totally by accident, Grant saw a picture of a stripper in one of the more shady hotels and recognized her as Danielle. They called the number on the poster and were directed to a small club off the Strip.

When Danielle saw them walk into the place, she immediately recognized Grant. "Grant, so nice to see you here!"

Grant nodded. He could tell Danielle wasn't completely at ease, although she was giving them her most welcoming smile. "We're actually here to look for Christy, and we thought you might know where to find her. She was saying something about you being able to get her a job in housekeeping for one of the large hotels?" Grant figured they would go farthest just appearing naïve about it all.

"Well I'll tell her you asked for her," Danielle said dismissively as soon as it was clear the guys weren't there for her services.

"We drove for eleven hours to see her, Danielle," Grant rebutted. "If you know where she is, you need to tell us."

She picked up a beer coaster off the bar. "Write down the name of your hotel and your room number and I'll ask her to call."

Grant was about to protest, but Hunter stopped him. "If she doesn't call by tonight, we'll be back to find you, Danielle. We came here to see Christy, and we're not leaving until we at least talk to her."

Danielle nodded, not looking straight at them. Hunter didn't really know Danielle, but he was pretty sure she'd be on the phone with Christy as soon as they left, so he ushered Grant out of the club.

"I wanted her to call while we were there, Cowboy," Grant said on the way over to their hotel.

"She wouldn't have," Hunter replied. "They're friends. Danielle is obviously covering for her."

"So you think Christy is stripping too?"

Hunter sighed. "It had crossed my mind."

Grant shook his head. "She wouldn't. She wouldn't sell her body like this. She's a typical small-town girl, Hunter."

Hunter took Grant's hand despite the fact they were still in the middle of the Strip. "People do desperate things in desperate times."

"I know," Grant said, barely audible. He couldn't wrap his head around it, but he was glad the way Hunter looked at him was more concern than pity or jealousy. Sure, he had feelings for Christy. At one point they were two lost souls who'd found comfort in each other. The knowledge that they'd always be there to cover each other's backs was something that had always given them strength. Now Grant felt he'd failed his friend.

Once inside their hotel room, Grant sank down on the bed, and Hunter joined him. "It's okay, Grant. She'll call," he said, placing a soothing hand on Grant's thigh.

"I failed her, Cowboy. I should have protected her better."

Hunter shook his head. "She's a grown-up. As grown-ups, we make our own choices, and some of them, in hindsight, aren't the best ones we could have made, but we made them and we'll have to live with them."

Grant was just turning into Hunter's soothing embrace when they heard a knock on their door.

Hunter got up to open it, and over his shoulder, Grant saw it was Christy. To Grant's relief, she looked the same as when she'd left him at Hunter's house, wearing simple, inconspicuous clothes. He'd been afraid she'd come in looking like a Vegas showgirl.

As soon as she took one step inside, Grant pulled her into a tight hug.

"Hey, put me down, you big lug," Christy said after a long time. "I'm fine."

Although he and Hunter had agreed they'd persuade her gently, Grant knew then he couldn't wait. "Come back home with us, Chris. Don't stay here. It's not good for you to be so far away from the kids. They need you."

IN THE end it didn't take much for Hunter and Grant to persuade Christy to come back to Idaho with them. Her job in the hotel barely paid enough to cover the rent on a single room, and when she'd tried her hand at stripping like Danielle, she'd found she couldn't do it. The offer to cook at the ranch was a godsend. And she admitted to missing the kids too.

The drive back was long, but Hunter and Grant spent it discussing what they were going to do to entrap Delco while he was executing his horse-stealing scheme. First thing the next morning, they stopped at the sheriff's office to get his cooperation, since they hoped they could catch Delco in the act and have him arrested.

Afraid that Delco might still have connections at the ranch, they worked out around-the-clock surveillance, with only a few people in the know of what was really going on. Those people were Hugh, Tim, and of course Hunter and Grant. Hugh had chosen not to involve Izzie because she was nearing the end of her pregnancy and easily upset.

Despite the new snowfall, they moved a handful of the horses a little farther away from the house to a meadow that had a nice, sturdy lean-to where they could hide and an excellent vista over the field from the shelter. The meadow was remote enough to make any horse thief feel secure, and they'd moved enough juvenile horses to act as bait. Now all they had to do was wait.

After about a week of dreadfully boring and freezing-cold stakeouts, everyone was growing restless. They'd perpetuated the myth of a cougar being on the prowl to cover up their story to the ranch hands who kept them company and who weren't in the know. That gave them an excuse to carry shotguns, in case Delco wasn't working on his own. It also kept them fairly sharp, since the ranch hands knew what a hungry cougar could do to a man if the animal was cornered.

Grant and Hunter usually took the night shift, because it gave them some privacy and an excuse to huddle close together to stay warm. Now that Christy was there to take care of the kids, they could afford to get away. They also figured that nighttime was the best chance to catch Delco red-handed.

They had just said their goodnights to the sheriff over the radio when they heard the sound of a truck. In the cold night air and the darkness of a new moon, the horses easily grew restless under the lean-to. Hunter was soothing them as Grant carefully stuck his head out to see if he could catch sight of anyone. It took some time, but eventually Grant came back in, blowing into his hands to keep warm.

"It's him, all right." Grant was smiling from ear to ear. "And he's not alone. There's another guy with him."

"Who?" Hunter asked, whispering.

"Remember Rory? That drifter Hugh hired just before me who didn't show after a few weeks? Looks like it's him."

"Damn, you mean Delco's actually been doing this since even before he broke up with Izzie?"

"Horses started disappearing before that guy started working here, right?"

Hunter nodded. "Snake," he spat, cursing Delco. "We need to nail them, Stud. I want that pea-brained rodeo cowboy put away for a long time."

"Even if we catch him he might be out again in no time, Cowboy," Grant answered pragmatically.

"I know." Hunter sighed. "So how do we do this?"

"Call the sheriff back. Tell him to get over here. You stay here and I'll walk around to catch them from the back."

"No," Hunter said urgently. "I'll go around the back!"

"This isn't the time to have our first big argument, Cowboy," Grant whispered, leaning into Hunter's personal space. He gave Hunter a quick peck on the mouth. "You talk to your sheriff buddy. They're your horses."

Hunter conceded, nodding at Grant. "Fine."

Grant took one of the shotguns and started to turn, but Hunter held him back, pulling on his coat.

"For Christ's sake, be careful out there, okay?"

Grant nodded. "You too. Make sure he doesn't corner you in here." He didn't linger, knowing full well he would much rather not leave the shelter for anything other than to seek out their warm bed. He wanted to put this behind them, though, so Hunter could stop worrying about his horses.

Walking away from where he'd seen the men exit the truck and trailer, Grant rounded the lean-to and ran toward a scattering of trees, hoping they'd give him enough shelter to get closer to the men as they neared the horse shelter. As he crouched down in the undergrowth, he saw them throw a heavy blanket over the barbed wire, pushing it down. Then Delco retrieved a makeshift halter and a few ropes from the truck before he and his helper started making their way to the lean-to. Grant saw them looking around to see whether there was anyone who could spot them, but this didn't slow their progress. Meanwhile, Grant hoped that Hunter had managed to persuade the sheriff to come out here in the middle of the night. It didn't matter that both he and Hunter were about a head taller than Delco; he didn't want to think what would happen if either of the thieves carried a gun and felt cornered.

Grant moved as they moved, trying to stay out of their direct field of vision but keeping his eye on them. They looked around some more before suddenly slipping inside the lean-to.

Grant's heart stopped. What if they spotted Hunter? His Cowboy had no place to go! He held back, praying that Hunter would be able to hide among the twenty-some young horses that were huddled together in the shelter. Then he heard shouting and the horses ran out, but no men followed. Grant stood up and didn't know what to do—give up his cover and run to the shelter or simply wait and hope he'd see the men emerge without Hunter.

# —38—

HUNTER knew it would only be a matter of time. The sheriff was on his way and Grant had his back. That said, he was still cornered. Delco and his compadre would have to come inside the lean-to to draw out the horses, and if they spotted him, they would certainly retaliate. He hoped Grant was only just behind them.

Hunter took a few deep breaths, trying to calm his nerves. He had to stay levelheaded. He wasn't just looking out for his own hide, but for Grant's too. And his horses. He couldn't forfeit those by acting irrationally or out of fear. No, he had to lay low, keep his head down until the absolute last moment.

They'd discussed how to catch Delco in the act. He'd have to be caught with clear intention of taking at least one horse with him. Preferably the horse would already be wearing some sort of makeshift bridle, so it would be clear that Delco was leading the horse away from the field.

Hunter pushed himself into a dark corner and felt reassured by the nearness of the horses. He would just have to bide his time. How much longer? He tried to listen for footsteps, but although he'd heard the telltale crackling of fresh snow when Grant had walked away, now he couldn't make out anything.

Suddenly the horses at the front of the lean-to stirred and started running out, closely followed by the rest. The cold of the outside air flooded in, and Hunter shivered as adrenaline started coursing through his veins. When he saw a frantically waving man run into the shelter, Hunter tried to disappear into the thin wooden wall behind him, though he knew he couldn't. He didn't breathe again until the man ran after the horses, apparently unaware of Hunter's presence.

Trying to will away the need to run outside, Hunter panted heavily. He would have to give Delco the time to round up one of the young horses, put a halter over it, and start his way back to his trailer. How long would it take? A minute? Five? Surely Grant would find a way to signal him? Damn! Hunter wished they'd spent their nights in the lean-to planning every move instead of trying to find pleasurable ways of keeping warm. They would only get one chance at this.

Then a shotgun blast rang through the frigid night air and Hunter ran outside so fast, his head was spinning. Almost automatically he cocked his rifle, pointing it at anything that moved, but there was chaos. The horses were running around the small corral with no means of finding an exit, and there were three men trying to do the same.

Grant was shouting at them to stop moving, and in a flash Hunter saw one of the men go down. It was too dark to see if there was any blood involved, but he said a quick prayer nevertheless. It was clear it wasn't Grant, though, since he was shouting Delco's name. Another shot pierced the air, and the horses scattered again. This time it came from the other side of the meadow, and everyone froze. Even Delco stopped moving, and from the corners of his eyes, Hunter saw Grant tackle the compact rodeo cowboy until he was sitting on top of him. Hunter managed to make his legs move and approached the other man, cautiously coming closer with his rifle at the ready.

"Seems you boys have everything under control," the county sheriff said in his usual ultra-cool voice. He walked over to Grant and Delco. "You again? Didn't I tell you to get the hell out of my county? I'm bringing you in, you punk."

Grant got up off the ground and let Delco go so the sheriff could pull him up by his jacket. "Doesn't look good, Delco," the sheriff continued. "Caught red-handed with the intention of stealing horses. And you didn't even change your MO to cover all the other horse thefts on this ranch. Would have helped if you'd robbed other people too, but I'm calling this stalking as well. You picked out this ranch to get back at these people, didn't you?"

"No way!" Delco cried out. "I stole from other places!"

"You did?" the sheriff asked. "Where?"

"The Hope Ranch," Delco spit out.

"Is that so?"

"They didn't even notice horses missing, they got so many!"

The sheriff shook his head and turned to Hunter. "I'll book them if you help me get them back to the station. I'll need to take your statements, but that can wait until tomorrow, after we've all had some sleep."

Grant moved to the drifter, who was still lying face down in the snow. He helped him get up, and the man followed without any struggle, so Hunter and Grant could easily take him to the sheriff's car.

The following morning the sheriff returned to take pictures of Delco's truck and the way he'd flattened the barbed wire with the blanket. He took Hunter and Grant's statements in the big house over a cup of coffee.

"What was the sheriff doing here?" Izzie asked when she crossed the three men in the hallway as they were showing the sheriff out. Grant couldn't help noticing she was starting to waddle. It almost looked like she was carrying more than one child.

"Let's go in here and I'll explain," Hunter said, putting his arm around his sister's shoulders as he guided her back into the living room.

He sat Izzie down, brought her a pillow for her back and a cup of tea before sitting next to her. By then she was almost frantic.

"It's got nothing to do with Hugh, right? Don't tell me Lisa's giving us a hard time? I don't think I could stand it. She promised she'd sign those papers before I had the baby!"

"Sssh, sis," Hunter said, stroking her thigh. "It has nothing to do with that. We caught our horse thief."

"You did?" The news seemed to light her up.

"Yes, and he's quite familiar with this place."

"Who is it? Someone who used to work here?"

"Rory, his right hand man, yes, but that guy isn't the brain behind the whole scheme."

"Come on, guys, this isn't twenty questions," Izzie said impatiently.

"It's Delco, Izzie," Hunter said calmly.

"Del…? That bastard!" In one unusually swift movement she was on her feet and her fists were balled. "What the fuck. Where did he get the balls to do this to us?"

Hunter pulled her toward the couch again, but she wouldn't sit down. "Take it easy, sis. The sheriff has him in the county jail, and they're trying to track down his buyer so they can indict that guy too. It looks like he was targeting us, but if his boasting held any truth, he hit the Hope Ranch as well, only they never filed any complaints."

"You okay, darling?" Hugh said, bursting though the door and moving directly toward Izzie. "I heard you shouting. Is everything okay?"

"Yeah, I'm fine." She swatted him away. "It's that damn Delco. I wish that man had never crossed my path. I can't believe I ever thought he'd be part of my life." Izzie seemed to mellow as Hugh put his arms around her. "I'm so glad I have you."

Grant was having a hard time not laughing at the rollercoaster of emotions Izzie was going through right now. Hunter was just glad she had Hugh now and wasn't crying on his shoulder for a change. It wasn't until Grant sat down next to him and put his hand on his knee that he realized how happy he was to have Grant by his side through all this as well. At least the tension over the horses going missing was over and the culprit was found. Hunter was happy it wasn't a cougar, since he hated shooting them, but he would have if he'd had to protect his ranch.

Hunter yawned and leaned against Grant as they watched how Hugh was comforting Izzie.

"Hey, don't fall asleep on me," Grant whispered.

"Didn't get a lot of sleep last night, with the stakeout and catchin' us a horse thief," Hunter said in an exaggerated Wild West accent.

Grant chuckled. "And you were pretty excited afterward as well."

Hunter nodded, remembering how he hadn't been able to sleep when they'd finally managed to find their bed. Grant had suggested he needed to be more worn out, so they'd had sex in the safety of their room, Hunter's room, with Hunter on his knees and his face buried in the pillow because he couldn't stop moaning.

"We really should get our own place," Hunter said quietly.

"Why don't we get some wood and stake out the perimeter? You have the plans, right?" Grant suggested.

"There's a few feet of snow outside," Hunter replied, stating the obvious.

"But it gives us something to look forward to."

Hunter had to admit it sounded tempting. With his livestock secure, he would have time to think of other things, and the house was at the top of his list. "I'll need to order the wood if we want to start building as soon as the ground clears."

"Not to mention we need help. We can't do this alone, Cowboy."

Hunter nodded. "Yeah, I know, but Flynn and Gable offered their help, and Tim and Hugh are going to help too. I think Hugh wants some excuse to get out of the house instead of playing nursemaid to Izzie."

Grant chuckled. "She *is* starting to look like a beached whale."

"Yeah, she probably feels like one too."

Hunter's pensiveness clearly wasn't lost on Grant. "Are you thinking about Miranda?"

Hunter shrugged. He hated to admit it to Grant, but he *was* thinking about her and how guilty he felt over not being there for her. "She's having my baby, Grant. And she has nobody to lean on." He nodded at Izzie, who had finally settled on the couch close to Hugh.

"Then you should go see her," Grant stated without hesitation.

Hunter sat up to take a good look at Grant's expression and realized Grant wasn't kidding.

"I mean it, Cowboy. You're no use to me all morose and bad-tempered. Go over there and talk to her. The better you get along with her, the better it'll be for the kid. Unless you don't want to be a part of your child's life."

"I do!" Hunter was quick to answer. "I want nothing more. I wish we could raise it here, on the ranch, like we're doing with your kids. One big, happy family. But Miranda won't even pick up the phone."

To Hunter's surprise, Grant got up and walked into the hallway, only to return with their coats. "Let's go."

"Where…?"

"I'm taking you into town, to pay Miranda a visit."

"Grant, I don't think—"

"Shut up, Cowboy. If the mountain won't come to Mohammed, Mohammed must go to the mountain. Or something like that."

Hunter didn't put up an argument. He was overcome by nerves, though. Could he do it? He looked up at Grant standing there, gesturing for him to put his coat on.

"I'd rather stake out the house," Hunter joked. Seeing Grant roll his eyes and shake his head made him give up his feeble attempt at protest. Grant was right, he couldn't keep putting this off.

All the way into town, he was glad Grant was driving, because he couldn't even get his own thoughts organized, let alone get them from A to B without hitting something. His heart sank when he saw Miranda's house. The curtains were drawn and the mailbox was overflowing.

"Damn," Grant cursed, glancing at Hunter with compassion. They both realized the reason Miranda wasn't answering her phone was that it seemed she hadn't been home in a long time.

"Her mother lives across town," Hunter said, vaguely remembering Miranda mentioning it once.

IT TOOK them two hours and a lot of asking around to find the house Miranda's mother lived in. As they exited the truck, they were greeted by a morose-looking woman.

"You Hunter?" she asked.

Hunter nodded.

"She don' want to see you."

"Is she okay?" Grant asked when Hunter didn't say anything.

"As good as she can be, given the circumstances, I suppose."

"The circumstances?" Grant asked.

"And who might you be?" the woman asked.

"I'm Grant, Hunter's… friend."

The woman didn't answer. Instead she turned to Hunter. "You can come in." Then back to Grant. "You stay out here."

Hunter looked at Grant for support before walking inside, but all Grant dared to do was wink.

# —39—

THE wait outside was endless. Grant paced on the sidewalk next to the truck, then got in and played piano on the dashboard before getting out again. He kept staring at the door Hunter had disappeared through. Damn! He wanted to be in there with Hunter, with his lover. He hated the fact that he would never be recognized as Hunter's partner. He would always be his "friend" and nothing more.

Just as Grant kicked the front tire of the truck in frustration, Hunter walked out. Grant couldn't read his expression; Hunter seemed excited, but he didn't look happy. That wasn't a good sign.

"So?" Grant asked when they were both sitting inside the truck.

"Start the engine."

"Not until you tell me what happened in there," Grant said, feeling more and more uncomfortable.

"Could you just drive me to Mercy Hospital, please?"

Grant started the car. "That's quite a drive."

"Just drive, Grant."

Grant pulled away from the curb and drove to the Interstate. At the last stop light before the on ramp, Hunter finally spoke.

"I'm a dad, Grant. I have a son."

Grant smiled and looked at his lover. "Congratulations, Cowboy. It's not all good, though, is it?"

Before Hunter could answer, cars behind them started honking their horns.

"Hang on," Grant said as he accelerated beyond the traffic light and found a space to park just before he had to get on the Interstate.

"You're going to have to tell me before I keep driving, because if you're going to spring things on me, I won't be responsible for the consequences."

Hunter grabbed Grant's hand and squeezed it on the bench between them. "Miranda was inside the house. She says she doesn't want to see him."

Grant's mouth practically dropped open. "She doesn't want to see her own son?"

"She says she can't cope with a sick child. Grant, just drive me over there so I can see him?"

"So what's wrong with him?"

"*Grant!*"

"Okay, okay." Grant pulled back into traffic. He was going to need all his concentration to drive safely, but he wanted to know what Miranda had told Hunter. What did she mean by "a sick child"? Was it just that he was born early and could still die? Or was there something worse?

Hunter didn't say anything all the way over to the hospital, and even as they pulled into the parking lot, Hunter remained eerily silent. Grant feared the worst.

Hunter seemed to know what to do, though. He had the name of a doctor to ask for, and they were directed to the pediatric intensive care unit.

"Mr. Krause? Miss Bocanovic told me you would eventually show up."

Grant wanted to defend Hunter against the female doctor's disdain, but he bit his tongue instead. Hunter was big enough to fight his own battles.

Hunter was surprisingly calm. "I just found out I have a son. I'd like to see him."

This seemed to mellow the doctor. "Very well. What has Miss Bocanovic told you?"

"She said he has some deformity and that he's going to need surgery?"

She nodded. "She signed a release but doesn't have the funds for the operations."

"There's more than one?"

Grant gently put his hand on the lower part of Hunter's back in support and hoped it wasn't too obvious. Hunter didn't react.

"He has spina bifida," the doctor continued in her professionally detached tone.

"What does that mean?" Hunter asked.

"It means he has a defect at the bottom of his spine. We need to operate on him to close it and reduce the damage. On top of that, we'll need to put a shunt into his brain to drain excess fluid."

Grant could tell the doctor's explanation was only adding to Hunter's confusion, so he stepped in. "Practically, what does this mean to the baby? Will he end up with a disability?"

"Most likely," the doctor answered matter-of-factly. "It's hard to predict, but most spina bifida children have significant problems walking and controlling their bladders and/or bowels, and some have developmental problems as well." She didn't stick around for more questions. "I'll go see if he's stable enough for you to visit him, Mr. Krause."

"We both want to see him," Hunter replied, much to Grant's surprise.

She looked at Grant and nodded, clearly not entirely happy with the situation but unable to deny them.

After she left, they were standing alone in the waiting room, and Hunter turned into Grant's arms. Grant squeezed him tightly. "It'll be okay, Cowboy," he said softly. "Everything will turn out for the best." Grant hated the empty words, especially because he didn't know if they were true, but he wanted desperately to comfort his lover.

"I know," Hunter answered. He pulled out of Grant's arms and ran his hand over his face.

Grant knew the strain on Hunter's face wouldn't disappear for a long time. He thanked his lucky stars that he had perfect kids, but he understood Hunter's worries all too well. The years of sneaking around to catch a glimpse of his children to see if they were all right were still vivid in his memories, after all.

A nurse appeared in the doorway. She had a much more accommodating smile than the doctor and invited them both to follow her. After scrubbing their hands and donning white gowns over their clothes, they were led to an incubator. Inside was a tiny infant with a cap on his head that looked too big and little tubes everywhere.

"He was born about a month premature, so he's a little one, but he's doing surprisingly well. You can put your hand through this hole and touch him. He likes to be touched," she said with a concerned smile on her face. "Don't worry too much about all the noises and beeping sounds. We'll look after those. If there's anything you need, just let me know."

She left the two of them alone, and they both stood there, staring at the tiny tot.

"Sit," Grant eventually said. "Do what she suggested. Put your hand inside and just touch him gently."

With some apprehension, Hunter sat down and did what Grant suggested. Grant put his hand on Hunter's shoulder and felt him slowly relax.

"He's so tiny."

Grant gave Hunter's shoulder a squeeze. "They all are when they're just born. He'll grow. Before you know it, you'll be teaching him to ride a horse."

"Not so sure about that," Hunter answered softly. "The doctor said he might not even walk."

Grant looked around and spotted a stool, which he pulled closer so he could sit down next to Hunter. "We can deal with that, right? We'll find a way."

"I just can't believe Miranda doesn't want to see him." Hunter was gently stroking the baby's fingers, and the little boy yawned, looking quite content.

"She might feel guilty or something," Grant suggested.

"She's his mother," Hunter hissed. "He needs her."

"I think you should give him a name," Grant said, in the hope it would distract Hunter.

"Who says he doesn't already have one?"

Grant shrugged and pointed at a small card stuck to the incubator. It had a teddy bear picture on it and the words "Male Baby Bocanovic." "Did Miranda mention a name?"

Hunter shook his head.

"Then I guess you can choose."

Hunter didn't say anything for a long while; then he suddenly took a deep breath in. "Think she'll let me name him after my dad?"

"Don't see why not," Grant said with a broad smile. "I think your dad would have appreciated it too."

"It's not like it's his first grandson. Danny was first."

Grant nodded and gently stroked the back of Hunter's neck. "Yes, but this is the son of his son, and although I'm sure he would have been proud of Danny, he'll be extra-proud of Matthew because he's a Krause."

"Matthew Krause. I like the way that sounds."


AFTER two surgeries and a bit of recovery, they brought Matthew home on a beautiful spring day. They took a detour to Miranda's mother's house, and Miranda agreed to see her son, but she didn't want to hold him, so Hunter and Grant drove back home with the bundled-up infant happily sleeping in his brand new safety seat.

At the ranch, Hunter introduced Matthew to his grandmother, his aunts, and cousin, and then walked him outside. Grant watched Hunter walk to the back of the house and couldn't resist following him. Under a large oak tree was a small family cemetery plot where Grant knew Hunter's dad was buried, among a few other relatives he didn't know. Grant smiled when he realized what Hunter was doing, and kept his distance, giving Hunter some privacy. He could hear his voice, though.

"Hey, Dad. Look who I brought to see you. Never thought there'd be another Krause on this ranch, but here he is. This is Matthew. Do you like the name? I know you'd probably think it's unnecessary to name him after you, but I couldn't think of a better name for my son. I'm so proud of him, Dad. He's a real fighter, this one, just like you. And since he's probably going to be my only one, I'd better get it right. I'll try my best, Dad, just like you taught me. Can't do better than my best."

When Hunter stayed silent for some time, Grant came closer and eventually sat down on the bench next to his lover. "Your dad would have been very proud of you."

"Oh, I know," Hunter said with an absent smile. "I wish he could have been here to enjoy his grandson. He's got the best view in the world, though." He nodded his head at the majestic fields in front of them. There were trees outlining them around the sides and horses grazing in the distance, but it was amazing how far you could see.

"All the way to where the earth touches the sky," Grant mused.

"There's no better place on Earth," Hunter agreed.

# —40—

THE leaves on the trees were coloring red by the time Hunter and Grant held their housewarming party. Despite last-minute changes to the building plan, the wooden ranch house, although smaller than the homestead where the other Krauses lived, still looked majestic. Hunter's mother remained in the old house with Izzie, Hugh, and their baby girl, Hugh and Lisa's son Danny, and Bernie, when she wasn't show-jumping somewhere else in the country. Christy had chosen to stay there as well, with her kids. It was easier for her, since she worked in the big kitchen, and the kids still saw Grant every day. Christy also looked after Matthew when the men were working, but at night, the baby boy was going to have his own room in his dad's house.

They'd added a ramp to the porch, and most of the rooms were on the first floor, just in case it became necessary for Matthew, but other than that, it looked like every other ranch house in the county.

Hunter was beaming with pride now it was finally finished.

Their guests arrived around noontime, bringing side dishes for the picnic and extra chairs. Calley brought her twins and told them Bill was too busy to make it. The twins spent more time on Flynn's lap than in their bassinets. Together with Izzie's daughter and Matthew, this brought the baby count to four. Danny played with the three other older kids, and Hunter's mother surveyed it all with the pride of a grandmother.

Everyone who'd helped out with the building arrived to celebrate the men moving in, and Hunter felt the love. He'd never imagined that the people who meant most to him would accept the man in his life so easily. The one he'd worried most about was Gable.

Gable had always been there for Hunter. He'd been Hunter's best friend for years, and Hunter had always been eager to help out when Gable needed him as well, but of course, Grant was Gable's ex, and they hadn't parted in the best of circumstances. For the longest time, Hunter had been afraid that his love for Grant would make him lose his best friend.

Gable and Grant had found a middle ground, though. They'd found a way to forgive each other, and now all Hunter felt from Gable was the quiet understanding he'd always wanted. Gable was a man of few words, but he'd diligently helped them build their house, and Hunter had even seen Gable and Grant laugh at things together, so this was more than he could have ever hoped for.

During the building, Hunter's appreciation for Flynn had grown as well. The man had two right hands and no fear of heights, so he and Grant had been the main men on the roof. Hunter had always felt that atop a horse was about as far from the ground as he felt comfortable, and the only visible reminder of Gable's bad leg was that he couldn't get up a ladder, so they were the ones to fetch material for the two roofers.

The way Flynn and Gable acted around each other in public made Hunter see that it was possible to show you loved your man without being all over him and embarrassing your mother. This was another big step. Hunter's mother had slowly warmed up to Grant and was now treating him like she treated her other son-in-law, Hugh. She wanted both of them to work hard and treat their better halves like royalty, and expected nothing less from Grant than she did of Hugh. Hunter wouldn't have wanted it any other way.

The big surprise came when Lisa arrived at the ranch. Hunter had put out a few feelers to figure out where she was and to invite her back home, but he hadn't received any confirmation, so her arrival was truly a surprise.

She and Jack drove up to the ranch in Jack's old truck, and Hunter worried that life on the Tennessee country music circuit hadn't been all she'd made it out to be. Lisa looked happy, though, and despite a short awkward moment between her and Hugh, the reunion with Danny was full of hugs and kisses. Lisa proudly showed off her baby bump, so Hugh teasingly congratulated his brother for knocking up his ex-wife.

Everyone ended up staying until the sun set, and then it was time to get all the kids to bed.

Although Grant and Hunter hadn't planned it that way, last-minute work had meant their first night at the new house was the evening after the housewarming. Everything still smelled new, and although they'd been careful to let the house air out to get rid of the painting fumes, there was no mistaking the fact they all still had to learn to find their way around.

While Hunter was checking on his sleeping son, Grant closed the heavy front door, shutting out the outside world. Hunter found Grant caressing the intricate woodwork he'd started carving the night they staked out the house, when there was still snow on the ground.

"It's by far the best-looking door this side of the Rockies," Hunter joked.

"And you're the best-looking man this side of the Rockies too," Grant replied, turning around to take Hunter in his arms.

"You mean there's a better-looking man on the other side?"

Grant poked Hunter's ribs. "There are lots of better-looking men, but I only want this one."

"I'm glad to hear that," Hunter whispered while kissing Grant's ear.

"Mattie asleep?" Grant asked.

"Like a lamb," Hunter smiled.

Grant chuckled. "He takes after his dad. Feed him well and keep him warm and he's asleep before you can say goodnight."

Now it was Hunter's turn to poke Grant in the ribs, which wasn't easy, because Grant held him in a tight hug. "We've been working hard. I don't see you lying awake much either!"

Grant's face turned serious. "So you think you can stay awake long enough to christen this house?"

Hunter pushed his lover against the intricately carved door and devoured him with a kiss. Then he pulled away. "As long as we can do it horizontally."

Although Hunter had crossed the hallway on the way to his son's room, he hadn't entered their bedroom yet. They'd quickly made the bed that morning, knowing they wouldn't have the energy to do it later, but hadn't been inside the room after that.

They hadn't put up any curtains yet, but there was a large banner tied to the curtain rail. It said: "Enjoy the rest of your life together." In smaller letters underneath was added: "We know we'll enjoy the quiet."

"Christy," Grant said at almost the same time Hunter said, "Izzie."

There was a huge fruit basket in the middle of the bed and rose petals strewn around.

Hunter snorted. "I wonder if they meant anything by that? Fruit."

Grant burst out laughing, then stopped as abruptly as he started and grabbed Hunter from behind, kissing his neck. Overcome by the sudden gesture, Hunter leaned his head back in the hope of moving even closer to his lover, until he felt teeth biting into his flesh. "Shit, you going all vampire on me?"

Grant held him tight. "Nope. You're my fruit, and you look so tasty I want to bite you."

Still embracing, they walked to the bed, where Hunter turned around and sat down, pulling Grant between his legs. "I'll show you how tasty you are." He looked up at Grant as he unbuttoned first Grant's jeans and then his own. Grant followed him with his eyes, a smile slowly spreading over his face until Hunter took Grant's semi-erect cock in his mouth.

"Fuck, I'll never get used to what you do to me," Grant said, with a definite grunt in his voice.

Hunter used his free hand to attempt to pull Grant's pants down further, but since Grant liked his clothes kind of form-fitting, it wasn't easy. "I'll do mine if you do yours," Grant finally croaked. Hunter reluctantly let go and Grant pulled his jeans down while he watched Hunter do the same.

Hunter put the basket in the corner and in one fell swoop pulled the duvet off so petals flew all around them.

Once they were naked, Grant tackled Hunter until they were lying on the bed in each other's arms. Hunter looked down at Grant and ran his fingers through Grant's dark curls. "Damn, I love you."

Grant didn't say anything at first, and then he slowly started smiling. "You know you say these things and I don't know how to react. If I say 'I love you' back, it sounds like I'm just saying it because you said it, and if I don't, then you'll think I don't love you. And you know I do. You know I've never felt anything for anyone else like I feel for you."

"Except maybe your kids?" Hunter said. All of a sudden his heart was racing, and he didn't know why. Over the past year and a half, their relationship hadn't been easy, mostly because they were both crap at talking about the really important things, but he knew they'd grown. Now they were both lying on their bed, in their own house. Anyone who mattered knew they were together. They were naked, which always resulted in sex. Urgent, passionate, no-holds-barred explosive sex. So why would Grant pick now to start a serious conversation?

"What I feel for my kids is different. I'm responsible for them. I need to make sure they're brought up right and happy, and that they grow up without having to worry about the realities of real life until they need to stand on their own two feet."

"And you don't need me to be happy?" Hunter asked. As soon as he heard the words, he thought they sounded needy and... well, frankly, like Miranda always sounded when she was whining.

Grant smiled at Hunter and shook his head. "That's the difference. You don't need *me* to be happy."

"That's where you're wrong," Hunter said seriously. "I was a morose, cantankerous bastard before you came." He snuggled closer into Grant's embrace.

"You were pretty cantankerous when I was already here," Grant corrected him.

"You changed that, and I'm glad you did. I didn't know how miserable I was until you showed me it could be different."

Grant caressed Hunter's jaw so he would look at him. "Pretty impressive, since I was just as uncomfortable admitting I really preferred men."

Moving to lay half on top of Grant, Hunter kissed him softly. He caressed Grant's sides and his soft chest hair, which was every bit as curly as the hair on his head. They were skin to skin, no fabric separating them, and it felt intimate rather than sexual, although Hunter had no doubt they'd end up making love. Part of him felt like such a wuss, enjoying this languid discovery of the man he'd been fucking for more than a year. He remembered how Miranda had complained about his wham-bam-thank-you-ma'am attitude in bed and how he'd never understood her—until now. These past eighteen months he'd learned to sleep next to Grant and enjoy the warm, firm body next to him in bed. He'd grown to miss the small, intimate caresses if he woke up and Grant had already gotten up. He'd surprised himself by still feeling lust for this man he'd spent almost 24/7 with for so long. And Hunter hoped he would still feel it for a long time to come.

While they were languidly kissing, the heat rose slowly between them. It was as if they'd suddenly realized they had time—and space—to just enjoy each other. As if they'd both come to the conclusion that making love was not a sprint, but a marathon; that it wasn't about getting off, but about what it felt like to share, to enjoy and give enjoyment; that it mattered more how they made the other one feel than how they felt themselves; that giving the other one pleasure would automatically ensure their own pleasure as well.

More than once, Hunter caught Grant looking at him, trying to catch his eye. It was starting to make Hunter feel uncomfortable, both because he didn't understand why things were different between them all of a sudden and because he was afraid Grant was having second thoughts, now that their relationship was as out in the open as it could be.

Grant letting go of him and falling to his back with a frustrated grunt only added to Hunter's uneasiness.

Afraid of opening a can of worms, Hunter didn't say anything and just looked away. With the full moon shining through the banner that was strung across the window, there was enough light to see clearly inside the room.

"What's wrong?" Grant asked, sitting up on the bed.

"Nothing's wrong."

Grant snorted. "Yeah, right."

"I just...." Hunter sighed and didn't finish his sentence. How could he tell Grant about his insecurities? How could he risk Grant acknowledging them and telling him he had doubts too? What if his fears became real and this white, fluffy cloud they'd been living on while they were building the house suddenly grew dark and menacing? What if Grant decided to continue his wandering life?

"If we're going to make this work, we're going to have to learn to talk to each other, Cowboy," Grant said softly.

Hunter didn't dare look at Grant. When had he suddenly become so scared? He hadn't thought twice about taking on the responsibility of bringing his son home when Miranda had pushed him away, yet now he was scared shitless. And of what?

Hunter got up out of bed and walked to the window. He pulled the banner aside and sat down on the broad windowsill where he could look over the field toward the trees lining the lower ranges. After a little while, Hunter felt a hesitant hand on his shoulder.

"Please talk to me, Cowboy. Don't shut me out."

Hunter put his hand over Grant's. He swallowed and took a deep breath in before answering. "I want... need to know whether you're here to stay."

Grant took a few moments to answer, and Hunter realized he was holding his breath. "Do you honestly think I built a house with my own bare hands just to leave again? Unless you want me...."

"No!" Hunter said loudly. He turned toward Grant and pulled him into his embrace. Placing his ear against Grant's chest, he inhaled Grant's scent and felt chest hair tickle his cheek. After a few moments of squeezing the buff body in his arms, Hunter pulled back just enough to look at Grant. "I was hoping this was happy ever after. I know you're a wanderer, and you told me you can never stay in the same place for long without becoming antsy, but I was hoping you could make an exception. Grant, I need you."

Grant smiled, and Hunter loved how his eyes became mischievous.

"But I'm an old-fashioned kind of guy, Grant."

Grant disentangled himself from Hunter's embrace and sank to his knees, chuckling when they cracked. He was still smiling when he took Hunter's hands in his. "So what are you telling me? You want to make an honest man out of me?"

Hunter shrugged. "I know we can't legally get married, but I need some sort of commitment."

"And here I thought building you a house would be enough to show you I was serious about you, Cowboy."

Hunter ran his fingers through Grant's tight curls and tried to gauge if Grant was joking. Although he was smiling slightly, Hunter felt like Grant meant what he'd said. "You want to settle down here? With me?"

Grant nodded. "Preferably with you, yes." The teasing smile playing around Grant's lips was back. "None of your sisters are my type, really, and your mother's a little old for me, although she's a much better cook than you are. I tried the guy that lives next door, but that didn't really work out, and although he's got a very nice-looking ranch hand, I don't want to fight Gable over him."

Hunter punched Grant's shoulder with his fist. "Stop that."

Grant's look turned serious. "I mean it, Cowboy. This is a great ranch, but it's not the only great ranch around here. I'm here because I like the owner, and I may be wrong, but I believe he likes me too."

"Asshole," Hunter cursed before taking Grant's face in his hand and kissing him. When they finally pulled apart, they were both flushed.

Grant put his hands on Hunter's thighs and pushed himself upright. "This floor is damn hard to sit on."

"Hey, you built it!"

Grant held out his hand and pulled Hunter to his feet. Then he kissed Hunter again. "Now come to bed, because Mattie's going to be up in a few hours."

Hunter watched Grant get into their brand-new bed, but didn't join him right away. Instead he walked to the bathroom and returned just moments later to get down on his knees in front of the bed. Grant eyed him suspiciously.

"Give me your hand."

Grant held out his right hand, still looking unsure at what Hunter was doing.

Hunter slipped a worn, shiny gold ring over Grant's ring finger. It fit perfectly.

"What is this?"

"It was my father's," Hunter answered. "When I was a child I used to crawl on his lap and play with his ring. I asked him once why he wore a ring, because I'd never seen a man wear one, and he said that, for my mother, it was worth wearing it. Because it showed everyone he belonged to her. He never took it off, not even to wash his hands or to work. After he died we had a hard time getting it off his finger, and once we did, my mom gave it to me."

"I don't think she meant you to find a guy to give it to, Hunter. I think she meant for you to wear it."

Hunter shook his head. "It's mine to give and I'd like you to wear it."

"To show I belong to you?"

Hunter cocked his head. "Well, not in the slavery sort of way, just…. I'm proud of what we have, of us. If it makes you feel any better, I'll get one too, and then we can belong to each other."

Grant fingered the ring. "It fits perfectly."

Hunter nodded. "You have his hands. That's one of the first things I noticed about you. I love your hands. They're large and strong but sort of elegant too."

Grant grabbed Hunter's hand and pulled him closer. "Come here before you really go all sappy on me."

Hunter crawled under the covers next to Grant.

"Shit, you're freezing, Cowboy."

They snuggled closer and started kissing again. Hunter was much calmer now that they'd had their little talk. Grant was here to stay, and he'd done what he'd dreamed about and given Grant his ring. That was as good as being married, he felt. And now that they had their own house, they could finally start their life together.

THE next morning, after breakfast, Grant walked into the kitchen of the main house. Hunter followed close behind, with Matthew in his arms, while Grant walked to the counter to pour them both a cup of coffee. Hugh was eating breakfast with his daughter on his lap, and Izzie was frying eggs.

"You're wearing Daddy's ring," Izzie remarked when Grant extended his hand to grab the cups.

Hunter noticed his mother had stopped eating, but he couldn't read her expression.

"Hunter gave it to me last night," Grant said softly.

Izzie smiled. "Looks good on you. It's about time it got worn again."

Hunter wanted some sort of acknowledgment from his mother, but she resumed eating without looking at either him or Grant. Hugh gave him an encouraging smile, but Hunter could tell he'd picked up on the tension as well.

"So are you going to throw us a wedding bash, Hunter?" Hugh said in an attempt at lightening the situation.

"Oh, like when you married Izzie?" Hunter rebutted. "Big dinner and a keg of beer?"

"Hey!" Izzie shouted from the kitchen. "I looked like a beached whale. I was afraid I was going to deliver her on the day of the wedding." She moved behind Hunter and placed her hand on his shoulder as she put a plate of bacon and eggs on the table. "We had our party last night, honey," she told Hunter. "Besides, one day you might want to make it legal, and then we'll really have something to celebrate."

Matthew started fussing, and Hunter got up to bring him to the living room, where the bassinets for both babies were set up so they could sleep during the day. He'd just tucked Matthew in when he heard the door open and close behind him.

"You gave Grant your father's wedding ring."

Hunter turned to face his mother. "Yes."

"I hope he takes good care of it."

"He will," Hunter replied.

"I hope he'll take good care of you too."

"We'll take care of each other, and together we'll take care of Mattie." Hunter resented her stone-faced look and wished he'd had a warmer mother. He vaguely remembered what she was like before his dad died. She was never the most lovey-dovey mother, but he remembered her smiling more when he was young.

"Like a real family?"

Hunter nodded, trying not to show the anger that statement made him feel. "We *are* a real family, Mother. It's not because I don't have a wife that we can't raise Mattie together. Would you rather have had me marry Miranda? At least now I have a partner who loves me and who helps me take care of my boy. *She* doesn't want anything to do with our son!"

"She does, but I told her not to come here."

Hunter couldn't believe his ears. "You talked to her?"

"She turned her back on my grandson. She doesn't deserve to be his mother."

Hunter looked from his mother, ignoring her dismissive look, to Matthew, who still hadn't settled. He wasn't happy with Miranda turning their son away, but he didn't want to have to explain to Mattie that he hadn't tried every avenue for him to have a relationship with his mother.

Swaddling his son in a blanket, Hunter lifted Matthew into his arms and walked back to the kitchen.

"Grant, can you drive us to Miranda's mother's house?"

Grant looked up with a questioning look, and Hunter didn't miss Hugh and Izzie's stunned reaction either, but Grant didn't ask any questions. He picked the keys to the truck off the kitchen counter and led the way.

"So what is this all about?" Grant asked en route to town.

"Apparently my mother told Miranda not to come to the house."

"Miranda wanted to see Mattie?" Grant asked, looking at Hunter.

"Watch the road," Hunter said sternly. He sighed. "I'm not Miranda's biggest fan, especially not after she left Mattie alone in the hospital, and I'm not doing this for her. I'm doing it for him. He might want to know who his mother is one day, and I don't have the heart to tell him she lives just down the road, but we didn't want him to know. If she's willing to acknowledge him, I'll find a way to explain to him why he's being raised by two men and not his mother."

Grant stopped the truck on the soft shoulder and cut the engine. He put his hand on Hunter's thigh. "What if she wants to start raising him, Cowboy?"

Hunter let his head fall back against the seat of the truck. He could feel Mattie's shallow breathing and fast heartbeat through his shirt, and remembering all the sleepless nights trying to get him to settle down made his eyes well up. When he looked at his son, a tear fell on the baby's soft hair, and he wiped it away.

"She gave him to me, Grant. If it hadn't been for her, I wouldn't have had a son. I'm his legal guardian, and I have every intention of raising him. She hasn't worked for over a year and lives with her mother. She doesn't have the financial means to support him."

Grant cocked his head. "I'm afraid the courts don't always take that into account. Around here, if she petitions for custody, they might very well give it to her simply because she's his mother."

"And I'm his father. I have just as much right. I'm the one who brought him home from the hospital. If it had been up to her, he would still be there."

Grant nodded, started the truck again, and pulled out onto the road.

Hunter knew Grant was right. In his heart, he felt he needed to give Matthew the chance to get to know his mother, but the risk was a real one. If Miranda understood that Mattie was a happy child, despite his disabilities, and that taking care of him was not the hardship she'd imagined, she might get it into her head that she wanted more than the occasional visit. Hunter couldn't bear the thought that he'd lose his son.

The truck stopped, and Hunter looked at his lover when Grant placed a hand on his knee.

"You sure about this?"

Hunter nodded. "Just stay with me, okay? I want her to see both of us with Mattie."

Grant agreed reluctantly.

Hunter knew the visit was totally unannounced, so he braced himself for rejection. To his surprise, it was Miranda herself who opened the door. She looked even smaller than Hunter remembered, although she wore a bright summer dress and looked healthier than the last time they'd visited, just before he met his son for the first time.

"Hi, Mir," Hunter said softly.

She smiled shyly and nodded at the men. "Hunter, Grant. Why don't you come inside? So what brings you here?" Her eyes traveled to the bundled-up infant in Hunter's arms and stayed there, even after Grant and Hunter walked into the living room and settled on the couch together.

"I thought it was time you got to know Matthew," Hunter said calmly.

Her eyes still stayed on Matthew. "You don't want him anymore?"

"For heaven's sake, he's not a puppy," Grant intervened, earning him a stern look from Hunter.

"No, Miranda," Hunter agreed. "To the contrary. I'll always be there to raise him, and so will Grant." Hunter looked at Grant again, who still sported a concerned look. "But I feel Mattie should have the chance to get to know his mother as well, especially if she lives in the same area. So I thought I'd introduce the two of you and offer an invitation to come see him at the ranch any time you like."

"Your mother doesn't want me there," Miranda said, barely audible.

"She can say who's allowed in her house, but I run the ranch, and I say who's allowed on the property. Besides, both Grant and I will gladly welcome you into *our* house." Hunter looked at Grant in the hope that Grant would acknowledge his statement, but Grant stayed quiet, his lips tightly pinched. Hunter knew Grant wouldn't contradict him, but he'd hoped for a bit more support.

"I heard you'd built your own house," Miranda said.

At that moment Matthew stirred, and Hunter pulled the blanket away from him a little. "You hot, little fellow?" Grant helped Hunter pull the blanket entirely off, and Hunter lifted him away. Matthew smiled at him, and then at Grant when Grant caressed Matthew's cheek, and the look on Grant's face made Hunter's heart swell. There wasn't a doubt in Hunter's mind that they'd do a good job raising the child. That wasn't what they were here for, though, so he got up and sat down next to Miranda.

"Miranda, meet Matthew. Mattie, meet your mom. You want to hold him?"

Miranda shook her head curtly.

"He's not shy around strangers," Hunter said, trying to encourage her. "At our house he gets passed around between enough people. He's used to it. Everyone adores him."

Matthew smiled broadly when Hunter lifted him up and handed him to Miranda. His smile disappeared when Miranda took him, though. Hunter didn't think he'd start to cry, but his lower lip was quivering, so he stroked Mattie's hair. "See, he's okay."

Miranda nodded, but Hunter could tell she was terrified. It wasn't until she relaxed that Matthew did as well.

"Any time now he's going to smile at you, and I promise you, you'll be sold." As soon as Hunter said the words, he felt Grant's stare and looked at him. Grant closed his eyes in exasperation. Hunter could almost hear Grant ask him whether he actually wanted to hand his son to Miranda.

To Hunter's surprise, Miranda pushed Matthew back into Hunter's hands. "I can't do this, Hunter. Not then and not now."

Hunter instinctively grabbed his son and cradled him in his arms. Matthew was none the wiser, and he'd never remember today, but at least if the question ever came up, Hunter would be able to say he'd tried.

"We better leave, Hunter," Grant said, handing Hunter Mattie's blanket.

Hunter looked at Miranda, who had also gotten up off the couch. "My offer stands. You're always welcome to visit Matthew at the ranch. And if you'd prefer not to come there, just give us a call and we'll bring him here."

Miranda led them out, but near the door, she held Hunter back. "Why, Hunter?"

"Why what? Mir, I never wanted to be a dad. Never had the feeling I was missing anything, but now I can't imagine not being his dad. And Mattie deserves a mom too."

"He's got Grant," Miranda said flatly.

"*I've* got Grant," Hunter corrected her. "And yes, Grant is Mattie's other dad, but one day he's going to ask me who his mom is, and I don't want to have to tell him I didn't want him to meet her."

When Hunter got into the truck with Matthew, he saw Miranda was crying. He knew it would be no use to walk back to her to comfort her. She wouldn't let him. The tension in the truck was thick too. Grant pulled into traffic as if he was chasing another car, and by the time they'd reached the quieter country roads, Hunter had had enough.

"Stop the truck."

"We're practically home," Grant said sternly.

"Stop anyway," Hunter said, trying not to raise his voice.

Grant pulled over roughly at the opposite side of the road from where they'd stopped earlier.

"I know you don't agree with me, but I needed to do this, Grant."

"You sounded like you were ready to leave him there if she'd asked."

Hunter shook his head and sighed dejectedly. "He's my son and I want what's best for him. If that means including his mother in his upbringing, then so be it. I thought you of all people would understand that."

"I thought it was clear that I did. He's my boy too, Hunter, or did you forget what you told me right at the beginning, when we brought him home? I missed out on raising my kids. I don't want to miss out on Mattie. I'd be gutted if she took him away from us, Cowboy."

Hunter scooted closer to Grant on the single seat of the truck and nuzzled Grant's ear.

"I'm sorry. I knew you didn't want me to do this, and I was afraid you'd try to stop me." Hunter kissed Grant's cheek, hoping to seduce his lover into giving in. Grant was usually easily persuaded, and this was no exception, although it took Hunter longer than usual. They were still kissing when Hunter heard the truck's engine kick into gear.

"What are you doing?" Hunter asked.

"Taking you home. We'll drop Mattie off with Christy, and then I'm taking you to our house."

Hunter's eyebrows almost reached his hairline. "It's the middle of the day."

Grant smiled and pushed the accelerator.

# —41—

GRANT loved makeup sex. He often wondered why Hunter and he didn't fight more, because being seduced into relenting by Hunter always proved worth swallowing some of his pride.

They'd quickly handed Matthew to Christy, with the excuse that they were late for their chores, but instead of going to the stables, they hurried to their house, barely able to wait until the front door had closed behind them. As soon as they were alone, Hunter's mouth was all over Grant and his hand was making its way inside Grant's pants.

"Are you going to let me fuck you?" Hunter asked breathlessly.

"Only if we can moan loudly and curse and scream."

"Is that why you haven't let me fuck you since that hotel room in Idaho Falls?"

Hunter's hand moved, and Grant felt like he was about ready to burst. "Fuck, Cowboy. I can't bite my pillow like you do. When I get fucked by a nice-size cock like yours, I don't want to be quiet."

Hunter growled into Grant's mouth and bit his lover's lip. "Damn, that's going to sound so sordid."

"Remember I want to hear you too."

"Oh, you will," Hunter said, removing his hand and walking away, leaving Grant hard and horny, leaning against the front door. If anything, Grant treated it as a dare. He knew he was going to have to bend to Hunter's will, but he wasn't going to bend willingly, for the sole reason that he knew Hunter enjoyed the challenge. Despite his jeans and shirt hanging open and the heaviness between his legs, Grant made it up the stairs before Hunter, and rushed to bar the way to their bedroom.

"What?" Hunter asked playfully. "Do I need a password to get into my own bedroom?"

Grant nodded teasingly.

Hunter moved closer to his lover, fluttering his fingers over the skin of Grant's abs.

Grant tried to resist as long as he could, but it tickled, and his reactions betrayed him. When Hunter started kissing him too, he let go of the doorpost and they burst into their bedroom. Grant held onto Hunter to keep his balance, and they both ended up on the bed, Hunter half on top of Grant.

Hunter stopped, looking down at Grant.

"What?" Grant asked, puzzled by Hunter's sudden reluctance.

"It's kind of depraved to be having sex in the middle of the day on a work day," Hunter said.

Grant raised an eyebrow. "We could just go to work."

"Hell, no. You promised me something, and I'm cashing in." Hunter ground his hips against Grant's erection. "I want you begging for mercy in three minutes flat."

"Begging?" Grant asked confidently. "I don't beg. Especially not for something I'm going to get anyway."

"We'll see about that," Hunter said, looking equally cocky while he slid off the bed and started taking his clothes off.

Grant watched him from where he was lying, his head supported by his hand, enjoying the show. Hunter had a tall, buff body that showed ample evidence of a good life of manual labor, combined with the tight buns and strong thighs of a horseman. Grant couldn't have been more turned on. After a short pause, he started pulling his jeans down. When he tried to take off his shirt, Hunter stopped him.

"Let me do that." Hunter straddled Grant and pushed his hands under the shirt to caress Grant's pecs.

Grant's muscles contracted under the ministrations, so his only recourse was to tease his lover. "Did you change your mind? Are you going to ride me, Cowboy?"

Hunter shook his head slowly, the tip of his tongue just sticking out between his lips. He was grinding his hips and basically driving Grant crazy, so Grant ran his hands over Hunter's hairy thighs.

"If anyone is going to do any riding it will be you, Stud, but I have other things in mind."

Grant raised himself up to kiss Hunter, but Hunter played hard to get. After he stepped off the bed, he crooked his finger at Grant, making him get up too. They were about the same height, and Grant pushed himself against Hunter to steal a kiss.

"Stop stalling," Hunter said with a broad smile, "and show me your nice ass."

Grant knew resisting any further wouldn't do any good. He knew what was coming and desperately wanted it, so the more he protested, the longer it would take. This was bigger than him, though. Hunter was usually the needy one and always eager to give in when Grant went all macho on him, but Grant found Hunter turning the tables quite enticing.

"What if I don't want you all over my ass?" Grant protested weakly.

"I'd say you were downright lying," Hunter replied, pushing Grant back toward the bed.

Grant let himself drop down on his back, a part of him still needing to put up a little bit of a struggle. He could see the lust in Hunter's eyes, which were even darker than usual, and smiled as Hunter crawled on top of him. He swallowed hard and bit back a moan when Hunter pushed his shirt apart and attacked his nipples.

It dawned on Grant that they usually didn't take their time. They'd explored some, of course, but never to distraction, like Hunter was doing now. It had always been in the back of their minds that they had to be quiet and not disturb Hunter's mother or his sisters sleeping down the hall. The kids were usually pretty good sleepers, luckily, but still, they could never quite let go in bed. Now he could let the moans escape from his mouth, and he cursed under his breath when Hunter's mouth ventured lower and started exploring his pubic hair and the area around his already achingly excited cock.

Almost automatically, Grant spread his legs, allowing Hunter more access, and Hunter didn't disappoint. When Hunter's fingers started exploring his balls and then the skin behind his sac, Grant's breathing sped up.

"Want to hear you," Hunter murmured.

Grant opened his eyes and looked down at his lover's face, which was hovering over the heavy cock lying on his belly. He wanted to wipe the smirk off Hunter's face, tell him to suck on his cock, but he didn't. Instead he decided to explore this side of Hunter he didn't see very often, the dominant side, the side of the man who ran a successful ranch and didn't take no for an answer. Was he the only one who got to see Hunter's softer side? He probably was, but then, how many people knew he could be just as commanding in the sack?

"What are you going to do to me?" Grant asked, hoping Hunter would already have a pretty good idea.

"Not telling you," Hunter teased. "Can you take it, Stud? Not knowing what's going to happen?"

Damn, his cowboy knew him too well. "You know what I like," Grant answered, not sounding as confident—or comfortable—as he would like. Hunter was smiling way too confidently, in Grant's eyes, but he told himself Hunter would never do anything Grant wasn't comfortable with. There wasn't much Grant wasn't comfortable with, come to think of it.

Hunter kept eye contact as he started circling Grant's entrance with his fingers. Grant's breathing sped up even more.

"Let me hear you," Hunter asked again.

Grant moaned loudly, then went silent again, biting the inside of his cheek.

"Oh, come on," Hunter protested. "You make me feel like what I'm doing to you isn't worth shit."

"You know what you're doing to me," Grant replied, his voice quivering from holding back.

"I need to hear you," Hunter repeated.

"What, you want me to talk dirty?" Grant asked, trying to put some strength behind his voice but failing as Hunter withdrew his fingers. He went limp on the bed, rolling his eyes. Why was Hunter pulling away from him? What had he done wrong? He looked up again. "Don't stop, Cowboy! Please?" Grant tried. Hunter *had* told him he wanted to have him begging.

Hunter returned, shaking his head and smiling. "Just getting the lube. Thought it would feel better to grease you up a bit first."

Grant chuckled at his own insecurities. Didn't Hunter understand that he was out of his depth here? Grant moved his hand to his cock, tugging at it a few times, and then cupped his sac, desperately needing more than he was getting right now.

The gel felt cold for a moment, but Hunter's fingers slipping inside his body warmed him up pretty quickly. Grant spread his legs a little more.

"Still not hearing the love here," Hunter said, a seductive smile playing around his mouth and one eyebrow raised.

"I can feel the love, though," Grant replied. He groaned to stress his point.

Hunter pushed forward and almost immediately found Grant's prostate.

"Fuck, yeah." Grant moaned softly as he felt pleasure shoot out from his groin. He rubbed his erection again, spreading the pre-cum around. It felt good to satisfy his need for more stimulation.

"Stop touching yourself," Hunter commanded.

"Fuck, Cowboy, move it along then," Grant complained. "It's the middle of the day. They're going to start missing us around this place!"

"Yeah," Hunter agreed. "But nobody will dare to come into the house. They'll just wonder what we're up to."

"So fuck me already."

Hunter chuckled. "I will. If you're good."

"Damn!" Grant shouted. He ignored Hunter's earlier demand and enveloped his cock with his hand again, just to scratch his itch. He also moved his ass in the direction of Hunter's unmoving hand.

Hunter rubbed Grant's prostate again. "Now stop touching yourself or I'm not doing that again."

"Stop teasing me then," Grant protested, but he raised his hands over his head anyway, looking longingly at his engorged erection. "Come on, Cowboy," Grant said breathlessly. "Either fuck me with those fingers or fuck me with your dick."

Hunter moved his fingers in and out, carefully brushing past Grant's bundle of nerves.

"Fuck, yeah. Oh, that's good, Cowboy. Right there." Grant spread his legs more, pulling up his knees, and as a result, missed Hunter diving in. It wasn't until he felt Hunter's tongue circling the fingers and stimulating the distended muscle he was trying to relax that Grant groaned loudly without holding back, even though his voice sounded loud in the otherwise quiet bedroom. There was nobody to hear them, anyway. "Uh… oh man!" Hunter had moved his mouth to Grant's cock and was sucking it inside, and he hadn't stopped pumping his fingers. Grant's spine tingled, and he could barely form a coherent thought, let alone a word or a sentence that made any sense. He let one of his legs drop and tried to watch Hunter bending over him when he noticed Hunter fisting himself. Seeing how much this was also turning Hunter on made the heat rise even more in Grant.

"If you're not… going to fuck me… now it's…." Grant didn't get to finish his sentence because his whole body contracted and he shot his load down Hunter's throat.

When Hunter released him, he was still twitching. Every time Hunter touched him on his way up the bed, Grant shivered. "Fuck me, Cowboy," Grant managed to say, but his voice had no power.

Hunter shook his head and kissed him softly. "You look like you'd crumble if I even tried to touch you."

Grant jumped involuntarily when Hunter put his hand on the side of his chest.

"See?" Hunter whispered as he tenderly snuggled up to Grant.

"Still want you inside me. Want to feel you come inside my body."

Hunter shook his head. "It's not about coming, Grant. It's this. The cuddling and the being together. I loved hearing you moan and knowing I was doing that to you, but what's really turning me on is that I'll get to fall asleep next to you and you'll still be there when I wake up."

Grant had to admit that even after more than a year of doing just that—going to sleep and waking up as a couple—hearing Hunter say it made it all seem so real that it frightened him.

"Come on, Cowboy," Grant said, making light of it. He turned to Hunter and put his arm around Hunter's shoulder, pulling him close. "I don't believe you don't need to get off right now."

Hunter didn't fight him when Grant pulled him on top and spread his legs. Grant was very relaxed, and it took next to no effort for Hunter to push his cock deep into Grant's tight body. Urged on by Grant grasping his ass cheeks and pulling them closer, Hunter started thrusting frantically. As Grant expected, it didn't take much before Hunter was moaning loudly and coming. Hunter buried his face against the side of Grant's neck, and Grant continued to hold him close. For a moment, Grant thought Hunter had dozed off, but although they were always a little sleepy after sex, they'd usually talk a bit more before falling asleep. Then it dawned on him that Hunter was hiding from the confrontation.

"I've messed up again, didn't I?" Grant asked softly. He kissed Hunter's hair by way of apology.

"No you didn't," Hunter answered flatly.

"Yes, I did. You went all romantic on me and I panicked." Grant sighed. He was no good at talking about his feelings, but this time was as good as any. "I love you, Hunter. You're my man. I've never felt this comfortable with anyone, and that's scary all by itself. I'm scared of losing all this. I've never had this much to lose in my entire life."

"You're not going to lose anything," Hunter said, looking up at Grant. His expression was so sad and compassionate Grant almost rolled his eyes. Almost. "You built us a house. Our house. For you and me and Mattie."

"Hey, you helped a lot!" Grant said with a smile.

"Yeah, and so did Gable and Flynn and Hugh and Izzie and Tim and all the stable hands, but you built this place with your own bare hands. You told the architect what you wanted changed about the plans, and you knew what to do. It's our house, and you built it for us."

Grant kissed Hunter's temple. "I'm glad it's made you happy."

"And I hope it means you won't leave it."

"Of course not, Cowboy. We've had this conversation before, right? How could I leave you to raise Mattie alone?"

They stayed like that for as long as they dared and eventually got up and showered before going outside to work. They'd missed lunch completely, and Izzie ribbed them over it, but Grant just had to look at Hunter to make him blush, and it made him not-so-secretly proud. He could get used to this: one big, annoying family neither of them wanted to live without.

# —Epilogue—

"THIS has got to be the best view in the entire state," Flynn said, sitting down on the bench next to Hunter. Grant was playing with Matthew in the grass and teaching him to roll over. The baby was giggling and laughing.

"All the way to where the earth touches the sky," Gable agreed. He sat down on the other side of Hunter and looked at the beautifully maintained headstone on Hunter's father's grave.

"What brings you two here?" Hunter asked his visitors. Hunter looked at Flynn, but Flynn gestured over at his lover, so Hunter twisted his head around.

"We drove into town this morning," Gable started. "By the west road."

"Past Miranda's house," Flynn added, as if he was eager to tell the story as well.

"The house was boarded up," Gable continued.

Hunter nodded. "Miranda moved in with her mother even before Mattie was born."

Hunter didn't miss the looks Gable and Flynn exchanged.

"We drove past Miranda's mother's house too," Gable said with a sigh.

"It's empty and there's a 'For Sale' sign outside," Flynn said.

Hunter swallowed and Grant stopped playing with Mattie. Matthew wasn't happy about that, and he started to cry.

"Calley says they're gone," Gable said softly.

Hunter got up and took his son from Grant, cradling the baby until he settled down. "Did Calley know anything more?" Hunter asked Gable after a tense silence.

Gable looked at Flynn again before speaking. "Calley heard that Miranda got a teaching job in Montana."

Hunter walked his son out to the edge of the large oak tree and into the sun. "Look, Mattie. All this is going to be yours one day. Right up to where the earth touches the sky."

Don't miss Gable's story in

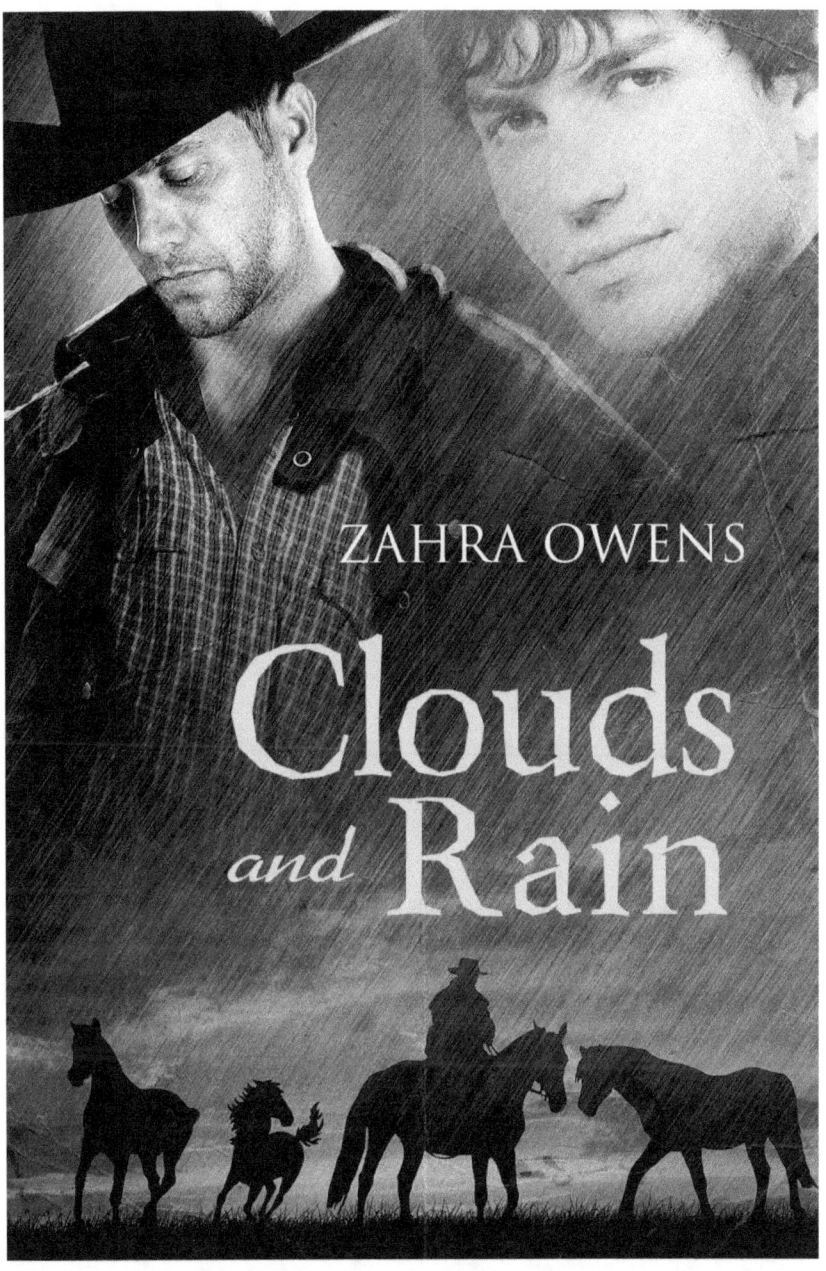

ZAHRA OWENS

Clouds
and Rain

http://www.dreamspinnerpress.com

ZAHRA OWENS was born in Europe just before Woodstock and the moon landing and was given a much less pronounceable name by her non-English-speaking parents. Being an Aquarian meant she would never quite conform, and people learned to expect the unexpected.

She started writing fairy tales in first grade; the same year she came into contact with her first group of English-speaking friends, a group which would eventually grow to include people from all over the world. On the outside she was a typical only child, accustomed to being with adults most of the time. On the inside, she sought ways to channel her wild imagination.

During the daytime she earns a living as a computer specialist, but it's her former career as an intensive care nurse that tends to seep into her fiction. Maybe this has to do with her weak spot for flawed characters and imperfect bodies, or maybe it's just her sadistic streak coming through. You be the judge.

Visit her web site at http://www.zahraowens.com/ and blog at http://zahra-owens.livejournal.com/.

Also by ZAHRA OWENS

Western Romances from DREAMSPINNER PRESS